The Garhole Bar

A PARKER MCLEOD THRILLER

By

A. Hardy Roper

The Garhole Bar
Copyright 2007 by A. Hardy Roper
Third Printing 2011

West Bay Publishing
www.westbay-publishing.com
Houston, TX

ISBN # 978-0-9840484-0-3

Printed in the US by: America's Press LTD

Reviews for The Garhole Bar

From the Galveston Daily News
Captivating and Engrossing, November 4, 2007
By <u>Margaret C. Barno "story weaver"</u> (Pflugerville, TX)

How long has it been since you've stayed up to the wee hours of the night so engrossed in a book so that you could read just one more page? It happened to me last night, or rather, this morning.

The Garhole Bar is a thriller, full of suspense, unexpected turns and many of these events unfold on the West End of Galveston Island. Its author, A. Hardy Roper, who called that location home for over twenty years, sets the novel, his first, at a bar owned by Parker McLeod. Named after the skeleton of an alligator gar jaw he had found and pried open, it is displayed prominently, hanging from the ceiling behind the bar counter.

The story's plot is complex; depth of character development, covering a sixty-year time frame. It is well executed, especially considering the fact that this is the author's first published work. The scenes initially shift from Germany and Galveston, eventually covering three continents.

Parker McLeod, a 19 year veteran, is struggling to get his life back together. While attempting to help an old friend and his granddaughter, Parker discovers skills learned during his military service come in handy in his new career as owner of a small bar on the west end of an island in the Gulf of Mexico off the coast of Texas.

Though there are a few aspects of the plot which could be tightened by a clarifying sentence, the story is well presented and kept my heart thumping to the last page. I hope that next thriller involving Parker McLeod is ready for press soon. My hunch is that A. Hardy Roper has a new venture as author that will keep him busy and his books in demand for years to come.

Review Written by wilhelmlette 🔖(Houston, TX USA)

Well done...had my interest from start to finish! December 11, 2007
Having been to Galveston Island many times, this book was especially fun to read. This novel will clearly be just as much of a page turner for those who don't know the island at all. A. Hardy Roper does a nice job of character development and successfully weaves the various storylines into a truly entertaining novel of intrigue. The book was an easy and entertaining read.

Acknowledgments

To each of my friends who helped me through the construction of this book, I owe more than simple thanks. I imposed on your time, and you rewarded me with your patience and grace. With much gratitude for your grammar and editing skills, I say thank you to Gaylene Miller and Patty Mayeux .

I give special thanks to my writing instructor and successful author in her own right, Donna Maloy. Thank you, Donna, for your insight, your ideas and final editing. Without your help, this creation would still be on the shelf of dreams.

I am perhaps, most grateful to my biggest fan and supporter, my lovely bride, Winkie. Thank you, dearest, for your endless hours of reading, editing and commenting. Your untiring encouragement kept me going when I was lost.

Photo credits belong to John Leech Photographers, Houston, Texas.

Prologue

On April 20, 1943, Adolph Hitler's birthday, the German submarine U155 entered the Gulf of Mexico through the Florida Straits. While running at periscope depth, Captain Johannes Rausch noted the bright lights of Miami, Florida thirty miles off the starboard bow. Rausch motioned his executive officer, Lieutenant Otto Kruger, to the periscope.

"Have a look, Lieutenant. The Americans do not practice blackouts. It is bad for tourism."

It was the first humor Rausch had allowed himself since disembarking from the submarine pens at Lorient, France. Two weeks earlier, Karl Döenitz, the admiral in charge of U-Boat Command, had instructed Rausch to sail to the Gulf of Mexico where he would receive further orders.

Something ominous was stirring. Rausch appreciated the need for secrecy, but on his ship, he was the Captain, the absolute master of his domain. He needed to know everything that might affect the safety of his boat and crew.

So, who was the stranger in civilian clothes that was secreted aboard only an hour before sailing? During their entire time at sea, his passenger had not come out of his cabin.

***

Behind the bridge in the cramped officer's quarters, Eric von Speigel heard the Captain announce they were entering the Gulf of Mexico. Dressed in civilian blue denims and a wool sweater with a "Made in USA" label attached, von Speigel stepped to the hatch of his cabin.

The seaman stationed outside had been assigned as his escort aboard ship, but von Speigel knew the man's real job was to watch him. He had expected it. A submarine was full of danger even when all was well. The Captain would not allow a stranger to have the run of the ship. That was fine with von Speigel. His mission was much too important to argue compromise. He had chosen to stay isolated. But now it was time to exert his authority.

"Inform the Captain I want to speak to him." Von Speigel's steel gray eyes relayed the urgency of a man on a mission.

"The Captain is busy on the bridge," his escort replied. The seaman broke eye contact quickly and turned away.

Von Speigel appreciated the seaman's tenacity, trying to protect his Captain. But von Speigel had no time for impertinence.

"I want to see the Captain now!" He pinched the man's collarbone turning him around, holding the seaman's eyes.

***

Moments later, in the privacy of his cabin, Captain Rausch confronted the intruder.

"You have orders for me, Herr von Speigel?"

It was the first words Rausch had spoken to the man since he had come aboard. He had been ordered to take him, but he did not have to like it. Communication would be as curt as possible.

"Yes, Captain," von Speigel, replied. He handed Rausch his identification papers and sealed orders. "And it's Major von Speigel."

"Yes, of course, Major."

Rausch tore open the envelope and studied the contents. No doubt now, thought Rausch. The man was Abwehr, the most arrogant of all Nazi spy groups. Without comment, he replaced the papers in the envelope and lifted his eyes to meet von Speigel's stare.

"Very unusual," Rausch commented, the disdain in his voice obvious. "The Captain taking orders from someone else aboard his own ship."

"Perhaps, Captain," von Speigel answered, abruptly. "But the orders are signed by Admiral Döenitz, and I expect you will carry them out." His inflection left no room for discussion. He clicked his heels in the German style and then turned and left the cabin.

A moment later, Lieutenant Kruger entered the Captain's stateroom. Rausch reviewed the orders with his second in command and then burned the papers in his lavatory.

"You have witnessed the orders, Lieutenant. We are to close within three miles of Galveston Island, send von Speigel ashore in a rubber boat, and hopefully get our men back undetected and get out."

"We are to leave him there. Is that correct, sir?"

"Yes, and good riddance."

"Who is this man?" Kruger asked.

"I don't know, but I will be glad to get him off my ship."

***

One week later, after running submerged all day, U155 surfaced just before dark a few miles south of the Louisiana coastline to charge her batteries. Tomorrow night, she would arrive off Galveston.

The last cold front of the year pushed down hard off the coast. Frigid waves splashed over the low-riding deck as the sub rolled starboard to port in ten-foot seas. The lone lookout, cold and seasick, huddled for warmth against the conning tower. Too late, he failed to see the approaching Coast Guard plane.

The plane's pilot spotted the conning tower rolling in the heavy seas. At fifteen hundred feet, he released a 325-pound depth charge that struck the ship square on the deck just forward of its 105-millimeter gun. Salt water roared through the jagged hole into the battery room below.

In the control room, the concussion knocked Lieutenant Kruger and several seamen to the deck, unconscious in the swirling water. Captain Rausch, himself hurled against the bulkhead, struggled to regain his senses. Bright red poured from a cut on his forehead. He pushed the blood from his eyes and managed to stand, holding onto the railing. Suddenly, a secondary explosion caused by the mixture of seawater and battery acid tore the bow from the ship.

Dumped from his bunk to the deck, Eric von Speigel instantly realized they were under attack. He had but one thought—the mission. The seaman outside was gone. Von Speigel hurried to the executive officer's cabin, hastily donned one of Lieutenant Kruger's uniforms, and broke for the bridge.

Before the bomb hit, the conning tower hatch had been left open to ventilate the ship. Water poured into the control room from both the open hatch and the severed bow.

Having received no damage control reports, Captain Rausch was unaware of the severity of the damage. In any event, he was too disoriented to order abandon ship. What was left of the ship's fifty-four man crew remained at their stations.

In his impaired state, Rausch thought the ship could still dive and evade another attack. He raced to the conning tower to climb the ladder and close the hatch.

Von Speigel appeared in the control room. The Captain shouted at him to help. Von Speigel ignored the plea, yanked the Captain to the deck and started up to escape. Rausch hit the deck hard but managed to grab von Speigel. Von Speigel whipped a pistol from his waistband and smashed the Captain's head, sending him crashing down again. Rausch's head dropped beneath the water, now two feet deep across the deck.

Outside the sinking ship, the Coast Guard plane dropped a raft for survivors. Von Spiegel climbed aboard in time to see the last of the conning tower sink below the turbulent water.

Just then, a figure popped out of the water and grabbed the other side of the raft. Somehow the guard from outside von Speigel's cabin had escaped the stricken ship—the only other survivor. The seaman stared wide-eyed in disbelief at von Speigel's officer uniform. Speechless, he turned one hand loose from the raft and pointed at the gold bars on von Speigel's shoulders.

Von Speigel jerked the pistol from his tunic, jammed it toward the exhausted seaman's tired and frightened face and fired, point-blank.

Hours later, a Coast Guard cutter plucked the weary Nazi from his raft. The ship's Captain radioed his base at Sabine Pass, Texas, just west of where the sub was sunk. "We have a survivor on board. He's a ship's officer. We are heading in."

"Roger that," replied the base operator.

The Captain kept a wary eye on his prisoner sitting handcuffed in the Executive Officer's chair. "What are they going to do with this guy?" he asked.

"I don't know," the operator answered. "Probably send him to Fort Crockett, that POW camp in Galveston."

Eric von Speigel, fluent in English, smiled inwardly. Yes indeed, he thought, all is not lost. To Galveston. He only needed to escape from the Prisoner of War camp, meet his contact, and collect the funds. Von Speigel did not know the exact amount of money he was to receive or what form it might take. He only knew his mission was of great importance to the Reich, and the funding would be generous.

Chapter One
Saturday, August 20, 1994

My name is Parker McLeod. I own a bar on the far west end of Galveston Island out among the prickly pear and rattlesnakes. When I'm not serving cold beer to tired fishermen, I spend most of my time trying hard to mind my own business. I have enough grief of my own without purposely tripping into someone else's sack of rocks. I learned a long time ago I can't save the world. But when the two Harley's rumbled into my parking lot, my sensory system jumped from sleep mode to high alert.

This time of year when the fishing is slow, we usually close early. But it was Saturday night and Lisa wanted to work so we stayed open longer than usual. I glanced at my watch. Almost eleven o'clock. Five minutes more and Lisa would have turned off the lights and closed the bar.

When the cycles turned off the highway, I was stretched out on the upper deck in my favorite Adirondack chair finishing a bottle of Famous Grouse. My shoulders ached and burned like always. I had shoved everything from aspirin to Vicodin through my veins, but nothing seemed to work except alcohol.

The windless bay water in front of me lay like a corpse, flat and still. An early front was due the next day, moving down from the north bringing cooler weather. But tonight, blowtorch air picked at my senses. Not unusual for late August.

I breathed deeply, struggling for relief, but drew nothing but the pungent aroma of salt grass and the residue of a million tiny sea animals decaying in the surrounding marsh.

Globs of sweat rolled down the back of my neck and mosquitoes as large as dragonflies honed in on my body. The one on my arm appeared too full of blood to fly. I wondered if the bastards got drunk feeding from a drunk. I slapped and blood splattered.

It was then I heard the bikes cut down the sand road to the bar. I shuffled through my bedroom to the window overlooking the parking lot and peeked past the shade. Below in the oyster shell driveway, two Hells Angels clones were dismounting their hogs. Under the light over the door, the tattoos on their arms glistened like a kaleidoscope with contrasting hues of purple, green and crimson.

I eased the shade to the window, slipped down the back stairs, and hid in the shadows beside the rear door. The two desperadoes stood at the back bar maybe twenty feet from me talking to Lisa behind the counter.

They were young, early twenties, on the thin side with pimply faces. The tall one talked through a joint hanging from his lips.

"Hey sugar, what'cha got shaking tonight?"

And then Lisa, only eighteen and new at the job, made her first mistake—she smiled at the bums. When a snake rattles, expect a strike.

Her low cut blouse tumbled open as she leaned into the bar. "Nothing much," she said, "We don't get a lot of business this time of night. What can I get you fellows?"

Her second mistake—giving the enemy information—announcing no one was around.

The shorter one raised his eyebrows and turned to the tall one. "Fellows? Did you know we were fellows, Jake?"

Jake passed the joint to the short one and laughed, "Why no, Punch, I didn't. You feel like a fellow?"

Punch inhaled deeply, then blew the smoke over the bar into Lisa's face. He took another hit, squashed the butt into the counter top, and dropped it to the floor. The smell of burning weed wafted across the room.

Lisa's eyes flared. She straightened, causing her blouse to rise and cover her chest. Then she backed to the sink behind the bar and pressed into it.

Punch pulled a crumpled bill from his jeans pocket and said, "How 'bout a couple of cold ones, Sug? We're kinda dry, you know?"

Lisa opened two beers and set them on the counter. "You're welcome to sit at one of the tables," she said, nodding toward the center of the room.

Strike three! Her move to put more distance between herself and the clowns showed weakness. When she opened the cash register for change, Jake, the tall one, leaned in a bit. I couldn't tell if he was going for her or the cash register. Either way it was not going to be pretty.

My little piece of heaven is less than a mile from the end of the island and the bridge over San Luis Pass that separates Galveston from the mainland heading south down the coast. The closest law enforcement is twenty miles in either direction.

I think the bad boys knew that. What could be more tempting? A lonely bar and a pup barmaid out in the middle of nowhere. Too easy too pass up.

Punch said, "You know, Jake, I think the bitch doesn't want us bothering her. She wants us to move to the table there and leave her alone. Not very friendly, is she?"

Lisa laid the change on the counter, then turned to Punch and said, "Look mister, it's closing time. How about you taking your beers on the road?"

Punch grinned, "Why, we can't do that, Sug. It's against the law."

While Punch kept Lisa's attention, the tall one, Jake, moved to the end of the bar.

I retreated into the shadows, looking around for something that would equalize the situation. Lisa's grandfather, Bully Stout, lived in a camping trailer behind the bar. He was out somewhere tonight, treasure hunting as usual, but an iron rod he used for probing the sand was leaning against the trailer.

I thought Jake was going to move toward Lisa, but he stopped at the end of the bar instead. With one quick move, he yanked the telephone loose from the wall, flipped open a pocketknife, and cut the cord.

As Lisa turned toward Jake, Punch reached over and hit the cash register button. The drawer flew open. He went for the bills. Lisa grabbed an empty beer bottle and smashed his hand. The money fell to the counter.

Jake rushed Lisa. He shoved her hard. She fell back against the sink and slid to the floor. He grabbed the money and jumped over the counter.

I hadn't moved in when my presence might have stopped the confrontation, and now I knew I couldn't take them both on without help. I broke for the iron rod while they headed for the front door. I raced around the side of the building to find them cranking their engines. I slammed the rod against Jake's knee and heard bone snap. The bike collapsed on top of him. Punch lifted his leg over his bike trying to dismount and come for me. I crushed the rod down hard on his shoulder, breaking his collarbone.

I pivoted back to Jake and raised the rod again yelling, "Drop the money! Drop the money!"

Jake reached into his pocket. I remembered the knife and slammed the rod against his trousers. He screamed with pain and withdrew an empty hand, fingers drawn and crushed. He motioned toward the saddlebags. I raised the rod again. He moved both arms up in a gesture of surrender. I held the rod with my right hand and retrieved the money from the bag with my left.

Punch sat slumped against the handlebars of his bike holding his shoulder, moaning in pain. I twirled the rod over my head like a kung-fu artist, yelling again.

"Get on your bikes and get the hell out of here. Now! You ever come back here, and your balls are crab bait." Wham! I slammed the rod against Punch's handlebars and screamed, "You got that?"

Punch managed to start his bike and somehow hold on with a collapsed right shoulder. He raced out the sand road toward the blacktop, leaving Jake behind. I stepped closer to the trapped Jake and swished the rod over his bike several times. He got the message, straightened his bike and took off, his shattered knee twisted out to the side.

Both bikes topped the sand road and turned right, south toward Freeport, away from Galveston. I heard the engines roar across the bridge and exhaled a long slow breath.

Lisa called from the back deck. I stuffed the money into my shorts and headed toward her. She came down the stairs wiping tears from her cheeks, obviously searching for me.

"Parker, Parker, where have you been? We've been robbed!"

She hurdled off the bottom step, arms out for an embrace. I pushed her back and held her shoulders at arms length.

"What? What do you mean robbed?"

"Two men, they...they stole the money from the register. Cut the phone. We can't even call for help."

Long, blond straggly hair whipped across her face. Some of the strands stuck to the wetness on her cheeks.

"Tell me what happened," I said.

She repeated what I already knew. I released her, then made a show of going inside and checking the cash register. I picked up the telephone and fumbled with the cut cord. She stood behind me leaning against the doorframe. She held her hands over her face, crying, eyes red and puffy.

I turned to her with the cord in my hand. "Well there's nothing we can do about it tonight."

She moved inside and leaned on the end of the bar, head down, her voice soft.

"I'm sorry Parker. I didn't know what to do. I...I..."

5

She collapsed into sobs. I moved toward her but stopped short. "Go to bed Lisa, I'll clean up here."

She looked up at me expecting sympathy, her face full of disappointment and hurt. For a moment, I saw the little girl I used to know. The one who would run into my arms when I was home on leave, laughing and giggling, begging me to take her into the marshes to study the birds.

But that was before and this was now. I didn't know the sad-eyed, splotched-face waif in front of me. Two years on the road with a drug-pushing scumbag. No, this was not the Lisa I knew. I lowered my eyes and turned away. She ran for the trailer, slamming the screen door behind her.

I reattached the telephone and thought about calling Marvin Klaus, the deputy sheriff who patrolled West Beach. But I knew he was probably in town at the donut shop, and I didn't feel like disturbing his routine and having him drive twenty miles out the west end for something I could handle.

Upstairs on my deck, I took several long pulls of whisky and thought about what I would do in the morning. Lisa obviously hadn't seen or heard the confrontation out front. I couldn't tell her I had recovered the money without her knowing I had witnessed everything. And if I witnessed it, why hadn't I come in to help her? I couldn't answer the question. I wasn't sure myself.

Lisa Stout, my little druggie niece, eighteen going on thirty. Two years ago, on her sixteenth birthday, she walked out of the girl's home in Galveston where she lived and simply disappeared. At the time, I was in Iraq, battling Saddam's finest, and couldn't do anything about it.

My aunt died while I was over there and her husband, Bully Stout, needed a place to live. He moved the trailer behind my house and with me out of the country, appointed himself caretaker of my property. I didn't mind it at the time, but who knew it was going to be permanent.

Then, two weeks ago, out of nowhere, Lisa showed up half-stoned and skinny as a cane pole with nothing but a scraggly dress on her back. She looked like a lost cat that had escaped from a sack someone dumped on the side of the road.

Bully begged me to let her stay. She moved in with him, sharing the squalid little camper like a couple of depression squatters.

I finished the bottle and lay back in the chair staring at the night sky. This time booze hadn't worked. A thousand tiny needles jabbed at my shoulders. The pain was almost constant now anyway and swinging that iron bar around hadn't helped.

A dark cloud moved in from the Gulf and crossed over the island blocking the moon. The Iraqi desert, torched oil wells, and a sky filled with boiling black death flashed before me. I massaged my shoulder as best I could and cursed the U.S. Army for the millionth time.

I shook the image away and closed my eyes. I felt satisfied the motorcycle potheads wouldn't return. Smoking dope and riding a bike was like sticking a gun in your mouth. And doing it with broken bones was pulling the trigger.

That kind of trouble was a stranger to the quiet lifestyle of the west end. Sure, we got an occasional thrill. Like when a strong undertow dragged someone offshore. Or when a drunk wiped himself out on the beach road. But real violence was as rare as a direct hit from a hurricane. And hurricanes only come along every twenty years or so. So twenty more years without any kind of trouble around here was all right with me. There was nothing I liked better than staying out of other people's way.

Chapter Two
Saturday, August 20

The huge Lufthansa Airbus lumbered into Buenos Aires International Airport on time at 11:45 AM. After clearing immigration, Günter Manfred went immediately to a bank of pay phones next to the luggage carousel.

Always use a public phone his trainer, had taught him. Hotel calls were too easily traced. One ring, then a voice in German, the tone high-pitched, demanding.

"*Speak!*"

"*I have arrived,*" Günter replied in his native language. No need to use names. He easily recognized the voice at the other end. Horst Frankin, his contact, had instructed him to check in upon arrival.

"*The woman?*" Frankin demanded, his voice surly.

"*Tomorrow afternoon,*" Günter replied. "*It is an eight-hour drive.*"

"*Eight hours? What is the name of the city?*"

Günter cursed—a slip of the tongue. He had not given them the woman's name or the city in which she lived. The more they knew, the less they needed him. And Günter could not take that chance. He had learned his lessons early. Keep your options open.

He had given them the rudiments of the story, of course, to get their interest, playing on their desperate need for funds. The Organization could not grow, or maybe even continue, without a large infusion of cash. And the story seemed plausible enough. He believed it himself, or he would not have agreed to undertake the mission, even with them funding it.

He had convinced the committee that his contacts would cooperate only if he kept their names secret. They bought in. After all, for the past twelve years, since he was sixteen, he had proven himself many times. They trusted him.

Günter, his voice smooth, ignoring the command, said, "*I will tell you when I get there.*" It was a lie, of course. He had learned growing up in East Germany with the Communists—trust no one.

Frankin's voice grew stronger, a high whine. "*You must confide in me, Günter. Remember, I am your contact. You report to me.*"

Günter paused. He held the phone away and took deep breaths. Staying in control was the most difficult part. Losing it had cost him before. He tolerated this imbecile because he had to, but the less Frankin knew the better. It was time to get indignant, he thought. The man was weak. Go on offense; put Frankin in his place.

Günter put his hand around the telephone receiver to muffle his voice, then shouted, "*Do you doubt me? You know the bargain! She must remain anonymous.*"

"*But...?*"

"*Are you questioning my loyalty? How dare you! After all I have done for the Organization.*"

"*Yes, yes, of course.*" Frankin answered, exasperated. "*It is just that we are low on funds, and we are financing you. I am getting pressure.*"

Günter softened, "*Do not worry, I will be successful. And you will be a hero for supporting me.*"

After a moment of silence, Frankin said, "*Well, I must report—Truth.*"

Günter repeated the motto, "*Truth*", and hung up. He retrieved his luggage, picked up his rented Mercedes and drove to the Intercontinental Hotel. He would spend one night in Buenos Aires.

The package he had addressed to himself in care of the hotel would not arrive until the next morning.

An hour later, he sat on a park bench across from the famed Casa Rosada absorbing every detail of the facade down to the faded pink plaster. A few yards away, a group of visitors was gathered with their guide to view the building and learn its history.

Some called it the home of the Presidents, but Günter knew better. The building itself was not the attraction, and the crowd could care less who was the current President. The tourists hoped for a miracle. They wanted to see Evita. Eva Peron, mistress, once wife of the army Colonel Juan Peron, who had become President in 1946.

Of course, it was impossible. This was 1994 and they had both been dead for years. But still, the imagery lived on—the glitz, the power.

Günter rose from the bench and stared along with the others at the balcony where Evita would have appeared to her subjects. He envisioned her there on a warm summer night, soaking in the adulation of the masses, waving to the cheering mob.

Günter loved the scene. He thought about how it must have been for Peron and Evita. Money and power, the twin aphrodisiacs. They had enjoyed both. It was Günter's dream, and the reason he was here in front of their palace, basking in the remnants of their glory. He had neither money nor power. But with success now, he could achieve both.

During the walk back to the hotel, he shifted his thoughts to his exchange with Frankin. He could be smooth or rough and switch gears as needed. Whatever the occasion required. But with Frankin, rough was easier. Tomorrow, he would have to be smooth again. The woman he would meet was old and probably frail. But that was tomorrow.

A newsstand caught his attention. A free magazine highlighted the nightlife of Buenos Aires—bars—women—sex. He walked to the corner and hailed a taxi. Smooth or rough? He had not had a woman in over a week, and for him that was unforgivable.

***

At a little after ten the next morning, Günter approached the main desk of the Intercontinental Hotel and took delivery of a large, manila envelope. He strode immediately to the hotel's parking garage, got into his car and checked the contents of the package. He then put the package in the trunk under the lining and eased out into the early morning Buenos Aires traffic.

A block from the hotel he hit his first interchange, a large roundabout with no stop signals. Horns blared from all directions as cars scurried around the circle, roaring in and out from each of the intersecting streets, swerving and hitting their brakes as needed. He glared at the drivers, fiery blends of Italian and Spanish and French that had mixed and mingled over the past several hundred years.

It seemed everyone here had a hot temper. His thoughts regressed to the dark-haired beauty he had encountered last evening at the Casa de Esquina Dance Club a block off the Reforma in the busiest section of downtown. She had arrived straight from work with tango shoes in hand. Soon her flashing, inviting eyes sent the signal he expected, and they ended the night in her apartment.

He had not intended to hurt her, but to his surprise, she had demanded money. He could not believe it. In Germany, he never paid for sex, even with the professionals. They never expected money; he was just too good. They only wanted him to return.

But this whore was different, and then...she got angry. Too bad. He'd had no choice but to show her who was in control. And then the fun part, instilling just the right amount of fear so she would not report him. But she had struggled, and his massive hands were too powerful and her neck too soft.

This morning he would do a quick reconnaissance and then leave the city as quickly as possible. Two blocks later, he turned onto a residential street lined with three story apartments. Ahead, two attendants loaded a stretcher into an ambulance. A sheet covered the victim's head. Strands of long dark hair spread beyond the sheet onto the stretcher. When one of the attendants glanced up, Günter quickly turned away and drove past. He turned back to the thoroughfare and entered the freeway erasing all thoughts of the woman from his mind. The dark-haired beauty from last evening had danced her last tango.

Chapter Three
Sunday, August 21

I should have known better. The night on the deck left me with a bad head and a thousand mosquito welts. I felt like someone had dragged me through a batch of prickly pear.

I struggled to the bathroom, hit the faucet handle and rubbed my face with cold water. The mirror wasn't kind. I pushed a few strands of black hair out of my face and stroked my beard. Specks of gray weaved in and out. I massaged the pouch under my eye, and attempted to push it back to normal. It didn't work. Jesus, the downhill slope at thirty-nine.

I made coffee downstairs and watched the sun cut the horizon through the window over the sink. The temperature climbed quickly, sucking the hot bay water into the air. As usual this time of year, the cold front had stalled out somewhere. It would be another sweltering day on the Gulf Coast.

A loud shriek came from the boat dock. I went outside and checked the makeshift cage hanging from the overhead deck.

"Sorry, Charlie. I forgot to feed you this morning."

I had found the bird on the beach hobbling around. Now, after two weeks of nursing, his broken wing seemed healed. I wanted badly for my ministering to work. Being caged was no life for a bird or for anything for that matter. He needed to soar. I dipped several mullet from a drum of water and pushed them through the wire cage.

I gave the bird my best reassuring smile and said, "You're almost ready, Charlie. You'll be free soon."

I moved to a table by the edge of the dock and gazed over the water thinking about last night. Lisa was the only blood relative left in my family, and I had left her in harm's way—why? I glanced at the camping trailer. The door was closed, no sign of life.

Customers would be in soon. I went inside and started a roux for lunch. The telephone sounded, a fisherman checking on the weather. If I answered the phone, the roux might burn. I ignored the call and continued stirring.

A few moments later, the telephone rang again. I swore inwardly.

A voice asked, "Are you okay?"

Startled by the interruption, I turned quickly and glared at the slumped figure in the doorway. Lisa's face appeared in shadow, backlit from the morning sun. It was better that way, not seeing the empty eyes and sunken cheeks.

She spoke again, "I see you fixed the phone. Who called?"

"Don't know."

"You didn't answer it?"

"No."

"Why not?"

I made a face and nodded to the skillet, still stirring. My eyes drifted past the rusted trailer and focused on the skiff in the boatlift. Lisa took a Coke from the beer box and leaned on the end of the counter, watching me.

"I thought it might be Poppa Bully," she said. "He's been out all night. I'm worried about him, that's all."

14

I continued staring out the window and said, "The boat's in the sling. He sure as hell hasn't been out running the crab traps like he was supposed to."

Lisa sipped her Coke, not saying anything.

I said, "If he's been out all night, he's out there somewhere digging again."

Lisa said, "You mean treasure hunting? At night?"

"That's what he does."

She shrugged and moved to a stool at the front of the counter. "I'm sorry about last night, Parker. How much did they get?"

Working over the stove with my back to her, I said, "Well, we got lucky. I found the money in the driveway out front. It must have fallen out of their saddlebags."

She bounced off the stool and screamed, "Oh, Parker, really? That's great. Oh, man, how lucky." She hurried around the bar and hugged my neck.

I shrugged her off and continued working.

She said, "Did you call the police?"

"No"

"What? Why not?"

"I take care of my own business. We've seen the last of those road jockeys. Besides we got the money back."

Lisa said, "Oh, man! I'm so glad."

I turned the heat off under the skillet and dropped in chopped onions to cool the roux. The onions bubbled and the roux turned a rich chocolate brown. I sniffed the pan knowing I would have to start over again if I detected the aroma of burned flour.

Lisa said, "I'm really worried about Poppa."

"Then why didn't you come in here and answer the phone," I said. "It rang earlier. Couldn't you hear it from the trailer?"

"Well...I...I wasn't in the trailer."

I turned to her. "What? What do you mean?"

"I spent the night in your truck beside the bar."

"What? My truck! Why'd you do that?"

"When Poppa's not here, I'm afraid."

"Afraid? Afraid of what? I told you those motorcycle bums wouldn't be back. It won't happen again."

We were eye to eye, a couple of feet apart, and had exchanged more words in the last two minutes than in the past two weeks.

Lisa took a deep breath and exhaled slowly. Then, trembling slightly she said, "It's...it's Denny."

I knew whom she meant—Denny Sader, the pimp bastard she had left Galveston with two years earlier. When I said before that she was eighteen going on thirty, the thirty part of it was the time she had spent with him. I had a pretty good idea what she had been doing.

I didn't know how to respond. I shook my head and turned back to the stove. My eyes drooped, a sign my body was shutting down. Exhausted from the booze and lack of rest, I turned to Lisa and said, "You finish the gumbo. I'm going upstairs."

I stretched out in a chair on the deck and closed my eyes to the morning sun. I dozed on and off, my mind wandering. Why had I ever let Lisa stay here? It was all Bully's fault—a beer-gutted old man with a wooden leg and a patch over one eye. His miniscule veteran's pension was barely enough to pay the electric bill on his trailer much less help out with the groceries or any of the other expenses. Sure, he made a few bucks selling crabs from his line of traps, but that was barely enough to pay for gas in his outboard. He was supposed to be out today getting crabs for the gumbo, but he had flaked out again.

And because I let him stay, now I had Lisa. She may be acting afraid of Sader, but I had no doubt she would go back to him soon. She would never kick the habit.

An hour later, I heard footsteps moving fast and a shout next to my head. Lisa shook me.

"Parker, wake up! Wake up!"

She pulled my arm.

"Oh, man. Parker, can you hear me? Poppa's in jail! Like, I'm really freaked. What should I do?"

I stirred. "Whaaa?" The sun beat on my eyes. I couldn't seem to open them.

Lisa straightened and leaned over my body. "Marvin Klaus called. Said he'd been calling all night."

I shaded my eyes with my hand and said, "What did you say? Jail? Who?"

"Poppa!"

"Bully's in jail?"

"Yes! What should we do?"

I pushed myself from the chair, arched my body, and pushed my thumbs into the small of my back.

"Nothing, absolutely nothing. That's what we'll do. Screw him! Customers will be coming in soon and they're going to be hungry."

"But..."

"But nothing," I continued, "He knows better. Now get down there and get ready for the noon crowd."

Lisa turned and ran down the stairs. I heard my truck start and the sound of tires spinning on shell. She raced out of the parking lot and up the sand road to the blacktop.

I sat on the edge of the bed and leaned back onto my elbows. I would get up in a minute and finish lunch. Just a few minutes of rest, just a few.

Chapter Four
Sunday, August 21

On the overnight flight from Munich, Günter had read about Santa Rosa de Calmuchita, the bustling Argentine city seven hundred kilometers west of Buenos Aires. He entered the town in the early afternoon, passing seventeenth-century churches and old-style colonial buildings commingled with modern office structures. Located in a valley between two mountain ranges, the local chamber of commerce advertised the city as a tourist Mecca, a perfect blend of outdoor activities and historical sites.

Although not mentioned in the guidebooks, Günter also knew the area was well populated with Germans. Over the past hundred years, thousands had emigrated to Argentina, many to the Santa Rosa area. At first, they had come for free land and jobs. Then later they helped build industries providing needed engineers, toolmakers and other skilled craftsman. Günter knew how it evolved. Soon they owned the businesses and with that came political pressure. By the 1930s and early 40s, Nazi propaganda heavily influenced Argentine decisions.

Günter continued through the city following the Santa Rosa River toward Lake Embalse, the huge body of water forty kilometers south of town. He lowered the windows and breathed in the cool mountain scents of eucalyptus and oak and pine. Halfway between the city and the lake, he turned right, onto the entrance road to the *Estancia Rosas*.

He passed under a stone arch and stopped. Fifty-foot tall cedar trees lined the gravel road that wound up to the compound. To the left was a long, low building, now empty, but obviously at one time filled with fine Spanish stallions. Weeds in front of the wooden doors held them closed. Off to the right was a large stone patio surrounding an empty swimming pool.

Behind the pool was the large colonial mansion itself, complete with huge arched windows and a red-tiled roof. Two enormous, if somewhat weathered, mahogany doors with tarnished brass hinges framed the entrance. All in all, he thought, an imposing setting. He reached for one of the large rings attached to the entrance and knocked soundly.

"Good afternoon, Señora. May I present myself? I am Günter Manfred, here from Germany to see Señora Rosas."

Her beauty astonished him—early twenties, flawless complexion. Lustrous black hair fell well below her shoulders. Deep, dark eyes captured his, and he was momentarily spellbound. She was small, five-three or less. He wanted to scoop her up and whisk her away. Whoever she was, this was not the woman who had corresponded with his mother.

He spoke in English, a language learned during training in the East German Army. He knew no Spanish, and he did not think the beautiful young woman before him, a younger generation, would know German.

She smiled and answered in English. "Of course, Señor Manfred. I am Mariana Villata, the Señora's niece. We have been expecting you. Your telegram seemed urgent."

He liked the way her eyes spoke, the message more than polite hospitality. He bowed slightly and smiled, "Thank you, Señora Villata. I am most grateful for your warm welcome."

"Please come in, and...it is Señorita Villata. But please call me Mariana."

"Of course, Señorita...uh, I am sorry, Mariana." He smiled broadly and clicked his heels together. He watched her turn, admiring her tight waist and erect walk.

He passed through the entry hall into a sitting room greeted by the smell of mildew and old carpet. A ceiling fan creaked slowly overhead, barely breaking the silence. Stale, musty air filled the room.

Frail but steady, holding a cane, Señora Rosas rose from a chair to greet him, her face deeply wrinkled and her hair completely white. Her presence emitted an air of old-world elegance.

She extended her hand and addressed Günter in German, *"Welcome to Argentina, Herr Manfred. My husband was a great friend of your grandfather."* Then, before he could reply, she switched to English. "I am afraid my niece does not speak your native language. Perhaps it would be best to continue in English."

Günter nodded slightly toward Mariana and then turned back to the frail woman in front of him. He took her hand and said, "But of course, Señora Rosas. And thank you for your kind hospitality."

Señora Rosas continued, "Not at all. I am pleased you have come this far to see me. Forgive me for not answering your last inquiry. I have not been feeling well. Please sit down."

Günter, too, was sorry she had not answered. It would have possibly saved him this out of the way trip to Argentina, not to mention the time it had taken. And time was important. He had successfully manipulated the Organization into funding the search, but their funds were limited. He needed to complete the mission as quickly as possible.

He offered a condolence. "I am sorry to learn of your discomfort, Señora."

Mariana had left the room, but now she returned holding a tray with a fine-china tea set. The curves of her breasts appeared as she bent to pour tea into his cup. Günter's pulse quickened.

Señora Rosas stretched her pale arm toward Mariana. "Isn't she lovely, Günter?"

He gazed at Mariana, their eyes met. He replied, "More than lovely, Señora. Exquisite, if I may be allowed."

"You are so kind," Mariana acknowledged, lowering her eyes.

Señora Rosas said, "How is your mother, Günter?"

Günter turned back and in a soft voice said, "Gone from us, I am afraid. She died of a cancer two weeks ago."

"I am sorry," the Señora replied. "I must apologize. You see, I did not know of your mother until recently. As you know, I was actually trying to locate her mother."

"My grandmother, Anna Manfred."

"Yes, dearest Anna." Señora Rosas said. Then she paused and with a small linen handkerchief dabbed a drop of moisture from her eye. "It was only a few months ago that I was able to confirm that Anna Manfred had died from typhoid fever in 1947, two years after the end of the war. To my surprise, I discovered she had a three-year old daughter when she died—your mother."

Günter nodded, then turned his face toward the windows and said, "Yes, it was a dreadful time in Germany then." His mind flashed to the post-war photographs he had seen: cities burned and ravaged, hunger and disease rampant, the once proud people appearing stooped and hopeless in soup lines. Then, another vision appeared—a distant memory. He was a small child, three or four. His mother was holding his hand, leading him along an alley as she searched trashcans for scraps of food, anything to eat. The old woman's voice brought him back.

"As you know, when I located your mother, I wrote to her immediately. We began a short correspondence. I told your mother about her mother's fiancé, Eric von Speigel, your grandfather."

The old woman's head shook as she spoke. A condition of some kind, he thought. Maybe it was a good thing he came when he did. She was the last link.

He hesitated, then spoke softly, "Thank you for your efforts, Señora Rosas. My mother was so grateful to learn more about her father. And I am in your debt for letting me know that Eric Von Speigel was my grandfather. That is why I am here. I want to know more about him. Your letter indicated that your husband and Eric were childhood friends in Leipzig."

"Yes, that's true." She handed him a photograph. "Here is a picture of my husband, Rheinhard and Eric together in Leipzig. You are so much like your grandfather, the military bearing—tall and erect. And your blond hair and blue eyes...so strong, so German." She turned to her niece. "Don't you think so, Mariana?"

Mariana offered an inviting smile, then said, "Yes, Auntie, Señor Manfred is quite handsome." She blushed slightly and reached for her teacup.

She was good, Günter thought. But he had already caught her measuring him earlier at the front door. Women were so quick. In a single flash of the eyes they determined everything they needed to know about a man. He knew this, so he had learned to watch for that instant in time, a quick glance, often peripheral, when they would judge their interest.

But he was good, too. So while she was appraising him, he had done the same to her. It was not something he learned in training, it was instinctive. Attracting women had always been easy for Günter. He had learned the art of manipulation early. After all, women existed to be used, interesting playthings for his enjoyment. And with his skills, he was always a step ahead.

Günter acknowledged their comments with a slight bow of his head. "Thank you," he said. "But, you embarrass me. My light skin turns red rather quickly I think."

Señora Rosas and Mariana both smiled. Then Mariana got up suddenly. "Señor Manfred, please excuse me. I must attend to lunch."

"Of course." He rose from his chair and watched her leave. He imagined her naked, his arms encircling her small waist as he pulled her into him. When she left the room, he turned to continue the conversation with the Señora and found her smiling. Had she read his thoughts?

A moment passed, her face turned serious. She said, "I am all Mariana has now, Günter. Her parents died tragically in an airplane crash several years ago."

Günter went along. "I am sorry, Señora. It is a sad thing."

Señora Rosas leaned toward Günter and in a quiet voice, said, "Yes it is true, a very sad thing, Günter. And as you can see, my health is failing as well. She will be all alone."

So, the message was clear, Günter thought, the proposition on the table. Señora Rosas had just offered her only niece. He glanced at the threadbare rug below his feet and understood. The weeds, the empty pool, the tarnished hinges—they needed money. But why him? What made them think he was the answer to their problems? It did not make sense.

Still he needed information, so he would play along. He rose and paced the room, then stopped in front of her. "Señora Rosas, your home and estate is very beautiful as is Mariana. A man could get used to such beauty."

He nodded slightly as if to say he understood her offer and was interested. She returned the acknowledgment with a slight smile and nod of her own.

"But, please forgive me," he continued, "I must know more about my family. Will you help me?"

She sighed heavily and after a moment said, "Of course, Günter. How can I help you?"

"What else can you tell me about Eric Von Speigel, Señora? I want to know everything."

"It was so long ago, Günter. So long ago," she said gazing past his eyes as if toward some distant memory. "Is it so important to you?"

"He was my grandfather, Señora Rosas. I have so little family. I came all the way from Germany just to learn more about him."

"Yes, yes, of course," she said.

He watched her closely. She seemed to be studying his face, searching, looking for something. But what? Trust? What did she know that was so...sacred? A moment later she continued.

"All right, Günter. But you must understand. Everything I tell you is in strictest confidence. It cannot leave this room." She rose, and began to pace with her cane. "We have to be ever vigilant. There are still those here who would harm us."

Chapter Five

Sunday, August 21

Bully Stout recoiled at the odor of stale tobacco, fouled perspiration and puke. The toilet had stopped up sometime during the night, and waste and urine gathered at the top of the bowl like a levee waiting to burst.

Hunks of slimy green plaster hung from the ceiling. He wondered if the next loud voice would break it loose and send it crashing to the floor. It was time to find out.

He rose from the cement bench, stretched to his full six-four, two hundred eighty pounds, and hobbled to the cell doors. A piece of the slimy green stuff hit his shoulder as he screamed down the hall, "Johnny, are you here yet?"

The words bounced off the concrete walls and reverberated down the cellblock. "Johnny, where the hell is Marvin Klaus? He knows damn well I ain't supposed to be here, so you just call him and tell him to let me out."

Bully couldn't believe his friend of sixty years had left him to rot in this stinking drunk tank. He yelled again, "Johnny, damn it. Are you there?" He knew his other friend, Johnny Weeks the jailer, worked the day shift and should have reported in by now. He was too old and too fat to do anything else.

Bully rocked back and forth, shifting weight from his bad leg to his good one. Marvin had arrested him for the second time, and he was getting damned tired of it. Marvin knew what he was doing out there at night, so what was the big deal?

Finally, Bully spied Weeks waddling up the hallway, puffing and wheezing under the load of his fifty-inch waist.

"Calm down, Bully," Weeks, said. Now that he was in the bowels of the jail away from the public, Weeks pulled his shirttail out, loosened his belt, and leaned on the cell bars. "Marvin ain't here, and you know I can't do nothing about it. You know you ain't getting out 'til you make bail. So sit down and shut up."

"Damn it, Johnny," Bully challenged, "Why'd he arrest me for diggin' holes? That ain't no forkin' crime."

"You were on state property, Bully. You know better."

Bully looked back at the foul-smelling refuse crowding the cell. One of the jailbirds threw up in the toilet bowl. Seconds later, the smell of fresh vomit reached his nostrils. In desperation, he turned back to his friend, motioning him closer. He lowered his voice to a whisper and pleaded again.

"Johnny, I'm close this time, really close. I can feel it. Maybe I'll cut you in."

Weeks pushed into the cell door. His huge belly melted into the bars filling the open spaces.

"Bully, don't be offering me no bribe now. We go back a long way, but I need this job. Those slime balls behind you hear you talking this trash and they'll scream discrimination. Besides, the last treasure you turned up weren't nothing but a damned old washing machine most likely buried in the last storm."

Bully waved Johnny off and limped back toward the seating area. Four Hispanics stood hunched in one corner talking quietly while three black men sprawled on the benches taking most of the space.

No one moved to offer him a seat. He slid his eye patch up to his forehead, dug into the socket with his finger, and held his glass eye up to the light. One of the Blacks made his way to the other end of the bench.

Bully put the eyeball in his shirt pocket and sat down. He dropped his artificial leg to the floor and rubbed the stump, the soreness constant now. The VA doctor had told him his weight agitated the nerve endings. Bully only knew it hurt like hell.

A big white kid moved across the room and eased beside him. When the kid bent down close to his ear, Bully sniffed stale alcohol and sour tobacco.

The kid whispered, "I seen what you did, old man. Getting a seat like that. You some kind of bad ass?"

Bully didn't respond. He had noticed the kid earlier, by size the biggest loser in the cellblock. Why was there always some punk wanting to be King Kong? Maybe it came with the territory and the type of habitual slobs who haunted jails.

Well, Bully Stout wasn't about to back off. He didn't get all crippled up fighting the world's biggest bullies to cow down to this redneck. Besides, he had been up all night. He was bone tired and not in any mood for wise guys.

He returned his eyeball to the socket, replaced the patch, and put his leg back on. When he was ready, he turned toward the kid and said, "Who the hell are you?"

The kid straightened, then put his hand on Bully's shoulder and squeezed it hard. "Watch it old man," the kid said, keeping his voice low. "You don't want no grief with me. Name's Bubba Shanks. I heard you talking to that fat jailer. You're some kind of treasure hunter, huh? How long you been searching?"

Bully gave him a hard stare. Shanks removed his hand and backed off a little.

Bully said, "Long enough, Sonny, long enough."

"So, you found any?" Shanks asked, a smirk on his face.

Better get up, Bully thought. Put himself in a better position. Shanks moved back a few steps. They were about the same height and maybe weight, but the kid had a lot of baby fat thrown in. Bully squinted his good eye. The kid might be fifty years younger, but he hadn't been digging holes in the sand for the last forty years.

Bully faced him straight on. "Do I look rich, you num-nuts?"

Shanks started at him. Bully raised his arm with his index finger pointing at the kid's chest. Shanks hesitated, staring at the gap where Bully's two middle fingers were missing, cut off at the joint. He laughed and waved his hand in a dismissive gesture. "Christ, old man. You ain't got much left. One leg, one eye, and one hand. You're a damned walking relic!"

Bully watched the fat boy's eyes. When Shanks glanced down at the wooden leg, Bully grabbed the kid's shirt, looped his thumb and index finger in over the top button and jerked him forward butting the kid's nose with his forehead. The kid dropped like a sack of sand falling off a truck. He hit the cell bars and slid to the floor. Blood oozed from his nose. The other inmates turned away.

"Bully! You okay in there?" Deputy Weeks called, coming back into the cellblock.

"Yeah, sure Johnny," Bully answered, looking at the kid sprawled on the floor. "I'm okay, but one of your lockups's got a bloody nose. It must be the altitude."

Weeks shook his head and said, "In Galveston?" He unlocked the cell door, ignoring Shanks. "You've been sprung," he continued. "Lisa's out front. Tell her I asked about her, okay? I'm glad she's home, Bully. Really glad."

Bully grasped his friend's hand and said, "Sure, Johnny, I'll tell her." Weeks had always been shy, but as with Bully's other friends, Johnny had known Lisa since she was born.

Bully pulled the steel door shut behind him and shuffled down the hallway holding onto the wall, his one good leg stiff from the hours spent in the damp cell.

He hugged Lisa at the jail entrance. "Thanks for coming, honey."

Lisa smiled and took Bully's arm. They maneuvered down the concrete steps outside the building and stopped at the bottom by the sidewalk.

Bully spied Parker's truck across the street. He put a gentle arm on Lisa's shoulder and said, "You didn't drive up here by yourself, did you, honey?"

"I'm sorry, Poppa. Marvin Klaus called about an hour ago. He said he called last night right after he put you in jail. But...oh man, Poppa! We were robbed last night. Two motorcycle dudes. They cut the phone lines. That's why I didn't hear Marvin calling all night and..."

Bully cut in, "Robbed! Are you all right, honey? Did they hurt you?"

"No, no, I'm okay, really. They didn't even get away with the money. Parker found it in the driveway this morning and..."

Bully put his massive arm around her shoulder and pulled her close. "It's okay, honey." He gave her a tight squeeze. "You're safe now with me. It's okay."

As they moved toward the truck, Bully said, "So where was Parker last night?"

Lisa said, "Drunk again."

Bully shook his head and mumbled, "That sum-bitch Parker. I oughta kick his ass. He shoud'a been there to help you." He pulled the stub of a cigar from his pocket, lit it, and said, "The closer to the end, the better these things taste." A stream of smoke disappeared into the moist Gulf air.

"How'd you get me out, honey?"

Lisa said, "Harry did it. He said he'd be in his office a little while longer if we wanted to come by."

Bully slapped his thigh, "Working on Sunday, huh? Good old Harry. Marvin must've called him last night after he tried to call you. Let's go thank him."

***

During the short ride to the law office, Bully thought about his friend, Harry Stein. No one had aged better than Harry. He kept his weight down and his hair on. Bully would never say anything, but he figured Harry used dye. The color never changed, shoe-polish brown with the same little pompadour swirl in front. He had that dapper lawyer look, always decked out in a freshly pressed shirt and tie. But Bully had him on height. Harry had quit growing at five-five. The same height he had been in the seventh grade when they first met.

Bully opened the office door and grasped Harry's hand as he walked in. They spoke and Bully thanked him. Then Bully turned to Lisa, put his hand on her shoulders and edged her forward.

Harry smiled broadly and said, "Hi Lisa. So good to see you. We missed you. Bully tells me you're doing a great job out at Parker's."

"Really?" Lisa said. Her cheeks turned a warm pink.

Harry spoke again, "You have your mother's eyes, Lisa. Such a pure blue and, like your mother's, they absolutely sparkle when you smile."

Lisa smiled. The pink edged toward red.

Bully silently thanked Harry for ignoring how Lisa really looked. She needed all the reinforcement she could get. Her face cried for makeup to cover the sins of abuse, and her tangled blond hair hung like frayed ropes around her neck.

Bully glanced at Harry with a knowing look, then said, "It's true, Lisa. I look at you and see your mother."

Lisa lowered her head, covering her eyes with her hand.

Harry turned to Bully and said, "So, Marvin caught you digging in the state park again, huh? Why don't you dig somewhere else? Get permission on some private land."

"I'll dig where I damn well please." Bully's voice rose as he spoke. "I was diggin' out there long before it was a park. It weren't nothing but a damned old swamp, full of stingrays and rattlers."

"Still after Jean Lafitte's treasure, huh, Bully? You ought to know better. How long have you been looking anyway, forty years?"

"Longer than that," Bully replied. "I was diggin' out on the west end while you were studying Texas history in the sixth-grade." Bully settled in a chair, loosened his artificial leg, and let it drop to the floor. It landed with a thud.

Harry said, "Still wearing that tree limb? Why don't you get one of those new titanium ones? They have to be a lot lighter, easier to walk on."

"Bullshit, Harry. This one works just fine. I carved it myself out of a piece of mahogany that'd washed up on the beach. That durn limb must've come all the way up from South America."

"Yeah, Bully," Harry said, "but the thing must weigh twenty pounds."

Bully waved Harry off. He knew the drill would never change. He would keep the wooden stump and Harry would continue to harass him.

Harry handed over the keys to Bully's truck. "I got it out of hock for you. It's parked in the back."

Bully reattached his homemade prosthesis and got up. He turned toward the door, pushed Lisa out before him and shouted over his shoulder, "Thanks, Harry. I'll pay you back real soon, with interest."

***

Bully's stump hurt from the rough night so they decided to leave his truck at Harry's. He would get a ride in tomorrow. Lisa drove out 23rd Street to the seawall. Along the beach, teenage surfers in neon swim trunks rode the waves, and girls in tight bikinis laughed and rubbed each other with oil.

Bully noticed her watching but said nothing. She had missed those years, and he shared the blame.

Further down the boulevard at 61st Street, they both managed another quick glance at the seawall. He guessed what she was thinking. Even after all these years, he couldn't come this way himself without remembering that night.

Caroline, his only daughter and Lisa's mother, drunk and driving too fast in a rainstorm, skidded past the light onto the rocks below. There was no one for Lisa then. She had gone to a state home for girls. Would she forgive him for not being there for her? Things would be better now, he would see to it.

A few blocks past 89th Street, the concrete barrier that protected Galveston ended. The road descended to sea level, and became FM3005. A sign announced San Luis Pass and the end of the island eighteen miles ahead.

A sheriff's car approached from the opposite lane. Bully noticed Lisa checking the speedometer. She didn't drive much, and he knew what traffic did to her.

"Oh, man," Lisa, said. "A cop. Like all I need is to get pulled over." She put both hands on the wheel and stared straight ahead.

Then Bully recognized the driver. "It's Marvin. Honk at him, honey. I want him to stop so I can read him off for arresting me."

"No way, Poppa." Lisa responded. "I don't have a driver's license. He'll throw me in jail like he did you."

Bully said, "No, he won't, honey. He was just doing his job when he arrested me." He reached over and squeezed Lisa's hand to comfort her. "People complain when they see me digging, so he has to do something. Anyway, he knows you don't have a license. He already told me that. He also knows you're too young to be serving beer. My God, Lisa, he's watched you grow up. There's nothing he don't know about you."

The sheriff's car slowed. Lisa's eyes cut nervously to the right, toward the barbed wire fence and the field beyond it. The truck drifted into the center stripe.

Bully yelled, "Look out!"

Lisa jerked the wheel abruptly to the right barely missing Marvin's car. Bully stuck his hand out of the window and waved over the cab. Deputy Klaus shook his head as he passed by.

Bully noticed Lisa checking the mirror. "You're okay, honey. Just keep driving, straight ahead."

The long night in jail had come and gone without sleep. Bully dropped his chin to his chest, closed his one good eye, and laid his head against the window.

Chapter Six

Günter sat transfixed, waiting for Señora Rosas to continue. What had she meant by her statement—*"there are still those who would harm us."*

She paced the room in silence, her face constricted with indecision. The old ceiling fan creaked in time with her walking stick, a slow painful dirge. He waited. Maybe he needed to say something, confirm his discretion.

Then, ever so softly, he said, "You have my word, Señora. Nothing will be learned from me."

She stopped pacing—a decision ratified. She pulled a small chair close to him and in almost a whisper said, "Very well, Günter. I do trust you. "

He nodded, carefully.

The Señora rose again and motioned Günter toward the back windows. A field of grass stretched before them down to a river.

She gestured at the landscape before them and said, "At one time, my family owned the largest *estancia* in the province. Our land stretched for several kilometers. Now, what you see today is all that is left, this house and the pastures down to the river in front of you."

She shuffled back to her chair and rested her head against its back with her eyes closed. After a moment, she opened them again and said,

"Do you know what the term *Criollo* means?"

Günter shook his head, feigning interest. "No, I do not," he replied. She tested his patience. How would any of this help him find Eric von Speigel.

"It means 'of Spanish origin.' Most Argentines are of European ancestry. They came from all over the Continent, and over the years, they mixed. But my family never did." She held out her arm, the skin sagging from her bones. "One hundred percent Spanish blood," she said. "And so is Mariana."

"This land has been in our family since the last century. I broke my family's tradition when I married my husband, Rheinhard Bauer. He was dashing, sophisticated, a German aristocrat. I was nineteen and in love. We married in August 1939. Two weeks later, Hitler invaded Poland and the war began. At first, Argentina remained neutral, helped by local German influence including my husband's."

Señora Rosas stopped for a moment, but her eyes never left his. She continued. "You see, Günter. What I did not know was that my husband was with the Abwehr, the intelligence section of the German Army. He was one of the top agents in Argentina, a spy, and...I am afraid...your grandfather was also." She paused, waiting for a response.

He winced slightly and took a quick breath. The words surged out, "My grandfather was a spy?"

"Yes, it is true." she said.

Günter was unsure how to react next. To complete his mission, he needed all the information about von Speigel the old woman had. He could not risk offending her, and he could not tell by her tone of voice how she felt about her husband and von Speigel being spies. The room was silent except for the creaking fan blade overhead.

Finally, she said, "Now, Günter, this next part is where I must trust you. Do I have your word that everything I tell you will remain in confidence?"

Günter opened his hands wide, palms out, as if again signaling his integrity. He said, "Yes, yes, of course, Señora. Your secrets are safe with me."

She said, "Do you know about the Nazi hunters?"

"You mean like the Jew, Simon Wiesenthal?"

"Yes, and as you know, Wiesenthal and his henchmen have hunted, those whom they termed 'war criminals' since the end of World War Two. It was Wiesenthal who tipped the Mossad to Adolph Eichmann's whereabouts in Buenos Aires. Eichmann, the infamous author of the *Final Solution,* the gassing of millions. The Mossad snatched him off the street and ferreted him to Israel where he was tried, found guilty, and hanged. And there were others as well. They found Klaus Barbie, known as the *Butcher of Lyon,* in Bolivia and deported him to France. They also tracked Josef Mengele, the death camp doctor who performed experiments on children, to Paraguay. And Günter," she continued, her eyes full of worry, "they are still active, here in Argentina."

Günter paused. Why was she concerned about that now? The fact that her husband and von Speigel were Nazi spies during the war shouldn't be a problem anymore. That happened long ago. Was she somehow afraid that the Nazi hunters would still get to her. But why would they want to?

He leaned forward and in a quiet voice said, "Surely, Señora, you are not worried now. Your husband has been dead for years. And he may have been a spy, but he wasn't involved in the concentration camps. He was no different than millions of other soldiers. They would not have put him on trial. He wasn't a War Criminal."

"You do not know these people, Günter. They are ruthless. We have heard stories that they have influenced the Argentine government to confiscate the properties of ex-Nazis's as a form of retribution."

"But, Señora..."

She waved him off. "No, Günter, my sources say it is possible. I have lived in fear for years. So much so, that after Rheinhard died, I changed my name back to Rosas. I must do what I can to protect our land here."

Günter leaned over and patted her hand. "Of course, Señora, of course."

"I can tell you more about your grandfather, but you must promise to be careful and respect our situation."

"I promise, Señora."

Seemingly satisfied, Señora Rosas continued, "You see...Eric was on a secret mission to America and Rheinhard was his contact in case anything went wrong."

At last, Günter thought, the mission. He edged forward in his chair. "Señora Rosas, please continue."

She answered in almost a whisper. "It was 1943. Eric was to be sneaked ashore on Galveston Island and..."

Günter interrupted, "Galveston Island?"

"Yes, in Texas," she said. "But, tragically, while en route, the American Coast Guard sank his submarine. He survived, but he was captured, and by coincidence, sent to a Prisoner Of War camp in Galveston. From there, he sent letters begging us to try and locate Anna Manfred to tell her he was safe."

Günter leaned back, a perplexed look on his face. "But, Señora. I do not understand. Why did von Speigel not try to contact Anna himself?"

"He had good reason not to, Günter," she insisted. "Corresponding directly with Anna would have violated his orders. Remember, he was on a highly secret mission. And the Abwehr was a merciless bunch. If they had intercepted one of the letters, it would have signaled that Eric had told Anna information he was ordered to keep secret. It would have put her life in danger.

"I understand," he said.

"And," Señora Rosas continued, "The Americans censored much of the mail. Eric was not using his real name in the POW camp. He had pretended to be an officer from the submarine. If the Americans had learned his real identity, he would have been executed as a spy."

"Then why was it safe to correspond with your husband?" Günter asked.

"He wrote to Rheinhard as a friend. The letters were innocent enough not to cause suspicion. But on the back of each sheet, Eric included secret messages written in invisible ink."

"Invisible ink?"

"Yes, the chemical was easily obtainable."

"What was in the secret messages?"

"Well, as I said, he asked us to notify Anna and tell her he was safe."

"And did you?" Günter asked.

"We tried, again and again. The first time we wrote, she had moved. By the time we got another lead, the Russians were overrunning eastern Germany. Attempting to communicate with anyone in Leipzig was impossible."

"Yes, of course, Señora," he replied. "It must have been difficult."

She nodded, acknowledging his acceptance, then continued, "And after the war, Leipzig was in the Russian zone. We could get nothing from the Communists. But Rheinhard was committed. Before he died, he made me promise to continue the search. So, after the reunification in 1990, I tried again—still nothing. Finally, I located a relative and learned that Anna had died. That is when I found out about your mother. I wrote to her immediately."

"Thank you for that," Günter said. He reached out to squeeze her hand and noticed the tears on her cheek. She breathed in short, shallow gulps, and her skin seemed moist and cool. He worried she would pass out at his feet, but he had no choice but to push on.

He offered her some tea, and she drank quietly. After a moment he said, "Señora Rosas, was there nothing else in the secret letters to your husband?"

She blinked twice and appeared to have regained some energy. "Yes," she said. "He also instructed Rheinhard to inform Berlin that because he had been captured, he had yet to make contact with the agent in Texas. But he would reach him after he escaped."

Günter interrupted again, "The agent in Texas? There was an Abwehr agent in Texas?"

"Yes," she replied. "Eric was to meet him and obtain the funds."

"The funds?"

"The funds for the mission. It was a very large operation, the biggest ever attempted by the Abwehr."

"And what was the mission?"

"To…to finance and train German operatives in the art of sabotage."

"Was he to train operatives all over America?"

"Mainly the Gulf Coast," she answered.

"A very expensive operation," Günter added. He was close now; he could feel it. Push on. "So did my grandfather escape and meet the contact? Did he obtain the funds?"

"We never found out."

"You…you never found out?" Günter stammered, the shock in his voice evident. Then he calmed himself and said, "Please forgive me, Señora. My impatience is inexcusable."

"Of course, Günter, I understand your anxiety," Señora Rosas replied. "He was your grandfather after all. The truth is, we do not know if he met the contact or not. Eric's last message said he was planning to escape, but we never heard from him again."

Günter straightened in the chair trying to conceal his distress, hoping the Señora had not noticed the color draining from his face. He had come all this way only to learn von Speigel had been rescued from the sinking submarine and then seemingly disappeared again. But wait, he thought, the contact.

He asked quickly, "Who was the man he was to meet?"

Señora Rosas did not answer immediately. She closed her eyes and seemed to meditate.

Patience, he reminded himself. You are so close.

Her hand trembled as she rubbed her forehead. After a moment, she opened her eyes, "I...I do not remember his name. It was so long ago. We destroyed all the correspondence to protect ourselves."

No! Günter thought. A dead end! His entire purpose in coming to Argentina was to gather enough information to continue on to America. What could he possibly accomplish in Texas now? They talked a while longer until he was convinced he had gotten all he could from her.

During lunch, they made small talk. Señora Rosas reminisced about her husband and their life together. She asked about Germany, the reunification. When Mariana cleared the table, Günter, disappointed, prepared to go.

"Señora, thank you for your hospitality. I am afraid I must leave. Have you possibly remembered the name of the operative in Texas?"

"No, I am sorry, Günter. It was just too long ago."

Günter glanced at his watch, four o'clock. When he rose to leave, Señora Rosas put her hand on his and said, "Günter, must you leave? Why not stay over? It is too late for your flight."

Günter studied Señora Rosas' face and then turned to Mariana.

"Yes, please do stay, Günter," Mariana added. "The evenings here can be quite satisfying."

***

An hour later, Mariana sat at her dressing table admiring herself in the mirror. Señora Rosas stood behind her brushing her hair. Mariana caught the Señora's eye in the mirror and said, "Your performance was incredible, Auntie. I only hope I can do as well tonight."

Señora Rosas stopped brushing and put her hands on Mariana's shoulders. They both faced the mirror looking at each other's reflection in the glass.

Señora Rosas replied, "Dearest one, with the lust that letch had in his eyes, I think you will have no problem."

"I think perhaps you are correct, Auntie."

"Besides," the Señora continued, "I wasn't acting. It is always easier to be convincing when one is telling the truth. And most of what I told him actually happened."

"Even the part about how valiantly you tried to locate Anna Manfred?"

"We did try, Mariana. It happened just as I told him. But then later, when we began to wonder about what happened to the funds for the mission, we needed to know if von Speigel ever returned or contacted her. So I do admit our reasons for finding her changed a little."

"A little," Mariana replied, a sheepish grin on her face.

Señora Rosas smiled broadly and tapped Mariana's shoulder playfully.

Mariana said, "So why did you choose to withhold the name of the Abwehr agent in Texas?"

Señora Rosas turned deadly serious, "Our sources in Germany tell us Günter is connected with a neo-Nazi organization. At this point, I do not know if the organization is involved or if he is acting independently. So, until we know it is best that we feed him one spoonful at a time. That is also why I demanded that he keep everything secret. I only pray that he does so. Because if he is working with the Nazi group, and our plan works, there is less chance someone else will be coming after us. We have enough of that now."

As Mariana turned and rose to take the Señora into her arms, she said, "I understand, Auntie. But rest assured our plan will work."

They embraced each other tenderly. Then, Señora Rosas said, "There is another reason I think it important to go slowly. This is our last chance, Mariana, our only chance. We cannot afford to lose.

If we proceed too quickly, he may become suspicious. I want him to trust us completely."

They each held each other for a moment longer, then Señora Rosas released the embrace and pushed Mariana back to arms length. And with dark purposeful eyes and a voice brimming with strength she said, "Now my dear, it is time for you to go and entertain our guest. Look in the cabinet. I think we have a bottle or two left of Ramefort '81."

"Yes, Auntie, nothing but the best Argentine cognac for our friend, Günter Manfred."

Chapter Seven
Sunday, August 21 & Monday, August 22

My eyes popped open at the sound of a truck horn. I checked my watch—three o'clock. Christ, I had slept through lunch. At the window in the back of my bedroom, I watched a pickup jerk out of the parking lot wondering how many customers had turned away?

I hustled downstairs and found several dollars on the back counter with a note. A customer had helped himself to a few beers and left. The room was stuffy and hot. A skillet of congealed roux from this morning sat on the counter. Several flies perched on the edge like guards in watchtowers.

I switched on the ceiling fans and propped the back door open, then sat at the counter with a cold beer and swept a trickle of sweat from my forehead.

Lisa appeared in the back doorway, her hair pulled back and fastened with a rubber band. Thoughts of a young girl laughing and reciting bird names flashed across my mind. I pushed them back.

Lisa said, "I'm sorry, Parker. I had to go."

I turned away. A beer sign on the far wall flickered on and off.

Lisa stopped at the end of the counter. "Did you feed Charlie yet?"

I noticed the solicitation in her voice, but ignored the question. Playing nice after screwing up didn't work with me. I had witnessed too many young officers sucking up to their commanders to be impressed by that tactic. Facing her again, I said, "I'm not paying you for the time you missed."

"It's okay. You don't have to."

I reached over the counter for another beer. "Damn straight I don't."

I gestured toward the stove. "The roux's no good. It sat out all morning. Check the leftover beans and rice in the refrigerator. Who knows, maybe we'll still snag a customer or two."

Lisa removed a large pot from the refrigerator, skimmed the congealed fat from the sausage off the top, and started the burner. She came around the counter, crossed the room to the front door and began struggling with the ropes that opened the wall of the outside bar.

"I can't lift the wall," she shouted. "Can you help me? Poppa usually does it and he's still out in the shed messing with his tools."

A stabbing pain shot across the side of my head. I winced, cursing that the beer hadn't relieved my hangover. "Oh, to hell with it!" I answered. "Leave it shut. Chances are we're done for the day anyway."

Lisa shouted again, "What'd you say, Parker?"

I looked back at her and yelled, "Screw it. Leave it shut. And forget about the chow." I waved her off and turned to leave.

Lisa approached my back. "Hey Parker. Like, ease up on me, man. Okay? Don't be such an asshole."

I pivoted, ready to lay into her but quickly sensed someone behind me. Fingers tightened on the back of my neck.

"Enough, Parker."

Bully's voice. I broke the grip and whirled around. We were close now, face to face. Tobacco breath streamed past the cigar clenched in his teeth. The unlit stub danced like a marionette. I gagged.

I stepped back and yelled, "Keep your damned hands off me, Bully."

His voice boomed past my ear.

"She's just a kid."

"A kid, my ass," I yelled again. "She's seen more at eighteen than a maid in a Mexican whorehouse. Now she's out here sponging off me."

Bully's left arm shot out and pushed me back. I twisted violently to escape the brunt of the blow. His good leg gave and he collapsed to the floor. I waited for the big mass to settle, then stepped over him toward the door.

Bully grunted, trying to right himself. He managed to prop himself on an elbow, then yell at me, "She ain't sponging off you. She earns her keep working in this forkin' dump. You sure as hell can't run it alone."

My temple pulsed. I turned quickly and sidestepped behind the counter. "Look who's talking about dumps? The Salvation Army wouldn't take that piece of shit you sleep in."

Lisa stooped to help Bully up. She put her hands under his armpits, then looked up at me. "You suck, man. You really do. You know that?"

I stared hard at Lisa but remained quiet. I had said enough already. I brushed past Bully and climbed the back stairs to my sanctuary.

***

Early the next morning I worked my cast net off the dock until I had caught enough mullet for Charlie's breakfast. I checked his bandaged wing, then pushed the mullet through the cage wires.

Afterwards, I moved to the concrete bench next to the bulkhead and watched the bay until the sun entered the sky. The front had arrived during the night and a slight north wind rippled the water. A flock of terns dived the bay hunting baitfish, squealing loudly, breaking the morning quiet.

Near Bully's camper, the bleached skull of an alligator gar hanging from a rope under the deck twirled in the breeze. Rows of razor-sharp teeth filled its foot-long jaw smiling back at me.

I had found the gar several weeks earlier washed up dead in a slough next to my house. They spend much of their time wallowing in deep, slimy holes out in the bay. But for some reason this one had ended up here. Gars are a smelly bunch. When the old salts around here don't like someone's appearance, you might here the saying, "He looks like he's been pulled through a gar hole." You get the idea.

Alligator gars are prehistoric throwbacks, evolutionary survivors. Their snout resembles that of an alligator, but they have the skin and fins of a fish. To call them ugly is being kind.

This gar was huge, seven feet and two hundred pounds. On a lark, I skinned the monster's head, boiled and bleached it white, and hung it from the deck to cure.

I walked over and inspected the head. It seemed dry enough. I took it down, wired its jaw open so all the teeth would show, and hung it from the ceiling over the back counter of the bar.

On a old piece of plywood, I hand-painted a quick drawing of an alligator gar and then added the name underneath, *The Garhole Bar*.

Funny how things turn out. I had actually backed into the idea of opening a bar. When I came home from the Army last Spring, the bottom level of my old bait camp was trashed out from a storm that had put two feet of water over the bulkhead. I had to clean it up anyway, and then I probably wouldn't have done much but sit there and drink. So why not turn it into a bar and charge others to drink with me. People drink when they are happy and people drink when they are sad. Sad was better. Misery paid dividends.

Turning the old camp into a bar hadn't been difficult. I scrubbed the concrete floor as clean as I could get it, then cut a hole in the front wall and hinged it to make a bar to the outside. Breezes from the Gulf could flow through the opening and exit the back window, cooling the interior. To liven the place up, I painted the walls a pastel, island colored green. I stuck in a few tables and chairs from a thrift shop, then wired in a couple of ceiling fans, added a counter in the back, threw in a beer cooler, hung some neon signs on the wall and presto—I was in business.

After hanging the sign, I hiked up the road to the highway, crossed the blacktop and swept through the sand dunes to the beach. I sat on a piece of driftwood facing the Gulf. The surf rolled steady and clear. The morning sun on my face gave me a lift, an affirmation that my life wasn't just some big horrible nightmare. The whole scene offered a sense of stability, of continuance.

Bustling sandpipers, willets and avocets dressed in tans and blacks ran the shore, searching for breakfast. Their cries reminded me of the early morning markets of the Middle East where vendors in white turbans hawked spices and rugs. I pushed the thought away, then picked up a shell and skimmed it down the beach scattering the birds before me.

I walked the beach and stopped to inspect part of a fishing net brought in by the morning tide. Maybe I could find a place for it in The Garhole—mount it on the wall or over the door.

The Garhole…. Yesterday had been the worst day since Lisa's return. I wasn't happy about the argument, but it was their fault, wasn't it? They had ganged up on me. I gave them both a place to live, and this was the thanks I got.

I climbed a small rise and looked back over the island. Black and yellow sunflowers danced in the breeze, and sea lavender was turning its fall purple. Acres of delicate spartina grass glistened in the early morning dew.

I could see all the way across the island to my house on the shoreline of West Galveston Bay. And as I had done a hundred times before, I sat on the sand dune and reflected on my life. I owned all the land between the beach and the house and from the end of the island to a mile further up the two-lane toward Galveston.

My mother's father had amassed the property during the depression in the 1930s when people were hungry and land was cheap. According to my mother, the old man loved the land even though she had often heard him say it was good for nothing but tough cattle and tougher men.

I was young when he died, and I barely remember him. But I have always felt the old man's love of the land in my veins. I know every sand dune and animal trail and marsh by heart. Growing up I had learned the names and colors of every bird species on the island. Many, like the gulls and brown pelicans, live here year around. Others visit according to the season. Purple Martins come in January, and dozens of songbirds—orioles, tanagers, and warblers— arrive in the spring. Ducks, geese, and sandhill cranes winter in the surrounding marshes.

When the old man died, my mother inherited the property. But there was no cash. We needed an income. I took odd jobs and weekend labor when I could find it. We scraped and saved.

Together, we built a bait stand with a bedroom on top. On my thirteenth birthday, we moved from town to run the camp. Each morning before daybreak, I dipped bait shrimp and sold ice and drinks to the fishermen. Business was good and we eked out a living. Life seemed simple.

And then there was Janie. We met in high school. Me, the all-star jock and her, the prom queen. We were from different sides of the tracks. While I scrapped along at the bait stand, she attended spring cotillions and her own coming-out party. Maybe the difference in our social status fueled the attraction. I don't know.

The marriage lasted until I came to the states for treatment in '93. It probably only worked that long because while I was stationed in Germany, she spent most of her time in Galveston.

I gazed back toward the beach. A typical late summer surf lapped at the shore. The weak, August front was almost finished by the time it crossed the Texas plains and settled down onto the coast.

I felt the breeze on my face and knew the island had blocked the north wind, allowing the surf to lay flat. The clear water would attract the baitfish, which brought the trout, which in turn brought the fishermen. The Garhole would be busy.

Chapter Eight
Tuesday, August 23

After leaving Santa Rosa de Calmuchita, Günter drove all day, arriving in Buenos Aires late in the evening. He spent the night in the city and arrived at the airport several hours before his scheduled flight. He had come too far to quit now; maybe something would turn up in Texas.

He dreaded the call to Horst Frankin, but he had no choice. The mission was to be funded in stages, and so far, only the trip to Argentina had been authorized.

"No, absolutely not," Franklin shouted into the phone. *"The committee is emphatic. No more funds without information. Where are you going in America?"*

Günter almost yelled into the telephone, the implied threat obvious by his tone of voice, *"Horst, you will get the permission I need. Remember, I will be home soon."* Günter was certain Frankin knew his history. Surely, he got the message.

A long pause, then Frankin's voice, *"I hear you Günter, but I can do no more."*

Günter glanced at the schedule board. The flight left in three hours, barely enough time for Frankin to wire the money for the trip. He took a deep breath. "*The old woman was helpful,*" he said, reluctantly. "*It is Galveston, a port city in Texas.*"

"*Ah ha, Galveston,*" Frankin, said. "*And who are you to meet there?*"

Günter expected the question. The idiot was persistent, if nothing else. He replied, "*I have a name, but under the same condition, it must remain a secret. They are very frightened.*"

"*Of what?*" Frankin asked.

"*I do not know,*" he lied, "*but it terrifies them.*" Günter had no name, but he was certain that if Frankin knew that, he would not send the funds.

Frankin stammered, and mumbled something unintelligible. Günter waited. Finally, Frankin said, "*Check with Western Union at the airport in one hour.*"

Günter slammed the telephone on its cradle. He would take care of the smug fool when he returned to Germany. For now, he could do nothing but wait for the flight. He bought a newspaper and settled into a chair. An advertisement for women's lingerie caught his attention.

His thoughts flashed to Mariana. It had happened during the night. She came to his room, her hair undone, a negligee quickly abandoned. She was inexperienced but willing, and so...accommodating, so...

His thoughts stopped. He never allowed himself feelings; they interfered with his goals. Anyway, the next morning, Mariana was gone. He had not seen her again.

He reviewed what he had learned. Some of what the Señora told him he already knew. Before his mother died, she had given him a letter that her mother, Anna Manfred, had left for her. Anna wanted her daughter to know that her father was Eric von Speigel, an honored member of the Reich's elite.

The letter disclosed that on the night before von Speigel was to leave for France, Anna had gone to him. He violated the rules and told her he was going on a secret mission to the United States, but he had not said where. He might not see her for months. He was to be in charge of a huge operation, involving many agents. It would require a great deal of money. Von Speigel had sworn Anna Manfred to secrecy, but later, after the war, when she knew she was dying, Anna wrote the letter to her daughter.

So, that much Günter already knew. He also knew from old war records that von Speigel's submarine had been sunk. He always assumed both von Speigel and the money for the mission had gone down with the sub. But then, out of nowhere, his mother received a letter from Señora Rosas. And over the next several weeks of correspondence, the Señora hinted that she knew more about von Speigel than she was admitting. So Günter, knowing the Organization was desperate for money, convinced them to fund his trip to Argentina.

From Señora Rosas, he now knew that von Speigel had survived, and the money wasn't at the bottom of the Gulf of Mexico. There was still a chance.

After von Speigel was captured, he had planned to escape. But what had happened to him? And where was the money? There were no records of Eric von Speigel being repatriated to Germany after the war. Was he still alive? The last Nazi in America!

Suddenly Günter heard his name announced on the airport's paging system. Who knew he was here? Was Frankin calling back, a problem with the funds? He stepped to the house phone.

"Günter, it is Mariana."

"Mariana! What a surprise. I wanted to see you before I left. I thought of you all the way to the airport." It was not a complete lie, he did have thoughts of her, or more like cravings—carnal cravings.

"I have been thinking of you, too. You will return, won't you, Günter?" Her voice was sweet, seductive.

"Of course, Mariana," the lie continued. "But I am leaving now for Galveston. I must learn what happened to my grandfather. Has the Señora remembered the contact's name?"

"That is why I am calling. Señora Rosas asked me to reach you. She thinks very highly of you, Günter. You remind her so much of her lost husband. After you left, she remembered she had not destroyed all of the correspondence. One letter had gotten misplaced, and she never burned it. She remembered it was from Eric."

"What was in it?"

"We have yet to locate it. She just told me about it moments ago. I wanted to reach you before you got on the plane. Call me from Texas."

***

At the *Estancia Rosas,* Mariana Villata replaced the handset into its cradle. A sly grin crossed her face. She turned to Señora Rosas sitting in the chair across from her. The ceiling fan creaked overhead, churning along as purposely as their plan.

Mariana said, "What do you think, Auntie? Was I good?"

"An excellent tease," the Señora answered. "I think he has taken the bait for sure. You are indeed a member of our family."

She rose from her chair and motioned for Mariana to take her arm. When they reached her bedroom, she released herself and sat on the edge of the bed.

Mariana said, "His arrogance astounds me, Auntie. He thinks he is such a great lover, ha! The man is an animal. If only we were not so desperate."

"But we are desperate," Señora Rosas responded. "Time is running out."

"How much time do we have?"

"Not much, and I fear this time the bank will not extend the note."

"Oh, Auntie. If you had only told me sooner about that blackmailer in Buenos Aires. I cannot believe it, a Nazi hunter turned traitor to his own cause."

"You weren't even born when it started," Señora Rosas said. "There was nothing you could do. The post-war years were very hard on us. Rheinhard was a playboy. His family in Germany had money, and they supported him, but they lost everything during the war. We were destitute. I sold off some of the *estancia* just to

54

support us. Then Rheinhard became ill, growing weaker every day. That is when that bastard Nazi hunter found us and started the blackmail. I could not let the hunters take Rheinhard. I was weak, I admit it. I had no choice but to pay to keep the Jew traitor quiet. Over the years, I sold off more of our land. Now we have nothing left but the house and a few acres, and it is mortgaged. The bank will foreclose in less than three weeks."

"I know how dreadful you must feel. The e*stancia* has been in your family for generations and..."

Señora Rosas interrupted, "And I want you to have it. At least we no longer have the threat from the blackmailer."

The comment surprised Mariana. She waited for the Señora to lie down and then helped her settle the covers around her. Then she sat on the edge beside her and said, "What do you mean, Auntie? We no longer have the threat?"

Señora Rosas reached into the drawer of her bedside table and removed a plastic vial containing a single capsule. She held it in front of Mariana and said, "Remember the trip I took to Buenos Aires last year."

Mariana nodded.

"I met with the bastard then." She shook the vial, rolling the capsule from one end to the other. "Rheinhard had two cyanide capsules issued by the Abwehr in case he was discovered. One for each of us." She stopped and placed the vial back on her nightstand.

"You...you didn't, Auntie."

"Yes, child, I did. I would have done anything to save what was left of our property for you. It was an easy decision. So my dear, with our blackmailer out of the way, all we need to do now is pay off the mortgage."

"Do you really think there is a chance Günter can find the money?"

"We must believe so, Mariana. I don't know what happened to the funds. Rheinhard and I tried to find out. All we knew for sure was that von Speigel was a Prisoner of War. After the war, Rheinhard went as far as he could with his contacts in the Abwehr.

No one seemed to know anything. And as I said, we could not find Anna Manfred. We even wrote to the agent in Texas asking for information. Rheinhard pretended it was official Abwehr business. The letters were returned unopened."

"We were so desperate we even considered going to Texas ourselves, but Rheinhard was too weak. His sickness overwhelmed us both. I had to focus on him. We were out of options, and then, when Rheinhard died, I grew weary and gave up. But then later, one of my contacts paid off, and I found Günter's mother and then Günter. There is no doubt he is after the money. This concern he shows for his grandfather is a lot of nonsense, simple pretext."

Mariana said, "Maybe the Abwehr agent in Texas sent the money back to Mexico and it was stolen en route. Or maybe the agent kept the money until the war was over and then spent it."

Señora Rosas said, "Perhaps. Anything is possible. But then again, maybe it is still hidden somewhere and Günter will get lucky and find it."

"And what if he finds it? Do you really think he will return here with the money?"

"Well, we know he is greedy. My offer was very plain. He could not have misinterpreted it. The entire *estancia* could be his." Señora Rosas took Mariana's hand and squeezed it, then winked. "And I am sure your skills only enhanced the offer."

Mariana smiled and then leaned in and caressed her aunt's cheek.

"However," the Señora continued, "you made a good point, my dear. We cannot know for certain if he will return. We cannot risk it. When he calls back, this is what we will do..."

Chapter Nine
Tuesday, August 23

I had left the beach yesterday thinking the clear surf would mean good fishing today and a decent lunch crowd. My intentions were to cook up a fresh batch of gumbo so the flavors would mix better overnight.

But back at The Garhole, I found Bully and Lisa holed up in their trailer. Our earlier argument was the worst we'd had since Lisa's return, and I wondered if they had locked the door planning to hide out all day.

Out of the mood to cook, I convinced myself that every now and then it was good to check out the competition. I cracked open a new bottle of Famous Grouse and spent the evening bar hopping up and down West Beach.

***

Other than finishing the bottle, the night had been uneventful. When I finally stumbled downstairs this morning the beer clock on the wall said 10:00 AM—a late start for preparing lunch.

I needed grease for a fresh roux, so I wiped the skillet with a cup towel and started the bacon. It wouldn't be my best batch, and if any of the regulars came in they would notice the difference and bitch.

So what! I never said The Garhole was Brennan's in New Orleans. The way my head pounded, they would be lucky if they got scrambled eggs.

The August heat had finally taken its toll on the garden. We were down to the dregs. I grabbed a bowl and started out to see what I could salvage.

Bully stepped out of the trailer, his unbuttoned shirt hanging loosely over his huge gut. He mumbled around the cigar clenched in his teeth. "Kinda late to start lunch ain't it."

I shot darts at him and continued toward the garden. I really didn't have anything to say. This was the first we had seen each other since yesterday, and I wasn't in a forgiving mood. Maybe I said some things I shouldn't have about Lisa, but that didn't give Bully the right to grab my neck. Nobody puts their hands on me. Nobody!

Bully stretched and yawned, then yelled at my back. "Check the refrigerator. Lisa thought you'd make it last night so she got the vegetables ready. You never showed up."

I ignored the dig. No sense getting provoked this early in the morning. I tried a reasonable tone of voice.

"Where is Lisa?"

"Why?" Bully answered. "Her hours don't start till eleven."

"Haven't seen her this morning, that's all."

"You mean you're gonna be human today. What'd you do, lay off the booze last night?"

I stepped closer to Bully, caught his eyes and said, "Screw you."

He removed the cigar from his mouth, waved it in front me, and started to say something. I left him with his mouth open, went back inside to the stove, and watched the fat burn out of the bacon.

Bully leaned against the back door. "She's out running the crab traps. You got to put something in the pot besides onions and okra."

I shook my head. "Deliver me." Bully didn't respond.

After a moment he said, "You know I'd told Marvin about those two motorcycle jockeys that harassed Lisa."

I didn't respond.

He continued and said, "Well, Marvin called earlier. Seems like they had a little accident after they left The Garhole. Somewhere between Freeport and Houston they hit a rainstorm and an eighteen-wheeler crossed over to their side. Hardly enough left to identify the pricks."

I smiled inwardly, relieved by the news. I had told Lisa not to worry about them returning, but somewhere in the back of my mind I hadn't yet convinced myself.

I added flour to the bacon grease and stirred. A few moments later, I added chopped garlic and got the rest of the seasonings ready.

Bully moved to a stool at the front of the bar, then reached over the counter for a beer, grunting as his stomach mashed against the edge. I turned at the noise in time to see him toast the gar-head before he drank.

He noticed me watching him and said, "Just showing a little respect. His kind's been around a long time. Maybe they know something we don't."

I thought about what he said. Maybe they did know something we didn't. They certainly had to be tough to survive this long, that was for sure. They were loners, only getting together for an occasional breeding romp. Nothing wrong with that. Sometimes, the fewer contacts you have with your own kind the better things are.

As the roux darkened, the magic aroma of bacon grease, roasted flour and sautéed garlic permeated the air. My gut rumbled, telling me I hadn't eaten since yesterday. When I turned to search the refrigerator for something to eat, Bully came around the counter and poured beer into the mixture. A half inch of cigar ash broke off and fell into the pot. He stirred it in.

I straightened, exhaled slowly, and shook my head. The word came out under my breath, "Asshole."

Bully said, "What?"

I said, "Add. Is there anything else you want to add?"

"I don't know," Bully said, continuing to stir. "What do you think?"

I wondered if Bully hadn't caught my sarcasm or if he had just chosen to ignore it. I stepped out to a front table and lowered my head on my arms. I had slept okay last night, but the tiredness hadn't gone away. Of all the symptoms, fatigue was the most persistent. I never felt rested.

I could have done without Bully's sniping. Why didn't I just kick them both out? Tell Bully to take his beat-up trailer and his whoring granddaughter and shove it.

A moment later, I sensed Bully standing at the table taking a deep breath. I knew what was coming; I had heard it before. First, the soft voice, then the sanctimonious lecture.

He said, "You know Parker, you could be nicer to Lisa. Cut her some slack. She's going through a rough time. After all, she is kin."

I sighed, my head still down on the table. Just as I thought, Bully's caustic approach hadn't worked so now he would try schmoozing. The combination of fatigue and Bully's manipulation had finally gotten to me. I pushed back from the table, veins bulging in my neck.

"Kin! She may be my cousin, but, by God, she's your granddaughter. Where were you when her mother died? I had an excuse. I was in the damned desert. But you! Why couldn't you be there for her? Her mother was your only daughter."

Bully's hot breath steamed at my face. "That ain't fair, Parker! That ain't fair at all. You know damned well I was sick—my heart and all. I was in and out of the V.A. hospital all during that time. I couldn't do nothin', I almost died."

"Yeah, well, Lisa did die," I yelled back. "Or she might as well have. You know she won't stay off the stuff. She'll be back with that pimp Sader in no time. Once a doper, always a doper."

Bully yelled back, moving his hands excitedly. His eye-patch slipped halfway off. "No, Parker. She's quit cold turkey. She left that bastard for good. Tried to kill herself—swallowed a whole damned purse full of valium. Thank God she woke up. Hitched down here with nothing but the jeans she was wearing. She's really trying now."

I raised my hand and waved Bully off. "Old man, she's sure suckered you."

Bully slammed the table. He sputtered and jerked, not able to get his words out. He turned in a huff and stormed out the front door as fast as his wooden leg would allow, pounding the cement floor with each step. Shell and sand spewed from the rear wheels of his pickup as he roared out toward the blacktop.

I rubbed the back of my neck and gazed at the ceiling. Bully's excuse never changed—too sick to do anything. He could have found some way to help. I sure didn't think it was my fault. I had been in the middle of a shooting war.

I went back to the stove, added the onions and okra to the pot, and turned the heat to low. I got a six-pack out of the cooler and went upstairs to the deck.

The cold front had dwindled out. The morning warmed fast. Late summer rays beat down directly from overhead. Perspiration gathered on my neck and soaked into my shirt. I opened a beer and drank steadily.

The sound of an outboard motor wafted up from below—Lisa back from the crab run. I got up and started for the stairs. It was for sure, the crabs weren't going to clean themselves and jump into the pot.

Günter Manfred fumed inwardly as he hustled along the crowded passageway. One would think the Americans would be more organized. Four planes had arrived within minutes of each other at the international terminal of the Houston Airport, and all of the passengers had been funneled into one walkway leading to the customs area. He stood in line with hundreds of other travelers waiting his turn to clear entry into the United States.

His thoughts returned to Argentina and his conversation with Señora Rosas. Rheinhard Bauer, her husband, must have been quite a man, he thought. Bauer had successfully evaded the Nazi trackers for years. The man had worked his options well. He had aided the Reich when Germany's standing with Argentine leaders was at its peak. Then, when Germany started losing and Argentina joined the Allies, Bauer had quietly regressed to his role as a landed aristocrat.

The message was clear—everyone used everyone. That was fine with Günter. He knew that trick well. When he was sixteen, his mother sat him down in their rat-infested kitchen and told him the truth. Until then, he thought his father had simply run away after learning his mother was pregnant. Günter knew he was a bastard child. He thought that was the reason he had been ostracized from society, treated like a leper. He sat there, waiting for his mother to speak, wondering how the story of his life could get any worse. And then he found out.

The border guards had caught his mother attempting to escape into the western zone and the Russian sergeant in charge of the detail raped her. A communist pig impregnated his mother and everyone except him knew it—the neighbors, his schoolmates. No wonder he had grown up a loner, without a single friend.

He hated the Russians for occupying his country and starving the people. He had eaten dogs and rats, and begged for food. Many nights he had nearly frozen to death. He already had good reason for retribution, but now with what his mother told him, revenge had become an obsession.

But his mother said no, revenge was not the answer. It would not free you from this life of destitution and hopelessness. If you are ready, she told him, an opportunity will present itself. But you must have patience. Meanwhile, she said—prepare yourself.

So he joined the German Truth Organization where he could do both—get training and revenge. They told him that only the revival of the Reich could save his country from the Communists. The ones who shaved their heads were called skinheads. Not too smart, he thought, making themselves so obvious. Better to keep your membership hidden, a secret. He could be more valuable that way.

So when the East German Army drafted him for his compulsory two-year enlistment, his GTO control encouraged him to transfer to the intelligence section. Günter became a double agent. The Army taught him how to infiltrate secret organizations, and the irony was that all the while he was reporting to the German Truth Organization.

The Army also taught him how to kill, using only his hands. That had come in handy. At the request of the GTO, he remained in the Army past his two-year enlistment. He had become too valuable to the GTO to quit.

Then after Reunification, when fear of the Communists receded, Günter quit the Army. The GTO could be more open now, but they still had to be careful. German laws were very strict against Neo-Nazi movements.

The line moved slowly. He must be patient, stay calm. He had planned his stay in America carefully. Soon he would pass through immigration control and disappear.

"Next," the immigration officer called out, beckoning Günter to cross the white line and approach his station.

"How long do you plan to visit America, Mr. Manfred?" the officer inquired, inputting the passport number as he spoke.

"Just a few days," Günter answered, using his best English.

"Business or pleasure?" The agent looked down, studying the passport.

"Some business, mostly on holiday." Keep the conversation minimal, he reminded himself. It was best not to be remembered. In practice, there was a fine line between the two, being too friendly or too reserved. He knew the agent was trained to be suspicious.

"And what is your business?"

The agent maintained eye contact now. Günter smiled to lighten the mood. "Export and import. I hope to get some ideas for German products I can export to Texas." It was more than he had wanted to say.

The agent didn't respond. He patted Günter's passport against his open palm as if trying to decide whether to go further with the interview. Günter waited patiently.

"Enjoy your stay, Mr. Manfred," the agent said, placing the passport into Günter's hand.

Before leaving Argentina, Günter had made a reservation at the Marriot Hotel in the Houston airport. He had also sent over-night the same package he had previously gotten in Argentina. And, again he would have to wait until the following morning to receive it. He checked in, took a shower, and ordered room service. He would remain in the room until morning. Nothing to do now, but wait.

The next morning after ten, he approached the front desk. "Anything for Günter Manfred?" He asked.

The desk clerk checked Günter's box. "Of course, sir. We have some mail for you."

Günter returned to his room and opened the sealed envelope inside the package. As Texas was his final destination, he would now switch to his new identity. He removed the fake passport and international driver's license.

Going through customs with false papers would have been too risky so he had used his real name. But now, when he left the hotel, he would be Alec Strauss. He would take his Günter Manfred identity papers with him. He needed them close in case he had to leave quickly.

People would notice his accent so Günter decided not to fake being from Germany. He would simply have two identities. He would use his real name, Günter Manfred, only to enter and exit the United States. While in Texas, he would use his alias. He would be a writer researching a story about early German settlements in Texas.

Then, if anything went wrong and he had to run, no one would be able to locate Alec Strauss. He didn't exist. Escape would be simple. He would merely travel to the closest border city and enter Mexico using his real name.

**

Two hours later, Strauss crossed the causeway connecting the mainland to Galveston Island and proceeded down Broadway, the main boulevard that extended through town to the beach on the far side of the island. An eclectic collection of buildings from old Victorian houses to shuttered businesses to fast-food restaurants lined the thoroughfare.

He turned left on 23rd Street headed toward the Tremont, a hotel in the downtown area of Galveston a block from the main shopping street known as the Strand. Better to stay in a crowded area, he thought—mix with the tourists, be just another visitor.

He passed the Rosenberg Library, an imposing structure of Italian renaissance architecture commanding an entire block. It was no doubt loaded with American propaganda, he thought. The Americans let people read anything. How foolish. But he might as well take advantage of their stupidity. What better place to get what he needed? Librarians are accustomed to people asking questions.

Strauss needed information, and he needed an excuse to ask questions when he arrived in Galveston. A writer could do that without raising suspicion. He had concocted his cover story after a GTO trainer had told him about the thousands of Germans who had emigrated to Texas through the Port of Galveston.

To the trainer, the emigrants were simply traitors running like frightened sheep when their country needed them most. The coming Fourth Reich could use their descendents now, he had said, especially after two wars, when so many of Germany's finest had sacrificed themselves for the glory of the State.

Günter Manfred, alias Alec Strauss, had no problem with sacrifice; that is, as long as it was someone else doing the giving. He had done enough of that. He knew about being hungry and cold. Years ago the GTO had rescued him from a pitiful existence. To a large extent, they were responsible for where he was today. He owed them for that. But, one thing he had learned for certain back on the streets of Leipzig, Günter Manfred would look out for number one.

Chapter Eleven
Tuesday, August 23

After lunch, Lisa cleaned the tables and took the empty beer bottles and paper bowls to the trashcan by the back door.

Bully sat at the outside table and watched her work. He thought about the short time she had been at The Garhole and how she seemed to love it. Everything excited her, from the morning sun on her face as she weeded and pruned the vegetable garden to running the crab traps and catching trout off the dock.

He had watched her serve lunch as the men came in from fishing. He wondered what she felt when she overheard their conversations about their wives and children. Maybe she would find someone nice and give him great grandchildren. It could happen, he mused. But it would have to be soon. He pressed his hand to his chest and pushed hard willing the pain to cease.

He was reading a map when she approached the table. She leaned in. "What'cha you doing, Poppa?"

"Just studying, honey," he answered, not looking up. "Been workin' on something."

She glanced at the map. "Poppa, I worry about you being out alone at night. All that digging you do and wandering around in the marsh. What if you fell and hurt yourself?"

Bully looked up and saw the concern in her eyes. "Don't you worry none, honey. I been doing it for years. I get stronger every day."

"I sure hope so," she said. "There's a bottle of pills by the sink in the camper that says nitro on them. What are they for?"

Bully waved his hand dismissing her question. "Oh, nothing, honey. Just some stuff to give me energy."

Lisa nodded, then picked up the map. She said, "Another treasure?"

Bully said, "Maybe. Listen honey, I've been thinking. Can you keep a secret?"

The answer squealed out, "Course I can, Poppa."

"Come with me, I wanna show you something."

Lisa followed him into the camper. He leaned over and pulled up the bottom trim board on the window behind his bed. From the space under the board, he removed a small canvas sack and shook two gold coins out onto the bed.

Lisa giggled and picked one up. "Oh, Poppa. This is awesome. You found that pirate's treasure!"

Bully said, "Maybe some of it. But I've had these for years. Dug'em up where Lafitte's old fort used to be before they put a new house on top of it."

"Are they, like...worth a lot?" she asked, studying the coins.

"Some, honey. Don't know how much. There're called doubloons. They used them for money back then. These were probably stolen from some treasure ship. If anything happens to me, I want you to have them."

Lisa dropped the coins on the bed and put her arms around his shoulders. "Oh Poppa, you're my treasure." A tear fell. She released the embrace and kissed his stubbled cheek.

Bully said, "Lisa, I wanted you to know about these coins, but there's something else."

"What, Poppa?"

"Most folks round here think I'm crazy, always looking for Lafitte's gold. Every inch around his old fort's been probed and searched. Most places out here too. Ain't no more of his gold on the island."

"But you're still looking, aren't you?"

"Not for Lafitte's treasure. I just use that story so people won't bother me."

Bully noticed the confused expression on Lisa's face and decided to explain.

"There's lots of other stories about buried treasures on Galveston Island. I know about a schooner that got caught in a hurricane. It broke up in the bay right behind the state park. With all the storms over the years, moving stuff around, I figured some of it might have washed in toward the marsh. When Marvin arrested me, I was way out at the shoreline diggin' in the mud. I thought I'd found one of the ship's timbers. "

"Well, was the timber off the schooner?"

"No. About the time he came by, I had already decided it weren't. But I ain't giving up. I still think the wreck might be somewhere behind the park, and I'm going back to look some more."

Lisa drew back, a concerned look on her face, "Poppa, don't do that, please. He'll arrest you again."

Bully smiled and patted her knee. "Don't worry, honey. When the moon is low, he won't be able to see me."

Lisa seemed to relax. She thought a minute and said, "Was there gold on the schooner?"

"Don't know. The bay back there is pretty shallow. Sometimes they had to use smaller boats to off-load from the larger ones. If it belonged to one of the privateers that used the island for a base, might have been some kind of booty on it. Tell you what. Bring those doubloons with you. I want to show you something else."

Bully pushed through the door of a shed behind the camper. Shovels of all descriptions and long metal rods lined the walls. He explained about using the rods as probes, hammering them into the sand. Saved a lot of digging, he said.

Lisa pointed at a large washtub with a framed screen over it. "What's that for, Poppa?" she asked.

"I use that for sifting sand, looking for clues." At the back of the shed, he picked up a long fiberglass pole. "Let's go back outside in the light."

"What's that thing?" she asked, looking at the strange contraption.

Bully said, "It's my gold machine."

"A gold machine? That's awesome." She took it from him and held it out like a broom. "You made this, Poppa?"

"Sure did, honey."

Lisa studied the contraption. A glass cylinder encased in brass and filled with a powdery mixture was threaded to the end of the pole. A brass tip protruded from the end of the cylinder. Two copper wires ran from the brass at the bottom of the cylinder to the other end of the pole and ended at a small battery.

"What's that stuff in the bottle at the end?" she asked.

Bully winked. "Secret formula," he said.

Lisa made a face.

Bully hesitated, then said, "It's a mixture of gold and mercury and some other minerals I read about."

"Does it work?"

"Don't know. I just finished making it. Throw those coins on the ground and let's see."

Bully poked the fiberglass rod against his stomach and pointed the end with the glass cylinder straight up into the air like a long divining rod. He took the copper wires in his fingers just above the battery as if waiting for a charge from his body to help energize the machine. He squinted and stared at the top of the pole and turned slowly in a 360° arc. Around and around he went, holding onto the wire. Suddenly, the gold-filled head bent toward the ground as if magnetized toward one spot.

Lisa clapped her hands and jumped up and down. She screamed, "Poppa, Poppa, it's pointing right at them!" Her eyes widened. Her hand went to her stomach and then to her mouth. "Oh my gosh, Poppa! It works. It really works."

Chapter Twelve
Wednesday, August 24 & Thursday, August 25

The woman in charge of the Rosenberg Library's Texas History Room smiled as Alec Strauss entered.

"May I help you, sir?"

She stood and came around the desk to face him as though he was the most important visitor of the day. She was tall, about five-nine, mid-twenties with brown hair and light makeup. She wore large, dark-rimmed glasses but removed them as she approached Strauss. She was attractive enough, Alec thought. Maybe if she let her hair down out of that bun...

"Yes, please. I am interested in the German migration to Texas in the 19th century. Do you have information on that?"

She moved closer, "Well, we do have quite a bit on the ships that disembarked here during that period. We have their manifests listing the passenger's names."

"Really," Alec replied. Maybe she got closer to compare heights, he thought. Or maybe she just wanted him to see more of her body. "Do you know where they went from here—their final destination? Or did they stay in this area?"

"Most left immediately to other parts of Texas," she replied. "But some remained in Galveston."

He followed her across the room. No panty hose. He noticed a red mark on the back of her calf where she had rubbed it against her chair.

She stopped at a shelf and turned her head. "Let me show you a book on the subject." As she bent slightly to retrieve the book, a ribbon of bare skin appeared between her top and pants.

"Yes, here it is." She slipped closer to him. "Galveston was incorporated in 1836, the same year Texas gained its independence from Mexico. German immigrants began arriving in the 1840s. The 1850 census indicated that forty per cent of the city's population was German."

As she looked up, their eyes locked. Alec could read eyes. The woman was interested. It was mutual. He liked her dark skin— Italian maybe, or a mix. Definitely southern European—hot blood. Full lips too. Even the heavy glasses added sensuality. She passed the book into his hands. They touched.

Still smiling she said, "And if you have particular names you want to check out, we have an excellent genealogy department on the first floor."

"Yes, thank you," he said, then hesitated. "Oh...I almost forgot. I also read there was a German POW camp here during the war." The effort was as casual as he could make it.

"Yes, that's true," she answered. "They kept the prisoners at old Fort Crockett over by the beach. Let me check the computer." She returned to her desk. "Yes, here we are. We have several articles from the *Galveston Daily News*. We also have a few copies of the post newspaper, *The Bugle*. Would you be interested in seeing them?"

"Well, as long as I am here."

"Oh, it's no problem. I'll get them for you. But it's against the rules to remove anything from the history room. You can read them here or make copies."

Alec spent the next two hours pouring through the information she had given him. Just before five o'clock, the librarian approached his table.

She leaned in slightly and said, "I'm getting ready to leave for the day. Can I help you with anything else?" The smile had turned impish.

His voice answered no, but his eyes said yes. He was sure she got the message. He waited.

"I don't mean to be intrusive," she said, "But I couldn't help notice your accent. Are you a visitor to our island?"

"Yes, I am just here for a short time, researching a book."

"Oh, you're a writer. How exciting!" She removed her glasses. A slight giggle. "I didn't mean to embarrass you about the accent. Actually, I find it interesting. You're from Germany, correct?"

Do not be paranoid, he told himself. She is not suspicious, just lonely.

"Is my accent that poor?" He asked, his expression fragile.

"No, no, not at all" she answered, her tone comforting. She squeezed his arm. "If there's anything I can do to help, please ask."

The words popped out. "How is the night life in Galveston? Anything interesting happening?"

A seductive smile. "Well, there's a nice jazz combo over at the Yacht Club. I was thinking of going there myself, tonight."

"Maybe I will see you there," he said. Their eyes locked again. Hers seemed adventurous, almost promising.

***

Later in his hotel room, Alec waded through the copies he had made at the library. He kept a few sheets on the fort but threw the immigration information into the trash. He considered what he had learned. The camp newspaper contained information about life at the fort for the American guards, but nothing about the internees. Not even a roster of the prisoners held there.

An article on the fort's history said it was outfitted with large coastal guns during the war. He chuckled to himself. What did they think? Germany was going to invade Galveston? Ha! Americans have so much money to waste.

All of the information he had gathered so far meant nothing. He would have to dig deeper, find another source. Except for the librarian and the possibilities for tonight, the afternoon had been wasted.

Alec arrived at the Yacht Club early and parked by the marina away from the restaurant. He listened to the night wind whipping the bay waters against the sides of the boats as they rocked gently in their berths. He studied the line of yachts, mentally measuring each one's length and speculating at the cost per foot. Expensive, he thought.

His mind moved to von Speigel. His mission would have also been expensive. The old woman in Argentina said it was to be one of the largest spy operations in America. What amount of funds had the Abwehr allocated to it?

A car pulled into the parking lot next to the Yacht Club. Not wanting to appear anxious, Alec remained in his car until the woman entered the front door. She sat at the bar and ordered a drink. The music combo had not started, and the club was almost empty.

Once inside, he walked directly to her and extended his hand. "Hi, my name is Alec, I am embarrassed that I did not introduce myself earlier."

She flashed an inviting smile then took his hand. "Mine's Julie...Julie Hanna. Get what you needed at the library?"

"Yes, thank you. But I need more than that," he said, waving for the bartender. "I need a drink. It has been a long day. Researching tires me out."

She emitted a deep-throated chuckle and took a sip from her glass of wine.

He ordered vodka. They talked for a while and sipped another drink. When the music started, they shifted to a table, then to the dance floor. Intimacy grew with each dance. When the musicians announced a break, they stayed on the floor, moving rhythmically to a slow ballad on the jukebox. He caressed her back, pulling her into him, and felt no resistance. Their hips merged, hers pressing. She massaged the back of his neck. They had not spoken much on the dance floor. Conversation wasn't needed.

When the tune ended, they eased back to their table, holding hands. He asked her if she wanted another glass of wine. She declined. The time was right.

"You live on the island?" He asked.

"Just a few blocks from here," she murmured.

He grinned, sheepishly. "All by yourself?"

"Just me.... You like brandy?"

"One of my favorites late at night."

"I've got a bottle at my place."

The next morning in his hotel room shower, Alec rubbed the hot steam into his skin. He enjoyed the game. Some women wanted to be romanced; others, like Julie, wanted to be taken. He could do either. Take what you want, he had learned. Berries are on the vines to be picked.

Naked, Alec postured in front of the mirror admiring his body. Daily workouts had sculpted the results he wanted. "You are the *Master Race*," he said softly. He posed again at the mirror, flexing. His hands were a gift, large and strong. Gifts should be used, not wasted. He was a killing machine. It had come easy, he discovered. A simple twist of the neck until the spine popped.

He flexed again, then relaxed and began to dress. He had work to do, the mission. But, he had hit a roadblock. His mind flashed to Mariana, her soft breasts snuggled into his chest, the whispered endearments as she stroked his back. Two days had passed since he last spoke with her. Maybe they had found the letter. Without thinking, he reached for the room telephone.

"Mariana, it is me, Günter."

"Günter, I am so glad you called. I have missed you."

"I have missed you too, Mariana. Your sweet voice is just as I remember."

"When are you coming back to me?"

"Soon, I promise. Mariana, my darling, my time is running out. I only have a few days in America to learn about my grandfather. I know it would be a great imposition, but could you...could you possibly search the Señora's papers for the letter we discussed?"

"I...I will try Günter. All of her personal correspondence and records must be around the house somewhere. I know she has a collection of letters from friends and relatives. I will see, but I cannot promise anything."

"Yes, of course, Mariana. And I do not want to burden you. It is just that...well, the letter may contain some information that would help me. I am running out of options here."

Humility was not one of Alec's stronger character traits. He hoped he had conveyed the right touch. Getting down to a woman's level was always so difficult.

"Perhaps I should come there." Mariana said, "I have never been to Texas. If I find the letter, I will bring it to you."

His mind reeled. Impossible, he thought. The one night with her had been a dream, but...

Her voice broke his thoughts. "Günter...are you there?"

"Yes, Mariana," he responded, quickly. "I long to see you my love, but Señora Rosas needs you there."

"But I want to see you, Günter. I can help, I know I can. I can be there in one day."

"Find the letter, Mariana, and I will be in your arms soon. I promise."

Günter Manfred alias Alec Strauss said goodbye and replaced the handset. He was well pleased with his performance. He could seem so sincere when he needed to.

Chapter Thirteen
Wednesday, August 24

The night sweats were worse than ever. The only relief came from the coolness of the soaked sheets and the pulsating fan on the dresser. I was never much for lying in bed feeling sorry for myself, so early this morning I had made the trek into Galveston for supplies and whisky.

I arrived back at The Garhole a little before noon. A new Lexus sat in the parking lot, its bright finish dulled by a fine layer of salt spray. I eased around it toward the back of the building wondering what crazy fisherman would drive a machine like that down to the wind and sand of West Beach. I thought it must be some high roller out of Houston taking the day off. I parked and rounded the corner of the building to find a woman's arm stuck into Charlie's cage.

"What are you doing, lady?"

She jerked her hand free and turned.

"Excuse me," she answered, her expression a combination of surprise and guilt. "I was just trying to pet the bird. Lisa said it was okay."

"Well, it's not okay. The bird's hurt, and I don't want him disturbed. His wing's almost healed."

I brushed past her carrying the groceries and a slightly dented bottle of Famous Grouse. Lisa met me at the back door.

"Don't freak, Parker. It's my fault. I told her she could do it. I didn't think you'd mind."

I ignored the comment, pushed past Lisa, and set the whisky and groceries on the counter. I took a short drink from the bottle and turned to see the stranger standing at the door mouthing a silent thank you to Lisa.

I got my first good look. Army training had taught me to size up a suspect with a quick glance. I would get a few seconds to observe a crowd of people and then be expected to detail each one. A good spy needed to know if he was being followed. The power of observation was a learned skill.

But I wouldn't have needed training to remember her: mid-thirties, auburn hair, about five four, trim. She hadn't been around here before, that was for sure. So why was she here? No one came to The Garhole for directions. It was the end of the trail.

Lisa served her a Coke at the end of the counter. Then she pivoted to me and said, "Parker, this is Claire Roberts. She's here to see you."

The woman smiled and said, "How do you do Mr. McLeod?"

It was hard staying angry at a face and figure like that. As tired as I was, I found myself wanting to continue some kind of dialogue. I took a glass from under the counter and poured it half full with scotch.

Claire Roberts moved a stool to the end of the counter and sat down. She turned to me and said, "The bird seemed lonely."

Her tone of voice was somewhere between patronizing and flirtatious. I wasn't sure which. I said, "Lady, that's a mature night heron. They spend most of their time alone. Besides, did you notice his bill? Sharp as a knife. You're lucky you have all your fingers."

She turned her hand over several times, studying it. Words formed slowly, "I'm really sorry, Mr. McLeod. Lisa said you fixed his wing. Will you be setting him free soon?"

I nodded slightly and drank from the glass. My eyes wandered over her body.

"I'm glad you're turning him loose," she said. "I don't like to see animals in a zoo or fish in a bowl. Should be a law against it, don't you think? They should be free. A friend of mine in Houston had a huge fish in her tank. The poor thing was so big it could hardly turn around. I finally talked her into donating it to that big aquarium downtown."

I didn't know if I was supposed to reply to her meandering thoughts or not. But as much as I was enjoying undressing her, the combination of the sleepless night and morning booze was getting to me. Worn thin, I shook my head suddenly too tired to keep my eyes open. In an effort to move along, I said, "What can I do for you, lady?"

She stepped toward me and extended her hand. "Do you have a few minutes, someplace we can talk?"

Her hand was warm, inviting. I didn't release until she did. "Well, I'm really tired. I was up late last night. Didn't get much sleep."

"Just a few minutes, I promise."

Her deep brown, almost black eyes were like vast pools of hope you could get lost in. I stared into her face, but my mind drifted back to Janie, my ex-wife. In the early days, we had spent hours wrapped in a blanket on the beach, searching each other's eyes, first one, then the other, then back. It was like that now, at least for me.

I shrugged and gestured to the outside table next to the water. She stood on the bulkhead facing the bay. I sat on a bench by the table.

"Wonderful view," she said. "You must have beautiful sunsets."

She turned back suddenly and caught me admiring the shape of her calves. I flinched slightly. If she noticed my reaction, she didn't let on. "Yes, we do," I offered. "Just over your left shoulder."

"How far is it to the other side of the bay?"

"About two miles. The Intracoastal Waterway is on the other side."

She lowered her sunglasses. "Where does it go?"

For the first time I noticed the freckles along the upper ridge of her nose, just below where the bridge of her glasses rested. Her nose wiggled when she spoke and the freckles seemed to bounce around. I liked the way she hadn't tried to cover them with makeup. It spoke of confidence. Accept her as she is, it said. She had nothing to hide.

"All along the Gulf Coast," I answered. "The part you see runs from Galveston to Freeport."

"Really," she said, moving closer.

"You wanted to talk to me, Ms. Roberts?"

"Yes, I'm sorry...."

She hesitated. I stroked my beard, pushed the long strands of my hair over my ears and said, "Okay. What are you selling?"

"Oh, I'm not selling anything, Mr. McLeod. I'm buying."

She moved quickly to the bench opposite me and sat down.

"You own almost three hundred acres here, including water frontage along West Bay and the beachfront. I represent a buyer interested in your property."

Of course, it had to be about my property. What else did I have? She sure wasn't here selling bar snacks. But she couldn't be a local realtor. They knew better. I didn't exactly have a reputation as Mr. Friendly.

"Not interested. Been in the family a long time."

I got up, stood on the edge of the dock, and faced out to the bay. A line of cormorants flying in wedge formation turned toward the shore. Such precision—necks erect, wings flapping in perfect unison—a group of heavy bombers on a final attack run. I pushed the thought away.

"Yes, I know," she said. "What about Bully Stout? I understand he is your uncle, and he lives here. How does he figure into the ownership?"

As if oblivious to her presence, I massaged one shoulder, then the other. A deep throbbing in my joints caused me to grimace. I responded a little rougher than intended and said, "He doesn't figure in."

I needed sleep. I started to get up. She touched my arm.

"Please, Mr. McLeod. I don't mean to be intrusive, just trying to break the ice."

The freckles bounced again. She seemed earnest. I settled back in my chair.

"So he just lives here with you?"

"That's correct."

"I see."

She seemed tentative, not certain if she wanted to continue. I waited.

"Well, Mr. McLeod, the west end of the island is filling up. New developments all over. They're very few properties of your size left. The client I represent has a very successful track record. He thinks he can get a permit from the Corp of Engineers to dredge a canal system that would crisscross the property."

I had heard proposals like this before. There seemed no end to developers wanting to build out every foot of West Beach soil. Tired or not, I would play out the game with her. She needed to know how I felt.

"Sounds as if this end of the island would change quite a bit," I replied. "That would get rid of the tidal pools and the salt marsh."

"Oh, yes," she said. "On the bay side, he would build a marina and clubhouse. He is even thinking about a nine-hole golf course. All of the swampy land around here would be filled in, built up."

"He must be willing to pay me a lot of money."

She continued, more excited now. "We haven't had it appraised, but I'm sure we could make you an offer you couldn't refuse."

"You mean like the Godfather?"

She smiled, "No, no. That is not what I meant at all. It's just that...well, soon the Galveston city limits will extend all the way to the end of the island, including your property. Taxes will skyrocket.

You could get out now at a fair price before the taxes become prohibitive."

I faked a frightened look on my face. "Oh gosh, quick, quick, where do I sign?"

Her smile faded. Enthusiasm drained from her cheeks like a deflating balloon. She sighed as she spoke.

"Okay, okay, I get the picture. You've heard this before, haven't you?"

I nodded, gently. She had hung in there pretty well, I thought. No sense beating her up anymore. For a moment, neither of us spoke. She leaned back and seemed to relax. The tension eased. She brushed something from her skirt. I rubbed my eyes. A moment later, her smile reappeared. Like a marathon runner, she seemed to have gotten her second wind. I felt another round coming.

"Mr. McLeod, I apologize. I really wasn't trying to bully you. It's just that you could be free. You could do what you want. Doesn't that have some appeal?"

Okay, it's time, I thought. Enough is enough. I leaned over the table as close to her as I could, my eyes steady into hers. I caught the gleam of her gold earrings and smelled her expensive perfume. It seemed familiar. In Kuwait, I had spent hours sampling dozens, attempting to find just the right one for Janie. I steadied my eyes, never leaving hers. In an even, firm voice, I said, "I do what I want now, Ms. Roberts. Money means nothing to me. You can only feed so many dogs."

"Dogs?" She looked puzzled.

"Just an expression," I said. "Listen to me, Ms. Roberts. This land has been in my family for sixty years. A lot has changed during that time. When my grandfather lived here, these were prime fishing grounds for redfish and trout. Grass covered the bottom of the bay. But now, thanks to the chemical companies across the bay, there's nothing out there but mud."

I stopped talking, thinking our conversation was over. I had told them all the same thing. I was surprised word hadn't gotten around to her.

She said, "If you're worried about the ecology, Mr. McLeod, I'm sure the developer would keep it in mind. There are, of course, government regulations in place. The Environmental Protection Agency has its rules."

I couldn't believe it. She had just rolled past everything I had said. I straightened in the chair, the words streamed out.

"Baloney! Politics! It's all about money and greed. Let me tell you something. The salt marsh that borders this house is one of the few remaining natural areas on the island. At high tide, the bay waters cover the flats to either side of us. Do you have any idea of the marine life that depends on this type of eco-system?"

"No, not really," she said. "But..."

I cut her off in mid-sentence. "Shrimp, crab, and almost all of our game fish are born in tidal marshes like this one. Without them, our fishing industry would die a sudden death, not to mention sport fishing. Mine might be only part of the system, but I damn sure intend to keep it that way."

I was on a roll now. The last of my energy poured out like a fast moving tide. I sat back again, exhausted—satisfied with my performance.

She blinked once, then said, "Yes...well, I see why you like it here Mr. McLeod. I really do. But aren't there places where you would enjoying going? Do some traveling? See the world?"

"Damn it, lady. Didn't you hear anything I just said? Don't you get it?" I was out of my chair now, flailing my arms in desperation, hanging on to the last bit of adrenalin rush.

"I love to travel," she said, her voice as soft as light rain. "Europe's my favorite. Ever been to Italy? Rome especially! The people gather at night and watch the waters swirl out of those lovely fountains. It's so much fun."

I stopped moving and exhaled a long slow breath trying to control myself. I sat down again across from her and leaned back.

"My God, lady. You never quit, do you? The Voice of America. You must have been vaccinated with a phonograph needle."

She blinked hard but didn't respond. I had overdone it. The pain in my shoulders was worse. I grimaced heavily and closed my eyes. After a moment, I gathered my best resigned look and with a firm voice said, "I've seen all I need to. I traveled in the Army—Germany, all of Europe, the Middle East."

I waited for a response, but she looked away. After a moment, she turned back and said, "I see. Well, okay Mr. McLeod. I'll leave now. I really didn't mean to upset you. Thank you for the visit."

It ended just that quickly. She stood and extended her hand in a farewell gesture, and I took it. Was the game over? Had I won? Won what?

As she walked away, I noticed the curve of her neck and the way her hips melted into her waist. It was my last conscious thought. Worn thin from the booze, I laid my head on the table and was fast asleep by the time her car pulled out of the driveway.

Chapter Fourteen
Wednesday, August 24

Denny Sader rarely opened his mouth. He managed to speak by just moving his lips. He would have made an excellent ventriloquist, but that would have required him to smile at the end of a performance, and Denny never smiled. Two many brown holes in his teeth. The gaps produced a whistling sound when he spoke.

Like the slimy reptile he was, Denny had slithered back into Galveston after a two-year hiatus. Between pool and drugs, he had done well here before, and he hadn't wanted to leave. But meeting Lisa had changed that.

Lisa Stout—jailbait. It was too risky hanging around Galveston with a sixteen-year old. Someone might recognize her. It was best to go somewhere where nobody knew them and wouldn't ask. They stayed on the road for two years, never long in one place. California, Nevada, anywhere he could make a buck, mostly hustling pool.

But his game wasn't good enough for the road, and Lisa kept bugging him to go home. She was eighteen now—legal tender. So they returned to Galveston.

It didn't take long for Denny to make a supplier connection and pick up his old clientele. Some of his old schoolmates were his best customers. He had stayed off the stuff himself. Denny Sader wasn't stupid.

In the back of The Eight Ball, by the jukebox, Denny hunched over a fourteen-year-old black kid. At six-foot two and a hundred and forty pounds, Denny's back curved like a sickle as he reached down and stuffed a sandwich bag filled with white rocks into the kid's pocket. He kept the kid's back to the entrance so he could see all the way to the street.

A quick glance at the front door and around the room confirmed they were alone. There were six pool tables, most of them with burn holes in the felt, a number of cheap plastic beer signs on the walls and several rusted folding chairs scattered about. His office was secure, ready for business.

And Post Office Street had a reputation for business, like that big white, two-story house on the corner. It was empty now, shuttered and crumbling, but thirty years earlier Denny knew it had been the biggest whorehouse in town. It was just one of many, both black and white.

In those days, Galveston had the most famous red-light district in the state. But the houses were all gone now, following the lonesome trail of prohibition booze and illegal gambling casinos. The cathouses and gambling dens were shut down back in the sixties by a state attorney general trying to make a name for himself so he could be elected governor. He didn't win.

Denny wished he had been a part of it then—the wild, rollicking, good time, wide open town. But all that was gone. Now, it was just drugs, and Denny aimed to get his share of the trade.

When Denny spoke to the black kid, the air hissing through the holes in his teeth sounded like the squeal of a dying rabbit.

"You got enough for two bags at twenty each if you split them up," he said. "You can double your money."

The black kid nodded; his dark eyes big as eight balls. "Business is good down in the Projects, huh, kid? Come back and see me again, soon." Denny pushed the kid away. So easy, he thought.

He chalked his cue stick. He needed to parlay the six ball into the four for a corner pocket shot and keep the cue ball from scratching.

. Pool had been Denny's first job. His mind drifted to the detention center across town where he had learned to play, hustling for small change. By the time he ran away and found The Eight Ball, he could beat all but the out-of-towners.

Detention Center. Sometimes, like now, when old memories tried to sneak through, he would squeeze his eyes real hard and will the bad thoughts away. The trick usually worked.

He had first mastered it at age eleven. His teacher had noticed him wearing a long sleeve shirt to school when it was ninety degrees outside. His arms were pocked with burns. His mother's boyfriend had used Denny as his personal plaything for more than a year.

After the state took him from his mother, he spent the next five years shuffling from one foster home to another, finally ending up in Galveston. He would have been out of the state's care at eighteen, but he knew the unwritten rule. In the last year of custody, you could run and the state wouldn't come after you. On Denny's seventeenth birthday, he walked out of the detention center and never returned.

But Denny had good genes. He had come from pros. Between welfare, food stamps, Workman's Compensation abuse, and gaming the Social Security disability rules, no one in his miserable family, including his mother and all of her boyfriends, had ever earned a legitimate dime. So with that family history, how could he miss? First it was pool, then drugs.

And Denny Sader never had any problems attracting women. He knew it was his height and build. Tall and slim like the models, the movie stars. He seldom ate. He had to keep his body.

Just then, someone came in the front door. He had seen her before, probably seventeen or eighteen, overweight and slouchy. Damn, he hated fat girls. Why couldn't they take care of themselves, like Lisa, nice and trim? He liked that.

He lined the balls up again and made the shot. The girl stood by his table and squealed, "Oh, Denny. That was awesome." He tried to ignore her. He hadn't been with a woman since Lisa split, but he wasn't this desperate.

She squealed again, "Buy me a beer, Denny? Please."

"Can't take the chance, Sugar," he said. "You got no ID." He wouldn't spend a nickel on her. He thought about giving her a line of coke, but he figured she didn't have any money, and he sure as hell didn't want to pimp for her. What hard-up shit would want her? He changed tables, hoping she wouldn't follow.

He thought of Lisa. He had met her just like this. She had wandered in one day while he was shooting pool. What a prize she had been; so young, so innocent. And now, she was gone. Bitch! How could she? He had been so good to her. Maybe he would just go after her. Yesterday, that big white kid, Bubba Shanks, had been in here talking about being in the drunk-tank with an old man who looked like a pirate. He had a wooden leg and a patch over his eye.

Bubba knew Lisa from around The Eight Ball, and he knew that she had come to get the old cripple out of jail. The pirate had to be Lisa's grandfather, the one she called Poppa Bully. She rattled off about him all the time. How tough could the old bastard be?

Denny stuck two quarters in the slot and released the balls. He loaded them on the table and racked them tight. He couldn't get Lisa off his mind. Where was she getting her hits? Surely she wasn't trying to go cold turkey. If he could just get her alone for a few minutes, she would be back on the stuff. She would be his again. It was that easy.

He looked back and noticed the ugly one still watching him. "Come over here, Sugar. I got something better than alcohol." Denny took her back to the restroom and locked the door.

Just for kicks, he thought, he would mess her up. One hit and she would be his. Not that he wanted any of her. Maybe he would put her on the street, let her work the docks and earn her next toke. Those hard-dick merchant marine types would screw a bush if they thought there was a snake in it. Especially after a long sea trip.

He thought about Lisa again. She was too good for the street. He had kept her for himself. But this piece of shit, no way. He turned his head and squeezed his eyes real tight. A memory he didn't want was trying hard to sneak in. But somewhere, something was telling him, all women were worthless, and this slut would pay the price.

Chapter Fifteen
Thursday, August 25

After his conversation with Mariana, Alec needed a break from the confinement of his room and time to consider his next move. He left the hotel and walked around the block to the Strand.

Along the sidewalks, visitors in shorts and sandals weaved in and out of the cheap souvenir and tee shirt shops like overfed rats pausing only to sniff and get directions. A horse-pulled cart clomped along the street, the guide shouting building histories to his sweat-soaked patrons. On the corner, an obese woman with wet circles under her arms scolded her four-year-old for dropping his ice cream on the street.

So this was America, Alec thought. Fat, lazy people—indifferent and bored. How had they ever defeated Germany? Alec shook the thought from his mind and picked up his pace. He moved with deliberate speed, neither slowing nor stopping, as if the rapid tempo alone would clear his mind. Using the telephone in his hotel room was certainly a mistake, he thought, but not an irreparable one. It was only Mariana, and at least she had agreed to continue the search for the mysterious letter.

No, the larger error was spending the night with the librarian, Julie Hanna. Had he said anything to make her suspicious, make her wonder what he was really doing here in Galveston? He hoped not. He would have to be more careful. It was best to be invisible. Use the training, he reminded himself. Stay focused.

At least the librarian had given him a name—Harry Stein. Learning that might have been worth the gamble.

Alec turned the corner to Mechanic Street and retrieved his rental car from the hotel garage. He drove to a convenience store on Broadway and used the pay phone outside.

"May I speak to Mr. Stein, please?"

The receptionist transferred the call. "This is Harry Stein. May I help you?" The voice was businesslike, firm and direct.

"Mr. Stein, my name is Alec Strauss. Someone at the library told me you are President of the Galveston Historical Society and that you may be able to help me. I represent a German magazine that engaged me to do a series of articles about German emigration to Texas."

"Really," Harry said. "How interesting."

"Yes, thank you," Alec replied. "But, while researching at the library, I learned that German prisoners were held at Fort Crockett during the war. I thought a story about the POW camp might be an interesting sidebar to my emigration articles."

"It might be at that," Harry said. "So, what can I do for you, Mr. Strauss?"

"Well, according to what I have read, after the prisoners were repatriated to Germany, some did return to America and become naturalized citizens. Do you know if any from Fort Crockett came back to Texas?"

Alec had his questions ready. Maybe von Speigel hadn't returned to Germany after the war and his repatriation records were fouled up. Or maybe he found he couldn't live in Leipzig because of the Communists, and he had returned to Texas. Or maybe he had just come back for the money.

"Don't know about that," Harry admitted. "But I'll tell you what. Galveston can always use favorable publicity. It's good for tourism.

Come by the office about noon. We'll have lunch and I'll tell you what I know."

Two hours later, Alec arrived at Harry Stein's office. When Harry entered the reception area, Alec stood to greet him, towering over the diminutive lawyer. Alec noted the probing eyes and protruding forehead. No doubt the man was bright, he thought. And well dressed, too—a tailor-made wool suit and expensive silk tie. He would have to be careful.

He introduced himself and they shook hands. Be polite, Alec reminded himself. Play the game. If this were 1939 Germany, the little Jew would have been arrested and shipped off in a boxcar. But now, because he needed him, Alec knew he would have to smile and act humble.

Harry Stein offered to take his car, and on the way to the restaurant, Alec considered his approach. Must not seem too obvious, he thought.

At Seawall Boulevard, Stein turned right, heading west along the Gulf front. The wind was calm and the blue-green water lapped gently at the shore. Children with shovels and buckets dug in the sand while their parents hovered under brightly colored umbrellas, maneuvering for tiny balls of shade. They passed the old Galvez Hotel, built in the early part of the century and survivor of numerous hurricanes.

Alec tried an icebreaker. "You have a lot of interesting architecture here," he said, pointing at the structure.

"Oh, yes, we certainly do," Harry said. "You might want to take one of the historical tours. It would help you get the feel of the island."

"Good idea," Alec said.

"Do you know much about our history?"

"No, not really," Alec answered. "They gave me the assignment on rather quick notice."

"Well, I'll give you the short version," Harry Stein continued. "In the early eighteen hundreds, Jean Lafitte, the most famous pirate of his time, operated out of here raiding the gold ships coming from

Mexico. Finally, the U.S. Navy ran him off. A few years later the city of Galveston was born and by the 1840s' it boasted the largest port on the Texas Coast. Even the Yankees thought it important."

"Yankees?" Alec was half-listening. The term caught him by surprise. He glanced at Stein, a quizzical look on his face.

"Oh I'm sorry, you're from Germany," Harry said. "You may not be familiar with the term. We called the northern forces Yankees during the Civil War. In 1863, their navy captured Galveston. It shook up the local folks, put them in a panic. Many feared the northern troops would pillage and steal. Legend has it some of the wealthier merchants buried their wealth, gold or whatever, out on the west end of the island."

"Really," Alec said. Be patient, he reminded himself. This man was a walking history book. Let him ramble. The less he spoke, the less Harry Stein would remember him.

"Yes, well, that's the story anyway." Harry paused for a moment, then continued, "Do you know about the Great Storm?"

"You mean the one in 1900?" Alec answered. "Only what I read about it in a magazine at the hotel."

"Winds reached 140 miles an hour," Harry said. Fifteen-foot tides swept over the island. Over six thousand people died. It is still the largest natural disaster ever in the United States."

Alec nodded, feigning interest.

Harry continued. "Afterward, the Corp of Engineers built the seawall we're riding on. They jacked up the houses and pumped in sand, raised the level of the entire city. We've had several hurricanes since then, but none as deadly as that one. Matter of fact, we are in the middle of hurricane season now. Could be one building as we speak. Know anything about hurricanes, Mr. Strauss?"

He forced an answer, "No, I'm afraid not."

Harry Stein cleared his throat, "Well, I'm not an expert either. But take the 1900 storm for instance. It formed off Africa five thousand miles from here, in late August, about this time of the month in fact. And...oh, here's the restaurant."

The International House of Pancakes restaurant at 53rd and Seawall Boulevard faced the water with a clear view of the surf. Alec and Harry sat at a window table and watched tourists stroll the seawall.

Harry picked up the conversation again, "So you're writing about German immigration, huh, Mr. Strauss?"

Good, Alec thought, an opening. "Yes, that is correct, Mr. Stein. As you know, thousands of Germans entered the U.S. through the port of Galveston and..."

Harry interrupted, "Yes, they did, Mr. Strauss. Galveston was a major port of entry then. Immigrants from all over Europe came through here. Italians, Czechs, Poles. In fact, my grandparents entered here, emigrated from Russia."

Emigrated like hell, Alec thought. They were Jewish, run out of Russia like the Füehrer ran them out of Germany. But enough of this. He needed information, and he was just about to ask about Fort Crockett when Harry spoke again.

"I know, I know," Harry said. "You want to know about the P.O.W camp here during the war. Okay, so you may be wondering why I brought you to a pancake house. Look through that side window. See across the street, the San Luis Hotel?"

"Yes, it is quite an imposing structure," Alec said.

"You see next to the hotel, that dirt-covered mound with the concrete façade? That's the only remaining bunker from Fort Crockett. It was an ammunition depot. They preserved it when they tore down most of the old structures. We're actually having lunch on part of the old fort grounds now."

Alec started to respond, but the waitress interrupted his thought. A tall blonde, thin as a pole. High cheekbones and fair skin. Alec made eye contact and smiled. She handed each of them a menu.

"What do you recommend?" Alec asked.

"Oh, lots of things," she answered. She touched the tip of her tongue to her top lip. "What are you hungry for? Anything special?"

An invitation. She wasn't asking about the menu selection. He knew that. They ordered, and when she left, Alec watched her hips glide across the room. He turned back to Stein and refocused quickly, speaking first to keep things on track. "So the fort extended to the beach?"

"Yes, the prisoners were allowed to exercise on the beach and bathe in the surf."

Interesting. Alec nodded making a mental note. An easy escape route.

"I'll drive you around the old perimeter when we're through here. That bunker across the street and a few buildings are all that's left."

Alec nodded an acknowledgment, then sipped his coffee and said, "Very interesting, Mr. Stein. But tell me, what do you know about the prisoners?"

Harry said, "Well, in 1943, when the Allies defeated Rommel in Africa, there were thousands of captured Germans soldiers the Allies had to deal with. There wasn't any room in England so they brought them to the United States. There were dozens of camps set up all over the country. Fort Crockett housed six or seven hundred, mostly officers."

Harry went on with more detail, more than Alec wanted to hear. He talked about what the prisoners ate and how they spent their day and how the camp was organized. Alec listened carefully, but nothing he had learned so far was helpful.

The waitress served the meal, and they ate casually, bantering back and forth. She returned several times refilling Alec's coffee cup, always careful to make eye contact. Maybe he would come back later.

After the waitress cleared the dishes, Alec said, "Were the prisoners treated well?"

"Oh, yes," Stein answered. "In strict compliance with the 1929 Geneva Convention."

Alec visualized his grandfather, Eric von Speigel, living here. He must have spent every hour plotting to break out to continue his mission. What had they done to him when he had tried to escape? Beat him? Torture? Why hadn't Rheinhard Bauer, his contact in

Argentina, heard from him again? Had he been murdered by the American guards and buried at sea?

"What about the prisoners themselves? Do you know anything about them?" Alec asked.

"Not really. Most of them came with nothing more than their clothes and their identification card."

"Yes, their Soldbuch," Alec added. He knew about the German Army's ID card. It contained personnel information such as date of birth, birthplace, military unit, and photo. "What if they had lost their card?" He asked. "What happened then?"

"Sometimes the camp administrator tried to get the personnel information from Germany through the International Red Cross, but those channels were slow and usually didn't work out. Mostly, they just took the prisoner's word for it."

Alec thought about that. It would have been easy for von Speigel to claim he had lost his identification when the U-Boat sunk and he was captured. As Señora Rosas had said, he would have pretended to be a crewmember and given them a false name. Otherwise, his captors would have gotten suspicious.

A light went off! No! He had screwed up. He had been so intent on learning the name of von Speigel's contact in Texas, he had forgotten to ask the Señora what name von Speigel had used in the prison camp. She had to know. Her husband had corresponded with him. He needed the name. How else could he track him?

Harry continued. "Many prisoners elected to work. They had jobs outside the camp."

Of course, Alec thought. Von Speigel would have needed money to escape. He probably volunteered for work.

"They actually got paid?" Alec asked.

"Yes, eighty cents a day. Of course it was scrip."

"Why scrip?"

"To discourage escape. So the prisoners wouldn't have any real money if they ran away."

"Interesting," Alec replied, wondering how far von Speigel could have gotten with no money. "But it was the duty of a prisoner to escape if possible, was it not?"

"Well, yes. I am sure it was," Harry replied. "We had the same expectations in our army."

Alec's attention was at its peak. The interview had come down to a final question. He leaned forward in the booth, his eyes focused on Harry's.

"But what about here, in Galveston?" he asked. "Were there any attempts to escape? Did any of the prisoners get away?"

Chapter Sixteen
Thursday, August 25

I envisioned Lisa about ten years old watching me clean a basket of crabs. I showed her how to determine males from females and measure them for size. And this time of year, when the females carried the bright orange egg sacks, I taught her to release them so there would be plenty for next year.

She would squirm and fidget, swearing she could hear the poor things scream when their backs came off. She was always a little squeamish that way.

Even now, she wouldn't clean a crab. But she loved to crank Bully's old outboard motor and take his skiff out into the bay to run the traps. This morning she had brought in a fine catch. Like gladiators in an arena, the big males were all twisted together in the washtub, their huge blue claws searching and fighting, performing a dance to the death.

I ripped off another back, hosed away the entrails and lungs, and tossed the hard, white body into a bucket of ice. It was the end of the season. The crabs had reached their maximum size, full of rich, succulent meat. Soon the cool weather would drive them to deeper water. This may be the last big batch, just enough for a good boil.

I had left a large aluminum pot filled with water and seasoned with bay leaves and cayenne pepper steaming on the stove inside. At the end, I would add whatever other spices I had, including a few cut lemons and a beer or two.

I had just cleaned the last crab and opened a fresh beer when Claire Roberts pulled her Lexus onto the shell pad in front of the bar. I finished the beer in large gulps and wiped my face with my hand. My bare chest and shorts were soaked and I hadn't shaved. I wet my hair with the hose and pushed it back with my fingers.

I watched her come forward—linen pantsuit and a crisp white blouse. Fresh looking, better than I had remembered, and I had tried not to.

Why had she returned so soon? Her sales training must have emphasized persistence. Keep at it—wear the opponent down. Eventually they would capitulate.

She strolled toward me waving toward the bay. "It's a beautiful morning isn't it?"

The smile appeared genuine, but the sunglasses hid her eyes. I was good at reading eyes, and hers were dark, I remembered, like a moonless night on the bay.

"Yes. Hello again, Ms. Roberts," I answered, my face passive. I wanted to test her, not give an inch, see how good she was.

She gestured toward the bar. "Something smells wonderful in there. What are you cooking?"

I pointed toward the crab bodies in the ice bucket and said, "Lunch."

She nodded.

I said, "Back so soon. Think I've changed my mind about selling?" My tone was non-threatening, but the sarcasm remained. I lifted the tub of crabs went inside and set it next to the stove.

She trailed behind. "No, I got the message yesterday. You were pretty clear about it."

What is this tack? I wondered. Reverse psychology? Now she'll act disinterested?

She leaned against the end of the counter, her arms folded across her chest. Then she surprised me and said, "Actually, I'm here to see Lisa. I brought her some clothes, some extra things I had. We talked yesterday, and she told me a little about herself."

Ah ha! I have it—an end run. But it wouldn't work. Did she really think she could get to me through Lisa? I turned to face her, and the words barreled out, "She doesn't need your charity."

Her smile vanished. "This is between Lisa and me, Mr. McLeod. You don't need to be involved. If she's here, I'd like to see her."

Whoa! I thought. A feisty little thing, all right. Well, after my lame remark, I couldn't blame her if she got defensive. If she would just remove her glasses so I could see if the freckles on her nose bounced.

I softened and jerked my thumb toward the outside. "She's in the garden behind the camper."

When she turned to leave, I tilted the tub of crabs over the boiling water expecting them to slide in one at a time. To my surprise, they all tumbled out at once. The boiling water splashed out, hitting my arms and naked chest.

"Damn it," I yelled, and dropped the tub back to the stove.

Claire jumped beside me. "Cold water," she shouted, pushing me toward the sink. She splashed tap water over my body, rubbing it as she went, gradually cooling my skin.

It seemed to work; the pain subsided. She stepped back, her hand still on my arm. "There, that should feel better," she offered.

I liked the feel of her warm breast on my arm as she pressed against me. My eyes fell on her water-soaked blouse clinging to her bra.

"Thanks," I said. Her hand released and I wished she hadn't let go. For a moment, our eyes held each other's gaze. But then an embarrassed look crossed her face and she turned away. The room went still as I silently grasped for words.

She moved to the door and leaned against the jam facing the bay. I grabbed a cup towel handed it to her over her shoulder.

103

"Sorry about your outfit," I said.

She turned, holding the towel across her chest. She seemed composed now, half-smiling, "Well, fortunately, I don't have any appointments this morning."

I glanced at her blouse and then quickly lifted my eyes to hers. "Too bad there's not a wet tee shirt contest on the beach." The words had just slipped out, and I wanted to grab each one and stuff them back into my mouth.

But Claire didn't respond immediately. Instead, she cocked her head and smiled again. The laughter erupted simultaneously as each of us seemed to relax.

Before either of us could say anything more, Lisa appeared at the back door. She guided Claire into Bully's camper, and I heard the hair dryer going. I slipped a beer from the cooler and moved to the outside table.

After a moment, Lisa went to Claire's car and returned with an armful of the clothes Claire had brought for her. Soon laughter and girlish screams spilled from the camper like a Friday night pajama party.

Then, Claire planted herself outside the trailer, and every few minutes, Lisa came out like a fashion model in a style show wearing a different outfit. Claire would inspect it, making a comment or two, and then Lisa would return to the camper for another change.

Finally, when the show was over, Lisa said, "These outfits are sooo fine." She rubbed some of the fabric between her fingers. "Thanks a lot, Claire. Wanna stay for lunch?"

"Well thanks, but no. I need to go home and change clothes. You really look good in those outfits, Lisa. I mean it."

Lisa said, "There're just awesome. My old clothes just suck so bad. I'll never wear them again." They both laughed again and hugged each other, then Lisa turned back to the camper.

Back inside, I lined newspaper on the counter and dumped the crabs out to cool. Hungry fishermen would be in soon to wrap a few crabs in paper, get a beer or two, and gather around the tables to eat.

Claire came in the back door and sat on a stool at the counter. "I really empathize with Lisa," she said. "She's been through a lot."

"Yes, she has," I replied. "Too damned much."

"What do you mean by that?" Claire asked.

"I'm just agreeing with you. She has been through a lot."

Claire gave me a questioning look.

"How much do you know?" I said.

"Well, she told me her mother died early, and she lived in state home for a few years."

"And?" I asked

"And what?" she replied.

"And nothing!"

I wanted to change the subject. It was up to Lisa to discuss her life with someone else, not me. Claire frowned, and looked hurt in a teasing way.

I stood my ground. "I really don't want to talk about it, Claire." The tone was final.

"You brought it up," she said.

"No, you did."

"Oh, I get it, Parker. You think I'm being nosy again. Guess it's the mother instinct in me. You don't want me to know anything more about you either, huh?"

"What do you mean by that?" I folded my arms in front of me and leaned back against the sink.

"Lisa told me you were in the Gulf War. She said you came home with some problems."

"You're right. That's not up for discussion either." I turned around and began washing my hands at the sink.

"Well, I don't understand," she said. "Were you wounded in battle?"

I shook my head and continued to wash, my back turned.

"Hurt in an accident?"

I shut off the water, took a towel from the drain board and turned around. "No! Look Claire, I really don't want to discuss it. If you're trying to soften me up so you can make an offer on my property, forget it. I'm not interested."

She seemed stunned by my remark. The smile faded. She hopped off the stool, removed her sunglasses and pointed them at me.

"Think what you want, Parker. I would like to sell your property for you, but as I've said, I know it's a dead issue. I respect that. So cut out the big-bad-wolf act and lighten up. Get used to me. Lisa needs help, and you don't seem interested. I guess you've got your own demons to fight."

I watched in awe as she turned and stormed through the front door, not waiting for a reply.

I slammed the bar with my palm and blustered out, "Good going, fool. You finally meet a woman who can stand up to you and you run her off."

I grabbed the Famous Grouse under the counter, brought the bottle to my lips, then stopped and set it down. Something changed though, I thought. We had actually called each other by our first names. How had that happened?

Chapter Seventeen
Friday, August 26

Lisa turned the burner off to cool the beans before putting them in the refrigerator for tomorrow's lunch. A lone customer sat at the bar drinking a beer. She wanted to tell him it was closing time, but Parker wouldn't like it. He paid her by the hour, so if he wanted to pay her to baby-sit red-nosed Neddie Lemmon, it was okay with her.

She thought about turning the lights off to see if he would glow in the dark. Be nice, she told herself. After all, who was she to criticize someone else? At least he had helped her close the big, outside bar window, something she couldn't do by herself. And besides, she couldn't remember not knowing Neddie Lemmon. Like the rest of Bully's friends, he had been around forever.

She made the last trip to the tables to pick up the empty bottles and wipe the tops. On the way back to the counter she said, "Business was slow today. Poppa told me things would be pretty much dead between now and October. What happens in October, Neddie?"

He turned on the stool to face her. His snow-white hair matched his perfectly trimmed, mustache and goatee. Both reflected off the deepest tan Lisa had ever seen. She smiled to herself and thought, except for his crimson snout, he would be a dead ringer for Colonel Sanders.

"Flounder run," Neddie, answered. "Late Fall when the cool weather hits, the flat fish move out of the shallow bays through the passes to deeper water. They stack up in the guts just off the end of the island. Flounder fanatics will come from Houston in droves. Business will be good then."

He leaned over and snatched another beer out of the cooler. He only paid for every other one so Lisa figured he felt guilty about her serving him every time. She had mentioned Neddie's alternating habit to Parker, but he had just shrugged it off.

"Any chow left?" Bully's voice boomed across the empty room. He hobbled through the back door and journeyed toward the stove.

Lisa turned quickly, startled by his sudden entrance. "Poppa, you scared me, yelling like that."

Bully grabbed a bowl from under the counter and turned on the burner. He spoke, the words circling the cigar that hung from his teeth, "Sorry, honey. I'm starved. Been out all day. How was business tonight?"

Lisa moved past him and around to a stool. "Slow, only three or four customers."

Bully turned. "Hey, Neddie. How are things at the hotel?"

"Same as always. Tips are lousy." Neddie turned the beer up and sucked out the foam, then immediately reached for another one.

He really should be paying for this one, Lisa thought. She nodded at Bully hoping he would say something.

Bully winked at her and turned back to Neddie. "Catching any fish?"

"Going in the morning, Bully. Got a little trout honey-hole those Houston boys don't know about."

Lisa followed the conversation. She wondered if Neddie's hair would stay so perfect out in the wind. She thought about her own. Claire had brought a special shampoo—something to make it softer. She hoped it worked.

"Got to get up early, huh? Why don't we give Lisa a break and let her close up now?" Bully said.

"Well, okay, if you say so, Bully. I will be going now. Thank you, Miss Lisa." He picked up the almost empty beer and toasted the gar-head, then finished the bottle. He looked at Bully and said, "Lisa told me about you toasting the gar-head. I kinda like the idea." He smiled and left.

"Come back to see us," Lisa said, smiling. She waved as he left and then turned to Bully. "Poppa, did you go to school with Neddie, too, like with Marvin and Harry and Johnny Weeks?"

"Yep, sure did, honey. Known him all my life. Old Neddie's probably the best fisherman on the island. He's always bringing some 'round here. Nothing better than fried trout."

Lisa picked up Neddie's empty bottle. "That why he gets free beer?"

"No, honey," Bully answered. "He gets free beer 'cause he's a friend."

"Cool," she said. She got the message. She had no friends, not one. Denny Sader had seen to that. Why did his image keeping popping into her head? How long would it take to wipe that clean?

It had been almost three weeks since she had left Denny, and stopping cold turkey hadn't been easy. She wanted to be strong. Deep down, she knew it was her last chance. Still, there were many nights she might have given in if she'd had a ride into town.

Bully continued, "Old as he is, Neddie still fishes almost every day. Works a few days a week as a bellhop over at the Tremont Hotel. All he's ever done. Before the Tremont, he bell-hopped for years at the old Galvez Hotel on the beach."

"Really," Lisa said. "I bet he looks awesome in a uniform."

Bully made a face. They both laughed.

"Where's Parker?" Bully asked, slurping the beans, bits of onion stuck to his chin.

Lisa said, "He came in a few minutes ago and snuck upstairs. Probably loaded. It's like, you know, like he doesn't want me to see him that way."

Bully nodded and wiped the bowl with a piece of cornbread.

Lisa said, "Sometimes I think the booze gets him worse than the stuff I used to do. Every time I'm around him he wants to flash at me like I'm some kind of...well, you know."

Bully put the bowl down, then reached across the counter and squeezed her hand. It felt good. She pushed her hair back and picked up a dishrag.

"You been out treasure hunting?"

"Yeah, I spent all day at the state park. Finally gave up on it. Guess I'll just have to wait for a new storm to turn something up out there."

Bully stuck the last piece of bean-soaked cornbread in his mouth and pushed the bowl away. "The beans ain't bad. Just need a few more peppers."

Lisa watched him burp under his breath, then strain his eyes toward the pot. He seemed to be contemplating another bowl.

"Try your gold machine?" she asked.

Bully turned toward the door and arched his back. He pushed his fingers deep into each side and massaged the muscles, moaning softly. "It didn't turn up nothing. There's something else I'm working on now, though. A load of whiskey."

Lisa squealed, "Whiskey! Really, that's cool."

"Yeah. Back in the thirties, during prohibition, there was a lot of bootlegging goin' on around the island. Rum-runners from Cuba brought in boatloads full."

"You funning with me, Poppa?"

Bully stopped kneading his back and leaned against the stove, facing the counter. "Serious as a case of the drips," he said. "Oh, shit! Sorry, honey. I shouldn't talk like that in front of you. Anyways, I ran into one of the boys I grew up with, Gus Riley. He's back in town now. His daddy was a bootlegger. Got caught and spent time in Huntsville prison. We got to talking about it and Gus said that part of the last shipment his daddy brought in was never recovered. Told me where the old man said it was. Turns out it's right here on Parker's property out by the oak motte."

"Awesome!" Lisa exclaimed. "Would it still be good, Poppa?"

"Hell, I don't know child," Bully said. "Good or not, I'm going out to look for it now. Why don't you close up? I'll see you in the morning."

"Can't yet," she replied. "Still another hour to go."

Bully said, "I thought that's why we ran Neddie off, so you could quit early."

"Well, we did. But I can't do that to Parker. He's paying me."

Bully nodded and went out the back door. Lisa wanted him to stay, but she wouldn't ask. She knew she had to get used to being alone. Besides, it was only another hour until closing. She was still embarrassed about admitting to Parker that she'd slept in his truck the night Bully was in jail. Tonight, she was determined to stay in the camper, alone or not.

She was a big girl now. But still, she wished one of the men were there. Either Bully's loud voice carrying on about something or other, or Parker drinking and screaming at her.

She had been cocaine-free for three weeks, not long enough to lose the need or even the urge. She had seen others go back, and she hoped she had the strength to stay away.

Lisa put the rest of the beans in the refrigerator and finished cleaning the stove. She glanced at the clock—almost nine. She was supposed to stay open until ten, but she didn't expect any more customers this late. She would just rest for a moment and then finish cleaning up. She went out to one of the tables, put her head down, and went to sleep.

Sometime later, Lisa awakened to the feeling of someone rubbing her neck. It wasn't a dream. She tried to get up but the hands moved to her shoulders and held her down.

"Hello, Lisa," Denny Sader whispered. A slight whistle emanated through the air as he spoke. His foul breath curved around her cheek and attacked her face.

She hadn't forgotten the scent or the voice. She tried to turn, to escape, but he was too strong. She wanted to scream, to yell for help, anything. Where was Poppa Bully? Parker?

Denny had his cheek against hers now, still holding her fast to the chair. The voice came back. "I've missed you," he hissed. "So much I came all the way out here to see you. Have you missed me?" He released a hand and stroked her hair, pulling it back through his fingers.

A chance, she thought. She twisted and elbowed him in the stomach. He winced. His other hand released and she ripped away from the table, shoving a chair in front of her. Denny hadn't changed much. His hair was longer, oilier. Or had she somehow missed that before?

She screamed, "Get out! Get out and leave me alone!" Her eyes shifted to the rear door. Could she make it?

"Bully will be back any minute," she said, frantically. "Leave before he sees you."

Denny straightened and rose to his full height, towering over her. My God, she thought. Those rotten teeth, the spaces. He was hideous. She backed to the counter.

Denny stayed with her. "You mean that old pirate with the wooden leg and patch over his eye? He won't be back. I watched him leave and followed him. I cut his tires. It's a pretty good walk from where he is."

Lisa reached for a beer bottle behind her. But Denny moved quickly to her, grabbed her, then flipped her around and twisted her arm behind her back, jamming her into the counter.

"Don't do this to me, Denny. I don't want to go back. Things are good now," Lisa said. Tears flowed over her cheeks. She tasted the salt on her lips. Denny mashed her tighter against the counter pushing the air from her lungs. She couldn't move or breathe.

"You're my girl, Lisa. I know you miss hanging with me. I've come for you. You need me. But you really need this." He pulled a package from his shirt pocket moved it in front of her eyes and pressed it to her lips.

She kicked and squirmed but couldn't break free. She got one hand up, reached back and scratched his face. He slapped her head. She kicked, trying to hit his shin, his knee, anything. She couldn't go back, she wouldn't. She had come too far.

"Denny, please, no," she begged.

He pressed harder. She felt his skinny body against her backside. His left arm tightened across her chest, locking her arms in. And then she watched in horror as he spread a line of white powder on the bar top. She shook her head violently, "No! No!"

He stuck his finger in the powder and wiped it across her lip. "Taste good?"

She struggled, trying to free her arms. He slapped her head again, and yelled in her ear, "Stop it, you bitch."

The slap hurt, but she continued to struggle—mustn't quit now. She begged, pleaded. "I'm clean, Denny. Since I left you. I have a chance here. Please."

He ignored her. "Here's a straw, honey. Put it in your nose like a good girl. You know you want to."

"Please, Denny. Please don't," she pleaded, her lungs bursting. He put his right hand behind her head and pushed. She resisted, but he was stronger. He pushed harder, tilting her head toward the counter, her chest pressed even more tightly against the edge. She weakened, the powder closer.

"Remember how it was, Lisa? How it felt? It takes away all the pain. Just this once...just this one time. It feels sooooo good."

Chapter Eighteen

Alec sat by the window in his room at the Tremont Hotel observing the entrance to the Irish pub across the street. He glanced at his watch—five o'clock. Several couples entered the bar within the next few minutes. Must be happy hour, he mused. The Americans seem to have a name for everything.

He rose from the chair and faced the mirror over the dresser. He wet his fingers and pushed his blond hair back over his ears, then began to pace the floor. The pub sounded good, but first, he wanted to focus on his mission and review what he had learned so far.

In 1943, Admiral Döenitz, the German spymaster, ordered Alec's grandfather, Eric von Speigel, to Galveston to organize a ring of saboteurs. But von Speigel had been captured en route and interned at Fort Crockett.

Von Speigel's superiors ordered him to escape and resume his spy mission. His last coded message indicated he was planning to break out, but his contact in Argentina, Rheinhard Bauer, never heard from him again, and he never found out what happened.

Alec had asked Harry Stein if there had been any successful escapes. Stein had promised to research it, but thought it doubtful. The prisoners were treated so well, why would any of them want to leave? And what could they do here in the states anyway, thousands of miles from the war?

Alec stopped in front of the mirror and stared intently at his own reflection. If he were von Speigel, what would he have done?

It was a soldier's duty to escape, and besides, a dedicated Abwehr member would never have forsaken his mission to the Reich. But if he had escaped, where had he gone? And where was the money? It did not make any sense. Unless...unless he escaped to get the money, the funds sent ahead to finance the saboteurs. But where would the money have been stashed? Did von Speigel's contact in Texas have it? And what form did it take—paper money? Gold coins? Diamonds?

Maybe diamonds, Alec thought. The Germans had confiscated millions in diamonds from the Jews. No, he thought, if it were diamonds, von Speigel would have brought them with him. And if he had, they would have gone down with the sub.

No! Señora Rosas said his contact in America was to supply the funds. Von Speigel left on short notice. There was no time to get the funds to him beforehand. Alec was stymied, no closer than before to the riddle's answer.

He stood by the desk and looked at the telephone, dreading the call to Germany. Frankin would press for information, and he would have no choice but to give the little bastard more details about his plan. He needed more time and more money. The committee would understand. They needed him and the funds he was after.

The police watched the GTO closely. German laws prohibited xenophobic activity and even Nazi paraphernalia. But anything was possible with money. They couldn't continue their plan for a Fourth Reich without more funding.

Or was it only the money they needed and not him? He wondered. There was no doubt he threatened the weakling, Frankin. He was sure Frankin would cut him out if he had the chance, and Alec wasn't in Germany to protect himself.

He calculated his position. What was the worse-case scenario? Of the twin aphrodisiacs, money and power, he might lose out on power. So what, he thought.

A picture of his mother crossed his mind, sitting in a threadbare kitchen telling him about his father. An opportunity would come along, she had said. But you must be ready for it.

His contact, Horst Frankin, was an idiot. Some of the others seemed smarter than that. But were they? Were they really fools enough to eliminate a man with his potential? Maybe they were, he considered. Well, what did he really owe them anyway? Nothing! Why was he even considering giving up the funds?

Not that he couldn't be a great leader if he wanted to. He thought about Adolph Hitler and his famous speeches at the Hoffbrau Biergarten in Munich. Alec had studied them all. He had practiced the tempo, the voice inflections. He closed his eyes and dreamed of the new Germany and what he would do to the Communists. Only he was strong enough to bring it about.

As he left his room headed for the happy hour across the street, his mind reeled in confusion—money, power, money, power, money, power.

***

Alec awoke early the next morning still disoriented. It was time to call Mariana. He hated to rush her, but he had to make things happen. This time he walked to a pay phone down the block.

"Mariana, my love. It is me, Günter."

"Oh, Günter...Günter, I am so glad you called. Auntie has had a stroke. She is in a coma, uncommunicative. The doctor said she has only a day or two left, no more."

Alec was stunned. What if she did not regain consciousness? The old woman gone! No! His last chance. He desperately needed the alias Eric von Speigel had used at Fort Crockett and only Señora Rosas knew that. Now, if Harry Stein did learn the names of any escaped prisoners, he had no way of knowing if one of them was von Speigel.

He wanted to scream out in disgust, but he caught himself in time and realized the stress in her voice.

"I am deeply sorry, Mariana. She is such a fine lady. I wish I could be there for you."

"Thank you, Günter. I want you here. I cannot run the *estancia* by myself. Did...did Auntie say anything to you about...us."

Yes, Alec thought. Something Señora Rosas had said—Mariana would inherit the estate. The old house and the land surrounding it were still valuable. And Mariana was so beautiful. The old woman made it clear to him. She wanted him there, with Mariana. No! He shook his head. Where was he going with that thought? Stay focused.

Alec ignored Mariana's last question and said, "It must be terrible for you now, Mariana, dealing with this tragedy."

"Yes, it is Günter. I am so distressed, I haven't slept at all. You will return, won't you?"

"Oh, uh, yes, of course Mariana, as soon as I have finished. But for now, I need your help."

"What is it, Günter?"

"Did the Señora ever mention the name von Speigel used as an alias in the POW camp?"

"No....No she didn't."

Silence followed. Alec wanted to press. The mission was failing, his dreams disappearing. He could hear Mariana breathing into the telephone, a soft sob. He waited, contemplating his next move.

Then, Mariana spoke again, excited now. "But Günter, I almost forgot. I have news. We never found the letter, the one I told you about from Eric von Speigel to Rheinhard Bauer."

Silence. Alec could not speak, he was finished. His last chance to the money trail would expire with the Señora's last breath. He started to hang up.

"But Günter, there was another letter."

"Yes, yes Mariana, go on."

"It was a communiqué from the Abwehr to Rheinhard. The Señora thought she had destroyed them all but somehow this one survived."

"Yes, yes, what does it say?"

"It mentions the name of von Speigel's contact in America, and where he lived. A small town in Texas, named Fredericksburg."

***

Mariana had taken Günter's call in Señora Rosas's room. She sat in a chair next to her bed. When Alec terminated the call, Mariana turned to her aunt.

"Well, the ruse was worth a try," the Señora mused. "We had to learn his intentions. We both made it very clear to him that you will inherit everything and that we want him here with you. He said he would return, but do you believe him? If he thought I was dying, I would like to have heard more commitment, more enthusiasm about returning here."

Mariana thought for a moment and said, "Auntie, we cannot afford to believe him when he says he is coming back here. We have too much at stake. Your plan was worth a try, but we still do not know. And you are right. No doubt he is going on to Fredericksburg. I think that proves he thinks the value of the money he is after is more than what he could get here. Maybe he knows more than we think. And for our sake, I hope he does."

"Maybe he intends to have both," the Señora added.

"A possibility, I suppose, Auntie. But if he is a dedicated neo-Nazi, he will not come here if he finds the money, he will return to Germany with it."

"That is true," Señora Rosas added. "And even if he is acting on his own, there is no guarantee he will come back to Argentina. He might just find the money and disappear in America."

Mariana nodded in agreement, then said, "It is fortunate that you really had forgotten the alias von Speigel used in the POW camp. At least he does not have that. Perhaps we should not have given him the name of the contact in Texas."

"No, my dear. Our plan has always been for him to find the money. We can't do it. We had to give him the information."

Mariana said, "Do you really think the money is still in Fredericksburg, after all these years?"

"I do not know." Señora Rosas concluded. "I do not even know if anyone there is still alive. But we have tried every trick I know. I do not know what else we can do from here, but we cannot give up."

Señora Rosas reached toward her nightstand. She grasped the vial with the cyanide capsule, held it to the light, and said, "We have much to think about."

Chapter Nineteen
Saturday, August 27

The performance began with one bird, a single piercing cry. Then, within seconds out of an empty sky, dozens of laughing gulls converged, hovering and diving over a school of shrimp.

Some innate survival instinct had instructed one bird to call for others. Teamwork—I must have missed that lecture. Growing up, I had learned to go it alone.

But the Army demanded teamwork, and I had given it my best shot. My old unit and I had worked well together. Then, when I came home after the war, the Army reneged, went AWOL. My incessant fatigue and pain proved it.

I heard Charlie squawk and started downstairs, massaging my shoulder as I went. I got another mullet from the barrel and stuffed it through the cage. He raised his wings defiantly and squawked again.

"Feeling trapped, huh boy? Ready to be free? Well, enjoy the easy life. Pretty soon you'll be like the rest of us, getting your own lunch."

The look he gave me said he was ready for that. His message was always the same. Am I ready? Am I ready? I couldn't look him in the eye anymore. What was this strange connection between the bird and me anyway? Envy? What responsibilities did a bird have? To exist? To eat and propagate? Simple, basic urges.

Trapped? Maybe that was it. Maybe I had an iron cage around me too. I couldn't remember being free, not really. As a teenager, I had worked my butt off slopping bait to support my mother and me. Then a marriage at nineteen and years of hit and miss with a wife I barely saw. Plus nineteen years of up at six to the sound of the bugle and yes sir, no sir. And then, even a bigger prison awaited—pain and booze. No way out.

I fed the night heron another mullet, then stepped as close to the cage as I could and studied the bird's movements. It had been several weeks. The wing should be healed. "You'll be out of here soon, Charlie. I promise."

My mouth felt like someone had stuffed a half-bale of cotton down my throat. I stumbled into the bar, grabbed a cold beer from the box and sucked down about half of it before stopping to breathe. Then I rolled the bottle along my cheek to cool my face.

I glanced toward the front of the room and cursed aloud, "Christ, not again." The front bar was closed, but Lisa had left the front door open. Why? When I came home last night she was talking to Neddie Lemmon. Not feeling like conversation, I scooted around the building and went upstairs to the deck. I had a few drinks and went to bed.

Just then, Bully stumbled in from around the side of the building and collapsed at the outside table. He removed his eye patch and rubbed his face with his shirt, toweling off as much sweat and sand as he could. Red, puffy splotches covered his cheeks and forehead. I went out and stood beside him.

"What's wrong with you, Bully? Where have you been?"

Panting heavily, he said, "Water, Parker, please."

I picked up the hose at my feet, turned it on, and handed it to Bully. He held the end to his mouth and drank greedily, then put it over his head, letting the cool liquid drench his face and neck. After a moment, he dropped the hose, then released his wooden leg and let it fall to the cement. He massaged the end of his stump talking at the same time.

"Tires cut, had to walk in from the oak motte. Took me half the forkin' night."

"Jesus," I said. "You cut a tire on some shell? Why didn't you change it instead of walking back?"

"No, sliced open!" Bully replied. "All the tires. Somebody cut all four of them."

"What! Cut them all? Who the hell...?"

Bully dropped his head and grabbed his chest, panting hard. His breaths came fast and shallow. He rubbed his chest in a circle.

"This damn wooden leg ain't made for walking a mile in the sand. Barely made it back." The words were chopped, strained. "Damn, my chest hurts. Parker—the nightstand."

I raced to the trailer for his nitro pills. He slipped one under his tongue. In seconds, his breathing slowed. As soon as he could speak, he blurted out, "Where's Lisa? Have you seen her?"

"I saw her last night with Neddie in the bar. She didn't close up again. Even left the lights on."

"No, I saw her with Neddie then, too," Bully said, alarm in his voice. "I mean did you see her after that, or this morning?"

"No, I haven't." I said.

"Where the hell could she be?" Bully pondered. "Your truck is outside."

"She knows better than to drive my truck."

"What do you mean?"

"I told her after she got you out of jail that my truck was off limits. If she ever drove it again, I'd kick her out."

Bully screwed his face up, "Jesus, Parker! What the hell is wrong with you? The way you treat her—I mean...listen to me, something's happened to Lisa, I know it."

I waved him off. "I wouldn't worry about it. She probably got the hot pants for some nickel-dick customer and went off with him. I've had it with her."

I rubbed my forehead, trying to quiet the pain from the hangover. This was the last straw with Lisa. Damn it! I had a business to run.

Bully reattached his leg, then got up and headed to the back door of the bar. "She wouldn't do that, Parker. Not now, she's come too far."

I yelled at his backside, "Three weeks? Hell, she's still drying out, Bully."

He was inside now, in front of the counter, shouting, "Why is this stool knocked over?"

I followed him in.

"And what's this white stuff on the bar?"

I dabbed it with my finger. I had tasted the substance before at an Army training school. "Cocaine! No doubt about it."

Bully's eyes widened, a scream erupted. "Sader! It's that damned Denny Sader." He slammed the bar with his fist. "I'll kill the sum-bitch."

"Wouldn't be him," I said. "He's not stupid enough to come out here. Had to be a customer. Someone new. Gave Lisa a hit, and she went with him. She's back doping again, Bully. It's not something you can shake cold turkey, like she tried to do. No one's that strong, especially a kid."

"No, it's that damned Sader," Bully yelled. "He must've been watching the bar. Followed me out to the motte and then cut my tires. It had to be him. No stranger woulda gone to that much trouble."

Bully turned and headed out the front door, yelling over his shoulder, "Parker, get someone out here to fix my truck."

I realized too late he would be taking mine and regretted leaving the keys in it. Before I could respond, I heard the squeal of tires as he roared out of the parking lot.

I thought about Sader and wondered if Bully could have been right about him. But then, even if Sader had come for Lisa, she had probably gone with him voluntarily. If Sader cut Bully's tires, it was just to keep Bully from following him. Lisa probably even suggested it.

I moved to the refrigerator, opened the door and studied the almost empty box. I knew I had to offer my customers something for lunch, but my mind wouldn't focus. I thought for a moment, then turned to the telephone and picked up the receiver to call a tire service company.

Chapter Twenty
Saturday, August 27

Bully rammed Parker's truck into a parking meter in front of The Eight Ball, smashing the bumper. The force knocked his leg off. He bent over and refastened it, grunting loudly. Seconds later, he entered the front door and barreled past the front tables.

The place was empty except for the day manager, a kid of about twenty behind the back counter, and Denny Sader. Denny was bent over a table making a shot, his back to the entrance. His long, lanky body stretched the length of the table.

The noise of the jukebox covered Bully's attack. He closed fast. "You son of a bitch, what have you done with her?"

Bully fell on Denny's back before Denny could straighten and turn. His massive frame pinned Sader's thin body to the table. He grabbed a handful of Denny's greasy hair, yanked his head back, and slammed it on the hard slate. Blood spurted from Denny's nose. One of his rotten teeth stuck in the green felt. Bully held Denny's face tight to the table. Blood soaked into the cloth like oil on cement.

"Did you hear me, you prick? Where is Lisa?" Bully shouted again. Denny kicked back, trying to get free. Bully jerked Denny's head back and slammed it to the table again. This time Denny's face hit the tooth that was stuck in the felt and more blood poured from a gash in his cheek.

The kid-manager started to move out from behind the counter. Bully yelled, "Stay where you are, you little shit, if you know what's good for you. This ain't none of your business."

The kid stopped and held up his hands in a gesture of surrender.

Bully wasn't finished with Denny by a long shot. He would pay for taking Lisa. But first, he had to find out where she was. Denny mumbled something. With his head still buried in the tabletop, Bully couldn't make out what he said. He grabbed another handful of Denny's greasy hair and yanked his head back for the third time.

"What did you say, boy? Tell me where she is, or I'll break your goddamned neck."

Bully had Denny's voice box stretched back so tight he could barely speak. The words squeaked out. "She's mine, old man. I took her and she's mine."

"Bullshit. I found dope on the bar. You made her do it. Now where is she?" Bully pulled harder on the hair bringing Denny's neck back to the breaking point. He would break it if need be; he didn't really give a damn.

A door slammed in the back by the restroom. Lisa came out through the hall. She slumped at the doorway holding onto the wall for support.

Bully shouted, "Lisa! Here! Lisa, look at me!"

Lisa looked up, her eyes glazed over.

"You!" Bully shouted to the kid behind the counter. "Get Lisa and take her out to my truck—now!"

The kid stayed rooted to the floor, glancing back and forth amongst Lisa, Denny, and Bully, not moving.

Bully's voice roared through the empty pool hall. "Now, damn it! Take her out to my truck, now!" The kid put his arm around Lisa's shoulders and helped her past Bully toward the front door.

Lisa looked up as they passed, "Poppa, oh Poppa. He made me, he made me."

"Lisa, get in Parker's truck and leave. Do you hear me? The keys are in it. Leave now!" Bully looked at the kid. "Put her in the truck, get it started, and get her out of here." The boy nodded as he half-carried Lisa to the front door.

Bully shoved Denny's head back into the blood-soaked felt and jerked it side to side, coating his face. Then he leaned down and whispered in his ear. "You bastard, I ought to kill you. You ever come 'round our house again you're dead meat. You hear me!"

Bully hadn't heard the footsteps behind him. Bubba Shanks, the big white kid from the jail, had come in the back door fresh from a delivery for Denny. Ever since Bubba had told Denny about Bully at the jail, Denny had been using the kid as a runner. Denny wasn't stupid. Let the kid get caught with the goods, not him.

The kid picked up a cue stick from an adjacent table and smashed Bully's wooden leg as hard as he could, breaking the stick in half. Bully collapsed onto Denny and then slid to the floor behind him.

Still bleeding from the nose and cheek, Denny took what was left of the cue-stick from Bubba. Bully was on his back on the floor with his hands up trying to protect himself. Blood dripped off Denny's face and splattered onto Bully's shirt and pants. Denny swung hard hitting Bully's hands, knocking them out of the way. Then he rammed the big end of the stick into Bully's stomach.

Bully retched, gasping for air. He watched helplessly as Denny raised the stick again. Somehow, he got his hands back over his gut and tried to roll out of the way behind the table.

Bubba grabbed Denny's shirt. "Hey, man. A cop just pulled up out front. The back door quick. Let's get the hell out of here."

Chapter Twenty-One
Saturday, August 27 & Sunday, August 28

A hundred miles west of Austin, on State Highway 290, Alec Strauss slowed to read the sign. *Fredericksburg, Texas, Population 7911.* On the main street, he noticed a number of stone buildings interspersed between newer wooden and brick structures. Some of the old rock homes dated from the 1850s'. Now they were bakeries, antique stores and gift shops.

At the visitor center, he approached a gray-haired woman behind the counter and asked for a map of the area.

"Of course, sir," the woman replied. She handed him the map and continued in German, "*Guten Morgen.*"

The language startled him. He caught her facial expression, questioning, asking for a reply. He didn't say anything.

She spoke again, in English. "I'm sorry, sir. Your accent seemed German. Do you speak the language?"

Alec answered too quickly, "Of course I do."

A mistake, he shouldn't have said that. People remember rudeness. Another mistake, with the racks behind him filled with local information, he shouldn't have asked for a map. A voice in his head echoed, *do not call attention to yourself.*

Well, it was too late now; he had gone this far. He smiled and said, "Forgive me, I did not mean to be short. It has been a tiring drive."

The woman nodded, as though she understood.

He continued, "I am curious. I understand German immigrants settled the town in the 1800s. Are there any descendants left in the area?" He waited for an answer, hoping the question seemed innocent, the normal observation of a tourist.

The old woman perked up, her eyes excited. "Oh my, yes. I'm fourth generation myself," she answered, her face beaming. "There are lots of us around. Check the phone book, you'll see. And if you're looking for anyone in particular, I know a lot of the locals."

Alec hesitated. In a small town, everyone knew everyone else's business. He decided to leave the inquiry where it was, hoping she wouldn't remember him. "No, not at all," he said. "Just passing through." He turned to leave.

She called after him, "Lots of good German restaurants here. And of course, we have the World War II Museum. Don't miss that."

Alec turned. "World War II Museum?"

She smiled again, "Yes, it was built to honor Chester Nimitz, our local hero. He was commander of the Pacific Fleet during World War II. Born in Fredericksburg. It is quite an exhibit. Lots of details about the war."

He nodded slightly in thanks, then turned and exited the building. The museum would be the last place he would go, nothing but American propaganda. Nimitz a hero? He laughed aloud, thinking, with the money and industry the United States possessed, anyone could have led their forces.

In their last telephone conversation, Mariana had given him the name Rudolph Hoff as von Speigel's contact in America. Both Hoff's name and the town were mentioned in the correspondence she had found. Alec stepped to a pay phone and checked the listings. No Rudolph Hoff. No one named Hoff at all.

Disappointed, he closed the book and sat on a nearby bench to think. If Rudolph was a spy, maybe he returned to Germany after the war. Even worse, was it possible he had been exposed and put in prison or even executed?

He looked up from the bench and noticed the courthouse a block away. Even though Hoff wasn't listed in the phone book, maybe he still owned property here. It was worth a try. He wanted to keep his inquiries as discreet as possible, somehow checking on Hoff without mentioning his name. People remembered specific questions. It made it more likely they would remember him.

He crossed the street and entered the county tax office. Another gray-haired woman sat behind the counter. Alec thought she could be the sister of the old woman at the visitor's center. The locals seem to match the age of the buildings.

When he approached the counter, she smiled and said, "I am sorry, we're closed today. I just came by to straighten a few things."

"Oh," Alec said, acting startled. "I understand. It is Saturday, isn't it. Well, I cannot be here on Monday. I am interested in purchasing a specific piece of property. Is it possible for me to look at your records."

"A special piece? Well, you must have either the legal description or the owner's name to find it."

He had no choice but to give her the name. "Hoff," he said. "Rudolph Hoff."

"Let me think," she said. She put her hand on her forehead and closed her eyes. "I have worked here for thirty years. It does sound familiar."

Hope surged. Could it be?

The gray-haired woman remained perfectly still for a moment, a look of consternation etched in her face. Finally she looked up and said, "Let me get the register."

She turned to a shelf behind her picked up a large computer-paper sized book and began skimming through it. After a moment, she said, "Well, we do have a Hoff. But it's not Rudolph, it Martha. She owns about fifty acres or so a few miles out of town."

The woman took Alec to a wall map and pointed out the direction and general location of the farm. He thanked her and walked briskly out to the sidewalk.

Martha Hoff. Could she possibly be related to Rudolph? Fredericksburg was without doubt a German town. But how many Hoff's lived here fifty years ago? There could have been many. It was a long shot, but all he had. If alive, Rudolph would be in his eighties.

It would be dark soon. He thought it better to lay low tonight, get a cheap room on the edge of town and eat in. If everything worked out, he could finish his business here in the morning and be back in Galveston by tomorrow afternoon.

He checked his watch again—5:00 PM. Harry Stein had promised to research escape attempts at Fort Crockett. But his office was probably closed as well, Strauss thought. He stopped at a pay phone outside the courthouse and got lucky. Stein answered the phone directly.

"Yes, Mr. Strauss. You caught me just in time," Harry said. "I was just leaving. You really got my curiosity up about the fort. I worked on it all afternoon."

Alec responded, "Really? Find out anything?"

"Well, I researched to the end of the war, August of '45. I found one escape attempt in late '43. It was unsuccessful. The prisoner's name was Otto Kruger."

"So did Kruger actually escape and then get recaptured?"

"Yes. He escaped, but he never got off the island. He was only out a few hours."

"So, no other escapes, huh?"

"I checked through to when the war ended, and that was the only one."

The conversation ended. Alec's mind reeled with possibilities. Was Otto Kruger actually Eric von Speigel? Who knows? Why hadn't he asked the old woman in Argentina when he'd had the chance?

But if Kruger was von Speigel, he hadn't escaped long enough to do anything. Unless he had somehow contacted Hoff before he escaped and Hoff had met him there. But Kruger was recaptured. So maybe Hoff still had the money. What had he done with it? Had he taken it back to Fredericksburg?

So then, if von Speigel died at the fort or was repatriated to Germany, maybe Hoff kept the money. And maybe it was still there, on Hoff's farm. Doubtful, after all these years. But still...

Live oak, cedar and mesquite trees covered the rolling hills on either side of the blacktop farm road. The trees were different, but the hills were similar to the countryside outside of Alec's home in Leipzig, Germany.

He wondered why the early immigrants had come here. Why had they left their homes in Germany to travel thousands of miles for this? There, the land was dark and fertile. Here, the topsoil was shallow and weak, too rocky for farming. They had taken the stones from the hillsides and built their homes with them. Every few miles he saw an old rock house, still standing and after a hundred and fifty years, still in use, built by good German stonecutters.

Twelve miles out of town, Alec turned onto a gravel road. A mile later, he turned into the entrance of the Hoff's property. Another stone house, he noted, two storied with a large chimney on one end, set back several hundred yards off the road at the top of a small hill. An orchard of peach trees, heavy with fruit, lined both sides of the road.

Alec had not let anyone know he was coming. Surprise was always better. The house was still, no signs of life. No lights, no automobile, and no animals. No one answered his knock. He stepped off the porch and peered through the front window. The shade was down, but there was a small crack at the bottom. He could see a sofa and some chairs. To the left of the room in front of the front door, a steep stairway rose to the second floor.

Alec checked the side windows of the house. The shades were drawn to the bottom of the windows. He could not see inside. Continuing around the side, he stopped suddenly at the back corner.

A noise. Someone hummed a tune, an old German folk song he recognized.

A woman bent over at the waist faced away from him, tending a rose bush, clipper in hand, busy with a flower. He approached slowly. From a side view, she appeared old, frail, her gray hair pushed back and tied behind her head.

"Hello," Alec said softly, not wanting to startle her.

She flinched, turned quickly, and took a step back, straightening. She didn't speak.

"Excuse me," he said. "I knocked on the front door. No one answered. Thought I would check the back yard. Sorry if I startled you. I am here to see Herr Hoff." He thought using the German address might settle her.

She said nothing, but continued to stare at him.

He spoke in German, *"If you are Frau Hoff, I have come a long way to meet you and Rudolph. Is he around?"*

Chapter Twenty-Two
Saturday, August 27

Bully hadn't said much on the drive back to The Garhole Bar. The pool cue Denny rammed into his stomach had left him nauseated. Marvin stopped once along the way to let him retch. When they pulled into the parking lot, Bully perked up and said, "There's my truck. Thank God, Parker got the tires fixed."

Confused, Marvin Klaus scrunched his eyebrows and said, "What do you mean he got your tires fixed?"

Bully didn't answer.

Marvin stopped the patrol car and turned to Bully. "Damn it, Bully! Tell me what this is all about so I can help you. What the hell were you doing at The Eight Ball? Who were you fighting with? A man your age–holy cow!"

Bully reached for the door handle and faced away from the deputy mumbling, "Personal business, Marvin."

Marvin put his hand on his friend's shoulder, "Sure, puking your guts out is personal business. Whose blood is all over your clothes?"

Bully gave Marvin a quick look. "You should have seen the other guy."

"Old joke, Bully, and not very funny. I think I got there just in time. Good thing Parker called me when he did."

Bully glanced at Marvin, "Parker called you?"

"Yeah," Marvin said. "I was just coming on shift, leaving the station when he called. They patched it through. Lucky for you. He said you were headed for The Eight Ball and were probably in trouble."

"Is that all he told you?"

"He wouldn't say what it was about. I don't know which of you is more stubborn. How did you get there anyway? Your truck's here."

Bully got out of the truck and shut the door.

Marvin leaned toward the open window. "Listen, Bully, you owe me. I was out of my jurisdiction at the pool hall. That was the police department's bag. I'm county, you know. I could've gotten into a lot of trouble."

Bully put his hand on the truck door to steady himself and said, "I didn't ask you there, Marvin."

Marvin slammed the steering wheel. "Goddamn it, Bully, don't do this to me. We go back too far."

Bully suddenly realized Parker's truck wasn't in the parking lot. Where was Lisa? She should have been here by now. Maybe Marvin was right, he thought. He would have to search for Lisa, and he couldn't count on Parker for help. Bully lowered his head. The stump of his leg hurt, and he needed sleep. He knew he could collapse any minute, exhausted from digging all night, walking in from the oak motte, and fighting with Sader. He knew Marvin was waiting for an answer. He wanted to tell him yes, please help, but different words came out. Some things a man takes care of himself. He raised his head, stared into the caring eyes of his old friend, and said, "Yes, we've been pals a long time, Marvin. That's why I gotta ask you to let me handle this."

After Marvin left, Bully got into his truck and returned to The Eight Ball. The only occupant was the kid who had driven Lisa away. The kid swore he had only gone a block or two when Lisa ordered him out of the truck and took off on her own. Bully spent the next two hours driving every street within several miles of the pool hall. But that still left a lot of ground to cover between the seawall on the south side of the island and the port area to the north. Too many streets; not enough time.

He crossed Broadway, the main north-south thoroughfare that divided the island, and pulled to the curb. He slammed the steering wheel, then yelled out to himself, "This isn't working, old man. Think, damn it!"

Where could Lisa have gone? There were only three ways off the island—the causeway to Houston, the ferry to Bolivar Island on the east end, and the toll bridge over San Luis Pass on the west end.

He considered each option. He doubted she would have made it onto the ferry in her condition. Anyway, why go to Bolivar? She knew no one there. Same with the causeway. She wouldn't have attempted to cross over it. She had nowhere to go in Houston. With no money, she couldn't have crossed the toll bridge. Besides, even in her condition, she would have recognized the cutoff to The Garhole before she got to the bridge.

Bully knew he could spend the rest of the day searching the back streets of downtown Galveston and still not find her. Time to play a hunch, he thought. She must be somewhere out on the west end, the area she knew best.

The island was shaped like an elongated spear. It ranged from several miles wide where the seawall ended to a few hundred yards in width at San Luis pass. On the west end alone, there were twenty miles of blacktop roads crisscrossing among open fields, backwater sloughs, and isolated houses and farms. Plus at least a dozen subdivisions interspersed along FM3005. She could be anywhere. The area was huge, and it was getting dark. Where was she and what kind of condition was she in?

He decided to swallow his pride. He stopped at a service station and called Marvin Klaus. "It's Lisa," Bully said. "That bastard Sader took her. I got her away from him at the pool hall, and she took off in Parker's truck before you got there. But she didn't make it home. She's out there somewhere, alone. Or maybe Sader found her. Christ, I don't know what to do."

"I knew it!" Marvin exclaimed. "It had to be Lisa. Damn it, Bully. I've known her since she was a baby. You know how I feel about her. Let me get on the horn. I'll get some help."

"No!" Bully yelled. "I told you it was personal."

"I'm not talking about more cops. Johnny's off-duty, and I'll call Neddie, and..."

Bully knew how his friends felt about Lisa. They would do anything for her, but he could handle this.

"No, I mean it, Marvin. We need to keep this close. I think she's out on the west end somewhere. You start at the end of the seawall and work west. I'll drive to The Garhole and come toward you."

Chapter Twenty-Three
Saturday, August 27

Marvin Klaus called to tell me about Bully's fight at the pool hall. He said Bully had found Lisa there and that Lisa had taken off in my truck. He had just started to tell me their plan to find her when Bully hobbled through the front door and leaned against the back bar panting short, rapid breaths.

I don't think he had slept for twenty-four hours. He looked ready to drop. I wondered how long the old man could go. I told Marvin Bully was there and hung up the telephone.

Breathing heavily, Bully said, "Parker, I still ain't found Lisa. I got a feeling she's somewhere between here and town. Marvin's starting from the end of the seawall and coming this way. It'll be dark soon, and I can't see a damn thing at night. I need your help."

If she was with Sader, I had no reason to think she hadn't hooked up with him voluntarily.

I answered, my emotions churning, "Who'll run The Garhole? It's Saturday night. I can't close on Saturday night."

"Damn you, Parker. Lisa needs us. Forget about your forkin' bar for once."

Bully moved to a stool beside me. Wheezing sounds squealed out from deep within his chest.

I said, "Look, Bully. If Lisa's not back here by now, it means she's with that loser Sader again because she wants to be. There're probably holed up somewhere smoking dope."

"Damn it, Parker! What's wrong with you? Lisa told me Sader kidnapped her. The bastard even admitted it while I was beating the shit out of him. I'll search alone if I have to. I won't let her down this time."

I knew what he was referring to. He hadn't been there for her after her mother died when she had gone into the state's custody. I should have known the way he felt by the way he begged me to let her stay when she showed up three weeks ago.

He lowered his voice, almost pleading. "For Christ sake, Parker. Come with me!"

It was his last, best effort. He had a hurt on his face I had never seen before. When I didn't reply, he turned and limped back through the room toward his truck, a dogged determination in his step.

I bolted past him, lowered the front bar, shut the front door, and climbed into the driver's seat. Bully hobbled around to the passenger side and got in.

He said, "She's out here on the west end somewhere. I know it."

We searched Bay Harbor and Terramar Beach, the oldest developments on the west end. To complicate matters, each development stretched across the entire island from the Gulf side across FM3005 to West Bay.

We headed toward Sea Isle and Indian Beach. We drove the beach side and then the bay side—nothing. The next development, Jamaica Beach, had several hundred houses and dozens of streets. I pulled the truck into the convenience store at the entrance to the subdivision.

"This isn't making any sense," I said. "We'll be out here all night at this rate. It'll take us an hour just to do Jamaica Beach and we've still got Pirate's Beach, Spanish Grant, and the back roads."

"We've got to keep trying," Bully exclaimed. "There's a pay phone. I'll call Marvin."

Back in the car, Bully continued. "No luck. He has a bigger area than us to search. He's working the developments by the beach along 3005."

I slapped my forehead saying, "Wait a minute! She doesn't have a driver's license. She wouldn't drive 3005 unless she had to. She probably came the back way, up Stewart Road. She would have passed Nine Mile Road."

"So?" Bully said.

"Nine Mile is the cutoff that goes back to the bird pond."

"You think?"

"Maybe. It's worth a shot. We went out there a lot when she was a kid. Remember? It's a fresh water pond with trees around it. Birds flocked to it during the spring migration. We used to alternate between that pond and the one at the oak motte. She might feel safe there."

We hurried past Jamaica Beach and the state park. At Thirteen Mile Road, we turned left onto Stewart Road. It split the island halfway between the beach and the bay. We drove past the golf course at Galveston Country Club and Pirates Cove subdivision.

"Here's Nine Mile coming up," I said. "I think there's a curve right at the entrance to the pond road."

Bully nodded.

I turned on the black top and raced toward the back of the island. A mile later, we approached a bend in the two-lane. I slowed the truck and yelled, "There it is!"

Sand ruts left the road and snaked through the grass. I knew they ended at the pond. The gap in the fence was open.

"Fresh tire tracks," Bully said.

We bounced up and down and sideways, the truck sloshing through the mud holes in the road. Bully grabbed the dashboard for support.

"There's your truck!" he yelled. "Hurry!"

I slammed to a stop. We were both out in a flash.

Bully reached the truck first. "She's here!" he shouted. "Lying across the seat."

Dried blood covered a small cut on her forehead. She appeared unconscious. Bully opened the door and eased her out.

He shouted to me, "My truck, quick."

I hustled to the back of the pickup and lowered the tailgate. Bully laid her down gently. He took his shirt off and placed it under her head. She moaned slightly.

Bully yelled, "She's alive."

I investigated the truck. "Looks as if her head hit the windshield. There's blood there and a crack in it. She must have been going too fast and hit that big mud hole. How is she?"

"Coming to," Bully replied. He checked the cut then her eyes. "She looks okay. Don't think there's a concussion."

"Hospital?" I asked.

"No," Bully answered. "Let's just take her home. I'll tend to her. We'll stop at the first phone and call Marvin."

Chapter Twenty-Four
Sunday, August 28

Günter Manfred, alias Alec Strauss, had traveled from Germany to Argentina to Galveston to Fredericksburg. The trail proved long and uncertain. But at last, he encountered a bit of good fortune, a stroke of luck. Mariana had found correspondence containing Rudolph Hoff's name and location. The woman standing before him was a Hoff. She must know something.

She seemed nervous, afraid to acknowledge anything. Of course, Alec thought. If she were related to Rudolph, she would be concerned about someone showing up on her doorstep after all these years, asking questions. He could be from German intelligence tracking the lost funds, or worse yet, from some Jewish organization tracking ex-Nazis. Of course, she would be careful.

"Who are you?" the woman asked, her voice tentative, unsure. The knuckles on her hand holding the clippers had turned white, her eyes flashed alarm. "Why did you call me Frau Hoff? Your accent? Are you from Germany?"

Alec saw tightness in her face and realized he must calm her, gain her confidence. He backed up a step, then spoke very softly.

"Yes, I am. My name is Günter Manfred. If you know Rudolph Hoff, I have come a long way to meet him. I need his help." Make yourself vulnerable, Alec thought. Non-threatening. Few people could resist a request for help. He waited for a reply.

The muscles in her face relaxed slightly. Her eyes seemed less frightened. She turned and moved slowly toward a lone live oak tree in the middle of the yard and sat on a bench by a garden table. Alec followed a few steps behind.

"May I sit?" he asked.

She nodded.

He moved to a bench across from her. Their eyes met.

She said, "I must tell you, Herr Manfred. For whatever reason you seek my father, he cannot help you. He is no longer living."

It was a punch in the gut. Alec had successfully tracked Eric von Speigel's contact in America only to learn the man was dead. Still, the woman had admitted she was his daughter. She must know something. Patience now, he counseled himself.

"I am so sorry, Frau Hoff," Alec said. "When did it happen?"

"Long ago, in the fifties," she answered. "It was cancer."

A silence surrounded them. Martha Hoff seemed immersed in some private world, far away.

Puffs of dark clouds moved in from the south and the ambient wind pushed a swirl of oak leaves past their feet. Behind them in the garden, rose bushes rattled and petals fell to the dark mulch below.

Martha Hoff's eyes cleared and seemed to focus. Alec watched as suspicion replaced nostalgia.

She said, "But you are much too young to have known my father. How could he have possibly helped you?"

Alec leaned forward, keeping eye contact. "Frau Hoff, I have been searching a long time. It has been very difficult. But...I know I am close, now."

"Close? Close to what?" She asked. "What are you talking about?" Her hands twitched. She pulled back slightly.

"I am close to finding my grandfather, Eric von Speigel," Alec said. He attempted a pained expression and waited for a reply.

Her hand sprung to her mouth. She inhaled quickly. "Eric had no children. He was not married."

There! At last, Alec thought. She had answered without thinking. She couldn't deny it now. She had known Eric von Speigel or about him. He followed quickly.

"I know it is a shock, Frau Hoff. And you are correct he wasn't married. But he did have a daughter, my mother. Eric von Speigel was my grandmother's fiancé. My mother was conceived before he left Germany for America. He never knew she was pregnant. He never knew he was a father."

Frau Hoff averted her eyes, then straightened and put both hands on the table as though about to stand. She seemed to be steeling herself, gathering strength. After a moment, she rose and faced him, her eyes defiant. "Why do you come here and tell me this? Why are you doing this to me?"

Alec pulled the photograph of von Speigel from his pocket that Señora Rosas had given him and thrust it in front of her. "I am Eric's grandson. See!"

She took the photograph into her hand and examined it closely. "My God," she said. "Are you telling me the truth?"

"Yes, please believe me, Frau Hoff. I am his grandson."

She broke a little. Her eyes glistened. "Yes, yes. I see it. Your eyes, your hair, even your bearing. It is true."

Alec was on track now; the scheme had worked. He could think of no other way to have approached Martha Hoff than to assume she had known von Speigel. If von Speigel had escaped, there was a good chance he would have gone to Fredericksburg. He would have wanted to reach his contact here in the United States. He would have needed refuge.

"I am sorry, Frau Hoff. I didn't know any other way to tell you. I am not here to cause you pain. Please, let me explain. I came because I am desperate to help my mother. She has spent over forty years in East Germany under communist rule. We have no money. My mother will die without the operation she needs. Like your father, she also has cancer. But with the right treatment, she has a chance."

The lie continued. Alec's mother had been dead for several weeks, but he thought this play on Frau Hoff's sympathies might work.

The shock about von Speigel having a child took a toll on her frail body. She sat back down, held her head in her hands, and cried softly, "I don't understand, Herr Manfred. How...how can I help you?"

Alec paused for effect. He lowered his eyes to the table taking the time to gather the expression of reassurance he wanted. Then he looked at her and said, softly, "Frau Hoff, I have no intention of harming your father's reputation or exposing him in any way. Your secrets are safe with me. I know he worked for the German government during the war. I know the purpose of my grandfather's trip to America. His contact in Argentina wrote to my mother and told her everything."

"Everything?" Frau Hoff replied.

"Yes, everything," he answered.

She didn't appear frightened at the revelation. He decided to continue. "I know my grandfather was a spy for the Abwehr, sent to Texas on a secret mission to recruit and train saboteurs. He was to obtain the funds for the mission from his contact here, your father. But he was captured and incarcerated in Galveston. He escaped and came here for help."

The last thought was a guess on Alec's part, but she had already confirmed part of it. Von Speigel must have come to Fredericksburg because Frau Hoff admitted she had known him. He could tell she wanted to say something. He waited.

She studied him for a moment longer and then said, "But if what you say is true, Herr Manfred, what does it have to do with helping your mother?"

Again, Alec waited. She would feel more in control if she answered her own questions. She seemed composed now, but suspicious again. Alec would have to be careful. He would try not to seem hurried, impatient.

Hoff spoke again, "Oh, I see," she said. "You want to know about the money? You think it could be used to help your mother?"

So she knew about the money. Good, he thought—keep going. "Yes, I'm afraid that's correct. I told you I was desperate. It is my mother's only chance."

Hoff didn't immediately react. She seemed to be searching his eyes for truth. Maybe if he changed the subject, took some pressure off.

"And I want to know more about my grandfather," he said. "I have no other family. I need the sense of existence, as though I am a part of something. Please, Frau Hoff, what can you tell me about him?"

Tears swelled, she took a tissue from her apron and dabbed her eyes. "No one here knows anything about this," she said. "It has been my secret for over forty years."

She had made her decision. She was going to trust him. He took on a gentle look and said, "I promise, Frau Hoff. I swear on my mother's heart, I will tell no one."

She took a few moments to compose herself. Her breathing slowed. She began in a long, slow voice. "Very well, Mr. Manfred. It was so long ago, but I will tell you what I remember. My father and I came here from Germany in 1935. I was fourteen at the time. My mother had died, and he told me we were moving to America for a better life. I didn't know it, but he was already in the service of the Abwehr, sent here as a sleeper agent as they called them."

"We came to Fredericksburg because it was predominantly a German area. In 1935, English was almost a second language here. We would fit in without raising any suspicion. It all seemed natural to me. I didn't want to come but, of course, I grew to love it here. I realized we had more opportunity, more freedom."

A dam opened. Her words poured out non-stop. She'd had this bottled up for years. Secrets too ominous to discuss with anyone.

"Then the war came. America joined in 1941 and in 1943, the Abwehr activated my father. They gave him a special mission. A shipment of money and gold would be brought from Mexico."

"Gold?" Alec interrupted, surprise in his voice.

"Yes, gold and currency," she said. "You see, the orders came on short notice. We had no money here. The German embassy in Mexico had funds that agents had brought in for a previously unsuccessful mission. It was delivered here to my father with instructions for him to meet Eric in Galveston."

"Did he do that?" Alec asked.

"He tried. He waited in Galveston for several days and when Eric never showed, he decided to leave the money there rather than take the risk of bringing it back to Fredericksburg and being caught with it."

Alec interrupted, "He left the money in Galveston?"

"Yes, he did," she said. "He knew Eric would eventually contact him. He could then return and retrieve the money for the mission. But time passed. He didn't hear from Eric or the Abwehr. One day, several months after the war ended, Eric showed up at our door. He told us his story. As you know, he had been captured and held prisoner in Galveston. That is why he hadn't shown for the rendezvous."

Alec broke in, "He came here several months after the war was over? I don't understand. They didn't release the internees here. They sent them back to Germany."

"Yes, but the POWs weren't sent back right away. There were prisoners in camps here until late 1946. A year after the war ended, he was still at Fort Crockett. He finally escaped and came to us for help. He didn't have anyplace else to go."

So, Alec thought, that is why Harry Stein hadn't found a record of a successful escape. Stein had stopped looking when the war ended. It was all making sense now, coming together. But there were still unanswered questions.

"Why did he escape after the war was over?" Alec asked. "Why didn't he just wait and return to Germany?" It must have been the money, Alec, thought. He came to Fredericksburg for the gold. He must have assumed Hoff still had it.

Hoff continued, "It had been announced that returning prisoners would be shipped to France to work in the coal mines for a period of time before they would be returned to Germany—restitution to the French government."

"So why didn't he just serve out his time in France and then go on to Germany?"

"Eric had borrowed the name of an officer on the Submarine, Otto Kruger, and used it as an alias in the POW camp. If he returned to Germany with that name, he would have been found out. He would have had to revert to his real name."

Of course, Alec thought. Otto Kruger was the name of the only prisoner who had escaped from the Galveston camp.

"So why would reverting to his real name back in Germany have been a problem?" Alec asked.

"Because," Frau Hoff continued, "he would have been repatriated to his hometown in Germany."

"Leipzig?" Alec said.

"Yes, Leipzig—the Russian zone," she answered. "Even then, we all knew the Russians would never give it up. Eric hated the Russians. He would never have gone back there."

Alec pushed the images from his mind. He also hated the Russians for what they had done to his country and...to him.

"So, you took him in?"

"Yes, that's when I found out my father was a spy. He confessed it all to me then. He told me about his recruitment by German Intelligence. He told me about the mission, the money. I didn't want to believe it but I had to, Eric was here."

The clouds moved in bringing rain. Pellets of water danced across the tabletop like soldiers marching in step. Frau Hoff pulled her collar up around her neck and started to rise.

It had all come down to this moment. His mother's revelation to him about his grandfather. The letter from Argentina. Mariana and Señora Rosas. The GTO and that bastard Frankin.

It was time now; he had to know. The rain drummed harder, and the wind howled across their backs. They rose from the table. As she turned to leave, he touched her shoulder. Their eyes met once more and he looked deep into the dark, lonely vista of her past and asked, "Frau Hoff, what...what happened?"

"What happened?" she replied, a quizzical look on her face. "About what?"

"To the gold!" Alec said. "What happened to the gold?"

Chapter Twenty-Five

Sunday, August 28

Harry Stein turned off FM3005 and eased down the lane at idle speed, his foot on the brake, picking up as little sand as possible. He knew the salt-filled bottoms of West Beach would attack his new Cadillac's undercarriage with the ferocity of a flesh-eating virus.

He recognized the four pickup trucks parked in front of The Garhole and realized he was the last to arrive. He eased around the side of the building and pulled to a stop away from the trucks. Harry liked to drive nice cars, but he didn't think of himself as pretentious, especially around his friends of sixty-plus years.

Bully Stout had called a rare meeting of the Dead Peckers Club. There were only five members left now. Three years earlier there had been eight. Harry smiled at the memories. He knew they should get together more often, but somehow they didn't. Still, he knew they would be there for one another if needed. That's what friends were for.

Bully had recovered several cases of rum from an old, sunken duck blind at the oak motte. What better excuse to convene the club? The rum had to be tested.

But Harry knew the real reason for the party was to celebrate Lisa's safe return. All the old geezers gathered here today had known her since she was born, her surrogate godfathers.

When Lisa disappeared from the girls' home, Marvin Klaus and Johnny Weeks had used their police department contacts in an attempt to find her. When their efforts failed, Harry pursued the agencies specializing in runaways. No luck. During that time, Neddie Lemmon had visited Bully daily. The two of them worried and fretted like two hummingbirds over a nest.

Then a miracle happened. Three weeks ago Lisa wandered into The Garhole Bar hungry and tattered. The Dead Peckers rejoiced all around. And then that bastard Sader took her again.

Harry entered the front door, and they all rose and shook hands. Empty Coke cans, squeezed limes, and several half-full rum bottles surrounded an ice bucket in the middle of the table.

Before anyone sat down, Lisa came from behind the counter and hugged Harry's neck. Harry put his hands on her shoulders and pushed her back, arms length.

"Wow, Lisa! You look terrific," he said. "If only I was fifty years younger."

Lisa giggled, her face flushed. "Oh, Harry," she said. "You're so cool. I bet you say that to all the girls."

Everyone laughed, then Bully shook his finger at Harry in a mock reproach and said, "Harry, you're a dirty old man."

Lisa giggled again and went back to the bar. Harry watched her leave, marveling at how a few more days of sleep and sunshine had transformed her. Her skin had regained its doll-like appearance, so beautiful and fragile Harry thought it might break if pinched. Except for the band-aid on her forehead, one night of reversal hadn't seemed to affect her much. She glowed.

Harry sat down with Marvin and Johnny at the table. Neddie Lemmon moved to his usual perch at the counter and began twirling the ends of his mustache, flirting with Lisa as she worked. He picked up his beer and saluted the gar-head.

Bully made a loop around the table, checking everyone's drink, then went out back and returned a few minutes later carrying a bucket of boiled shrimp.

Harry wanted to help, but he knew Bully would read him the riot act for thinking he was helpless, an old cripple. The man had his pride.

Bully dumped the shrimp on top of the taped-down newspaper spread on the table. Steam rolled off and wafted up to Harry's sinuses, causing him to sneeze and rub his eyes.

"Damn it, Bully! Too much red pepper," he said, reaching for a handful of shrimp.

"Malarkey!" Bully exclaimed, "Can't have too much." Bully's face took on a serious look. "See you brought your new wheels."

Harry put his hand over his eyes acting embarrassed and said, "I was hoping you wouldn't notice. I parked it around the corner so I wouldn't have to take your grief about it."

Bully said, "We've known each other too long. You know that's not going to happen."

All smiled as Harry reached for a paper cup and filled it with ice. Just then, the sound of wheels crunching shell came from the parking area and they all turned to see a new Lexus pulling in next to Harry's Cadillac.

Bully said, "Looks like you got some competition, Harry. One of those dang foreign jobs."

The men sat silently mesmerized as a striking redhead dressed in tailored gray slacks and a light green blouse got out of the car and entered the front door.

For a moment, the room remained strangely silent, but then Lisa ran from behind the counter shouting, "Claire, I'm so glad you could come."

They met in the middle of the room and hugged and then Lisa guided her toward the table saying, "Claire Roberts, I want you to meet Poppa Bully and his friends."

All the Dead Peckers immediately stood and Lisa introduced each one. Then Claire said, "My goodness, Lisa. You're a lucky girl, having these gentlemen as godfathers."

The men all smiled, their faces turning various shades of red. Lisa pulled a chair over for Claire and everyone sat down. Bully hobbled off to the back for more shrimp. Harry raised his glass and said, "Ever had a Cuba Libre before, Miss Roberts?"

Claire smiled and said, "Please call me Claire. And no, I don't think I have. What's in it?"

"It's a fine drink—rum, Coke, lime. Invented in Havana back in the old days before Castro, when things were jumping there."

Claire nodded toward the bottles. "Well, Lisa told me about Bully finding the rum. You think it came from Cuba?"

"No doubt," Harry said. "Bootleggers brought it in during prohibition. Cuba made the best rum in the world then." He winked at Claire and said, "Unfortunately, for us, only a few bottles survived."

Claire said, "I've read a little about Cuba in those days. It must have been quite a place."

"You got that right," Harry said. "I was in Havana myself in '55. Gambling, booze, wome..." He stopped in mid-word and cleared his throat. "Of course Galveston was like that too in the thirties. We had it all then—ladies of the night—gambling. We were Las Vegas before there was a Las Vegas. You probably don't remember Alice Faye, the movie star. She and Phil Harris were married at the old nightclub and casino, The Hollywood Dinner Club over on Stewart Road . And then there was another casino, The Balinese Room, built on a pier over the Gulf."

"Exciting day, I guess," Claire said. "What happened to it all?"

"Times change. The Texas Rangers shut it all down back in the '50s." Harry looked off, reminiscing. He had made an occasional visit to the clubs himself to throw the bones a little. Everyone did in those days, he remembered.

Harry finished mixing the drink and handed it to Claire.

"Oh, this is quite refreshing," she said. "Goes well with the heat and humidity of the island."

After some conversation passed with Claire at the center of attention, Lisa motioned Claire to join her and they went out onto the dock.

The party lasted all morning and the old men grew tired, full of shrimp and rum. After a couple more rounds, Marvin, Johnny and Neddie left. Bully went into his trailer for a nap worn thin from the bustle of the last few days. Harry was cleaning the table when Claire and Lisa came back in.

Lisa said, "Let me do that, Harry." She gathered an armful of paper plates and empty cups and took them out to the trash.

Harry pulled out a chair for Claire and they both sat down. Claire smiled and said, "You and Bully have been friends for a long time, haven't you?"

"Since the fifth grade," Harry answered. He looked away, his thoughts off in the distance. "I gave him his nickname."

"Really," Claire said.

"I was always small for my age. One day on the playground, two kids were giving me a hard time. Bully ran the little scoundrels off. I called him the bully-beater. Toughest name I could think of."

Claire laughed. "I love it," she said. "So, how did Bully get hurt? What happened to him?"

Harry filled a fresh cup with ice, added Coke and the last of the rum, and squeezed in two limes. "Care for a drink, Claire?" he said, offering the cup.

"No thanks," she said.

Harry felt his eyes moisten and his throat run dry. With a half-smile and gentle voice, he said, "It's the last one. The end of an era."

Claire put her hand on his around the cup and said, "Why don't we share it."

Harry poured half the drink into another cup. They touched the cups together in a silent toast and took a sip.

"It was World War II," Harry said, his voice soft but controlled. "Bully tried to enlist right after Pearl Harbor in '41, but he was too young, still in high school. Finally made it in '44, just in time for the Normandy landing. Fought all the way through France into Belgium."

"Is that where he got hurt?" Claire asked.

"Yeah, during the Battle of the Bulge in December of '44. More than hurt. His lieutenant wandered into a minefield and froze up, scared to death. Bully went after him—picked him up. On the way back, Bully stepped on a mine. Blew off his left foot, two fingers on his left hand and tore out his left eye. The lieutenant made it out with a little shrapnel in his butt."

"Some story," Claire said.

"Yeah," Harry continued. "Bully got the Silver Star for that one. Wouldn't think he was a war hero, would you?"

Claire shook her head.

Harry said, "And...as bad as that was, it wasn't the worst part. Ever hear of the Malmedy Massacre?"

"No, I haven't."

"Well, a couple of weeks before he stepped on the mine, a German Panzer division breached American lines and surprised a U.S. truck column bringing reinforcements to the front. The German tanks shot up the column. Then they rounded up the survivors, sprayed them with machine guns, and finished them off with pistol shots to the head. Left them there, like dead crows, scattered in the snow."

"Against all the rules?" Claire said.

"Completely," Harry said. "Eighty-six Americans slaughtered. Bully and a few others survived by feigning death. He had nightmares about it long after the war. They murdered a lot of his friends there."

"He must hate Germans," Claire said.

"Not all Germans, just Nazis," Harry said. "It was an S.S. unit that murdered his friends—Hitler's worse fanatics."

Harry looked away. Neither of them spoke, both absorbed in their own thoughts. Claire finished her drink, staring at the ice in the bottom of her cup.

Lisa came in the back door, stepped quickly to the table and said, "Well, I just about got it all cleaned up. These empty rum bottles are the last of it." She gathered all the bottles and took them to a trashcan out front.

Harry watched her move—the bounce in her step, vibrant and alive—the effervescence of youth, he thought. His thoughts flashed to his own youth. At just a few years older than Lisa, while he was shuffling between classes at the University of Texas, Bully was getting his leg amputated at a field hospital in northern France.

Bully gave more than his share then, protecting them all. Harry wished he could do more for Bully now. Getting him out of jail was something, but he owed him more than that. He rose from the table, hugged Lisa and told Claire goodbye. He thought it best to leave them to their own youthful conversations. This wasn't the time to share his feelings with either of them. They wouldn't understand.

Chapter Twenty-Six
Sunday, August 28

After a restless night, I had finally dozed off around daybreak. I slept off and on through the ruckus of Bully's party and awakened sometime after lunch drenched in sweat. The air was thick with moisture sucked from the bay by the afternoon sun. I could have rented my room out as a sauna.

I strolled out to the deck in my shorts, arched the small of my back, and pulled my elbows in to stretch my shoulders. At the top of the stairs, I heard the sound of women's voices from below. I eased back to the railing and leaned in slightly to get a view.

Lisa came out and dumped an armful of paper plates and cups into the trash barrel. Then Claire appeared at the door and thanked Lisa for inviting her to the party.

Lisa said, "I'm so glad you're here, Claire." Then she felt her forehead. "You think the cut will leave a scar?"

"Let me see," Claire said. She peeled back the band-aid and took a closer look. "No, it'll be all right. It's already beginning to heal."

"I'm glad you can stay a while longer," Lisa said. "We can talk some. I knew the Dead Peckers wouldn't hang around long. After all that rum, they needed their naps."

Claire said, "Dead what?"

"Poppa's friends. There're all over seventy. They call themselves the Dead..."

"Never mind, Lisa. I get the picture."

I envisioned an embarrassed look on Claire's face and stepped back from the railing to avoid being seen. I wondered if the freckles on her nose had turned the color of her hair. Pictures of her smile clicked through my mind like a camera on auto forward.

Lisa said, "They ate most of the shrimp before you got here. You must be hungry. Poppa made some duck chili. You want some?"

A dark mass bubbled on the bottom of a cast-iron skillet sitting on top of a charcoal grill. Claire leaned over the pot and inhaled.

"Thanks, Lisa," she said. "But I can smell the peppers. I think I'll pass on the chili." She pulled a tissue from her pocket and dabbed her eyes.

"Probably smart," Lisa said, giggling. "Parker says Poppa's chili would melt the chrome off a trailer hitch."

Claire laughed and said, "Where is Parker? His truck is outside."

Lisa pointed to the deck. "Probably sleeping one off."

Just as she said that, I shifted back to the bedroom. They both glanced up to an empty deck.

I rubbed my face to still the itch of morning stubble. I had shaved my heavy beard to rid the gray and gotten a haircut. My first in weeks. I pulled my tee shirt away from my body and winced at the smell of stale whiskey and salt-air sweat. I showered and shaved, slipped on a fresh shirt, and combed my hair. As I approached the table, Lisa went inside. I sat across from Claire, my hair still wet.

Claire smiled and removed her sunglasses. Her eyes sparkled in the shade under the deck.

"Wow, Parker. You clean up good."

I grinned and said, "Thanks, Claire. Guess I did need a little scrubbing."

"Sorry you missed the party," she said. "I met all Bully's friends. Some characters, huh?"

"Yeah, it doesn't take long to pass the word around when free booze is available." Her face was smooth, just two slight dimples in her cheeks where the smile ended.

She said, "Bully hit the jackpot this time, didn't he?"

"I'll never hear the end of it."

"You didn't feel like coming down?"

"No, it was Bully's doings. They're his friends, not mine."

"Guess you don't have any, huh?"

I caught her raised eyebrows and questioning pose, the mock frown on her face. Here we go again, I thought.

"That's right, I don't have any," I answered. "So, are you playing rescuer today, and I'm the rescuee?"

"Do you need to be saved?"

"Ah ha! More sales training, huh? Answering a question with a question. Well, don't give me any of your psycho-babble. I had enough of it in the Army."

"No alcohol today?"

She wasn't going to back off. Well, neither would I. "No," I answered. "I thought I'd better be sober so I could read the offer you brought me."

Claire seemed to study me for a moment before responding. She turned serious, the teasing apparently finished.

"Parker, I told you last time I wouldn't bug you about that anymore. I came out here because Lisa invited me."

I paused long enough to digest her last statement. She seemed to have changed course. I felt relief. The bantering between us had grown tiresome and besides, she really looked good today. In a softer voice, I grinned and said, "Well, I'm glad she invited you."

She seemed surprised at my comment. I was myself.

She said, "Really? Well that was a nice thing to say. Thanks, Parker."

She rose from the bench and looked out over the water. The breeze from the Gulf pushed over the island behind us, rippling the bay. As she turned back, a strand of hair caressed her cheek and blew across her lips. She pushed it back and smiled.

I said, "I'd like to show you something. Take a ride with me?"

I drove slowly down the hard-packed sand road. The scent from the red and yellow blossoms of wild lantana bushes freshened the air in the afternoon sun. A half-mile into the salt marsh at the top of a sand dune, I stopped the truck. I motioned to a wooden bench that overlooked a small lagoon and handed Claire a pair of binoculars.

I pointed out over the pond and said, "Focus on that group of live oak trees on the other side of the water. We call that an oak motte. See how they're growing, all leaning in the same direction. The prevailing Gulf breeze forms them that way. It takes years for them to look like that."

"Yes, yes, I see," she said, the words bubbling out. "They're lovely—an art form in themselves. It's almost as if they were sculpted by some divining hand."

"There are only two or three of those mottes left on the entire island. Developers took the rest."

Claire lowered the glasses and rested them on her lap.

After a moment, I nodded toward the lagoon again. "Look at the base of the trees."

When she raised the binoculars, I touched her back to move her in the direction I wanted her to look and said, "See the bird on the ground?"

"Oh, my gosh! It's beautiful. What is it?"

"Purple gallinule. See the different hues? Violet neck, blue and green front and wings."

While Claire studied the bird, I kept my hand on her back. "Wow! I love it," she said. "Red bill with a little yellow tip on the end—so vivid. It could be a painting."

The smallness of the bench forced us close. I felt her warmth and realized she must feel mine too. For the next hour, we sat there quietly, studying the birds. I had pointed out eight or ten different species noting their colors and the difference between male and female when suddenly she rammed her elbow into my side.

"Oh my gosh, Parker. Look, flamingos!"

"Where?"

She pointed toward a corner of the slough. Two large, pink birds waded near the shore. I grinned broadly, trying not to laugh.

"No, no, Claire. Those are roseate spoonbills. Many people mistake them. We don't have flamingos here." I said it softly, trying not to embarrass her.

"Really? How can you tell them apart?"

"Well, for starters, flamingoes are much taller and lankier. They have small bills but very long necks. They can reach all around and preen their bodies. Roseates have the heavy, flat bills you see there." I motioned toward the birds in front of us.

"We almost lost all the Roseates in the 1920s. There were probably less than two hundred of them left on the Texas coast. Plume hunting was big then." I raised my hands up to both sides of my head. "Remember the big feathered hats?"

Claire frowned, "Sure, Parker. Blame it on the women."

We both laughed. A moment later, she rose from the bench and looked across the marsh. Acres of sea lavender and goldenrod waved back at her.

"This is a lovely setting, Parker. Thank you for sharing it with me."

"Yes, it is my favorite. I've spent a lot of time here."

"Why is this place so special for birds?"

"Well, in the spring a lot of song birds migrate up from Central America. They fly over the Gulf of Mexico, and by the time they reach here, they're pretty pooped. They need places like this to rest before going further. We've logged over a hundred different species here."

"We?" Claire asked.

"Yes, Lisa and me. I built this bench so we could sit and watch the birds. She was so young then. When I came home from the

Army on leave, she often stayed out here with me. In the evenings we came here."

"You guys were serious bird-watchers, weren't you?"

"Yeah, well, it was fun. We were close...then."

"Then?"

Claire sat back down and slipped her arm through mine. I smelled the freshness of her hair and a hint of perfume. After a moment, I said, "When Lisa's mother died, I couldn't get home. I was in the Middle East. She ran off with that loser and got into drugs. Ruined her life."

Claire pushed against me and squeezed my arm with her other hand. "Oh, Parker," she said, her voice soft, comforting. "You were close before and then she got into trouble. Try not to judge her so harshly."

"Think I'm being to rough? Look what she's done to herself."

Claire released my arm and leaned back, studying me. "And what about you?" she said.

I cocked my head. "Me?" I said. "What do you mean, Claire?"

"Don't you see the parallel?" she said, positioning her hands like a railroad track. "You're both into drugs, and you're both down on yourselves. I understand Lisa. She's just a kid. She was lost and got into some bad company. At least she's trying now. But you..."

Where had that come from? Now she was Claire the counselor. We had been sitting there close—sharing thoughts and then bam, she'd blasted into me.

"What do you mean I'm into drugs?" I shot back, a tinge of righteous indignation obvious in my tone.

She didn't respond. She just sat there quietly, as if waiting for me to continue. Finally I got it.

"Oh, you mean the alcohol." I rose from the bench and walked to the edge of the rise. A blue heron coasted to a soft landing in the lagoon. I watched it set up, leaning slightly forward, its massive wings folded to the sides as though frozen in time, waiting for the strike. I marveled at its patience. I needed some of that now.

"Was it the marriage?" she asked softly.

I refocused. "Janie? No, I'm long over that," I answered.

Claire stood from the bench and moved between me and the bird forcing my attention. "Tell me about her."

"Oh, she was the most popular girl in school. Came from old money, shipping and insurance. We were high-school sweethearts. She got pregnant on prom night. We married and lived out here."

"And then?" Claire asked.

"The next year I got drafted and..."

Claire interrupted, "But, you were married with a child. How could they draft you?"

"Janie miscarried. And by then they were drafting married men. I was only nineteen."

She reached for my hand and squeezed it. "I'm sorry about the baby," she said. "You were married a long time. No more children?"

"Well, I stayed in the Army and of course we moved around a lot. But she never got used to being away from her mother. Sometimes she stayed here for months. We would see each other when I came home on leave. One of those long-distance marriages you read about."

"So it's been a year since the divorce, and you say you're over it. Then what's with the booze and self-pity?"

From somewhere deep inside, the impulse shot out the top of my head. I exploded—a blowout. I twisted away, thrashing my arms and moving about, cursing.

"Damn it, Claire! You push too much! It's not the divorce. It's the pain. It never stops. My shoulders, the headaches. I don't sleep. I have blackouts. It was the damned war and the goddamned Army afterwards. I fought the system for a year, trying to get help and..."

I waved her off, then turned and surged down the slope toward the lagoon, scattering the birds as I went. The anger had come from nowhere, streamed out like steam from a boiler. Later, I would try to figure out what had happened. For now, I was just too damned mad to do anything. I passed the oak motte never looking back.

Chapter Twenty-Seven
Sunday, August 28

A late summer thunderstorm moved in over the farm, rattling the windowpanes. Martha Hoff and Alec Strauss had moved from the outside table into the kitchen to escape the rain. Frau Hoff handed Alec a cup towel and motioned toward the door. Alec pushed it under the jam, abating the wind and noise.

Lightning struck somewhere close, rattling dishes in the cupboard. Frau Hoff appeared visibly shaken and a bit confused.

Alec knew she hadn't verbally invited him in. He had simply followed behind when the rain increased. She stood by the kitchen counter, her eyes averted. Alec pulled a chair from the table and sat down, signifying his intent to stay. He rubbed his eyes and sighed heavily—appearing weary, waiting for her to calm herself. After a moment, she heated a kettle of water on the stove and placed two porcelain teacups and saucers on the table.

Alec needed information and this frail, old woman was his last hope. So far, she had been very helpful. He now knew Eric von Speigel had escaped from the POW camp in Galveston and made it to the Hoff farm in Fredericksburg. But the money and gold was left in Galveston.

When the kettle began to steam, Martha Hoff placed tea bags in the cups and poured them full. "I know you want to know about the money," she said, her face expressionless.

Alec noticed her eyes seemed to have regained composure even strength.

"This may seem odd to you," she continued, "but I convinced my father not to return to Galveston for the money."

"He...he never went back? But why?" Alec asked, his tone incredulous. It was getting more difficult to stay composed. The thought of the money consumed him, overwhelming his judgment. He wanted to reach over and slap the information out of her.

Hoff raised the teacup to her lips, holding it with both hands to steady her trembling fingers. Alec judged it was from her age, not emotions. She seemed calm as she spoke.

"I was afraid if they caught my father retrieving the money he would be discovered as a spy and executed. We lied to Eric and told him we had never gotten it from Mexico. Eric was an escaped war prisoner, he had no place else to go. He stayed with us. And then...well, he was so handsome, so confident, so..."

She paused for a moment, as if remembering, then continued.

"We...we grew to love each other. But even then I didn't tell Eric about the money. What if he had been caught and sent to prison or back to Germany? I might have lost Eric and my father. The money meant nothing to me. We had our farm. I had my father and Eric. It was all that was important. I even sent the letters back to his contact, unopened."

"Letters, what letters?"

"From Argentina, his spy contact there. They sent several, even after the war."

So, Alec thought, either Rheinhard Bauer or Señora Rosas had sent letters to Rudolph Hoff in Fredericksburg. Why? Were they just trying to learn about von Speigel, or did they already know he was there? Maybe it wasn't von Speigel at all they were after. Maybe it was the money. Was that why the Señora and Mariana wanted so desperately for him to return to Argentina? No! He refused to believe it. Señora Rosas was so sincere. And Mariana, no! She could not have faked *that*.

Martha Hoff's voice trailed off. She turned her face toward the window. Wind driven rain pummeled the outside, sending rivulets of water racing downward.

Alec vacillated—push or ease up. Timing was critical. He desperately needed to know more, but he managed to hold back. He took another tack to break the tension.

"Frau Hoff, did Eric ever mention his fiancée in Germany, my grandmother, Anna Manfred?"

Martha Hoff turned back to him. "Yes, he did," she replied. "Through his contact in Argentina, he tried very hard to locate her to let her know he was alive, a POW. He never got a response. So, when he learned the Russians had captured Leipzig, and he couldn't contact Anna, he assumed she was dead."

"So Eric lived here with you and your father on the farm?"

"Yes. We had a wonderful life together. He only died a few months ago. We had no children, and now it's just me, here on the farm, with my memories." She closed her eyes and put her hand to her forehead. She seemed to be fading, almost as if she had given up.

Outside, the wind and rain diminished. The storm passed and the room became quiet. Neither of them spoke. This was not the time to press, he thought. Give her a few minutes to compose herself. He sipped his tea and considered his next move.

Finally, he said, "Frau Hoff, I am glad that you were able to bring happiness and peace to my grandfather's life. It must have been wonderful for the two of you here."

"Yes, it was," she said, making eye contact again.

"Yet, it is sad to think Eric never knew he had a daughter."

She nodded, her eyes glistening in the light from the overhead bulb.

Alec said, "I know he would have wanted to help her now if he could. Don't you think so?"

171

"Help her...now?" she answered. "What do you mean? How could he help her now?"

Alec didn't reply immediately. Again, he wanted it to be her idea. He held her eyes, waiting for her to speak.

She said, "Oh. The money, the gold. For your mother's operation."

"Yes."

"Well, I don't know where the money is. I destroyed the map."

"The map?"

"Yes, the map indicating where the gold was buried."

"On Galveston Island?"

"Yes. I told you he decided not to risk bringing it back to Fredericksburg with him."

"So it is still there?" Alec's voice grew stronger, more excited.

"I don't know. I only know he never went back for it."

"Where...where is it buried?"

She grasped the teacup with both hands as if to steady herself. "I don't know. I burned the map. I didn't want anything here that would connect Eric or my father with the operation. I only remember a few things—a few landmarks. My father knew the name of a German in Galveston who owned land out on the west end of the island. He kept a few cattle out there. My father contacted him on the pretense that he was visiting from Fredericksburg and wanted to see his animals. Maybe he could learn something, he said. The German agreed. They went out there, and then later my father went back and buried the money."

"What was the German's name?" Alec asked.

"I...don't remember," Frau Hoff said. She shifted a hand to her mouth to quiet her lower lip. Then, she started to get up, to move away.

Alec put his hand on hers, pressing slightly. "You must remember," he said.

"I don't know. Maybe my father never told me his name."

Alec was close now. The money was still there, buried somewhere on Galveston Island. But which property and where on the property?

"The landmarks?" Alec said. "You mentioned landmarks. What were they?"

"I remember a little," she said. "A corral, an old corral. A windmill. Somewhere around or between the well and the corral. A tree or some trees." She stopped.

Keep pushing, he told himself. What else does she know? He would appeal to her sense of patriotism, her love for the mother country. She was the older generation, she would understand. "You must remember more," he said. His voice grew stronger. "We need the money. We must have it. It's for the Fatherland, the Reich must continue."

Alec rose from his chair and moved to the end of the table. He stared down at her. His throat pulsed and his hands shook. Power replaced control, but he didn't care now. He was so close! So close. She must know more. He moved beside her.

"What...? What did you say? The Fatherland? The Reich? The money. It's not for your mother? You want to use it for...oh my God! You're...you're a Nazi. One of them—evil!"

Frau Hoff pushed up hard from the table, but Alec leaped behind her and held her shoulders. He leaned in slightly and whispered into her ear, "Your father was a true German, Frau Hoff, but he failed the Reich. You can make up for his failure. You owe it to him."

"No!" she screamed. "I hated the Nazis. They were against everything I love. I was glad we left Germany. Do you hear me? We were free here! Free! I almost turned my father in to the authorities when I found out he was a spy and Eric, too. It was horrible. But, he was my father. I couldn't do it. And Eric...oh, Eric."

"So you did not report them. You helped them."

"Not for Germany. It was for us. Eric promised he would never do anything to harm America. And I trusted him. My father did the same. They kept their promise. We had a good life here."

"They were both traitors to Germany. You seduced my grandfather and made him a traitor. You did not deserve him. He was a great man and you turned him." Alec moved his hand to her neck.

"No, I didn't have to change him. He knew. He knew Hitler was the devil and the Nazis were the devil's spawn. You're right, your grandfather was a great man, but not because he had been in the Abwehr. He was a loyal German, but he was never a Nazi. He loved his country, but he hated Hitler. He grew to love America, and he loved me."

"You are lying, Frau Hoff. It is all a lie. My grandfather would never have deserted the Füehrer. What else do you know? Tell me!"

"Nothing! I know nothing more," she said. Then she relaxed in his hands as if to say she was ready. She seemed to know what was coming. It had been a good life. Everyone she cared about was gone. She had nothing left.

Alec placed his right hand on her forehead and his left hand behind her head. With a quick jerk, he twisted her head violently to the right breaking the cervical spine between the third and fourth vertebrae, causing instant death. Her head dropped to her chest.

Alec lowered his face to her ear and whispered, "A pity, old woman. But you know too much now. I could not leave you alive."

Chapter Twenty-Eight
Sunday, August 28

Somewhere past the oak motte, I heard my truck start and looked back to see Claire leaving. Why did she always have to challenge me so? Well, I would probably never see her again anyway. So what. It was her fault, wasn't it? She didn't have any right to be that nosy.

I curved around the oak trees to the path along the shoreline that led back to The Garhole. A ruby-throated humming bird fluttered over a lantana bush. The fall migration had begun. Birds by the hundreds would soon rest here before moving south on their final journey home.

Moving on. Not a bad idea, I thought. Maybe Claire was right, maybe I should sell and get out. What did I have here but a cranky, old, one-eyed man, a girl with a drug problem, and now...a woman who wouldn't give me a break. Hell, I couldn't even be miserable on my own terms.

What was I hanging on here for anyway? My grandfather? I barely remembered the old man. Everyone else was selling out. Some of the families here had owned land for years, even longer than the McLeods. But money talks. So to hell with the birds and the fish and the crabs and the shrimp. No one else seemed to care about them anyway. It was all just about making money, raping the environment. Maybe I should get my share.

Let that hungry developer from Houston make an offer. I'd show him how to be greedy. I'd get more money for my three hundred acres than I could spend.

Maybe I'd get a boat and sail the Caribbean. I'd never been there. Or what about Australia? I could get lost in the outback, go on a walk-about. No, better yet, I could get a Harley and cruise the western states—Nevada, California. Maybe find a hippie commune, free love. So what if I got some God-forsaken venereal disease? Who gives a damn?

Off to my right, a huge brown pelican folded its massive wings and dove to the water. I stopped to watch, trying to clear my mind. The bird hit with the force of a bomb, and then straightened. A small fish flapped in its bill. Soon the pelican stretched its neck straight up, as high as he could get it, and the fish slid helplessly to the waiting pouch below.

The bird's pouch reminded me of Bully's huge gut. Bully Stout, yeah great. Thanks to him, The Garhole had suffered another day without profits. Free rum and no beer sales. I shook my head as I walked, thinking I would even have to pay Lisa for her time.

My thoughts drifted to my conversation with Claire. She should have been on my intelligence team. She could sure drag stuff out of me—things I didn't want to talk about. It was the first time I had discussed my divorce with anyone.

Janie. How was she doing? It would have been nice if I'd had her support when I got home from the war, the basket case that I was. But it didn't happen. And now she's married to that oil executive in Houston. Her mama must be proud. Of course she could have waited until the divorce was final before taking off to live with the guy.

Back at The Garhole, the tables had been cleaned and the empty rum bottles were stacked in a cardboard box by the front door. Still, the place reeked of cigar smoke and stale rum and boiled shrimp. I turned the ceiling fans on high and walked out to the deck.

Charlie squawked, and I realized I hadn't fed him. He sat silently on his perch, his black eyes following my every move. "Here you go old boy." I offered a fish through the wire and watched as the night heron devoured it.

I opened the door and eased my hand around the bird's back, wary of its razor like beak. With my other hand, I slowly unwrapped the bandage on the bird's wing and removed the splint. The wing seemed healed, the movement natural.

"Okay, Charlie. This is it." I eased my hands out of the cage and backed away leaving the door open.

Charlie raised both wings high over his head and squawked a challenge. Then he dropped off his perch to the floor of the cage and moved slowly forward. He came tentatively at first, but soon his head, then his neck and body reached the opening. He sat at the edge of the cage and bobbed up and down as if asking for permission. Was it time?

For a moment the bird and I remained transfixed, our eyes glued to each other. Then, I nodded slowly, very slowly, as if saying yes, Charlie. Yes! He leaned forward, craned his head in both directions, and then back to the center, looking at me one last time. Then he pushed from the cage and lifted his wings. And with a great swoosh, Charlie was free. I watched him go, proud of my accomplishment yet envious of his freedom. He circled once over the top of The Garhole, squawked loudly and soared away.

Chapter Twenty-Nine
Sunday, August 28, & Monday, August 29,

Alone in his room at the Tremont House, Alec Strauss stood before the mirror positioning his huge hands as though Frau Hoff's head was in them. Crack! He mimicked the sound of vertebrae breaking as he twisted her neck.

The Army had trained him well; he killed quietly and quickly. Using a weapon was risky. The East German police were ruthless. If he had been caught with a gun, they would have shown no mercy. His skill with his hands was so well honed and fine-tuned that he had become the GTO's primary assassin. Whenever they wanted a particularly nasty job done, they gave it to Günter Manfred.

The immigrants were the easiest—Gypsies, Turks, Africans. After all, none of them was a son of the Fatherland. Sometimes he killed without orders, just for practice.

And they weren't the only foreigners in his homeland. The Russians were there too. They came like the plague, raping and murdering. He took a Russian guard when he was sixteen, his first prize. A test, they said. Go out and kill a Russian pig. It had been easy. A bastard like that had raped his mother. He only had to imagine he was killing his own father. As his energy flowed through his hands into the Russian's body, he felt sure the bastard could feel his thoughts. No words needed to be said. The Russian would know how deep his hatred was.

He had felt the same energy flow when he twisted Frau Hoff's neck. That is why she relaxed, he thought. She knew she deserved to die. He twisted his hands again. Crack! He wished she were in them again.

Alec turned from the mirror and looked down on the bar across the street. Calmed now, he began to think. At least he had gotten something from Hoff—a real lead to the money. He was sure she had confessed all she knew. Rudolph Hoff had buried the money on a ranch on Galveston Island belonging to a local German family. But who owned the property now, and was the money still there?

There was still work to do, but now he had a plan. He would call that little Jew again, the history expert, Harry Stein. Stein seemed to know everyone on the island.

The bartender was alone when Alec entered the Irish Bar across the street. It was Sunday, the bartender said, not much going on. Alec sat at a table to avoid conversation. He nursed a beer and considered his options. Stein wouldn't be in his office on Sunday. He would have to wait until tomorrow morning to call.

Earlier, in his room, he had reviewed a map of the island. He considered driving out to the west end and looking around. But what good would that do? The area was twenty miles long, and the gold could be anywhere.

His eyes landed on a beer poster of scantily dressed girls at a football stadium. His thoughts turned to Julie Hanna, the librarian. He found her name in the telephone directory.

"Hello Julie, it is Alec."

"Hey, big boy. Where have you been?"

Her voice was soft, inviting. He imagined her naked, under him. "Doing research, out of town. I have missed you. Are you busy tonight?"

After drinks and dinner at the Yacht Club, they went to Julie's apartment. She made them a drink and then turned to put a tape in the sound system. Alec rubbed the back of her neck.

"That feels so good," she moaned. "Press a little harder on the shoulders, here." She guided his hand to the spot she wanted.

Alec massaged her gently, gradually working the shoulders until his fingers surrounded her neck. He pressed his thumbs in the area just above the third vertebrae. She moaned again. He was in position now. One quick jerk and it would be over. She was expendable. The last time had felt so good. He loved the sound of bones breaking, so crisp, so efficient.

Just then, Julie reached around with her right hand and stroked his thigh. Alec lessened his grip on her head. She turned and took his hand and led him into the bedroom.

Sometime in the middle of the night, he left. He had played a little rough, but at least he hadn't killed her. He had broken Frau Hoff's neck and had almost done the same to Julie Hanna. But Hoff was alone, too many people had seen him with Julie. She was a lucky girl...still alive. Maybe she could cover the bruises with makeup and clothes.

Back in his hotel room, he studied his face in the bathroom mirror. What a fool he had been. He was so close now. A sudden hesitancy crept into his eyes. He had been so sure, so confident. It had started again, like Germany, losing control. What if the librarian talked? No, he had seen her eyes. A mirror of fear. She knew better than to kiss and tell.

Was the gold worth the risk? He hadn't planned to kill the Hoff woman, it just happened. What if they traced the Hoff woman to him? He could quit now, take the first flight back to Germany. So he had failed, so what? He would be no worse off than before.

And there was also Argentina. Mariana would inherit Señora Rosas's estate. He could do worse. Wasn't that what the Señora and Mariana wanted? And Mariana—so lovely. He felt a twitch in his groin. She had called again today. Fortunately, he had been out. The messages were piling up. She wanted him.

No! He slapped himself. Why was he thinking these thoughts? He finally had a good lead. Get control, he told himself.

He slept a few hours, then went downstairs to the pay phone. Stein agreed to see him.

Alec stood as Harry came out of his office, "Thank you for meeting with me again," he said.

"Glad to help," Harry answered, smiling. He waved him into his office.

Alec glanced at the walls decorated with plaques and tributes to Stein's work for the Historical Society. Harry sat behind his desk and Alec took a chair in front.

"If you plan to be here much longer, you may encounter a new experience," Harry said.

"Oh?"

"Yes, remember when I told you about hurricanes? Well there's one out there now." Harry pointed to a map on his desk and motioned for Alec to take a closer look. "Fifteen degrees north and sixty three west. That's about 125 miles northwest of Martinique."

Alec leaned closer, and in an effort to appear interested said, "That is a long way off."

"Sure, but these storms are totally unpredictable. If it comes this way, it could be here in a few days." Harry drew a simulated path that ended in Galveston.

"Well let us hope not," Alec said, dismissing the man's enthusiasm. He did not think he would be here much longer in any event. Getting more funds out of the GTO would be difficult. Something had to happen soon. He continued, "Mr. Stein, I spent the weekend at the Rosenberg Library reviewing everything I could find on Germans in Galveston. I was surprised so many entered through the port here."

"Think you've got enough for your articles?" Harry said.

"Well, after studying the ship's logs and tracking a few of the immigrants, I am not sure their story is that interesting on its own."

"Really? What about the POW angle?"

"Yes, that is a possibility. But I think I need something more exciting. Something you said piqued my interest. You mentioned that during the Civil War, some of the merchants here buried their gold when the northern troops invaded Galveston."

"Well, that's the story anyway," Harry replied.

"So do you think it is true?" Alec asked.

"Who knows?" Harry said.

"But if it is true, what happened to the gold?"

Harry laughed and slapped his thigh. "You don't think it's still buried, do you? Don't you think they dug it up after the Yankees left, or can we now add Civil War gold to all the other tales about buried treasure here? Who knows, it might be more than Jean Lafitte left."

Alec didn't appreciate Stein's humor. He was busy trying to sell him on the idea.

"Maybe some of them did leave it buried just in case the northern troops returned. Or maybe one of them went off to fight the war and never returned. It is possible," Alec said.

"No way," Harry said. "You write that, you'll be writing fiction."

"Well, that's another idea," Alec commented. "Fiction. Several of the successful merchants in Galveston at that time had come over from Germany. I could tie the German angle into a story about Civil War gold. I think my readers back home would really enjoy a good adventure story about their countrymen who came to Texas. You know they still have visions of Texas as the wild west with cowboys and Indians."

"Hard to believe," Harry commented, shaking his head.

"It is true," Alec continued. "Well, anyway from my research over the weekend, I really believe some of the gold may still be buried on the island. So first, I am going to try very hard to find it, and if not, well then I will consider turning the story into a novel."

"You're kidding, right?" Harry said.

Alec noted Stein's sarcasm. It was apparent he was not buying the story. Alec switched to flattery.

"You know more about Galveston than anyone. You know all the buried treasure stories. Will you help me? I need to know more about the ownership and location of the ranches on the west end. I know some of the merchants had property out there."

Harry said, "Let me understand. You want to write a story about German immigrant merchants in Galveston who buried gold during the Civil War and left it there. Is that right?"

"Yes."

"And you want me to give you the names of some of the Germans who owned property out there at that time. Correct?"

"Yes, that's right."

Harry rose from his desk and walked toward the door. Alec remained in his seat but followed Stein with his eyes.

"Well," Harry said, "if the gold was left there, wouldn't you need to know who owns the property now?"

The old Jew was smart, Alec thought. Trying to trap him. Alec said, "Well, yes I would unless some of the ranches out there haven't changed hands. Is that possible?"

Stein scratched his chin and said, "The same family owning the property for a hundred years, that's what you think?"

"If it is possible," Alec said.

"Well, it is possible, I suppose," Harry said. "But unlikely the way west end real estate has increased in value."

Alec hoped Stein didn't think the idea too far fetched. He really needed to know which German families owned ranches in the 1940's, but he couldn't come up with another idea on how to ask Stein, so he had pressed the Civil War theory. He felt Stein's eyes boring into him.

Harry said, "What do you know about searching for buried treasure?"

Alec hesitated, "Well, not much, but..."

Harry Stein burst out laughing. "This is the most far-fetched bunch of malarky I've ever heard," he said. He opened his office door and motioned for Alec to leave. "I can't spend any more time with you. I thought you were a serious writer. We're proud of our history here in Galveston. We have a lot to offer the serious student, but you've wasted enough of my time. There's only one other person on this island who could possibly help you. You need to see Bully Stout."

Chapter Thirty
Tuesday, August 30

Lisa shook me awake and said Claire was here to see me. I stumbled into the bathroom holding my head. Nothing I could do about the circles under my eyes. Sometimes a hot shower would dissipate the darkness a little, but I had no time for that now. I threw on some shorts and a shirt and eased down the back stairway holding the handrail.

Claire sat at the back counter drinking a Coke, appearing radiant in a brightly colored blouse of red and yellow roses set off by looped gold earrings and a thin gold choker. No resort attire here. She was dressed to kill.

"Good afternoon, Parker."

The words flowed out as easy as her smile. The freckles on her nose bounced. So cheerful—such enthusiasm. I abandoned her at the oak motte two days ago, and now she was back. Why? I would find out soon enough. For now, I was just glad to see her. I mumbled hello and turned to the sink to fill a glass of water.

"Hope you slept well," she said. "It's after twelve o'clock."

It was the same old Claire, starting with a dig. But at least it was a cheerful dig as though nothing had happened.

"Well, bartenders keep late hours," I replied, trying to match her catty tone. "And we have to get our beauty rest."

"Sure you do," she said, grinning broadly. "By the way, thanks for the use of your truck. I would have gassed it up but there were no stations between the lagoon and The Garhole."

A small rebuke, but I guess I deserved it. I managed a smile. "I apologize for Sunday, Claire."

"You should, making me drive a stick shift. Not very gentlemanly of you."

It wasn't the answer I wanted, too flippant. Maybe she was just being careful. Couldn't blame her, after the way I had exploded. I turned toward the refrigerator and opened the door. Cold rice, some eggs, a few peppers. That would do. I removed the containers and turned to Claire, "You hungry? I'll whip something up."

She answered with a straight face, "Thanks, but we don't have time. The appointment's at two o'clock."

"Appointment?"

"Yes. Grab a quick shower and let's go," she said, shooing me with her hand. "We'll barely make it now."

"What are you talking about?"

"The title company. You've got to sign the papers," she answered with a straight face. "Last night when I came back, you agreed to sell."

"You...you were here last night?" The head pounding increased, the room swirled about. A ray from the ceiling light bounced off the gar-head's teeth. Was it laughing or sneering?

Claire answered, playfully, "Good lord, Parker. You are having memory lapses. I could have molested you on the deck for all you know."

I acknowledged her tone and smiled. "You're wrong, Claire. I think I would have remembered that."

She put her hand over her face in mock embarrassment. I watched closely, hoping the freckles would move again.

She lowered her hand and said, "Seriously Parker, you do have an appointment. My ex knows the head man at the VA hospital in Houston. They scheduled you on an emergency basis."

My smile vanished. "Not interested. I've been that route." In a show of finality, I turned toward the stove, broke some eggs into a bowl and lit the burner. I tossed a hunk of butter into the pan and folded in the eggs.

Claire said, "What do you mean, you've been that route?"

I added chopped peppers, then picked up a wooden spoon and stirred the eggs. I turned back to Claire and said, "When the war was over and my unit returned to Germany, my symptoms worsened. I sought treatment at two different centers there. No help. Then back in the States, the same thing. They don't give a damn. So, no thank you."

Claire said, "Parker, listen to me, please. It's been almost a year since your discharge. You haven't kept up with what's going on. You don't watch television. You don't even have a radio and..."

I held up my hand to stop her rant and said, "I have a radio, Claire."

She frowned and said, "Yeah, right, a weather radio. So you know what the tides are doing. Big deal." She twirled her finger, then added, "All you really do is sit out here and mope. They've got a name for your problem, now Parker. It's called Gulf War Syndrome."

It was my time to twirl my finger now. I did so and turned back to the stove. "Whoopee! Gulf War Syndrome, huh? Am I supposed to jump up and down about that?"

I stirred the eggs and peppers again and added the leftover rice. The aroma of sautéed butter wafted through the air.

"If you won't do it for yourself, will you do it for me?"

Her voice was whiny, weak. I looked back at her. She had a pitiful, poor-me expression on her face.

She said, "I hope I didn't get all dressed up for nothing."

I said, "You're going to take me?"

"Of course!"

I considered the offer. Except for being with Claire, it would be a waste of time. Nobody at the VA was interested in me. But she was right about one thing, I hadn't kept up. Was it possible there was an effort afoot to legitimize my problem? Maybe it was worth a try. Besides, I could do worse than spend the day with Claire.

"Okay, Claire, okay. You win. I'll go." I dumped the egg and rice concoction onto paper plates and passed one to her. "But first...let me take you to breakfast."

A few minutes later we jumped into her Lexus and headed for Galveston. As we drove over the causeway, I said, "Believe it or not, I haven't been off the island since I came home last year."

Claire grinned and said, "Knowing you, Parker, I believe it."

I returned the laugh, then pulled the visor down and studied my face in the mirror.

Claire said, "You look great, Parker. Relax. We're just going to the VA."

"Well, I'd hate to embarrass you in front of your friend."

"My ex's friend."

"Right."

"Actually, Parker, I haven't left the island much either. Of course, being a woman, I do have to shop from time to time in Houston. But those days are becoming fewer and fewer for me, too."

"The island lifestyle is really growing on you, isn't it?"

"Yes, I love the laid back atmosphere. People aren't in a big rush—island time."

I realized how little I really knew about Claire. I had been too self-absorbed to consider anyone else. "Your ex-husband is a doctor?"

"That's right."

She didn't elaborate. But the roles were reversed now, so too bad if she didn't want to discuss her personal life. I pressed on.

"Were you married long?"

"Five years."

The short answer, definitely a closed attitude. Where was the old effervescent Claire?

"What happened?" I asked, as innocently as possible.

She didn't answer—kept her eyes on the road. I waited—kept my eyes on her. Finally, she smiled.

"Okay, okay, I get it," she said. "Turn about is fair play."

"Exactly."

"I was a nurse. We met while he was in medical school."

"Oh, no! Not that old story. He dumped you after you put him through school."

"It does happen, Parker." Her voice toughened.

I looked away, wanting to diffuse the comment.

Then a coquettish smile appeared and she said, "He traded me for a younger version."

I turned back in time to catch her flirting look. "Version or virgin?" I said. We both laughed.

"I know what you're thinking," she said. "How could he have been stupid enough to lose me and still smart enough to get through medical school?"

We both laughed again. It felt good. It had been a long time.

Chapter Thirty-One
Tuesday, August 30

A mile before the entrance to The Garhole Bar, Alec Strauss passed a Lexus headed toward the city. The driver, a striking redhead, seemed absorbed in conversation with the other occupant.

A few moments later, Alec turned down the road to the bar. He crunched to a stop on the shell driveway, then got out and entered the front door.

The girl behind the bar faced the other direction, but he liked the way her blonde hair caressed the back of her neck.

"Hi," he said. "Must have been quite a party?"

Lisa turned suddenly, surprise on her face.

Gesturing at the empty rum bottles stacked by the door, Alec smiled and said, "Sorry if I startled you."

Beautiful, he thought. Her hair seemed natural, and those blue eyes, as pure as his. Her loose-fitting dress hung low on her chest hiding what Alec suspected was a lovely body.

Lisa smiled, "Can I help you, mister?"

Alec moved to a stool at the bar and pointed at the gar-head suspended from the ceiling. Its long rows of jagged teeth rocked gently in the breeze. "Is that a fish head or some kind of animal?" he asked, grinning as he said it.

Lisa glanced at the gar-head and then back to Alec. "You're not a fisherman, are you?" she said.

He shook his head.

"It's the head of an alligator gar. You must not be from around here."

"Well, no, I am not," he answered, trying to keep the conversation light. "I am looking for Bully Stout. Is he around?"

She leaned over the counter, wiping it with a rag. The dress fell away from her chest. "He went to town for groceries. Should be back soon. He's my grandfather. Can I help you with something?"

He knew the game; she wanted him to look. He glanced down quickly and made sure she knew it. "Well, if you think Mr. Stout will be back soon, I will just wait. That okay with you?"

"Cool," Lisa answered, straightening her posture as she said it. "You can keep me company. Want something to drink?"

"A beer, maybe."

She handed him a can out of the cooler. "I'm fixing lunch. You hungry?"

"What are you making?"

"Shrimp Creole from yesterday. Well, not making. Just heating it up, really." She laughed a little and said, "Want some?"

"I am not sure what it is."

"Really? It's awesome." A smile lit up her face. "Just shrimp and onions and tomatoes and things. Here taste it."

She leaned over the bar with a wooden spoon full of shrimp and rice. The dress opened again.

"It's good," he said. "Maybe I will have a bowl." Her eyes invited him. He had seen the look, the appraisal, when he had first entered the bar and she turned around. He had passed inspection then. "You say Bully Stout is your grandfather?"

"Yeah. I hang here with him in a trailer out back." She turned away to fill a bowl.

"I understand he is a treasure hunter. Do you think he would be interested in helping me in a search?"

She twisted back, "Buried treasure! Sure, that's what he does." She pointed at the empty bottles. "He just found all those a few days ago."

"He did?"

"Really. He found some old bootlegger's rum. He said they'd been buried out there for forty or fifty years. Too bad you weren't here Sunday."

"Yes, I can see that. Are there supposed to be a lot of treasures buried on the island?"

"I guess so," Lisa said. "You ever heard of Jean Lafitte, the pirate?"

"I read a little about him. Does Bully think his treasure is still here?"

"Dunno. You'd have to ask him, but he did find some old gold coins."

"Are you kidding? Real ones?"

"Yeah, it's awesome," she said. "Wait a minute, you'll see." She went out the back door.

Alec eased to the door and watched as she went into the camper. She bent over and pulled something from beneath the window. He slipped back to the barstool. She came back in holding a gold doubloon in her hand.

"See this? Poppa found it years ago. It's part of Lafitte's treasure."

"Wow! That's nice," he said. "Did he find a lot of them?"

"No, only two." She answered with obvious pride. "He's saving them for me."

Alec leaned over the counter to examine the doubloon more closely. He placed his hand underneath Lisa's. With his other hand he turned the coin over, examining it closely. He took his time, all the while lightly massaging Lisa's palm.

"Very interesting," he said. He smelled the freshness of her skin and the sun in her dress. After a few seconds of eye contact, Alec closed her hand over the piece and sat back down.

"So, it is just you and your grandfather living out here, huh?"

Lisa set the coin on the bar, picked up a knife and sliced a loaf of French bread. "No, Parker's here, too."

"Parker?"

"Yeah, he owns the place. He's my cousin. Poppa Bully was married to my grandmother who was Parker's mother's sister." She hesitated for a moment. "Wow, that's confusing, isn't it? Didn't mean to make it so complicated."

"It is okay," Alec said. "I think I followed you."

"Well, anyway," she continued. "The three of us live here—me and Poppa Bully in the trailer and Parker upstairs." She pointed overhead, then pushed the bowl of creole and a piece of bread across the counter.

"What about your mother?"

"Momma was killed in a car wreck when I was fourteen."

Alec noticed the sadness in her voice. "Sorry to hear that," he said, his voice soft. "And your father?"

"Don't know much about him." Lisa averted her eyes and turned back to the stove.

"So, you've lived with your grandfather since then?"

She put the knife down and faced him again, leaning back against the sink next to the stove. "No, he was sick when my mother died. I lived in a state home. It sucked, big time. Then..."

The back door flew open and Bully Stout came in carrying two sacks of groceries. He swept by Lisa to the refrigerator behind the counter, ignoring Strauss. He was busy unloading the sacks when Lisa said, "Poppa, this man's here to see you."

Chapter Thirty-Two
Tuesday, August 30

"So you wanna go treasure huntin', huh?" Bully said, sizing the man up as he spoke.

They were about the same height, he noted. The stranger appeared powerful, a strong build hidden under his clothes. He noticed the man's huge hands and mentally compared them to his own. Except for the blond hair and blue eyes, fifty years ago Bully could have been looking at himself in the mirror. He pegged the accent as German and wondered why a Kraut was interested in buried treasure?

"Yes, I do," the man replied. "My name is Alec Strauss. I am a writer here to do a story on Galveston. Your friend Harry Stein recommended you. I need your help and, of course, I would expect to pay you for your expertise."

Bully raised his eye patch and rubbed his eye socket, a stalling technique while he considered the offer. Harry had recommended him? For a moment, Bully thought it must be some kind of joke. Harry had put the man up to it. Payback for bailing him out of jail. Well he would go along for a while. He replaced the patch, slowly shaking his head. "Expertise?" he said. "Pretty big word for what I do. What are you looking for?"

"Well," Alec elaborated. "I understand that some of the wealthy merchants who lived in Galveston during the Civil War buried their money out here on the west end. Are you familiar with the story?"

"Yeah, I know about it," Bully said. He reached into the cooler for a beer and popped it open without offering one to Strauss. He took a long slow pull.

Alec said, "And my research indicates that some of the merchants may have been German immigrants."

"Well, lots of Kra...uh Germans lived here then. So you think some of it's still out there. Is that it?"

"Yes, I do," Alec responded. "I have done some research, and I think it is possible. I am willing to pay you for your time and split anything we find. How about it, Mr. Stout? Up for a little adventure?"

Bully brushed past the challenge. "So you're a writer, here from Germany to look for Civil War gold." He scratched his head. He wanted to look confused, pull more out of the man. He finished the beer and set the empty bottle on the counter.

Alec said, "Yes, I came originally to do research for a book on early German immigration through the port of Galveston, but I think this story might be more exciting."

Bully didn't answer. The idea seemed a little far-fetched, even to him. But if the Kraut wanted to pay him for his time, he really didn't have anything to lose. He could use the money to buy some things for Lisa. He started to say he would do it, but Strauss continued talking.

"Do you know anything about the German families that owned property out here during the Civil War?"

Bully laughed, "Hell no. I'm not that damned old."

Alec smiled and said, "Well, I was just wondering if any of the ranches have remained in the same family since then?"

Bully scratched his head again. "It's possible, I suppose. I've been coming out here since the 30s, hunting and fishing and such. I know 'bout a couple of old German folks that lived here then. But a hundred years ago? I dunno."

Alec blinked hard. "You have been coming out here since the 1930s?"

"That's what I said," Bully answered. "What's the matter? Don't I look old enough for that? Hell, son, it was only sixty years ago. Come on, I wanna show you something." Bully walked out the back door and led Alec to the shed behind the camping trailer where he stored the gold machine.

"Does it work?" Alec asked.

Bully heard the challenge. He considered demonstrating the machine, but he didn't want to get a coin out of the camper in front of the stranger. Instead, he grinned and said, "You'll know when we find the gold."

"Sounds good." Alec returned the smile. "So you will do it? Can you get us access to the places we need to search?"

Bully stepped closer and lowered his voice as though they were fellow conspirators. "Well, it's all posted land. We'll have to go in at night. You up for that?"

Strauss seemed anxious to get started. With plenty of afternoon left, Bully suggested they drive a few of the back roads. He wanted to show Strauss the terrain in the daylight before they explored it after dark.

When they turned left onto FM3005, Bully said, "You wouldn't know it 'less you lived here, but this end of the island gets skinnier every year."

"Really?" Alec said. "What do you mean?"

Bully pointed toward the Gulf. "Every storm peels the beach back more and more. Just in my time, the island's lost several hundred feet in width."

Alec said, "So I guess anything buried near the beach would have probably been washed out to sea by now, right?"

"Yeah, probably so," Bully said. He took the stub of a cigar out of the ashtray and lit it. Smoke filled the cab. Strauss coughed and rolled his window down. Bully enjoyed the reaction. He puffed again and blew toward the windshield. The smoke slid around to the passenger seat.

Alec leaned toward the window. "So they probably would not have buried anything along here."

"Probably not. They knew what the storms did to the beach. And anyway, this road didn't exist then. Only way to the end of the island was by way of the beach. The land this far out wasn't used much. Too hard to get to. The ranches and farms were on the bay side and closer to town."

"But you found the rum out here?"

Bully, confused, looked at Strauss. "Rum? Oh, yeah. But that was buried in the 30s. I was talking about the 1860s."

"Oh, yes," Alec said.

"But, even in the 30s, this road didn't go all the way to the end of the island. The bootleggers offloaded from larger ships in the Gulf and came through San Luis Pass in small boats. They'd stash the goods somewhere on the bay side and pick them up later. Each one had his favorite place."

"So how many ranches were here in the 1860s." Alec asked.

"Don't know for sure," Bully answered. "They weren't all ranches. I think one was a dairy. Some truck farms too. They grew cantaloupes, watermelons, squash, beans. Galveston was pretty self-sufficient in them days. Lots of sturdy, hard-working folks."

"Mostly German immigrants?"

"Mostly, but not all. There were others too. Even a few Jewish folks from different places in Europe."

Bully added the last part about the Jews for effect, having a little fun with the German. Strauss looked so much like the typical Nazi, he couldn't help but test him. He thought he saw a slight grimace on his face. Strauss looked out the window. Neither of them spoke for a few minutes.

Bully drove up the blacktop and turned onto Thirteen Mile Road, following the same route on Stewart Road he and Parker had traveled earlier.

Just past the country club, Bully pointed to the left. "See that clump of trees there? It's an old Karankawa Indian burial ground.

Tough bastards. Some say they were man-eaters. When Jean Lafitte was here, some of his men came out and killed a bunch of them Indians. They called it the Battle of the Three Trees. Anyway, a few years ago, some of them professor types from Rice University in Houston came out and dug up a lot of artifacts. You know, pots and flint and such. They even found skeletons and a skull or two."

"Really?" Alec said. "Have you ever found anything interesting? Maybe some of that buried treasure I read about?"

"Only a couple of old coins. Years ago, I heard about a man who found part of an old Spanish sword somewhere around those trees. And of course there's the story about Lafitte's treasure."

"What is that?" Alec asked.

"Well, supposedly, right before the U.S. Navy ran Lafitte off the island, he divided his loot up into three bunches. He buried one bunch in some oaken kegs out here somewhere. Later, his men came back and dug up the other two, but not this one. Then, during a fever, Lafitte kept mumbling about trees and treasure. Three trees, he said. Everyone has always thought this was the place. Same place where the Indians were bushwhacked. It's been searched a thousand times. I searched the whole area myself and never found nothing."

A few minutes later Bully turned off Stewart Road down a blacktop lane and wound back toward West Bay. He drove to the end and stopped. A sign on the gate read "Posted, Member, Southwestern Cattle Association."

Bully said, "This is the old Schindler ranch. I used to come out here years ago. I think I remember them saying it had been in the family since the 1840s. Don't know who owns it now." Bully got out of the truck and lifted the chain that ran between the gate and the fence post. "Locked up tight," he said. "Used to be nobody locked their property around here. Now it's different. Too forkin' many Houston people down here on the weekends. Can't trust nobody no more."

They looked past the gate at a grove of tallow trees and a slightly-used cattle pen.

Bully continued, "I see why it's posted. Somebody's still runnin' cattle here. You can tell because there's no weeds in the pen."

"How old do you think that cattle pen is?" Alec asked.

"Old?" Bully replied.

"Yes. How long has it been there?" Alec asked again.

Bully, puzzled at the question, didn't reply immediately.

Strauss continued, "From what I've read, most of the early citizens lived in town. They only came out here to work their land. So I figure they would have buried the gold someplace they could have remembered easily. A landmark of some kind, like a corral or an old windmill."

Bully got the drift. "Oh, you mean was the pen here in the 1860s. Oh, hell no. Hardly nothin' lasts a hundred years out here. Not even the trees. Even if they'd had a pen then, there is no telling where it would have been located. Everything's been washed away by the storms."

"How many storms have you had this century?"

"This century? Well, after the big one in 1900, there was one in 1915, and another in '43. Then Hurricane Carla in 1961 and Alicia in '83. That doesn't count all of the smaller ones."

"So when do you think this cattle pen was built?"

Bully wondered where Strauss was going with this. The guy asked a thousand questions. He had already told him the pen wasn't there a hundred years ago during the Civil War.

"Well, as I said, I used to hunt this ranch as a kid back in the 30s. It's been here since then at least."

"None of the storms since then destroyed it? Not even the one in 1943?"

"No."

Alec studied the area. It is possible, he thought. A corral and a stand of trees. But if the gold was here, where would Hoff have buried it? The possibilities were endless. There were trees here and a corral but no windmill he could see. But two out of three wasn't bad, he thought. He turned to Bully and said, "Let's start here tonight."

Chapter Thirty-Three
Tuesday, August 30

Army medics and technicians stripped, poked, fingered and fondled me for two hours, then left me sitting naked and cold in a treatment room. After thirty minutes of freezing my tits off, I still hadn't seen a physician.

I mumbled aloud to an empty wall, "You arrogant bastards! Why do you invariably think your time is more valuable than the patient's?"

I caught my reflection in the wall mirror talking to myself. Maybe I did need treatment.

I checked my watch and reached for my clothes. Forty-five minutes! I'm outta here. No, hold on, I admonished myself. Do it for Claire. She had made an effort to help, probably had to cajole her ex-husband into arranging the appointment.

Her husband—wait a minute! Something was not right. Her husband dumped her for a hard body and she's still friendly with the guy? Strange.

I thought about our earlier conversation on our way to Houston. What did I really know about her relationship with her ex-husband? Not much. Claire was slick. She gave me the Reader's Digest version, scrubbed and cleaned. There was obviously more to their divorce than what she told me.

My thoughts changed quickly back to my naked body and the cold. I rubbed my thighs and arms. Claire or no Claire, I'd had enough.

"Screw this!" The words tumbled out to the empty room. I dressed hurriedly and yanked the door open only to meet head on with a short, prematurely balding man wearing a white smock.

"Major McLeod?"

"Yes."

"I'm Dr. Faust."

The physician pushed past me into the treatment room. I sized him up quickly. No smile or offer of a handshake. No eye contact. Young, not too long out of medical school. Short-man complex, superior. Too good for the VA.

Faust glanced at my chart, then set it on the table and folded his arms in front. "You must be quite special," he said. "The normal waiting period for a new patient is over three months, and you're not even a General."

No humor intended, just sarcasm. Here we go again. How many times had I experienced this? Another Army doctor paying his dues, waiting for his discharge.

I got close to his face. My blood pressure surged, the words streamed out, "Yeah Doctor, I'm special. I'm a U.S. Serviceman. That ought to be enough for you. But then, on the other hand, I guess I'm not special enough."

"Really, why not?" Dr. Faust said, the cynicism obvious.

Before I answered, the doctor made a fatal mistake, he matched my eyes. With the hard, cold stare of a predator, I said, "Well, if I had been that special, I wouldn't have drawn you for a doctor."

Faust flinched slightly. He had probably tried not to, but my trained eye caught the movement. Score one for the Major.

Faust turned and closed the door. "Look, Major McLeod. I have seen plenty of your type. You spend a few months in the desert and then come home whining for a disability pension. Most of you weren't even close to the action, yet you've got every ailment you can think up or read about."

"Oh, really," I said, stepping closer. "Well, I'm sure you're *very* busy, doctor. So why did you bother to see me at all?"

"The request came from the Chief of Staff here. Seems you have a friend on the inside."

"Ah ha," Parker exclaimed. "So without my connection, you would've been conveniently swamped, just too busy."

"Probably so," Faust said, mocking my answer.

I reached over and patted the good doctor's shoulder. "You must not be a career man, huh, Bub? Those brass bars getting a little heavy?"

"What do you mean by that, Major?" he demanded, getting huffy.

"Let me tell you something, Doc. You saw my chart. You're right, I didn't get a Purple Heart. But at least I was there. More than I can say for pukes like you. Since I got back, I've seen a dozen of your type. What are you, about thirty, maybe? You're pissed, right? You couldn't afford medical school, so you joined the Army and got a free education. Now you're just doing your time. Right Faust? It's a prison sentence, isn't it? You can't wait to get out and make the big bucks."

Faust seemed stunned, momentarily set back. I was pleased. He may run over some of the poor saps in here, but it wouldn't work with me. To my surprise, he recovered quickly and fired back.

"You know, you guys come in with these...*symptoms*. No two of you are ever alike. It gets old, seeing a bunch of malingerers. But you are correct about one thing, Major. I am paying my penance here. One more year, and I'll be paid for my ability. As a matter of fact, I'm already set up to work with the finest heart surgeon in the medical center right next door."

Faust panted now, breathing hard. I loved it.

"Faust, do you care about any of these guys in here? I don't give a shit what you think about me, but some of the men here have real problems. Like the ones who can't move their arms or legs. Little things like that. They went over there for you too, you know."

"Well, it's a volunteer service. They didn't have to join."

I grabbed his coat lapels lifted him off the floor and shoved him against the door.

"I'm leaving now, you little jerk-off, but if I ever hear of you mistreating a serviceman, I guarantee I will be back for your ass. You got that?" I turned the little squeak around, lifted him up onto the bed and slammed the bed against the wall.

Within seconds, I cleared the floor and headed down in the elevator. Claire barely made it in before the door closed. When the door opened on the ground floor, I held her by the elbow and pushed her across the parking lot to her car.

"Damn it, Parker. Slow Down!" she yelled. "I'm about to trip over myself.'

"Sorry, Claire...I've...I've got to get the hell away from here."

Minutes later, we sat mired in the late afternoon traffic on I-45 South inching our way toward Galveston. As the car's air conditioner struggled to cool the car in the scorching heat, the normal forty-five minute drive doubled. Finally, after miles of silence and stop and go traffic, Claire said, "Okay, Parker. Enough is enough. What happened?"

I turned my face toward the window. Even the feeder roads were full.

"Can't imagine it," I said, almost under my breath.

Claire glanced over, "What?"

"I said I can't imagine it. Why would anyone want to fight this stuff every day?" I gestured toward the traffic.

"What? Damn it, Parker! Talk to me! What happened back there?"

I kept looking out the window, not saying anything. By the time we reached the causeway to the island, Claire had withdrawn to her own little world. We had reached a standoff, no quarter asked or received.

Thirty minutes later, I watched the tail lights of her Lexus vanish up the sand road in front of The Garhole. This could be it for us, I guessed. But hey, so what? First, the yo-yo was up, and then it was down. It wasn't exactly a relationship anyway—more like two cats in heat. Well, at least one anyway. I managed a weak smile.

With my good friend, Famous Grouse, I climbed to my favorite hide-a-way, the deck off my bedroom. I took a swig, then set the bottle down and rubbed my arms.

The wind increased as a late-summer squall raced in from the East. Fast moving clouds swirled and danced. First there was a slight rippling on the water, then the wave action increased, changing to white caps as the force swept closer. As the storm intensified, all hell broke loose driving hard sheets of rain across the bay.

A storm. Maybe that was the answer. Something big enough to wipe me out, once and for all. But hurricane season was almost over and no storm this year had even come close to Galveston. The Gulf of Mexico remained quiet. There was a tropical disturbance mentioned on the radio. But it was fifteen hundred miles away off Martinique, way down in the Windward Chain and headed west, probably to the Yucatan.

Just my luck.

Chapter Thirty-Four
Wednesday, August 31

Alec arrived back at the Tremont House in the early pre-dawn hours, exhausted from the all-night search. The light on his room phone blinked steadily, bathing the room in a quiet, red glow. He flipped on the overhead light and went straight to the handset. He had been so careful. Who knew he was here?

He held his hand on the receiver, debating. Maybe he should check out immediately, change hotels, not even listen to the message. But, no. If they found him once.... He dialed the extension. The message was clear, call immediately. Frankin answered on the first ring.

"*Speak!*"

"*What?*" Alec replied, his tone curt.

"*A report of course,*" Frankin said. "*It has been several days.*"

Frankin's condescending attitude disgusted Alec, but he held back. It would wait. He would take care of the little bastard when he returned to Germany. "*I am making progress. That is all they need to know.*"

"*What progress? Tell me!*"

Alec stalled. He rubbed his eyes and face. Twenty-four hours without sleep. He put his hand on the dresser, steadying himself. *"I think the money is still here— in Galveston. I have a lead."*

"What lead? Where?"

Alec realized he wasn't thinking clearly. He had made a mistake. Told him too much. He said, *"Not now. I'll call you later."* He jammed the receiver onto the cradle and unplugged the phone from the wall. Of course Frankin could track him, he thought. The GTO had provided his false identity. They knew his alias.

He couldn't afford any more mistakes. He needed rest. Tonight he and the old man would try again. The Schindler place excited him because it had a corral that Stout said had been there since the 1930s. But there was no windmill.

***

Alec slept a few hours and then drove directly to The Garhole. He hoped to convince Stout to search during the day. Tolerating the ignorant old man for hours at a time tested his resolve, but his only choice was to continue with him. Time was short, every hour counted.

Alec visualized Stout swinging the gold machine around as if he were casting a fly. Then he would stop and hammer a long iron rod into the ground. The man had the stamina of a special-forces soldier.

When he arrived at The Garhole, the front and back doors were both open, but the room was empty. The wind had quit, and the room was stuffy. A ceiling fan creaked overhead stirring dust from the floor. Above the bar, the gar-head stared down, a relentless glare. It was as though the monster with white teeth and hollowed eyes knew his thoughts.

He crossed to the back counter and stood behind the door. He recognized Lisa and Bully's voice coming from the trailer.

"So, Poppa, ya'll didn't have any luck last night?"

"No, honey. We searched all over the Schindler ranch until the battery on the gold machine ran out."

"Maybe it's not the right place, huh, Poppa?"

"Honey, there ain't no right place. But I guess as long as this Strauss fella is willing to pay me I'll go try. A couple more places we can look."

"I hope you keep trying," Lisa said. "Man, that Alec is sooo hot!"

"Hot?"

"Yeah, hot. You know like...hot." Lisa rolled her eyes.

"You mean good lookin'?"

"Waaay past that."

"Don't you get no ideas now, sugar. He's too damned old for you."

"I like older men, Poppa." She gave him a big hug. "Especially if they're as cool as you are. You get some rest now, okay?"

"Yeah, honey, I need some sleep. If that Strauss fella comes while I'm napping, tell him he'll just have to wait."

Alec ducked back around the counter and hurried out the front door. He leaned into the door of his car and fumbled in the seat as though he had just arrived and was searching for something.

He wasn't surprised at Lisa's attraction toward him. She wasn't so bad herself. Not too smart, but...he thought about yesterday when she leaned over the counter. No, he admonished himself. Play it safe with this one, too much at stake. He glanced up and noticed Lisa looking out toward his car. He got out and re-entered the front door.

"Hi, Lisa. Where are all the fishermen today?"

Lisa said, "Oh. Hello, Mr. Strauss. Didn't see you pull up."

"Call me Alec. I'm not that much older than you."

"Well...okay, Alec. You're the first customer today. Don't know where everybody is. Maybe it's too hot for fishing." She pressed a cold cup towel to her forehead and cheeks.

"I came out to see if Bully would go out again this afternoon. Is he around?"

"He's worn out Mr...uh, I mean Alec. He said to tell you if you came in early to go home and come back at dark."

Alec already knew the answer. He had no choice now but to go along with Stout's wishes and come back later. He sat at the counter across from her, leaned in, and spoke in a lowered voice. "It's all right with me, Lisa. I'll have you all to myself for awhile."

She flushed, and turned toward the refrigerator. She opened the door and leaned into it.

"Sorry Lisa," Alec said. "I did not mean to embarrass you. It is just that I think you are very pretty. I should not have teased you."

"It's uh...okay. I don't know what to say. Nobody ever told me that before." She shut the door and stood across from Alec.

"That you are pretty?"

"Yes."

"Really? You have never had a boyfriend?"

It happened so quickly, Alec didn't know how to react. Lisa turned away with her face in her hands. She wiped a tear with her hand. A few seconds later she turned back. Alec started to speak, but suddenly Lisa turned away again and leaned against the stove. This time her tears flowed freely.

Alec hurried around the counter and pressed her to his chest. He stroked the back of her hair. "Lisa, I am so sorry. Did I say something wrong?"

Slowly, she calmed herself. They remained clinched together. Her body heat excited him.

"It's not you, Alec. It's me."

Alec continued to hold her tightly against him. He moved his hand to her back and gently rubbed up and down. She pressed into him.

"Tell me, Lisa. Please, what is it?" Alec raised her chin with his hand and kissed a tear on her cheek.

She pressed her cheek against his and whispered, "Can...can I trust you, Alec?"

"Of course you can. Tell me."

Lisa told him everything—her life story. How she was abandoned at fourteen when her mother died. How Bully was sick and couldn't help and how Parker was off in the Army. How she met Denny Sader in the pool hall and what he had done to her and how much she was afraid of him. She told Alec how he had kidnapped her once already and how Bully had saved her. It all came out like a fast ripping tide—a total catharsis—until she was too weak to stand.

Alec didn't speak during her entire admission. They went out to the front and sat at a table. "It is okay, Lisa. You are here now, away from him. You are safe."

"No, no, you don't understand." Her lips quivered as she spoke, "I'm never safe from him. He's coming for me again, I know he is."

Alec spoke softly, "I promise, Lisa. Nothing will happen to you. Trust me." He eased back. She seemed to be studying his eyes searching for assurance.

"Oh, I do, Alec. I do trust you."

"Good," he said, squeezing her hand. "But I have to go now, Lisa. Get some rest myself. I will return later tonight."

Breaking away from Lisa's inviting body hadn't been easy. A part of him wanted to take her. Another part wanted to roust Stout out of bed. They could be searching now. Why wait? Stout had said there were other places to look. He hesitated, glanced toward the camper. No, he told himself—patience. Play the game.

On his way out the driveway, he noticed a man walking along the sand road toward him. They locked eyes and the man's glare bore into him as they passed each other. He had seen the look before, penetrating, searching. Where? Yes, he remembered. It was in the eyes of an East German policeman while interrogating a prisoner. It was more than curiosity, it was trained.

Chapter Thirty-Five
Wednesday, August 31

I hiked the beach at daybreak, moving quietly along the shore, listening to the gentle lapping of the surf. I found some sea-beans from South America and a few broken sand dollars. Shorebirds of different sizes and colors scurried along in front of me probing the sand with their long beaks. Life at its simplest.

As the sun broke free from the horizon, I knew I would not let the day go by without calling Claire. I pocketed a few shells and moved quickly across the field to the highway.

When I crossed the blacktop and entered the lane to The Garhole, I passed a rather plain four-door sedan leaving the parking lot. The license plate pegged it as a rental car. A quick look at the driver's face triggered something in my past. I had seen the profile many times, not here, but in Europe—the strong face, thick neck, blond hair, blue eyes.

Who was he, and what was he doing at The Garhole? He certainly wasn't local, not even a Houston regular. In fact, no one I had ever seen before. I was sure of it. He was definitely northern European, Scandinavian or German.

I intended to ask Lisa or Bully who he was, but when I went inside Bully was asleep in his camper, and Lisa was out in the garden.

The crab traps hadn't produced overnight and the freezer was empty. Fortunately, this was the doldrums time of year on West Bay. The bustle of the summer crowd had come and gone. Business would be slow until the weather cooled enough to move the fish. It looked as if the tired old garden might come through one last time. Lisa had left enough okra and tomatoes on the counter to make a stew for lunch.

I washed the tomatoes and had just started chopping the okra when Lisa came in with another armful. I said, "Lisa, who was that...?"

The telephone rang and Lisa answered it. She stretched the phone toward me and said, "It's for you, Parker. Colonel somebody."

Colonel? The caller must be Army. Probably some puke calling to read me off about my little rhubarb with that jerk Faust at the VA. But I was no longer on active duty, so what could they do to me? I decided to play along.

I summoned up my gruffest tone, "This is McLeod."

"Yes, Major. My name is Kennon. Colonel Ben Kennon. I am the Chief of Staff for the VA Hospital in Houston. You came in yesterday for an appointment?"

"If you can call it that." A colonel this time. I really rated today.

Kennon said, "I see you received a battery of tests, but there is no report from a physician. Was there a problem, Major?"

"You might say that, Colonel. The medics that ran the tests were okay. But I waited an hour buck naked for an exam before your jerk-off doctor accused me of malingering and a few other things."

Kennon's reply was slow in coming. To his credit, he ignored my tirade and said, "I have reviewed your chart, Major. My specialty is working with Gulf War veterans. Could you please come back this afternoon so I can examine you and discuss the results of your tests from yesterday?"

"What about the other doctor?" I asked.

"The physician you saw requested reassignment. He hasn't been in this morning."

Reassigned! That felt good. I wondered about the good men the little runt had intimidated. So many broken bodies and crushed souls stranded at the VA. The last thing those poor guys needed was a self-serving prick like Faust.

But Kennon sounded different. I agreed to come in, then hung up and called Claire.

"Hi. It's me, Parker."

No answer.

"Hello. Are you there?"

More silence.

"Claaaaire."

"What!"

At least she had answered. Yesterday I left her like a school kid after an argument. It was time to suck up.

"Claire, I'm sorry."

"What are you talking about?"

"You asked me what happened in the doctor's office, and I wouldn't discuss it. He was a real jerk, Claire. Insulted me and all the Vets. I blew up, told him off."

"You couldn't tell me that?"

"I'd already lost my temper at the oak motte. I didn't think you'd want to see my worst side two days in a row."

She didn't respond, so I continued, "The VA wants to see me again today. A different doctor. Would you please go with me?" Had I actually used the "P" word? I pushed the telephone hard against my ear...waiting. The pause seemed forever. More silence.

"Claire, I'd really like to see you."

I waited.

"Well...okay, Parker. On one condition."

She explained, and I readily agreed. She could be present in the session.

When we arrived at the VA two hours later, Colonel Kennon immediately examined me. Afterwards, he ushered Claire and me into his private office and directed us to the couch. He was taller than me, thin and ramrod straight, with a graying mustache to match his salt and pepper hair.

He pulled a chair close to us and sat down. He nodded toward Claire and then turned to me and said, "Thank you for coming in, Major."

If the remark was supposed to set me at ease, it didn't work. I narrowed my eyes and held him tight.

Ignoring my obstinance, Kennon opened a thick file and glanced at a sheet or two. He said, "You have been out of the service almost a year now, Major McLeod."

I nodded.

"According to your records, you spent nineteen years in the Army. You couldn't make it one more?"

I knew what he was getting at. Twenty years offered a lifetime retirement. I studied the Colonel's expression. Was he being earnest or condescending?

I said, "Well, I regret that I didn't, but if you have my complete record, you know what happened." I waved toward the file in the Colonel's hands, thinking he must have read about all about my medical evaluations.

Kennon glanced at the file again, then back to me. He closed the folder and set it on the coffee table between us. "Yes, I see. Tell me, Major, you were drafted, so how did you become an officer?"

Where was he going with this? What did this have to with my medical problems? I fidgeted in my chair and glanced at Claire. She nodded encouragement. I would go along for a while.

"Well, during boot camp the Army discovered I had a knack for linguistics. They sent me to Defense Language School West at Fort Ord in California. My next duty was Munich, Germany."

Kennon interrupted, "You were in Intelligence, correct?"

"Yes, I specialized in the German language. The cold war was hot and heavy in those days. Most of the so-called spies were East German." I paused for a moment, then continued. "Anyway, back to your question. The University of Maryland has an extension school in Munich. Going at night, I was able to get my degree."

"So you were accepted into Officers Candidate School?"

"Correct. Then I spent time at Fort Huachuca, Arizona for a military intelligence program and then finally back to Germany again."

"Thank you, Major. Now if I may, let me get right to it. During the Gulf War, you were close to the front lines. Did you see any action?"

"Want to know if I'm shell-shocked?"

Claire's heel jammed the top of my shoe. She pushed down hard. I winced. Okay, so the sarcasm was out of line. But what is with all the sudden attention? After fighting the system for two years and getting nowhere, why was the chief of the Veterans Hospital in Houston sitting across from me acting as if he cared?

Claire cleared her throat. I caught a side view of her frown.

The Colonel said, "Don't be a wise-acre, Major. I'm trying to determine your exposures."

"Exposures? Oh, yes, Colonel, I had exposures. Torched oil fields...a boiling black sky so heavy we couldn't breathe. Some of the men got pneumonia, almost died."

"Anything else you recall?

"Oh, nothing much. Just SCUD missile launches with who knows what in them. Want to hear more?"

The doctor picked up the file and made a note, then he said, "Frankly, no, not with the attitude you're showing. I'm trying to be helpful here, Major. Now, do you want to continue or not?"

Claire jumped in, "Yes, he does, Colonel." She motioned to me, "Tell him you do, Parker." Her smile said—get with it, Parker!

I straightened a little and said, "I want to continue, Colonel."

"Thank you, Major. Now, you have listed your symptoms as fatigue, recurrent headaches, muscle and joint pain, and insomnia. Are there others?"

"Those are the main ones."

The Colonel leaned back in his chair. "Major McLeod, I have personally examined several hundred Gulf War veterans. In addition to your symptoms, they have complained of memory loss, coordination problems, nerve damage, swollen lymph nodes, swollen gums, low blood pressure, and weight loss, just to name a few. Have you experienced any of these?"

I ran through my memory. "Well, yes…. Maybe I had some of those earlier on. But now, only the ones I listed bother me."

Kennon continued, "After every war our soldiers have returned with health problems. From this one, several thousand servicemen and women are complaining of the various symptoms we have discussed. No two veterans seem to have exactly the same problems, but they all share a least a few of them."

"Yeah," I replied. "And I know for a fact that many of the old-timers didn't come forward with their symptoms because they were afraid they'd be phased out of the Army prior to retirement."

"You really believe that, Major?"

"You're damned right I do. No one got satisfaction from the system. I got out of the Army because my health was so bad I couldn't do my job, and I couldn't get any help. I have been tested in four different facilities. I can tell you what they say I don't have—multiple sclerosis, inner ear infection, teeth and jaw problems, exercise induced asthma, and oh yeah, mononucleosis and panic disorder."

"Quite a list, Major," Kennon said, "So, your current disability rating is thirty per cent, correct?"

"Yes sir, that's correct."

"I think we can do better. I'm quite sure we'll get it increased."

I sat there speechless. I glanced at Claire then back to the doctor. "How can you do that?"

"You've been out of the loop a while, Major. We don't know exactly what the causes of Gulf War Syndrome are, but we've got enough facts now to at least improve your status."

I focused hard. Was he being straight?

Colonel Kennon continued, "Just a couple more questions, Major McLeod. What medications were prescribed for you?"

"Well, Valium and Xanax for anxiety and sleep, and Doxycycline as an antibiotic."

"What are you taking now?"

"Straight scotch. I didn't want to be a prescription junkie."

Claire's heel hit my shoe again. I squirmed.

The doctor said, "Not funny, Major, but that brings us to your test results. Most were negative. It's difficult to pin- point anything specific. However, I do believe your symptoms are real and not imagined. I am going to detail a treatment program for you that I think will work. But Major, you have a much more serious problem. Your liver is enlarged, and you are quite jaundiced. Haven't you noticed the yellow in your eyes?"

I turned to Claire. She had mentioned it on our way into Houston. She mouthed, "I told you so."

Colonel Kennon straightened in his chair and exhaled slowly. The overhead light bounced off the brass eagles on his shoulder and beamed toward Claire and me. I focused on the brass and then on the doctor's eyes.

The Colonel stood and reached out for my hand. He held it for a moment and said, "Major McLeod, we will do what we can, but...I am not sure we can fix that."

Chapter Thirty-Six
Wednesday, August 31

The news hadn't shocked me; death could bring relief. Still, out of instinct, I wanted clarification. "What are you saying, doctor? My liver is irreparably damaged? If I don't quit drinking, I could die?"

Colonel Kennon placed the test results back in my folder, then sat the file on his desk. He met my eyes and said, "Not could, Major. If you don't stop drinking you *will* die. It might already be too late. But your only hope is to give your liver a rest."

I held the doctor's eyes waiting for a blink. None came. I lowered my head and exhaled a long, slow sigh.

Claire spoke, "Colonel Kennon, can't the liver repair itself?"

"In some cases it's possible," he answered. "But, as I said, there are no guarantees."

Kennon handed me a folder. "As for your other symptoms, we have prepared a plan for you—a special exercise program that seems to have helped in other cases I've studied. There is also behavioral therapy, such as learning relaxation techniques and activity pacing."

Claire said, "Similar to a holistic approach, Colonel? Is that what you're recommending?"

"More or less," he answered, responding to Claire. "Best treatment we have right now, and as I said, we've had some success with it. There are so many symptoms with GWS that no particular drug seems to work. Too many of the guys have gotten hooked on pain killers."

Kennon turned back to me and said, "You'll be in a control group under my direct supervision. The diet I want you on is included in the information I am giving you, and of course, you have to stop the alcohol. It is all we can do right now. See me on the schedule I have outlined, and we will monitor your progress."

"No miracle cures?" Claire asked.

Kennon shook his head.

Claire continued, "Dr. Kennon, Parker told me about the SCUD missile attacks. Do you think they were the probable cause?"

"We don't know. I have studied many service personnel who were around the attacks. Some have these symptoms and some don't. Our forces were exposed to all kinds of possible threats. We thought perhaps the low-level bombing of Iraqi chemical factories might have spread nerve gas across the desert. But then, no animals died. We're looking at everything—uranium depleted artillery shells, pesticides used by Iraqi farmers, sand storms, allergic reactions, you name it."

Colonel Kennon stood and extended his hand. In an act of dismissal he said, "See you in two weeks Major McLeod."

Neither of us spoke when we left his office. I could tell by her sideways glances that Claire wanted me to open up, but I was too balled up inside.

A few blocks from the VA, Claire pulled into a coffee shop. We sat by a window overlooking a busy thoroughfare. Cars clogged the street. I thought about the view from The Garhole, birds hovering for breakfast and trout making feeding circles in the front of the dock.

As the waitress delivered water and menus, I saw a man and woman in a car with two kids in the back. Normal people, living normal lives. They drive to work, perform their functions, and then go home to their families. They have dinner together, the kids do homework and watch TV and maybe the husband and wife make love. What in hell happened to me?

When the server left, Claire leaned across the table and said, "Oh, Parker. I just want to reach over and choke you. I'm so tired of your self-pity I could throw up."

She had caught me at my favorite past time—whining to myself. Not about to admit it, I summoned my best-feigned indignity and said, "What do you mean by that?"

Claire replied quickly, "You know what I mean. You have just been told you may be dying and you sit there like it's hopeless. Where is the tough, spy man, Army officer who protected our country for nineteen years?"

"Somehow I don't feel so tough. What do you want me to do, talk about how I feel about biting the big one?"

"You should," Claire said. "You've been killing yourself for months. Why not talk about it?"

"What's to talk about? If I die, I die. Who gives a shit?"

Claire picked up her napkin and threw it at me. It hit my face and slid to my lap. She sighed heavily and rubbed her temples, resignation in her eyes.

Her valiant effort touched me. I turned back toward the street for a moment. Then suddenly, thoughts spilled out like water from a glass—nothing planned. I just started talking.

"The Army was my father and they deserted me. I didn't deserve it. I gave them twenty years of my life. The first time I really needed them, they weren't there for me."

I held her eyes. I guess I was looking for compassion.

She said, "So, you're feeling abandoned, huh?"

I thought about it a moment and said, "Good word, I guess. Reminds me of the bastard who conceived me."

Claire said, "Okay, you got me. What's with your father?"

"Don't call him that, the son of a bitch."

"Whoa! Hit a nerve, eh? Sorry."

"Yeah, you hit a nerve all right. His name was Carl Varden, a ship's captain from Denmark. Met my mother at some dive in Galveston when he was in port here."

"Tell me about him, Parker."

"I only saw him a few times a year. What I remember most were the language sessions. He wanted me to learn Danish so I could go back to Copenhagen with him on one of his return trips. So he said anyway."

"What happened?"

"I learned it. Even studied the book he left me between visits."

Claire said, "So that's why you picked up German so rapidly?"

"I guess so. It did come easy for me."

"So, what happened that you disliked your father so much?"

"Damn it! I mean it Claire. Stop calling him that."

"Sorry."

"When I was about twelve or so, my mother told me he drowned at sea."

"I'm sorry, Parker," Claire answered, her voice soft.

"Don't be. I wish the bastard had drowned. I believed it at the time. Then, when I was sixteen, my mother announced she was going to New York to live with a museum curator she had met in Houston. She said I was old enough to run the bait camp by myself. Sixteen! Can you imagine that!"

"So she left you too, huh? But, I don't understand. What's that got to do with the man who conceived you, as you put it?"

"I'm getting to that. She said she'd had enough of the hot, sticky air that melted the salt to her skin. She wanted lights and people. She said she had to have something else in her life besides fried shrimp. What a statement! What was I, a frigging shrimp? Anyway, she said she was sorry she had lied to me. It seems that during the entire time they were together, Varden had another family in Denmark, a wife and two kids. He hadn't drowned, he'd deserted her."

"And you too."

"I suppose so. Then she told me they were never married. Next day, I changed my name to McLeod, my grandfather's."

"Your mother's father, who owned the land you now have?"

"Right," Parker answered. "I've always felt a strange connection to him. I guess it's the land. He never quit. Toughed it out like you're supposed to."

"As you've had to do?"

"Since I was a kid."

"Is your mother still in New York?"

"No, a few weeks after arriving in New York, she was murdered on a subway by a hopped-up teenager."

"I'm sorry, Parker," Claire said. "So you've been on your own since you were sixteen, huh?"

I nodded.

"You've certainly had your share of grief. All that abandonment, your father, your mother, the Army. Now I understand why you're so angry with Lisa. You were close once. Then she ran away and got into drugs. Maybe you feel as if she abandoned you too, huh?"

"Playing the psychologist again, huh, Claire? Trying to get into my head?"

"Just listen, Parker. Think about this. Lisa was abandoned too, by her whole family. Her mother died, Bully wasn't able to care for her. You weren't either. And...just like you.... She was a kid."

I thought about it and said, "Okay, so what?"

Claire said, "Come on, Parker. Get off that poor-me stuff."

I didn't respond. The waitress brought coffee, giving both of us a chance to temper the conversation.

After a pause, Claire said, "You know, Parker, I've had a few lumps myself. No pun intended. I had breast cancer two years ago and..."

I interrupted, "Jesus, Claire! Are you okay?"

"Yes, they said they got it all. But my doctor slash friend slash husband couldn't take it. He said the chemo treatments were too tough on him." Claire laughed. "Can you believe that? Too tough on him. I guess I was lucky to find out about him when I did. So I moved to Galveston to start over. And I'd had enough of the nurse routine, so I decided on real estate."

I smiled and said, "Good decision."

"What? Moving to Galveston or getting into real estate?"

"Both," I answered. "Otherwise you wouldn't have met me."

Claire laughed and shook her head in mock disgust.

I said, "Ever see him anymore?"

"Well, even the jerk that he was, I don't burn bridges. He got you into the VA on short notice, remember?"

I twirled my finger and said, "Whoopee! As if I asked for that."

Her smile turned into a smirk. "Well, someone has to take care of you."

"I take care of myself," I said, somewhat defiantly.

She chuckled. "Parker, you're disgusting. Do you know John Donne's poem that begins with 'No man is an island'?"

"The one about 'Each man is a part of the main' or something close to that. What's your point, Claire?"

"Hello, island!"

That hit hard. I recoiled momentarily, but then barked back, "Yeah, I'm an island all right. Babysitting Bully and Lisa. And Bully isn't even really kin. He married my aunt, my mother's sister, that all."

"I'm sorry, Parker. I didn't mean to stir you up like that. I guess I was being too invasive with the island comment, huh? You needed to distance from me, didn't you?"

I blurted out, "Claire, for God's sake. Quit analyzing me. How would you feel if I badgered you with a thousand personal questions?"

"Maybe I'd feel as if you cared," she answered, hurriedly.

"Okay, so here's one for you," I said. "The line you gave me about him trading you for a younger version was a bunch of baloney, right?"

"Oh no. He did that all right. Got one with two real boobs. Big ones too. Not like my little mangoes—or should I say mango." Claire's mouth curved into a sad frown.

I laughed. A vision of Claire's wet breast pushed against my chest returned. A nice mango, I thought.

I said, "So you've run away too, huh,? All the way to Galveston."

"You might think that." she said. "But I consider it running to something. At least I don't drown myself in alcohol."

I thought about that and said, "Yeah, well, like they say, rehab is for quitters."

Claire frowned. She shook her head and focused on her coffee. We paid the check and started the drive back to Galveston.

The disappointment on her face remained. I had screwed up, trying to be funny at the wrong time. It was the first time in months I had felt humor coming back into my dying existence, and I had chosen sarcasm. Not smart. Not now, with her. She was obviously no longer in a joking mood. I reached over to her in the car and touched her shoulder.

"I'm sorry Claire. I'm not used to people caring about me."

"It's okay, Parker," Claire said, a small smile appearing. "I'm just worried about you, that's all."

I rubbed her shoulder, then gently squeezed it. "You're probably right, Claire. I need some worrying about."

An hour later we drove past the last exit of the freeway before the causeway, I rolled the window down. Warm, salt air rushed over my face. I pointed to my jeans and sneakers.

"It's too early to go home, and I'm all dressed up. How about having dinner with me tonight?"

Claire smiled broadly and said, "Well, okay. I'll have dinner with you. But first, I need to ask you one more question. Then we'll drop the therapy, okay?"

I covered my face with my hand and sank down into the seat. "Claire, give me a break."

"Just one, okay?"

I sighed, heavily.

"How much longer are you going to play this victim role?"

We were on the down slope of the causeway now, the entrance to the island. I dropped my hand and straightened in the seat. To the left was the great expanse of Galveston Bay. A tug pushing several barges of liquefied gas had just cleared underneath the bridge, heading east following the Intracoastal. At a point several miles out into the long stretch of water, the tug would bisect the Houston Ship Channel and thread its way between the steady stream of tankers and freighters chugging northward toward the Port of Houston.

On the right was West Bay. A shallow water, bordered on the north by the mainland and on the south by Galveston Island. Pleasure boats of all descriptions darted from one secret spot to another chasing the game fish. A scattering of oyster reefs and tidal islands stretched across the water for twenty-odd miles past the booming real estate developments and struggling estuaries, down to the end of the island and The Garhole Bar.

There was something magical about crossing the causeway. I felt my pulse slow and my blood pressure lower. I was at home now.

As we left the bridge and traveled onto the island, I realized I hadn't answered Claire's question. I felt her eyes boring into me. She wasn't going to let it go.

She glanced at the road in front of her to check the traffic then turned back to me and said, "Well?"

"I'll let you know," I said.

Chapter Thirty-Seven
Wednesday, August 31

Alec's gut roared with anticipation. The second hand on his watch ticked louder and more demanding. As Bully's old truck coughed and sputtered its way up the sand road toward the highway, the clatter of its engine did little to drown out the watch's incessant ticking.

At the blacktop, Bully switched to high beams and Alec watched the dark shadows on the road disappear into the moonless night.

He willed his heartbeat to its normal rate of fifty, the pulse of an athlete in prime condition. He had to pace himself, stay in control. He had lost it with the Hoff woman and gone a little too far with the librarian.

The sound of Bully's voice broke through the engine noise. "We'll go to the old Boehm place tonight."

Surprised, Alec said, "The what? I thought we were going back to the Schindler ranch?"

"No," Bully answered, "I think we covered it pretty well."

Alec frowned. He had wanted to try the Schindler ranch again. The place seemed right, the corral and the grove of trees. He protested, "Let's try the Schindler ranch one more time before we give up on it."

Bully snorted, "I told you we searched it pretty good. So we'll try the Boehm place tonight. If we don't have any luck there, I'll call Harry. He'll help us."

Alec doubted that. He remembered the way Stein dismissed him from his office with a wave of his hand, his skepticism obvious. Alec chuckled inwardly, thinking, if Stein only knew. Nazi gold buried on the west end and the search for it financed by the German Truth Organization. Such irony. Stein, a Jew helping to build the new Germany.

Alec cut his eyes toward the old man. The wooden leg and patch over the eye almost made him laugh—a crippled washout who thought himself a reincarnated Caribbean pirate. Ha!

Then Alec remembered the conversation he'd overheard between Bully and Lisa in the trailer. Bully told Lisa he would look for the gold as long as Alec was willing to pay. Alec wondered if he had been set up, the whole thing a scheme so Stout could pick up a few extra dollars. Searching but never finding.

Bully's cigar bounced with the rhythm of his voice as he spoke. "The Boehm place is closer to town so the island's wider there. And it's back on the bay side where there's not much development. There's less chance we'll be seen."

They drove up FM3005 past several subdivisions and turned left toward West Bay. They turned right on Stewart Road, followed it for a mile and then turned left again on a lonely black top that twisted and turned, winding back to the ranch.

Bully pushed the eye patch up and rubbed his glass eye. "This ain't like the Schindler place," he noted. "The area is pretty low, a lot of marsh. It'll pretty much flood over with some of the high tides we get."

Alec considered the comment. Earlier, Stout had told him the old ranchers knew the effects a storm could have on the island. That is why they wouldn't have hidden anything close to the beach. So, why would Hoff have buried the gold in a low area close to a marsh? It did not make sense. But since Hoff was not from Galveston, he might not have known about the tides and the storms. Alec shook his head trying to clear the confusion. The fact was, the gold could be anywhere.

When they reached the entrance, Alec focused on the beam from the truck's headlamps. He looked for the landmarks the Hoff woman had mentioned. Nothing appeared. He nodded toward Bully, "There is no lock on the gate. I guess they are not too concerned about trespassers."

"Couldn't be any cattle on it or they would have locked up," Bully answered. "The land's pretty poor here. See all them prickly pears and palmetto? Salt water from the high tides and storm surges kills all the good grasses."

They opened the gate and followed the ruts in the road plowing through the salt grass. The wind had stilled and the scene was eerily silent except for the thousands of marsh mosquitoes attacking the truck's windows.

Bully spoke again. "I don't see an animal of any kind. Looks like whoever owns it might've given up on raising beef. Probably some goddamned land syndicate out of Houston."

He lowered the window and tossed out the stub of his unlit cigar. Then he worked up a mouthful of spit and blasted it through the opening into the weeds below. A wad of insects charged into the truck.

"Bully," Alec screamed, swatting vigorously. "Roll that window up."

Ignoring the outburst, Bully reached to the glove compartment for another cigar. "The smoke will take care of the critters. We'll park behind the barn there—hide my truck from the road."

Alec had not noticed the barn, half hidden behind a stand of salt-cedars. Maybe there was hope, he thought. He looked for the remains of a corral and windmill by the barn and trees. "You said this was a big ranch, huh, Bully? Who owns it now?"

"I told you the Boehms," Bully answered. "I went to high school with one of the boys. We duck hunted all out there." He pointed toward the darkness. "You can't see it now, but that's all potholes and marsh grass."

Alec strained to see through the pitch-black night. He imagined water everywhere. If the gold was on this ranch, it was probably on the high ground, somewhere close to where they were now.

Bully spoke again. "I ain't been on the place in years. I never searched it 'cause I never heard about any booty being stashed here."

You certainly would not have heard about this booty, Alec thought. He stepped out of the truck and stared at the stand of salt-cedars close by. A grove of trees. At least he had that. His pulse raced. Could he be this lucky?

Bully got out of the truck. Alec watched as he rubbed under his armpits, gathering perspiration. He rubbed the sweat from his underarms to his face and the back of his neck.

Alec gave him a disgusted look. "What are you doing, Bully?"

"Best damned mosquito repellant money can't buy," he answered. Then he moved his hands toward Alec and said, "Want some?" Bully laughed as Alec recoiled away.

Alec found an almost empty can of bug repellent in the truck and sprayed himself, cursing that he had not thought to bring more.

Bully fired up the gold machine and worked it toward the trees. Alec followed. They searched until the early hours, prodding likely spots with an iron bar and occasionally digging down several feet with a shovel.

Hour after hour, they repeated the drill. Bully insisted on refilling each hole to mask their presence. The extra work doubled their effort. By 3:00 AM, perspiration soaked their clothes and scratches from the tall grass covered their arms. They had completed a full circle around the barn for several hundred feet in each direction. Alec had not found any remains of a windmill, but just in case he had missed something, he cajoled Bully into working out several directions from the trees. Nothing! No corral, no well, and no gold.

They had forgotten drinking water, and Alec's throat ached. Each time he figured the old man was ready to drop, Stout would work up a glob of something and spit it out. Alec couldn't muster enough moisture to lick his lips.

Back at the barn, they sat on a bench to rest. Neither had spoken much during the search. Alec mopped the sweat from his brow and rubbed the mosquito bites on his arms. He tried working some moisture into his throat. Nothing. Nothing at all. Another wasted night. He thought again about the conversation between Bully and Lisa. Maybe Bully was a fraud. The longer he sat there swatting mosquitoes, the angrier he became.

Suddenly, without thinking, he blurted out, "You think that crazy machine of yours really works?" The frustration in his voice surprised him.

Bully swatted a mosquito on the back of his neck and wiped the blood on his shirtsleeve. Then he rubbed his neck again as if checking for more and said, his voice rising, "I told you I never heard of nothing being buried on this property. But it was German owned. That seemed to be a big deal to you."

He took a breath and waved his arm toward the blackness. "So we spent half the night out here in this forkin' swamp. But if you want to keep looking, I'll do some checking tomorrow on some other locations. It's up to you."

Alec observed Bully more closely. The old man didn't seem nearly as tired as he was. Where did he get his energy? Alec was in perfect physical condition, trained and honed, yet he was exhausted, even mentally tired.

"Well," Alec said, his resignation apparent. "Harry Stein strongly recommended you." He lowered his head into his hands and mumbled, "Maybe it was just all a big joke."

"What?" The comment seemed to energize Bully. He straightened. His volume increased. "A joke! You mean about the gold being buried out here or about Harry recommending me?"

Alec did not like the challenging tone of Bully's voice. He didn't react well to veiled threats.

"Maybe you do not know what you are doing, old man. The only thing you have ever found is a few cases of rum. Maybe I need to find someone else. You and Stein are probably just screwing me around. Splitting your fee."

Bully jumped off the bench. His wooden leg caught in the heavy grass. He almost fell. Alec tensed.

Bully regained his stance, rose to his full height, and yelled, "You asshole. You can't talk about my friend like that. You think we'd be in cahoots just to split the lousy few bucks you're paying? I don't need your forkin' money." He raised his arm and pointed toward the road. "Get your ass out the gate and walk back to town."

Alec's first impulse was to charge Bully and smash him into the marsh. He got halfway up then caught himself and eased back to the bench. He would take him if he had to. Physically they were similar in size, both over six feet and strong. But Alec was not yet thirty and Bully was well over seventy. Plus the old man carried a huge midsection. It would be so easy, Alec thought. A couple of pops to that huge gut, and the old man would crash to the ground like a sack of dung falling from a truck.

He remained motionless on the bench. Bully railed at him again to leave, but Alec had regained enough composure not to move or say anything. He realized too late the tempest he'd created. He hoped Bully would calm down.

Bully kicked at the grass and cursed again. Then he turned and stormed off to his truck. Alec followed, but too late—Bully was gone.

Alec ploughed his fist into the gate, denting the aluminum railing. What a fool he had been—a mental lapse. It had happened so quickly. He was tired to the bone, but that was no excuse. He should have been stronger. He was out of time, out of money. How was he going to find the gold now? The old man had said there were a few more places they could search. Alec did not know the area, and he could not risk being caught trespassing.

He had no choice but to walk back to town and hope the local police would not pick him up along the way. How would he explain being out on a lonely blacktop, miles from town, in the middle of the night?

Chapter Thirty-Eight
Thursday, September 1

The morning broke bright and clear. I hopped down the back stairs down to the bar and put on a pot of coffee. The pot shook in my hands. My system cried for alcohol. I glanced at the beer box, thought better of it, and leaned on the counter to steady myself.

Rows of jagged teeth stared down at me. I gave the relic the evil eye and said, "I don't think I like what you're thinking, big boy. Nothing happened last night."

I'm not sure it believed me, but nothing had happened. After dinner, Claire and I stopped at her condo. She changed into shorts, and we drove to the beach across from The Garhole. We strolled along arm in arm for a while. Afterwards she dropped me off in the parking lot and went home. And that was that. Not that I hadn't wanted more. I just wasn't about to push it.

I took my coffee outside. Out in the bay an early morning fisherman was driving his outboard toward San Luis Pass. The boat ran smoothly on the slick surface creating the only ripple on the water. I raised my cup in salute. The fisherman waved.

I sat on a bench, laid back against the table, and closed my eyes. I thought about Claire, a strand of hair blowing across her face and she smiling and pulling it back. The warmth of her touch in the late evening breeze.

My thoughts flashed to Janie—a hot summer night on the beach, young lovers full of lust and mystery, our bodies pressed hard against each other.

Then, suddenly, Claire's body replaced hers. The kisses were more controlled, the lovemaking less frantic. A moment later, we lay spent watching the moon's rays shimmering over the calm water.

My eyes popped open, and I realized how mushy it all sounded. But then I thought, so what? Maybe I was getting a little soft. I had never gotten anywhere being hard. I smiled at the pun.

A rumble in my gut reminded me I'd gone twenty-four hours without booze. I poured another cup of coffee, walked up to the deck, and stared across the marsh beside my house. The Colonel said exercise would be good for my GWS problems and help keep my mind off the withdrawal symptoms.

I laced on an old pair of tennis shoes, hiked up the sandy lane to the blacktop, and crossed through the cord grass to the beach. I walked the shore for two or three miles, tracing the route Claire and I had taken the night before, my pace increasing with each step. A fisherman I knew was out in the surf wading for trout. I waved. He smiled broadly and held up a stringer with several fish.

***

Back at The Garhole, I hosed the dock clean and emptied and scoured the refrigerator. I cleaned my room and hung my clothes, things I had put off for weeks. By mid-morning, I was back in the bar de-boning a chicken.

Bully limped through the back door, grabbed a beer from the cooler, and moved to a stool at the counter. He slurped half the bottle without stopping to breathe.

I faced away from him, busy at the sink. Neither of us spoke. I opened the refrigerator door and leaned forward, studying the contents.

He demolished the rest of the beer, then said in an apologetic tone, "Parker, if you're looking for the biscuits, I didn't make it to the store."

I shut the door and turned toward him. "Well, it's no big deal. I should have stopped on the way home myself last night. Okay, so no chicken and dumplings. We'll have soup for lunch." I opened the door again and took out some carrots and a couple of onions.

Bully's arm went over the top for another beer. I finished chopping the vegetables, then turned to face him.

"What's going on, Bully?" I asked, my tone conciliatory. "You've been moping around all morning. I know you were out half the night. Did someone beat you to Lafitte's gold?"

Bully replied quickly, "I was out all night all right. And no, Parker. No one beat me to Lafitte's gold." He finished the second beer, then stood and heaved it toward the trashcan behind the counter. It broke against another empty bottle and the sound bounced back. "You really want to know?"

I just looked at him.

He said, "That asshole that Harry sent out here pissed me off. I sent him packin'."

Puzzled, I said, "What are you talking about, Bully?"

"You know, that Kraut that's looking for buried gold. Lisa didn't tell you?"

"No, she didn't," I answered and then realized I had seen little of either Lisa or Bully during the last few days.

"What do you mean 'Kraut'? Who is the guy?" I asked.

"Hell, I don't know who he is. He said he was over here from Germany. Supposed to be a writer or something. Said he thinks some Civil War gold is buried out on the west end. He wanted my help and said he'd pay me so I thought I'd do it. Lisa needs some clothes."

"You mean the old story about some of the citizens burying gold when the Yankees were here?"

"Yeah."

"Bullshit!"

"I know."

"So he's been out here several times and Lisa has met him, too?"

"Yeah, you must have been in Houston with that real estate woman."

"Her name is Claire Roberts," I said, raising my voice.

Bully ignored my rebuke and said, "Lisa likes the guy. I don't."

"What do you mean, 'Lisa likes the guy'?"

"You know what I mean," Bully responded.

"How old is he?" I asked.

"Hell, I don't know. Late twenties or so."

"Wait a minute," I said. "Is he a big guy, blond hair?"

"Yeah, about my height," Bully answered.

"I did see him—yesterday, leaving The Garhole as I came in. Lisa's way too young for him and too...vulnerable."

"Vulnerable?" Bully said. "You mean...you think...?"

"I don't know what I think," I said. "Where's Lisa now?"

"That real estate woman, uh...I mean Claire took her shopping, I think."

Claire hadn't told me she was coming. She must have picked Lisa up while I was on the beach. I felt relief knowing where Lisa was.

I said, "So what did this guy do to piss you off?"

"He accused me and Harry of bamboozling him to take his money. Said we were double-teaming him. Can you imagine that? Me, maybe. But Harry, bamboozling somebody? Ha! It really set me off."

"Hell, Bully, you've still got a hang-up about Germans. And after what you've been through, I can't say that I blame you. But it was a long time ago. You're not ready to forget and forgive?"

Bully's voice softened. "I could forgive the wounds. Losing a leg and an eye by stepping on that mine was combat. Those things happen in war. But I'll never forgive the massacre at Malmedy—

pure murder. All those boys lying in the snow...almost a hundred of them."

Bully's eyes glazed over. He was back in 1944 again—the Battle of the Bulge. So many friends lost. I almost reached over and touched him, but held back. I turned back to the stove, put the chicken into a pot of water and walked out onto the dock.

No doubt, I thought. Something strange was going on. A German writer looking for gold in Galveston? It didn't compute.

For the first time in weeks, I cranked up the outboard and pushed out into West Bay. It was the first day of September. The next few days would be among the hottest of the year. The noonday sun bounced its unrelenting rays off the boat's aluminum hull. I squinted past the gleam in my eyes and focused on the heat rising from the windless water.

A flock of pelicans crossed in front of me, their huge wings rising and falling in perfect harmony. I thought of Lisa and our times together in the marsh behind The Garhole Bar, studying the birds. I pictured her smile and her innocence, a child without a father. With a mother who was more interested in nightlife than her daughter.

Then I saw myself at sixteen, sitting on the dock waiting for the sunrise—hoping a fisherman would come along so I wouldn't be alone. I turned the boat back toward shore and pushed the throttle down hard to full speed.

Chapter Thirty-Nine
Friday, September 2

I had always been fond of Harry Stein. A success story deserved respect. Harry had grown up in the projects by the docks and worked his way up from nothing to become the island's premier attorney and President of the Galveston Historical Society to boot. Harry cared about the community and its people. He probably did more pro bono work than any lawyer in town.

When I learned Janie was pregnant, I turned to Harry for help. Janie Whitten, the daughter of a society queen. Harry met with Janie's mother and convinced her I was an honorable boy—a good person. He told her I would be a good father, and I would care for Janie and the baby.

Janie's mother wanted to send her to a home for unwed mothers and give the baby up for adoption. Harry convinced her otherwise. Let them get married, he urged. It was the best solution.

Harry bounded into the reception area, hand extended.

"Parker! Good to see you. Missed you at the party. But then you're not quite eligible for the Dead Pecker's Club, are you?"

I laughed. "Some days I feel like it."

He gave me a bear hug, then stepped back. "Well, it's official. We've got another storm out there."

"Really?"

"Yeah, they just announced it—Hurricane Dorothy. Two hundred miles south of Haiti heading westward toward the Yucatan Peninsula. Sure hope it stays out of the Gulf."

"Yeah, me too." I said, averting my eyes. I really wasn't sure how I felt now. Only a few days ago, I had thought a class five storm may be just what I needed. Wipe me out completely. Get me the hell out of here. But now, with Claire...

Harry waved me into his office, gesturing toward a large leather chair that fronted his desk. I sat down and Harry moved around the back of the desk to his chair. Then he leaned toward me and said, "Can you believe Bully found all that rum?"

I grinned, "Yeah, and on my own property, too." We both laughed. Then, I turned serious, "Listen, Harry. I need your help."

When I said that, I saw the concern of an old friend in Harry's eyes.

"Sure, Parker, anything," he said. He opened a drawer and retrieved a pencil and yellow tablet.

"No need for that," I said, nodding to the pen and paper. "I just need to ask you a few questions."

Harry shoved the pad aside and folded his hands. "You look disturbed, Parker. How can I help you?"

Good old Harry. Get right to the meat of it. I moved to the edge of my chair, eyes focused, and said, "Tell me about this Strauss character."

"Uh, oh!" Harry exclaimed, leaning back. He shook his head and exhaled slowly. After a moment, he straightened, his face somber, professional. "I referred him to Bully. I thought he could make a few harmless bucks. Hope I didn't screw up."

"No, no," I said, quickly giving Harry a dismissive wave of my hand. "It's nothing you did. When Bully took him treasure hunting, Strauss got upset because they hadn't found anything. He accused you and Bully of teaming up to fleece him. Bully blew his top and made him walk back to town."

Harry slammed the desk. "I love it!" he yelled. "Bully made him take a hike, huh? Great! The guy's a jerk, Parker. The second time he was here I couldn't stand him either."

"The second time?"

"Yeah, I've met with him twice," Harry said. "The first time he said he wanted information about German immigrants in Galveston. Said he was writing a series of articles."

"Bully said he was a writer."

"That's what he told me," Harry responded. "He claimed he represented some German magazine. Came here to do research."

"What do German immigrants have to do with buried treasure?"

"Good question. But, the gold thing didn't come up until later. When he got to the office, he seemed more interested in the POW camp at Fort Crockett during the war than he was with the immigrants. We had lunch on the seawall across from the old fort. I told him all I knew."

"Now I'm really confused," I said.

"I know what you mean," Harry added. "It is confusing. He said he wanted to use the POW angle as a sidebar to the immigrant story. He wanted to know if any of the POW's ever escaped. I told him I would research it."

"What did you find out?"

"I found out one of the prisoners did escape, but he was recaptured."

"What's that all about?" I asked.

"Who knows?" Harry said, waving his arms in front of him. "And then, a couple days later, he came in wanting to know about buried Civil War gold."

I straightened in the chair and cocked my head. "He switched from German immigrants to the POW camp to buried Civil War gold?"

"Yes. He said I had mentioned it to him during his first visit and he thought it would be a better story. You know how I am, Parker. I probably rattled off lots of stories about Galveston. No telling what all I told him. Anyway, he said he had researched the subject after our conversation, and he thought the story was true. He seemed convinced that at least one German merchant buried gold when the Yankees captured Galveston."

"That story has been around for years, Harry. You're an expert on Galveston history, what do you think about that?"

"Maybe some was buried then, but the federals were here such a short time that..."

I cut him off in mid-sentence. "Surely they dug it up again right after the Yankees left."

"Exactly," he added.

My head swirled. German immigrants—Fort Crocket—escaped POWs—Civil War gold. "What the hell is going on, Harry?"

"I wish I knew," Harry replied. "You worried about Bully blowing up at him?"

"No, that's not really any of my business. Bully can take care of himself."

"Well, what then?" Harry asked.

I hesitated. "It's...it's about Lisa. Bully says she likes the guy. And Lisa, well....She's not exactly in a place where..."

"Oh hell, Parker," Harry interrupted. "I am sorry."

Chapter Forty
Friday, September 2

Following the blow-up with Bully, Alec spent the next night searching the same mosquito infested areas he and Bully had covered. More time wasted.

After spending the morning massaging sore muscles and scratching bumps on his arms, he realized he desperately needed Bully's help. His mind focused on a plan.

Full tables and the sound of smashing pool balls greeted Strauss as he entered The Eight Ball. A screaming country western song blared across the room, overpowering the mumbling voices of the players and hangers-on. Orange smoke hung like sulfured clouds below the table lights.

A razor-thin kid about twenty made change for a customer while talking through a cigarette. When he turned, Alec followed him across the room. He spoke to the kid's back. "Hey, man. I'm looking for Denny Sader. Is he around?"

The kid didn't answer. This was Sader's home turf, Alec thought. Surely, the kid knew him. Alec stepped in front and blocked the kid's path, towering over him.

"Did you hear me?" Alec said, squeezing the boy's shoulder.

The kid stopped, his eyes focused straight ahead, never above the level of Alec's shoulder. He said, "Yeah, uh, okay but..."

Alec removed his hand and said, "It's all right, man. I'm not a cop."

The boy glanced around nervously and nodded across the room. "That's him. The tall one at the table in the corner."

Alec studied Sader as he edged across the room. He noted the greasy hair and pocked face. He thought they were about the same height, but Alec guessed he had at least a hundred pounds on him.

Alec laid two quarters close to the money plunger. "Next game," he said. He pulled a stick from the rack of pool cues on the wall and pointed it toward the light checking its shape.   Sader   moved beside him chalking his cue stick as he spoke, his voice hissing as it escaped the holes in his teeth. "This is a private game, dude. Know what I mean?"

Alec turned and replaced the stick in its holder. He took the gold doubloon he had purchased earlier at a coin shop out of his pocket and twirled it in his hand. "I'd like to talk to you outside if you got a minute. Something special."

Denny glanced at the coin, his eyes widened. "You a cop?"

"No. Lisa Stout gave me this to show you." He let Sader have another quick glance, then shoved the coin back into his pocket.

Denny dropped his cue stick on the table and followed Alec outside. They walked to the corner of the building, away from the entrance.

Denny lit a cigarette and inhaled deeply. Smoke streamed from his nose as he spoke. "Okay, man. Whassup up with this?"

Alec stepped in. "Lisa told me to tell you she wants to come back, but she's afraid of Bully."

"That right? The bitch wants to come home, huh?" Sader took another drag and blew a long column of smoke past Alec's ear. They were close now, eye to eye. "Well, who the hell are you anyway, man?"

Alec went into a long story about meeting Lisa and about searching for buried treasure with Bully and how Bully had deserted him in the middle of the night miles from town.

Denny flipped the cigarette out into the street and immediately lit another. "So what's that got to do with Lisa?" He asked. "Why you pimping for her?"

"I want to get even with Bully for dumping on me. I want to see him lose Lisa and the gold. It would serve him right, the old fool."

"Gold? What gold?" Denny responded.

"The gold he's got stashed."

"Bullshit," Denny responded. He started walking back toward the front entrance.

Alec addressed his back. "What about Bully's gold?"

Denny turned and came back a few steps. "Ha, that's a scream, man. That old bastard's always looking for pirate treasure. He's the joke of the island."

"Really? What about the gold coin? Lisa says Bully's got more, a bunch. She knows where he hides them."

"So why tell me?" Denny said, "You know all this, you go for it."

"Go for what?" Alec said. "I told you. I'm just out to get even with that fat bastard, Bully. Lisa wants you. Talked about you the whole time. She wants to get the hell out of there. Be free. Go back on the road."

"Really?" Sader said, his tone sarcastic.

"She's fed up living in that dump," Alec continued. "Figures the coins will give the two of you a good start. She says he's got a shitload of them."

"And you don't want any of them? You're just doing this for spite, right?"

Alec nodded.

"More bullshit," Denny said.

"Well, I would like a small cut. Whatever you think is fair."

"More like it," Denny said.

Bubba Shanks, the kid who was in jail with Bully, sneaked in behind Strauss. He brought a knife to Alec's back and whispered, "Head around to the side of the building. No tricks."

They shuffled to the alley, then Bubba stepped in and shoved Alec against the brick wall. Alec hit hard, off balance. Denny stepped in, flipped him around, and kneed his groin. Alec fell to the ground, feigning more damage than had been done. He moaned softly. Shanks put his shoe on Alec's neck and said, "Don't move or I'll break your neck."

Denny searched Alec for a weapon. He took the gold piece from Alec's pocket, studied it briefly, then shoved it into his jeans.

"I'll be keeping this for the time you've wasted," he said with a smirk. Then he opened Alec's wallet and studied the international driver's license. "You from Germany?"

"Yeah," Alec replied, his voice strained by the kid's shoe on his neck.

Denny motioned for Bubba to remove his foot.

Alec rubbed his neck and said, "Look, man. I'm just a writer doing a story for a German magazine. I've been hanging around The Garhole with Bully searching the island. I got to know Lisa. She confessed to me how miserable she was. Then she told me about you, and the coins, and what she wanted. I just want to get even with that asshole Stout, and maybe make a buck or two. But I don't need this shit. Let me up, and I'm outta here. You can keep the coin. I'll tell Lisa to forget it."

Alec hoped he had shown the right amount of nervousness. He could take them both now if he wanted to. It wouldn't be difficult. A quick chop to the kid's kneecap, then grab Denny's balls with one hand and shove him against the wall with the other. Easy. But not now. He would take care of Sader later. No way he would let this skinny prick get away with humiliating him.

"Let him up," Denny said.

Alec stood and brushed himself off, acting scared.

Denny waved Shanks off, ordering him back to the pool hall. After the kid left he said, "Tell me about the coins."

Alec said, "Lisa says Bully's been collecting coins and other stuff for years. She says she'll take it all. But when you come out to get her, make sure Bully's not there. She wants to leave town the same night. Says Bully won't miss the stuff for a few days. He won't think to check it."

Denny didn't say anything.

Alec continued, "We can both get even with him. Those doubloons gotta be worth some good dough. You get the gold, and...you get Lisa back."

Denny took another drag and blew the smoke into Alec's face. Alec didn't flinch. Denny smashed the cigarette with his foot and closed in, almost touching. And with eyes as cold as sleet, Sader bored into Alec's eyes and said, "So what's your plan?"

Chapter Forty-One
Friday, September 2

The message light on Alec's room phone blinked steadily. He hesitated for a moment then decided it would not hurt to listen.

Mariana Villata had left several more messages. How had she known where he was? Of course, he remembered. He had stupidly called her from his room. She must have somehow traced it through the telephone exchange in Santa Rosa de Calmuchita. Her aunt probably knew someone there. But why did she seem so desperate to connect with him? Had the old woman finally kicked off. He hoped so. Returning to Argentina for Mariana was one more ace in his hand.

He retrieved his car and headed out the West Beach road, his thoughts on Denny Sader. He cursed and pounded the steering wheel as he drove. No one had ever treated him like that, no one. Sader would pay.

His plan was working. Sader was as hooked as one of his crack smokers, the fly headed for the web. In fact, other than the shame he had to endure, the meeting with Sader had gone perfectly. Everything was proceeding nicely.

The next step was to get Lisa on his side. He knew how to do that. He had seen it in her eyes. She would do anything he asked.

He backed into a path to the beach past The Garhole Bar and waited. The lunch crowd was leaving, only two trucks left. Minutes later, when the lot emptied, he parked by the front door and went in. Lisa sat at the bar, staring out the window toward West Bay, sipping a drink with her back to him.

Alec slipped behind her, put his hands ever so softly over her eyes, and kissed her lightly on the neck. His warm breath flowed into her ear. "Guess who, my lovely?"

She turned quickly, smiling. "Alec! Oh man, I'm so glad you came." She bounced off the stool and hugged his neck. "I was freaked that you'd split after what Bully did to you."

After what Bully did? Good, Alec thought, the old man hadn't turned her. "I missed you. It's that simple," he said, pulling her closer.

"Oh, Alec. You're teasing me." She blushed and pushed him away, playfully.

He touched her cheek, then let his hand fall gently over her shoulder. He pulled her into him and felt no resistance. She tilted her head upward, staring into his eyes. He had seen the look dozens of times—the hunger, the loneliness, the incessant need for reassurance.

He spoke softly, "You are not angry with me."

"Angry? How could I be?" Lisa answered, putting her head to his chest.

"Well, about what happened between Bully and me," he whispered. "He told you, didn't he?" Alec stroked her hair and felt her heart racing against his chest.

She pushed back and twisted away, smiling. "Oh, Alec. Really! I'm not mad at you. Like, I know how Poppa can get gruffy and tired sometimes. But he is pretty bagged at you. What happened anyway?"

Alec moved to a barstool and sat down. "Oh, I said something I shouldn't have. I'm really sorry. We were out all night. I was overtired."

Lisa sat on a stool opposite him and took his hand. Alec said, "I really do appreciate what he is doing for me." He dropped his smile and slid into a poor-me face. "Would you tell him for me?"

Lisa winked and squeezed his hand. "I'll do what I can. I know how to butter him up."

"Thanks," he said. "But maybe I should just come back later and talk to him myself. Do you think he'll be around tonight?"

"Don't know. Why not just wait?" she said. "The crowd's gone, and we could talk or...something." She moved his hand around her body and drew him closer. They both stood.

Alec put his cheek to hers and felt her warmth. He smelled the powder on her skin and the freshness of her hair.

He whispered, "Lisa, you feel soooo good." He touched her blouse outside of her breast. She moaned invitingly. Then, out of nowhere, thoughts of other conquests raced through his mind. It would be so easy, but...

He pulled back slightly. Just in time, he knew. One moment longer and... He took both her hands and held them in front of him creating a space between them.

"It would be better if I came back later," he said. "Maybe at closing." He squeezed her hands and gently pushed her back. "We could take a ride to the beach."

She released her hands suddenly and broke away, nodding toward the front of the bar. "It's Parker. He just drove up."

Chapter Forty-Two
Friday, September 2

I left Harry's office more puzzled than ever about our new friend, Alec Strauss. Which was he—a desperate, neophyte writer stirring up fantasy stories, or a con artist with a game plan of some sort?

Nineteen years in Army intelligence hadn't left me paranoid for nothing. I had interrogated thousands of East German refugees trying to sort out the good from the bad, and my radar was definitely humming on this one.

When I arrived back at The Garhole, Strauss's rental car was there. I hurried through the back door, my arms filled with two paper sacks full of groceries. I sat them on the counter and walked around to where Lisa and Strauss were standing.

He was taller than me, with a lot better physique, and youth. He looked like Mr. Clean with hair. Put that together, and I knew if we ever tangled I'd need a crowbar on my side. His blond hair and blue eyes were so perfect he could have been one of the Reich's test-tube babies. The perfect master race specimen. I know it sounds stereotyped, but that's the way he looked.

Lisa said, "Hi Parker. Glad you're back."

"Put the groceries up, will you, Lisa? I'm going upstairs."

"Sure Parker," she answered.

Strauss was watching me closely, probably waiting for me to acknowledge him. I wanted to appear disinterested. No sense alerting the perp. I got the feeling he was trying to determine where he had seen me before.

He was so obvious, I couldn't let it go. I turned toward him and met his eyes. We were locked in a Daniel Boone stare-down, only he wasn't acting like the bear. Maybe he thought I was supposed to be one.

Lisa said, "Parker, this is Alec Strauss."

Strauss managed a quick hello. I nodded slightly and grumbled an acknowledgement. Lisa's voice broke my focus.

"Parker, before I forget, Claire called and said she would meet you at Guido's for dinner. But it'd have to be late because she's got some business to do first."

I cut my eyes quickly to her and acknowledged the message with a quick nod. It meant my initial confrontation with Strauss was over. I had blinked first. It was better that way, letting him think he had won the intimidation contest. And maybe he had.

I forced an accommodating tone of voice and said, "So you're the writer that's been treasure hunting with Bully, huh?"

The muscles in his face seemed to relax ever so slightly.

He said, "Yes, it is interesting. Bully seems to know a lot about Galveston treasures."

I spoke in his language, *"You are from Germany?"*

Hearing his own tongue caught him by surprise. He responded in kind. *"Yes, I am. You speak German well, Mr. McLeod. Where did you learn it?"*

"In the Army," I responded. *"I was stationed in Munich for several years. So where are you from in Germany?"*

Strauss paused at my question. His eyes narrowed slightly, a tell-tale sign of suspicion. I imagined little antennas rising out of his head. I think he realized I was after something but didn't know what.

"Freiburg," he answered, still in his language. *"It's a small village south of Stuttgart close to the French border."*

"I don't know it," I replied. *"But I spent a lot of time by the East German border before reunification. Do you know that region?"*

"No, not at all," he continued. *"I have never been to that area."*

Lisa broke in. "Hey guys, like, start talking English. I'm here too, you know."

We ignored her interruption. The game continued. I changed to English. "So what kind of writing do you do?"

"Magazine articles mostly."

"Really? Which magazine?"

I would probe as much as he would let me. Bait him. Maybe he would give me a name, something I could check.

"I'm freelance," Alec, answered. "I haven't decided which one to approach with the articles."

I nodded. "Oh, so you came all the way here to research a story you haven't sold yet. You must be pretty talented."

My sarcasm must have increased his wariness. He broke eye contact without responding and turned to Lisa.

"Nice to see you again, Lisa. I really must be going." Then, he turned back to me and offered a quick salute, *"Auf Widersehen, Herr McLeod."*

After he left, I dissected the conversation. I hadn't been subtle about pumping him. Maybe I was a little too anxious, but I wanted him to know that if he was planning something, he would have more to deal with than a crippled old man and a lonely young girl. Lisa wasn't exactly pure after two years on the road with a drug-pushing punk. But she was my cousin and the only blood relative I had left. That ought to count for something.

Chapter Forty-Three
Friday, September 2

Guido's Restaurant faces the beach on Seawall Boulevard. Patrons come from Houston for the day just to drive along the water, breathe in the clean Gulf breezes, and dine on fresh seafood.

The waiter indicated this might be the last weekend for sautéed crab. The season was almost over. When the weather cooled, oysters would replace crab as the favored dish. I ordered crab and Claire selected charcoaled shrimp, another house specialty. The meal had come and gone, and we were enjoying our second cup of coffee.

"Thanks for suggesting Guido's, Parker," Claire said. "I wasn't disappointed."

"It was good at that," I answered. "Next time we'll dine at The Garhole. I might even scrape up a white tablecloth."

Claire smiled, "Hey! Lisa told me about your culinary skills. I'm looking forward to the feast."

Our gaze drifted across the boulevard to the seawall. The wind had laid and the night was still. A couple with small children sat on a concrete bench watching the waves slip gently onto the beach. The man pointed at the moon as if explaining something. The boy and girl, each about six or seven, sat with tilted faces eagerly absorbing their father's words of wisdom.

Claire reached for my hand, squeezed it lightly, and said, "You're way out there somewhere, Parker. Want some company?"

Her question broke my thoughts. I blinked and said, "What?"

"I asked where you were. Obviously not here with me."

"I'm sorry, Claire. I was thinking about my lost daughter."

"Tell me," she said, and squeezed my hand again.

"We hadn't even given her a name. I was wondering what I would have told her about the moon.

"What do you think you would have said."

"Oh, I don't know. Maybe I would have explained how the gravitational pull of the moon created the tides."

"Really? On a night like this, sitting on that bench on the seawall, you would have lectured her on science?"

"Not a lecture, Claire. Not like that...I mean…"

"Okay, not a lecture. Is that it, then? Is that all you would have said?"

"No. I would have told her about the different phases of the moon, and…"

"And what, Parker? For goodness sake! How about the heart, Parker? The moon's effect on the heart and how for centuries young lovers have come under its spell."

When she said that, I glanced beyond her through the window. The moon had risen to a spot just above the outline of her hair. I gave her an impish grin and said, "Don't look now, Claire, but that big yellow ball is right over your head." I leaned over and kissed her on the lips. "It's like a big bunch of mistletoe, and I couldn't resist. The darn thing must be casting a spell on me now."

In the dim light of the restaurant, the freckles on her nose seemed to dance like they had the first time we met. The corners of her mouth turned upward in a slight smile.

She said, "Really, Parker. You're under a spell? I think I like that."

We ordered more coffee and bantered on about nothing for a few minutes. A young couple at the next table got up to leave. The girl, in her early twenties with long blond hair, reminded me of Lisa.

My thoughts jumped to earlier in the afternoon. I told Claire about my encounter with Strauss at The Garhole and my concerns about Lisa.

She listened patiently and said, "Is it possible you're overreacting, Parker? Maybe they really like each other."

"But Strauss is like twenty-eight or nine—maybe thirty," I said. "And she's just turned eighteen. You know what I mean?"

Claire, looking as cool as a glass of white wine, said, "Well, Parker, for every Jack there's a Jill."

I closed my eyes and exhaled slowly, trying to control my anxiety. I took a deep breath and said softly, "Damn it, Claire. Get serious, will you?"

Claire dropped the smile. "Listen, Parker. Like you said, she's eighteen. And she does have hormones after all."

"What do you mean by that?"

She put up her hands, palms up, in front of her and said, "Nothing, okay? I give. You got me."

The waiter brought our check. I pulled a money clip from my pocket all the while avoiding eye contact with Claire. I started to get up.

She reached across the table and put her hand on mine. "Easy, Parker," she said. "I'm sorry. I see how upset you are. It's just that, well—she must like the guy. Cut her some slack."

I jerked my hand back and waved it in front of me. "Cut her some slack? Bully said the same thing, only it was when I was down on her. Now you say it when I'm trying to protect her. I'm telling you, Claire, there's something strange about Strauss. He's changed his story several times. And this Civil War gold thing is a bunch of hooey." I shook my head and said, "What's he really after?"

"Sounds like a rhetorical question," Claire said.

"What do you mean by that?" The words came out rougher than I had intended, but I wasn't in the mood for games. "Be direct, damn it!"

Claire answered, her voice soft, "I only meant, why don't you check him out?"

"Check him out? How?"

"You're the intelligence expert."

I blinked again, my face contorted. "Claire, look at me. I'm a wreck. I can't sleep. This alcohol withdrawal thing is killing me. At least the booze kept my mind off the pain."

I flexed my shoulders and stretched my back, then turned back to the seawall. The couple with the children had left. I glanced around the room. Claire and I were the last ones in the restaurant. The lights in the other areas were off. The waiter stood at the far end of the room, pretending to study something in his hand. My eyes came back to Claire's. She had not moved.

"Okay, so you don't want to hear the whining."

"Exactly," she said.

I thought for a moment and said, "You're right, Claire. I am the expert. Thanks for reminding me."

I settled the bill, then excused myself and went to a payphone in the lobby.

"Marvin, it's Parker. You working tonight?"

"Yeah, I'm working," the deputy replied, chuckling into the phone. "Just finished a pizza. What do you want? The Garhole get robbed again?"

I held the phone away from my face in case Marvin's garlic breath somehow seeped through the wires. "I need a favor."

"A favor! You got your nerve, Parker. We was having a Dead Pecker's meeting out at The Garhole and you wouldn't even come in to say kiss my royal...or anything. You missed some damn good rum, too."

I was in no mood for Marvin's slam. I gritted my teeth and moved on. "It's not for me, Marvin. Listen! Bully's been hired to search for buried treasure. I want to check out the guy who hired him. Will you help me?"

Marvin screamed, "They'd better not be on somebody's property without permission. And he knows better than digging at the state park. I just hauled his ass in last week."

I ignored the outburst and said, "Harry Stein referred the man to Bully, but now he wishes he hadn't. He thinks something weird is going on and I do, too. The guy's a German citizen supposedly over here working as a writer. His name is Alec Strauss. That's about all I know about him."

"A German? Bully's working with a friggin' Kraut? I don't believe it."

"I don't have time to fool around with this, Marvin. Now damn it! Do you want to help or not?"

Marvin gave a long exhale through the phone. After he had calmed a little, he said, "Okay, okay, what do you want me to do?"

"Find out what you can—where he's staying. Check out his passport. Maybe you can find something that way."

"I'll do what I can, Parker, but I can't just pick the guy up with no cause and look at his passport."

"I'm telling you, Marvin, this is serious. I saw a car rental sticker on his car. How about calling them under some pretense and goading them into giving you his passport information."

"I can't do that. I could get into trouble if anybody found out. Anyway, Bully can take care of himself."

"Maybe," I said. "But the guy's also hitting on Lisa."

"No!" Marvin burst out. "Why didn't you say so? What'd you say the name of the rental agency was?"

A few moments later, Claire and I crossed the street to the concrete bench on the seawall and sat there quietly. She put her head on my shoulder. A patch of dark clouds wandered across the moon and hid its light. A shadow passed over us. I took it as an omen, and not a good one.

We drove to Claire's condominium. If the cloud had been a warning of something ominous ahead, at least it wasn't intended for Claire and me. I had cleared that hurdle. The good night kiss lasted until after midnight.

Chapter Forty-Four
Friday, September 2

Denny Sader and Bubba Shanks backed into a cutoff to the beach and parked behind a small dune a short way past The Garhole. Denny killed the engine and lit a cigarette, leaving the windows up to keep the mosquitoes out. The temperature in the car rose quickly. Perspiration mounted on their faces like steam from a kettle.

Denny took a deep hit off his cigarette and exhaled a putrid mixture of smoke and saliva that whistled through the holes in his teeth and spewed out. "This won't work. Too damned hot," he said, cracking the car door for air. A hoard of flying tigers roared through the opening.

"Jesus, shut the friggin' door for Christ's sake," Bubba screamed, batting the bugs around his face. "Turn on the motor and get some air in here."

Denny eased the door shut. "Can't. Don't want to attract anybody who might be behind us on the beach."

"Who the friggin' Christ would be out here this time of night?" Shanks said, wiping his face with his hand.

"Fishermen or maybe some high school kids copping a feel. Anyway, can't take a chance," Denny answered.

He glimpsed Shanks out of the corner of his eye. The kid panted heavily with quick short breaths. Grease from his hair mingled with the sweat on his forehead producing a glistening effect like the phosphorous on the gulf water behind them. What a slob, Denny thought. But it was the best he could do. He needed a lookout and Bubba, fat boy, Shanks was it.

No problem. He would grab Lisa and the coins, dump the kid, and be out of this shit-hole before Bully or anyone else knew what happened. Denny Sader hadn't come to town on a load of oyster shells.

He and Lisa would head back to California or maybe Nevada. Lisa would be his again. He squeezed his crotch and moaned softly. He turned to Shanks. "Listen kid, the last truck is leaving the bar now. Lisa will close up soon. You stay here and I'll walk in."

Shanks nodded. Denny opened the door and dropped the cigarette into the sand. He leaned back in. "And be sure to honk if a car turns into the road to the bar. Got it?"

"Yeah, I got it. Are you going to bring Lisa out to the blacktop?"

"No, I'll blink the light on the front of the bar when I'm ready. You come in and pick us up. That jerk-off Strauss was right. That fat-bastard grandfather of hers must be out treasure hunting."

A moment later, when the last pickup pulled out on FM3005 headed for Galveston, Denny knew Lisa was alone.

***

The Garhole's last customer had rambled on about a hurricane off Cuba. The Weather Bureau said it could go anywhere.

While the man talked, Lisa thought about her home. What if the storm came to Galveston? Where would she live if a hurricane wiped them out? Talk like that scared her.

Before the customer left, Lisa had him close the big shutter on the front of the bar. She waved goodbye and locked the front door. She glanced quickly around the room and decided tomorrow morning would be soon enough to sweep the floor. Business had been slow for a Friday night. She looked at the clock. It was just after ten.

She gathered the empty beer bottles off the counter and dumped them in the trashcan by the back door. Being alone sucked. She used to enjoy a few minutes by herself now and then, a relief from Parker and Bully's constant sniping at each other. But not anymore; things were different now. Now she wished they were here all the time. Especially at night.

Usually, when Poppa Bully was out treasure hunting, Parker was there. But since Parker had met Claire he was gone a lot, too. She knew they were out together again tonight, but he should have been back by now. He had promised to help her close up.

A noise! She grabbed the edge of the counter, not wanting to look around. The back door creaked on its hinges. The night wind. She exhaled, slowly.

She switched the interior light off and left through the back door, headed for the camper. The moist September air stuck to her skin like paste. Maybe she could sneak into Parker's bathroom for a quick shower before he returned. She headed up the stairs with a towel and a change of clothes.

She showered and dressed quickly and had just begun to comb her hair at Parker's bathroom mirror when a voice just outside the bathroom door said, "Hello Lisa, it's me. I'm baaack."

She froze, afraid to turn.

"I've missed you," the voice came again. Denny Sader leaned against the jam blocking the doorway.

Could she jerk past him? She made for the door, but he caught her at the waist. She kicked back, trying to hit his shin or knee and knock him off balance but Denny held tight. She screamed. Her voice bounced out to the deck and across the bay, lost in the night sky. A night heron rose from its perch on the railing outside and screeched back but got no answer.

Denny wrestled her onto the bed, staying on top, his mouth at her ear. "Why are you fighting me, bitch? We're leaving tonight like you wanted. Back to California. I've got some really good stuff for you, too."

Lisa freed an arm and reached for his hair, hoping to pull his head back. With enough strain on his neck, he might relinquish his hold. She could slip away. Race for the stairs. She grabbed a handful of hair and began to yank backwards, but he caught her wrist and pulled her arm sharply under her.

"Please, Denny. You're hurting me."

"Really? Then stop this. I'm here like you wanted."

"What? You're crazy," she said.

He let go of her wrist and slapped her hard across the face. Blood trickled from her mouth. She moaned softly and tasted a warm salty liquid on her lips. Denny unbuckled his belt. She screamed, "Denny, no! Please!"

He reached for his zipper.

A powerful forearm encircled his neck. He gagged, his breath cut off. Alec Strauss put his lips by Denny's ear and whispered, "Hello, Denny…. Surprise!"

Denny, unable to speak, struggled to break free, but the hold was too tight, too strong. He was running out of air.

Alec whispered again, "You didn't really think I would let you get away with what you did to me at the pool hall, did you? Ha!"

Alec yanked him off the bed. Denny kicked out but could find no leverage. He felt helpless at Alec's mercy. Alec dragged him across the bedroom floor to the outside deck.

At the railing, Alec flipped Denny around to face him. Before Denny could catch his breath and react, Alec placed his left hand on the back of Denny's head and his right hand on his chin and jammed his neck hard to the right until he heard it pop.

"Goodbye, you fool," Alec whispered. He raised the lifeless body and pushed it over the railing to the concrete below. The body bounced hard on the apron and settled, arms and legs twisted.

Lisa staggered from the bedroom, her hand cupping the blood dripping from her mouth. "Alec, oh Alec. What happened? Where's Denny?"

"We struggled," Alec said, acting slightly confused. "He...he fell over the railing."

She came to him. He took her in his arms and said, "Lisa, you're bleeding. Go to the bathroom and stay there until I come for you. I want to make sure it is safe. I'm going downstairs to check on Sader."

Alec hurriedly rifled Denny's pockets for the coin Denny had taken earlier. He didn't bother to check Denny's pulse. He knew he was dead when he went over the railing.

He rushed to the trailer and grabbed the coins from Bully's secret hiding place under the window. Things looked good. Sader was dead, and Lisa thought he had saved her. Perfect. He had Bully's gold coins, and soon would he would have the rest of the Nazi money and gold.

Nothing like precision planning. He had arrived earlier and parked down the road that led to the oak motte. He watched Sader and Shanks arrive and pull into the side road just past the entrance to The Garhole. When he saw Denny leave the car, he ran quickly through the salt grass and got to The Garhole in time to see Lisa going upstairs. He waited for Denny and followed him up to the bedroom.

Now he was back at Denny's car, approaching it from behind. He ripped the door open, yanked Bubba Shanks out and shoved him against the car. He slapped him hard twice and kneed him in the groin. Bubba groaned and went limp.

"How did that feel, fatso? You want some more?"

Shanks moaned again managing a weak, "No, no, please, no more."

Alec pushed him up against the door. He forced his forearm under the kid's neck. "Denny's dead," he said. "You want part of this, or do you want to get the hell out of here? Your choice!"

"I'm...I'm gone," Shanks said, barely able to speak.

Alec pushed him into the front seat and within seconds, Shanks started the engine and roared off down the blacktop toward the city.

Alec hurried back to his car and rushed it quickly to the parking area.

Lisa sat on a barstool with her head in her hands. When Alec came in, she ran and threw her arms around him. "Oh, Alec. Is he...dead?"

"Yes."

"You saved me, Alec. You saved my life."

Alec brushed her hair back and tilted her face to meet his. "It's okay Lisa, it's okay. I'm just so thankful I was here in time."

"I wish Bully or Parker were here," Lisa said. "I don't know what to do!"

They both turned at the sound of a police car wailing in the distance. It seemed to be slowing as if turning onto the road to The Garhole.

"You called the police?" Alec said, surprised. "I told you to stay upstairs."

"Yes," she said, "911. You were gone so long!"

This was not part of the plan. Alec knew they would have to call the police, but he had wanted to talk to Lisa first. "Quick, Lisa. What did you tell them?"

"That a man was dead and to hurry."

"That's all? Did you tell them I did it?"

"No, I told you what I said. What's wrong Alec?"

"You must help me," he said.

"Help you? Of course Alec, anything."

Alec told Lisa what he wanted her to say. Time was short. The deputy had banged on the front door and was coming around the side. So far, so good, he thought. If only Lisa would cooperate.

Chapter Forty-Five
Saturday, September 3

After leaving Claire last night, I had planned to get my tired bones out of bed early and jog on the beach. But then I saw the flashing emergency lights at The Garhole and the night dragged on. I finally dozed off about four in the morning after Marvin Klaus and the county coroner left, and Lisa and Bully had gone to bed.

My eyes had barely closed when the morning sun forced them open again. I rolled out of bed, probing the area below my right rib cage as I stumbled toward the bathroom.

So my liver was supposed to be twice its normal size, huh? Well, I couldn't feel it. Colonel Kennon had said to quit alcohol and start exercising 'or else'. Right now, I thought 'or else' didn't sound too bad. I hadn't counted the hours since my last drink, but it felt like a year or maybe a minute. The musty aroma of oaken barrels hung in my olfactory senses, a constant invitation to return to the bottle.

I splashed cold water on my face, then slipped into a pair of shorts and headed down to check on Lisa. At the bottom of the stairs, Bully shouted and waved me into the bar.

He sat at an end stool protected by four empty beer bottles on the counter. "I'm telling you Parker, Strauss saved Lisa's life." Bully's voice echoed across the empty room. "And by God, I'm just glad he was here to do it."

By God all right, I thought. By God, I needed a drink, and Bully slugging down one beer after another didn't help much. I had looked forward to exercising this morning, not continuing the lecture Bully had started last night. But between the pain in my joints and Bully's sudden turnaround attitude toward Strauss, all I wanted now was to go outside, lean over the dock, and throw up.

Yesterday, Bully was ranting about Alec Strauss, the loser. Now, he was praising him for saving Lisa. I wanted to put my hands over my ears.

"That bastard Sader came for Lisa again," Bully said. "No tellin' what he would have done to her."

"Bully, calm down," I interjected. "I was here last night, remember? I heard what Lisa told Marvin Klaus. She was struggling with Denny at the edge of the deck when Strauss showed up down below and yelled at them. Sader got distracted and fell over the railing."

"So? He saved Lisa's life." The tone in his voice was final, no room for speculation.

I tried anyway. "What was Strauss doing here, showing up at that time of night?"

Bully stopped drinking long enough to light the stub of last night's cigar. The stench from the stale tobacco mixed with the smoke and wafted toward the ceiling. I thought I saw the gar-head gag.

"Lisa said he'd been here earlier. Wanted to apologize to me. Said he'd be back later to see me."

"How convenient," I smirked.

"Think what you want, Parker. Marvin believed them. The coroner believed them. They told Lisa not to worry about anything. Poor girl, she's worn out—still asleep. I just wish I'd been here when Sader showed up. The bastard got what he deserved."

I couldn't argue with that, no matter what had happened. I had doubts about the story, but this wasn't the time to discuss them with Bully. It was best to let it go.

My years in Army intelligence had taught me to trust my instincts, and they were telling me something was not right. I had interrogated hundreds of East German agents who had infiltrated into Berlin and West Germany. I had more training and experience questioning witnesses than Deputy Klaus and half the Galveston Sheriff's Office combined.

Lisa had seemed overly nervous when she related her story. She kept looking back at Strauss as if for reassurance. Had she been prompted? Strauss was cool—too cool. He had just seen a man fall over a railing and break his neck, and he was not the least bit ruffled.

Exercise would have to come later. I was out of the mood for it now, anyway. I wanted to call Klaus, but I needed to get Bully out of the bar. I walked to the back door, peeked out toward the trailer, and then returned to where Bully was sitting.

"Bully, have you checked on Lisa lately? I haven't heard a peep out of her all morning."

Bully looked up. "You're right, Parker. I ain't neither. I'll go see." He finished the last of his beer, slipped off the stool and headed toward the trailer. I grabbed the telephone.

"Damn it, Parker. Couldn't you have waited 'till I got some sleep? I've been up half the damn night. Holy cow!"

"Sorry, Marvin. It's important. What do you and the coroner think about Strauss and Lisa's statements?"

"What do you mean what do we think? Why wouldn't we believe Lisa? That jerk-off Denny Sader had already kidnapped her once. Good riddance is what we think. Now let me get some sleep."

"Is the coroner doing an autopsy?"

"Autopsy? Hell no. The coroner said it was obvious the asshole's neck was broken, and we have a witness to the fall."

I had one more question. "So how did Sader get out to The Garhole, and where's his car?"

273

"We think he had an accomplice who took off when he heard my siren."

"So why didn't Lisa or Alec see the accomplice?"

"We found some recent tire tracks in a cutoff down from The Garhole. He was probably waiting there."

"Any idea who that was?"

"No, but we're looking for Sader's car. It'll turn up."

"Check The Eight Ball. Bully said there was a big white kid that took him off Sader when Bully had him down. He thinks he was Sader's gofer."

"Okay, we'll check it out," Marvin replied, his tone hurried. "Is that all?"

I ignored the last comment. "Did you check on Alec Strauss like I asked you?"

"Just got a call. Some other fool trying to keep me awake. I called the car rental agency last night and badgered the night clerk into giving me his passport number. Hope I don't get fired over it. Only thing we've found out so far is there's no such number."

"No number? How could that be?"

"Hell, I don't know," Marvin, said. "Probably some snafu at Immigration. I'll find Strauss later and ask him about it."

Marvin slammed the phone in my ear. I sat at the counter and considered my next step, my mind clouded by lack of sleep and alcohol withdrawal. I needed a drink. I had moved the last bottle from my room to the downstairs bar to keep it from being so handy. I stared at the bottle under the counter, a short reach away.

I stepped to the back door again and studied the railing Denny Sader had fallen over. Sader wasn't a huge man, but he was much larger and stronger than Lisa. He could have handled her easily. Falling over the railing? I didn't think so.

I wanted to ask Lisa about her story, but I wouldn't wake her. Bully hadn't come back from the trailer, so I figured they were both asleep now.

The morning fishermen would be in soon. I had forgotten to stop for groceries last night. I checked the refrigerator, then the freezer—nothing but frozen shrimp. I grabbed some onions out of the basket on the floor and started chopping.

Maybe I should find Strauss and interrogate him myself. My old boss, Colonel Moore, had taught me the tricks of the trade. We had made a fine team together from Munich to Kuwait City. Our finest coup had been questioning a captured Iraqi officer who had disclosed the position of a Scud Missile launcher enabling the Air Force to take it out. I made Major over that one.

Colonel Patrick Moore—friend and team mate—still on active duty. Wait a minute, I thought. Of course, that's what I could do—call the Colonel.

I heated oil in the skillet, added shrimp and onions, and started the rice. I reached for the telephone and called Information in Washington D.C. Saturday morning, Moore should be home.

After exchanging a few pleasantries about family and friends, I said, "Pat, I need your help. Some family business down here."

I explained the situation and then said, "Our local Sheriff's department can't find a record of a passport entry. Can you check it out for me?"

"I don't know, Parker. It's not official Army business," Colonel Moore replied.

I pushed. "Pat, why would an innocent man lie to me? He said he was from southern Germany, but his accent was definitely East German. Yet he claimed he'd never been to that area."

"You could tell that?"

"Are you kidding? It's like comparing the Bronx to East Texas. We trained for an attack from East Germany. Remember? We had to be able to distinguish exactly what region a suspect was from."

"You're sure, huh?" Moore questioned.

I chuckled. "Pat, during the Gulf War, I couldn't tell you the country a man was from. But in Germany, you give me a city and I can tell you what block the guy was reared on."

"Too bad the Army lost you," Colonel Moore offered.

"They didn't lose me. I lost them, remember?"

Moore didn't reply so I said, "Pat, I wouldn't ask if there were any other way. Use some of the back channels."

I waited. Sometimes silence was the best pressure. Finally, after a few seconds of delay, Moore answered. "Okay, Parker. I'll do what I can."

Chapter Forty-Six
Saturday, September 3

Bully sat at the back counter blowing smoke up through the gar-head hanging from the ceiling. He enjoyed the game. The thin, gray cloud entered the monster's elongated jaws coating rows of razor-like teeth with yellow stench as it roamed steadily upward, searching for escape. The final exit came through the hollowed eye sockets at the top of the head. Cheap entertainment.

After his early morning encounter with Parker, he had slept most of the day. Then, late in the afternoon, Parker rousted him, banging on the trailer door. Parker said he needed someone to run the bar so he could go into town. It was either him or Lisa, and she was still out cold from last night's trauma.

He stuck the cigar back in his mouth and reached down to release his wooden leg. It hit the floor with a thump. He massaged the sore end of his stump thinking more than his leg hurt. The tight pains in his chest had returned. It was as if a vise had closed, squeezing breath from his lungs.

He thought about Lisa inside the trailer, tucked safely into a fetal position wrapped in a blanket. If only he had come back earlier last night. But who would have thought Sader would return to The Garhole? Bully was sure he had taught him a lesson at the pool hall.

Thanks to Alec Strauss, Lisa was okay and that was all that mattered. It irritated Bully that Parker couldn't see that. And why was Parker so fired up against Strauss anyway? Ever since Lisa's return, Parker had ignored her, treated her as if she didn't exist. Now he cared?

Bully blew another puff directly at the gar-head and said, "So what did you see?" The long jaw glared back at him.

He rubbed the stump again and massaged his chest, then popped another pill. Getting to be a habit, he thought. A pain, then a pill. More and more frequent. Maybe he should quit, take it easy, give up the ghost on treasure hunting. Sixty years was enough. He would have to figure out some other way to help Lisa. She said she wanted to go back to school, maybe even college. But that took money.

He raised the patch over his eye, rubbed the itching socket and considered his options. It took all his Army disability pay just to keep the old truck running and pick up a few groceries. Right now, Alec Strauss was the only source of cash he had. Maybe he shouldn't have lost it with him.

He looked out toward the parking lot. Where were the fishermen? Not a single customer since Parker left. He turned to see Lisa stumbling in.

"You feeling okay, honey?"

Lisa rubbed her eyes and reached into the cooler for a Coke. "Yeah, Poppa. I'm okay. What time is it?"

"Don't know, honey, but it's late. There's some shrimp on the stove if you're hungry."

She mumbled something unintelligible, slopped some shrimp onto a plate, and ambled out to the dock. He knew she was probably still in shock from last night, so he let her go without pushing the conversation.

He reattached his leg, walked to the front bar, and gazed out toward the highway. Not a car in sight. Screw it! He would close early. Parker would never know. He was gone for the night anyway.

Just then, Bully saw Alec's car coming down the sand road. He pulled into the parking lot and entered the front door.

"Hello, Bully. I came back to check on Lisa. How is she?"

"She seems okay. She slept all day, but she's up now."

When Alec got closer, Bully extended his hand. "Glad you came, Alec. I wanted to thank you for last night. You saved Lisa."

Alec grasped Bully's hand and held it. "Well, I just felt fortunate to be here. No telling what that Sader character might have done."

Bully shook his head. "You're right, I shoulda been here."

"Listen, Bully, I want to apologize for what I said the other night."

"Forget it, you saved Lisa," Bully said, waving his hand in dismissal. "I owe you. You still wanna look for that gold?"

"You mean tonight? Do you feel up to it?"

"Yeah, I'll be fine."

"Well, yes, sure. That sounds great, but I do want to see Lisa before we go."

Bully directed him to the back patio. Alec walked around the chalk outline of Sader's body drawn on the cement. Lisa sat on a bench watching the sun fade into the haze just above the horizon.

"Hello, Lisa," Alec said, approaching her back.

She turned suddenly, then stood and rushed into Alec's arms. "Oh, Alec. I'm so glad you're here."

"It's okay, Lisa. It's all over now. You're safe."

"I can't believe it happened," Lisa said, holding onto Alec, staring at the outline of Sader's body on the concrete. "Denny's really dead."

They sat together on the bench as the night shadows covered the bay. Neither spoke for a few moments, then Lisa took Alec's hand and turned to him. "Alec, I'm really confused. I don't understand. You saved me. Why did you want me to tell Deputy Klaus that you were downstairs when Denny fell over the railing?"

Alec had anticipated the question. Lisa wasn't the smartest dumpling in the pot, but she seemed bothered by not telling the truth. He hoped the next lie would work. He put his arm around her shoulder and pulled her close.

"Lisa, before I left Germany, I hurt a man badly. My mother's boyfriend. He got drunk and hit her. I told him if he ever did it again, I would kill him."

"Did you?" Lisa asked, her voice soft, trusting.

"No, but I beat him badly. He was an evil man, Lisa, an ex-Russian border guard." To Alec, the phrase, *"Russian border guard,"* was like accusing the devil himself, but Lisa didn't seem to react to it in the same way.

She squeezed his hand and leaned against his chest. "If he hurt your mother, I'm glad you did it."

"Last night, I was afraid if we told the police I was with Denny when he fell over the railing, they would run a check on me. And with the violence in my background, I was afraid it would cause trouble."

"Alec, Deputy Klaus is a friend of Bully's. It would have been okay."

"Maybe, but police in my country do not like foreigners. I thought it was the same here. I was afraid they would send me back to Germany, and I do not want to leave...you." He kissed her cheek and pulled her close.

"Oh, Alec."

He wiped a tear from her eye. "Anyway, we can not tell them now. Changing our story would look too suspicious. It is all over anyway. Let us just keep it like it is and not tell anyone."

"Not even Bully or Parker?"

"Not even Bully or Parker. If they found out you lied, well...it would hurt them too much."

Lisa pressed against his chest. He felt her heartbeat quicken. Was she apprehensive about being disloyal to Bully and Parker or just excited about being close to him. Could he trust her?

***

Bully loaded his pickup with propane lanterns, shovels, iron rods, a sledgehammer, and his gold finder.

"Got everything?" Alec asked.

"Yeah. Need some gold now," Bully replied.

"Let's go back to the old Schindler place," Alec said, as they pulled out of the parking lot. "I want to check around that old corral again."

"Okay, Alec," Bully answered, shaking his head. "But I told you that corral wasn't there during the Civil War."

"Well....Do you have another place in mind?"

"No, not yet," Bully answered. "I ain't had time to think on it."

Alec considered the options. He sure didn't want to go back to the Boehm Ranch where he and Bully had argued. Plus, they had searched it pretty well anyway. The Schindler ranch seemed like the best bet.

With the moon at its fullest, and the night as clear as freshly-cleaned glass, they roared off in Bully's old pickup, spitting smoke and dreaming of gold.

They worked hard through the night, each with his own agenda, sweating and fighting mosquitoes, probing and digging, their search occasionally interrupted by the hoot of an indignant barn owl screeching across the barren marsh.

Chapter Forty-Seven
Sunday, September 4

Lisa shouted from the bottom of the stairs, "Parker! You got a call, long distance."

I rolled over and looked at the clock—6:00 AM. The image of a scotch bottle jumped across my mind. Seventy-two hours without booze. My headache had cleared, but the joint pain lingered on. I moved my hand up and massaged my shoulder.

Lisa called again from halfway up the stairs, "Parker, did you hear me? Telephone! Do you want to take this call or not?"

I didn't respond. Lying there half-awake, I was thinking about the strange relationship between Bully and Strauss. They were big buddies again. It didn't make sense. Were my suspicions unfounded—alcohol induced paranoia? I shook my head to clear it and started downstairs to the telephone.

"Yeah, McLeod here."

"It's Pat. We ran the check. There is no Alec Strauss."

"What?"

"No one named Alec Strauss has legally entered this country in the past six months. We're attempting to track the name through

German authorities, but we need more to go on. Got a home address or anything?"

As Moore spoke, I guzzled a bottle of water from the refrigerator. The cold went straight to my sinuses, and a sharp pain shot across my forehead. I massaged the spot just over my eyebrow attempting to chase the pain away.

"Parker, are you there?" Moore asked.

"Yeah, yeah, Pat. I'm here," I answered, still rubbing my forehead. "I don't get it. He does have a passport in that name. We got the number from the car rental agency."

Moore responded, shock in his voice. "Parker, we've had this discussion before. You can't go nosing around like that without authority. You're invading the man's privacy."

"I didn't do it, Pat. The sheriff did."

"Oh, Jesus. Even worse. What kind of law enforcement do you have down there?"

"He took a chance," I answered. "He's known Lisa since she was born." Growing tired of Moore's chastising, I said, "Listen Pat, I don't have time for protocol. I need your help. Are you with me on this or not?"

While waiting for the answer, my eyes fell on a small scar in the palm of my hand. The Gulf War. I was in a tent with Colonel Moore, the temperature well over a hundred. Sweat poured from our bodies and flies hovered everywhere.

A long line of foul-smelling prisoners were lined up for interrogation. They had surrendered in mass, leaving no time for a thorough search. One pulled a knife and was almost on Moore when I intercepted him, taking the knife blade in my hand.

Thankfully, I only needed a few stitches, but Moore ranted that I had saved his life. He insisted on putting me in for a Purple Heart. I laughed it off.

I closed my fist and felt the scar tissue tighten. I hoped I didn't have to call that chip in, but I would for Lisa.

More silence. Finally, Moore spoke. "Sorry Parker. Of course I'm with you."

I sighed silently.

Moore continued, "Something's going on, all right. Either he sneaked into the country or he has another passport. I'm calling in the FBI."

I considered Moore's analysis. The FBI might be the smart way to go, but then Bully and Lisa believed Strauss. Maybe I should just trust their instincts and back off. Maybe there was a mix-up at Immigration as Marvin suggested. All I really knew at this point was that he was might be using a phony name and that he had lied about where he was from. I needed more facts.

"No, please Patrick, it's a personal matter. Do what you can on the sly, but..."

Pat cut in, "Parker, make up your mind. You want my help or not?"

He was right of course. My indecision was shining through. I'd hate to hear a tape replay of the last few minutes.

I firmed my voice. "Yes, I want your help. Just give me a few hours. I'll get back to you soon." I terminated the call and moved to the back door.

Lisa stood on the edge of the dock throwing the cast net out for shrimp. She held the center ring with her left hand, grabbed one side of the inner edge with her teeth and the outer edge with her right hand. Then, with a high arc, just as I had taught her years ago, she twirled it out into the water.

Each movement accentuated her body. Full breasts and mature hips. She was a woman now. Where had the time gone? I visualized her at ten, giggling and laughing, learning to throw the net.

She tossed the net again, let it sink for a moment, then pulled the cord to tighten the draw strings. She raised the net onto the dock, dropped the bottom into a washtub, and released the strings. Shrimp jumped from the tub. Lisa bent over, picked up the loose ones that had escaped, and dropped them back into the washtub.

Maybe I should talk to her now. Tell her about the phony passport. Would she believe me? Maybe, maybe not.

Instead of talking to Lisa, I called Marvin Klaus again and got the same answer—nothing new on Strauss. I needed more facts before I confronted Lisa and Bully. Klaus gave me Strauss's home address from the passport, and I called it in to Colonel Moore.

Minutes later, I was rolling down FM3005 toward the city. Once in town, I turned off Seawall Boulevard onto Rosenberg Avenue and headed toward the Strand. Sunday morning was a good time to be in downtown Galveston. Except for an occasional homeless person stumbling to life from a back alley, the streets were deserted.

I circled the Tremont Hotel looking for Strauss's rental car. No luck. Either Strauss was not there or the car was in the hotel's parking garage. I entered the lobby through a side door, hoping not to run into Strauss in the lobby. Fortunately, Bully's friend Neddie Lemmon was working today.

"Finally got off the dog-watch, huh, Neddie?" I said, approaching the bell-desk. Neddie looked up quickly from the morning paper. His goatee was neatly trimmed and his silver hair perfectly coiffured.

"Parker! What are you doing here?" he said, almost whispering. "It's barely light outside—way too damned early for you."

I stepped closer. "Need a favor, Neddie." I explained what I wanted.

"Can't do it, Parker," Neddie answered nervously, glancing to both sides as he spoke. "It'd mean my job."

I leaned in and spoke softly, "Neddie, how many free lunches have you had at The Garhole? Plenty, right? I'll bet Lisa even threw in a beer or two."

Neddie stammered. Light from the desk lamp reflected off his nose, exaggerating the redness.

My voice rose, "Damn it, Neddie!"

Neddie put his palms out indicating he wanted me to lower my voice. "Okay, okay," he said. "Is your man tall, German type, blond hair, blue eyes, well built?"

"Sounds like him."

"I helped check him in. Didn't tip a damned nickel. Cheap bastard. He's got the meanest eyes I've seen. Looks like a cat ready to pounce. He's serious about something."

"Yeah, serious about doing something with Lisa." Mentioning Lisa had worked with Marvin Klaus. I figured it would work with another Dead Pecker member.

"What?"

"Lisa."

"No."

"Yes.

"Damn! Why didn't you say so? He just left the hotel. I sent him for breakfast to a Mexican restaurant off Twenty-Fifth Street across from the police station. It's about four blocks up. He ought to be gone at least thirty minutes, but let me call his room to make sure he didn't come back through the side door."

I emerged from the elevator with a master key in my pocket and opened the door to a pitch-black room. The room phone blinked incessantly. I picked up the handset and listened to the messages, the newest one only an hour old. All from the same woman, Mariana. She sounded like a looker, damned sexy voice. Wanted someone named Günter to call. Was Günter Alec Strauss? Or did Strauss have a confederate in this madness? Strauss was from Germany, but she had called from Argentina. If Strauss was this Günter, the bastard did get around.

I searched Strauss's room and found nothing—not one piece of identification that would indicate the German's real identity. No laundry marks or monograms, nothing in the bathroom but normal toilet articles. No briefcase or papers of any kind—a sterile environment. It was almost as if the occupant had been trained in intelligence work. I couldn't have done a better job myself of being a non-existent person. It was too perfect.

The phone rang—a signal Strauss had returned and was in the lobby. I left quickly, careful to leave everything exactly as it was. I exited down the stairs and out the back of the hotel through the emergency door.

I eased my truck into the narrow entrance of the hotel's garage and parked next to Strauss's car. The garage seemed deserted. I shattered the car's side window. The towel absorbed much of the noise, but pieces of glass covered the seat.

I checked under the seats and rifled the glove compartment—no passport. Nothing but the car rental papers in Alec Strauss's name and a Texas map.

I popped the trunk. Empty. As a last effort, I pulled the spare tire from the wheel well and stared at the empty hole in the frame. As I rolled the tire back into the well, a cloth bag appeared taped to the bottom side of the tire.

I removed a small key from the bag and turned it over in my hand. No. 1019. Where had I seen a key like this one? A safe? Strauss wouldn't have a safe. A safety-deposit box? No. Not that type of key. A locker! Sure, a locker key. But wait, there are no lockers at the airport now—too much of a security risk. Someone could rig a bomb in one.

I replaced the tire in the well, shut the trunk lid and left as quietly as possible. The only lockers I could think of were at the Galveston Bus Station four blocks away.

I arrived at the station and checked the timetable. The bus for Houston had just left and there was nothing else scheduled until after lunch. The ticket agent appeared busy with paperwork, and outside a lone maintenance man swept the driveway.

The key fit in 1019. I removed a manila envelope, shut the locker and eased into the restroom. Bonanza! I couldn't believe my luck— a German driver's license, credit card, and passport. All in the name of Günter Manfred.

I copied the contents at a pay machine in the terminal and then carefully returned the envelope to the locker. I went back to the parking garage, replaced the key on the tire, and proceeded to break out the windows of two additional cars. Just another routine theft in Galveston.

On the return trip down West Beach, I had but one recurring thought - Günter Manfred? Who the hell was this guy?

Chapter Forty-Eight
Sunday, September 4

I noticed Bully's truck at The Garhole, but the boat was gone. The empty camper indicated both he and Lisa were out in the bay, probably running the crab traps.

I picked up the phone and dialed Colonel Moore's number. "Patrick. It's me, Parker."

"Parker, I'm glad you called," Moore replied. "You guys worried about the storm?"

Absorbed with what I had learned about Strauss, the question caught me off guard.

"Storm?"

"Yes, Hurricane Dorothy. It's turned north. Should break into the Gulf tomorrow."

"Really? Well, it's still days off. I've got a bigger tempest brewing here."

"Yeah, and it's not in a teapot either. The address you gave me on Alec Strauss is bogus. I don't think the guy exists."

"You're right, Pat, he doesn't. I found his real passport. Check out this name—Günter Manfred." I took a minute to communicate his address and passport number.

"Parker, we really need to check this guy out. Something's going down. Let me call the FBI."

"Just a little more time, Pat. Give me that."

I could almost see the Colonel fidgeting in his chair, nervous about going against regulations. Before Moore could speak, I continued, "Call our old unit in Germany, Pat. See what they can come up with."

More silence. Finally, Moore's voice returned. "Parker, if this backfires on us..."

"I can handle it, Pat. I'm a pro, remember."

"Okay, Parker. I'll get back to you as soon as I can on the new name. But listen. For God's sake, be careful. This guy's had some training somewhere. It's the old two-passport trick, the real one to get in and out of the country without suspicion, and another one so no one will know where he is and what he's doing. How did you get the real one?"

"I found a key to a bus station locker in his car."

"You searched his car! Was it unlocked?"

"Not exactly."

"Parker! You're going to get me into a shit-load of trouble."

"We've been there before, Pat."

"Yeah, but I'm still on active duty. You're not."

I added a touch of disdain to my voice. "Don't worry Colonel. I'll keep you out of it."

"Damn it, Parker. Don't say it like that. We've been through too much together."

"Sorry, Pat. I just don't have much time on this."

"Okay, okay. Was there anything else in his car?"

"Just the car rental papers."

"Nothing else?"

"No....Oh, yeah. A Texas map."

"Had the map been used?"

"Used?"

"Yeah, like opened or anything?"

"No.... Wait a minute. It was open, folded to...folded to...a section of the state west of Austin."

"West of Austin?"

"Yeah."

"Why there?"

"Who knows?" I answered. "The only decent size town in that area is Fredericksburg."

"Fredericksburg? What's in Fredericksburg?" Colonel Moore asked.

"Well, I went there once when I was stationed at Fort Sam in San Antonio. There's the Admiral Nimitz museum and a bunch of tourist shops and some German restaurants."

"German restaurants?"

"Yeah, the town was founded by German immigrants back in the 1840s and...hold it! That's it, Pat. Germans!"

Moore said, "Germans? You think...?"

"Yes, that has to be it. Something in Fredericksburg drew his attention. He's probably either been there already, or he's going."

Chapter Forty-Nine
Monday, September 5

After an exhausting search Saturday night, Alec slept most of the day Sunday. Monday morning the valet brought his car to the front of the hotel. "I'm sorry, Mr. Strauss. Your front window is smashed. Someone broke into several cars at the garage. Please check to see if anything is missing."

Alec quickly looked inside. "No. I didn't have anything in the car."

He drove to a deserted street, then stopped and popped the trunk switch. He lifted the spare tire out of the wheel well and checked the cloth bag. The key appeared undisturbed. The valet had said several other cars were vandalized. Still...

He drove quickly to the bus station and checked the locker. All seemed well. Close call, he thought. He couldn't afford any mistakes at this stage of the game. Bully and Lisa both trusted him now. He was close to the end. He could feel it.

He felt confident they would find the gold, and he would be out of here and back to Germany, mission accomplished. As soon as he got home, that smug bastard, Horst Frankin, had a little surprise coming. With Frankin out of the way, he would be one step closer to the top. But he wouldn't just hand over the money. He would demand more status first, maybe even a spot on the committee.

Of course, that might depend on how much money he found. And if the money was enough, why did he need them at all? Money or power? Money or power? Which? Were both possible?

Confused thoughts raced through his jumbled mind. It was as though a huge picture of the mission had suddenly turned into a puzzle, and it was breaking apart and falling around him in a thousand pieces.

And what about Mariana? A detour to Argentina might be worth it. Maybe more than a detour. She owned the *Estancia* Rosas now. It could be a good life. Money or power? Money or power? The puzzle pieces fell around him.

But there must be no loose ends here. Just find the gold and leave, right? Wrong! Bubba Shanks—a big loose end. He knew too much.

Alec drove to the pool hall only to find it closed. The sign on the door indicated it would open at noon. He drove back to the hotel and left the car with the valet. The hotel had offered to exchange his rental car. He went to his room and waited. At noon, he walked the short four blocks back to the Eight Ball. The same skinny kid he had seen before was there brushing a table. Alec dropped a twenty-dollar bill in front of him.

"Looking for the big white kid that hangs with Denny Sader. You seen him? I have some business for him."

The kid pushed the bill into his pocket. "Bubba hadn't been around here lately."

"Know where he lives? It's important," Alec said. The kid stalled. Alec leaned closer. His frame completely blocked the light from the kid's face. He put his massive hand on the kid's shoulder and whispered close to his ear.

"You have twenty dollars of my money. You want to be smart and tell me about Bubba."

The kid responded without looking up. "Two streets over to Mechanic, then straight up a block or two. On the left side, it's the first garage apartment you'll come to."

Alec decided not to wait on his car. He walked over a few blocks, then turned up Mechanic Street. The neighborhood changed from run-down commercial buildings to paint-bare houses with broken screens and doors. Black kids and multicolored dogs played in the street. The kids stopped to stare as Alec negotiated the two blocks.

He noticed Denny Sader's car parked behind the house by the garage apartment. He climbed the stairs and walked in past the open door. The radio blared heavy metal. Bubba Shanks lay passed out on the couch surrounded by empty beer bottles.

Alec slapped him hard twice and let him slide to the floor. "Get up, you dumb shit," Alec screamed. "We have some talking to do."

He yanked the kid up and shoved him back onto the couch. He started to slap him again, but the kid put his hand out in a protective gesture and hollered, "Okay, okay, I'm awake now."

"You stupid idiot. You were supposed to get rid of Sader's car. Leave it here and the cops will be questioning you soon. You want that?"

"No, No. I'll lose it."

"You know where Sader lived?" Alec asked.

"We always met at the pool hall. I'll dump the car on the other side of town."

"If the cops ever find out you were at The Garhole with Denny, you will be charged as an accomplice. Ten years in prison. No booze, no pills, no grass."

"I'll be quiet."

"You will be more that quiet! Leave town today or you are dead meat, got it?"

Alec wanted badly to finish him off now. But if they found the kid's body before he left town, the police would connect him through the kid at the pool hall. No, best to scare the hell out him.

Fear sprung from Bubba's eyes. "I got no place to go," he said.

"Dump his car and take the bus as far as this will take you."

Alec stuffed three twenties into Bubba's pocket. Then he slammed his fist into Bubba's stomach. Shanks doubled over and fell sideways on the couch. Alec pushed him to the floor, rolled him to his back, and sat astride him. He grabbed the kid's neck and began choking him. Bubba gasped for breath. His eyes bulged.

Alec released his grip. "Any questions?"

Blood spurted from Bubba's mouth. The words came out gargled. "No, no, don't worry, Alec. I'll never squeal. I'll leave town today—okay? I'm outta here."

Chapter Fifty

Monday, September 5

One thing about a little intrigue, it sharpened the mind. My brain hadn't been this active since Desert Storm. Things moved quickly now.

When Claire called, I realized the problem with Strauss had enveloped me so completely, I hadn't spoken to her at all on Sunday. The bubbling sound of her voice excited me.

"Hi, Parker! What's for lunch? I've just finished showing a property not far from you. I think I might have a sale. I feel like celebrating. If you're not busy, I'll drop by."

"Absolutely!" I said, delighted with her call. "We're having Chicken Cacciatore today. Bully and Lisa will be glad to see you."

"Only Bully and Lisa?"

"Well the rest of the Dead Peckers aren't here."

"Funniee."

She arrived a few minutes later. I hugged her close, not wanting to let go. She didn't resist at first, but then with the breath squeezed out her she pulled back, removed her sunglasses and said, "Gee, Parker. I think you missed me."

I realized how much when she said that. I nodded and said, "I'm so glad you called."

She searched my eyes for a moment and said, "What's wrong? What's going on?"

Holding her so tightly must have set off some kind of warning bell. Her intuition cooked full steam. I wanted to tell her what I had learned about Strauss. But when we last talked at Guido's restaurant, she seemed so doubtful I decided to take the easy way out and keep the information to myself until I knew more.

"Gee, Claire. Can't I just miss you?"

She gave me a wary look and said, "Okay. Keep it in then. I'm not going to play therapist today." She reached for the refrigerator door and a bottle of water, then squeezed by me and went around to a stool in front of the counter.

I waited for her to settle and said, "So you think you've got a sale working, huh?"

"Yes," she answered, smiling. "And it's a good one. One of those big three storied houses on the beach."

"Good, you can lay off trying to sell me then."

"Paaarker," she said, drawing it out. "I told you..."

I interrupted in mid-sentence, "Just kidding, Claire. You know that." I grinned and pushed a plate of chicken in front of her.

She took a bite. "This is so good, all the mushrooms and onions. What's your secret?"

"Lots of garlic," Bully answered from the back door. "And he didn't cook it, I did."

Claire smiled at Bully. "Really, I thought your specialty was duck chili."

"That too," Bully said.

We all laughed. Lisa came in behind Bully. She hugged Claire and sat at the counter beside her. Claire reached over and fluffed Lisa's ponytail.

"Your hair really looks good, Lisa. That shampoo I gave you must be doing the trick."

"Yeah, it's awesome," Lisa replied.

"And I bet your complexion has never looked better. Are you using the lotion I gave you?"

"Sure am."

Claire took Lisa's hand and said, "Lisa, you've really been through a lot since you came here. Thank God, it's over now. And I just want you to know...I'm here for you."

Lisa closed her eyes. When she spoke, a tear rolled out. "Oh, Claire. What would I do without you?"

I was happy to see Claire, but it appeared the women wanted to visit. Plus, I needed to think. I walked out to the dock and sat at the concrete table facing West Bay.

I wanted to tell Bully and Lisa what I had learned about Strauss. But did I have enough to convince them something was not right? Probably not, I concluded. The way Strauss had ingratiated himself, it was a good bet they would rationalize anything I had to say, no matter how disturbing.

Claire came out beside me. She snapped her fingers in front of my face. "Parker, where are you? Come in, earth."

"What? Oh. Sorry, Claire. How was your lunch?"

"We've already had this discussion. It was wonderful as usual. So how's the new regimen coming along? Are you feeling any better? Have you been exercising?"

"What you really want to know is—have I been boozing?"

She grinned, "Read me like a book, huh?"

"Well, the answer is, I feel like hell. I can't sleep, and I get the shakes. I'm running a little on the beach, but probably not enough to do any good."

"And?"

"And what?"

"Come on, Parker," she nudged.

"And no, I haven't had a drink since we left the doctor's office. Okay, mommy?"

We both laughed. Bully and Lisa joined us at the table. Claire said, "Parker, did you know Lisa was thinking about getting her GED?"

I turned to Lisa and smiled. "Your GED. That's wonderful. And what about after that?"

Lisa looked puzzled. "After my GED?"

Claire broke in, "I think Parker means college, Lisa."

"College? No way, I'm not that smart."

I shot back, "I think you are, Lisa. You could start with the community college in town and go from there."

"Really? You think so, Parker?"

"Yes, I do."

An awkward silence. Everyone stared at me. It was the first time I had smiled at Lisa since her return.

The telephone sounded. Lisa went inside to the bar. "Telephone for you, Parker. Colonel Somebody."

I went inside. "Hi, Patrick. Got something so soon?"

"Do you remember Sergeant Cartwright from our outfit?"

"Josh Cartwright? Sure, Master Sergeant. He retired after Iraq, right?"

"Correct. But I was telling one of the men here about your problem. Can't do all the tracking myself. Anyway, Cartwright's name came up. He was a Texas boy, remember? Well, surprise, surprise. It turns out Cartwright lives in Fredericksburg. He volunteers at the Nimitz Museum there."

"Nimitz was Navy," I said. "What's an Army man doing at a Navy museum?"

"It's a small town. They need all the help they can get."

"Think he can help me?"

"He was in our unit. Best damned intelligence outfit in Desert Storm."

"I'll call him right away, Pat. Thanks for the tip."

"You know our business, Parker. Chase every lead."

I stepped into the doorway and shouted, "Got to make a quick phone call, Claire. It'll just take a second."

I called the Museum and got lucky. Sergeant Cartwright was working. "Josh, it's me, Parker McLeod."

"Major McLeod, great to hear from you. How'd you track me down?"

"Colonel Moore told me. How have you been?"

"Good days and bad," Cartwright replied. "Eating Valium like popcorn. Can't sleep, night sweats, vision's all screwed up."

"Not getting any help?"

"Hell no, I gave up on the Army. I'm pretty close to Fort Sam in San Antonio, but they don't know shit. I still think they gassed us. You still have your problems?"

"Yeah, but I've got a new doctor at the VA in Houston. Maybe he can help. I'll get you the info."

"Worth a try."

"Josh, I've got a problem. It may sound strange and I don't know if you can help me, but...." I explained the situation then added, "I don't know what I'm asking for. I'm not even sure he went to Fredericksburg. It's just a hunch. That's all I can tell you. But he has lied to us all the way from his phony identification to the reason why he's here. I guess what I'm asking is...has anything strange, out of the ordinary, happened there recently?"

Chapter Fifty-One
Tuesday, September 6

An unusually strong northeast breeze blew my bedroom door open and awakened me from a sound sleep, my first in weeks. Had Dorothy hit during the night? No, my stirring mind convinced me it couldn't have. The door wasn't secured, that's all.

Last night's advisory had indicated the storm was still seven hundred miles southeast of Galveston. It had cleared Cuba, crossed the twenty-fifth parallel, and headed west, predicted to hit Mexico.

"Parker!"

Lisa's voice broke my thoughts. She yelled again. "Telephone for you. You sure got popular all of a sudden."

I jumped into a pair of shorts and stumbled down the stairs. "McLeod, here."

"Major, it's me, Cartwright. I checked the newspaper. It's a weekly, one of those regional jobs. Mostly local color and ads and stuff. There was nothing of interest in it, so then I called the two most logical sources of information—the sheriff and the Chamber of Commerce. The sheriff is a friend of mine. I ride with him sometimes as a volunteer. Something unusual did happen here just a few days ago."

"What?"

"A murder! First one here in years. An old German woman was killed on her farm outside of town. She was pretty much a loner, but she did talk to the mailman every day. After a couple of days not seeing her, he asked the sheriff to check. At first, they thought it was an accident. They found her at the bottom of a staircase, a real steep one. It looked as if she had tripped and fallen down the stairs."

"But she didn't?"

"No, they did an autopsy. Coroner said there's no way it was accidental."

"Why?" I asked.

"Her neck. The way it was twisted. The vertebrae completely severed. Coroner said no fall would do that. It was a set up. He said she died a very violent death. Poor woman."

"Anything unusual about the scene?"

"No. Nothing disturbed. No sign of a robbery."

"What was her name?"

"Martha Hoff. She was in her early seventies, lived by herself. Her father, Rudolph Hoff, died back in the fifties. And no one has seen the other man in several months."

"The other man? What other man?"

"Folks say another man lived there with her. I called my mother-in-law who's older than Martha Hoff. Older than dirt, actually. Anyway, she used to live out that way. Turns out she knew the Hoffs. Knew Martha and the old man. They came over from Germany in the 1930s and settled here. Martha was a young girl then."

"What about the other man?"

"Well, according to my mother-in-law, one day Martha just quit being friendly. She didn't visit or go to town as much. Hardly ever left the farm. That was in like, 1943 or '44. Definitely during the war anyway. Mom would drive by and sometimes she would see a man there, someone new. But she never met him. In fact they say he never left the farm."

"Isn't that a little strange?"

"Yeah, but according to mom, folks around here were pretty private then. It was mostly a German community and not the tourist Mecca it is now. And, of course, we were at war with Germany."

"So nobody knows who he was or where he came from?"

"Right."

"Is he a suspect?"

"Probably. At this point, the sheriff really doesn't have anything else to go on. I also spoke with my wife's aunt who works at the chamber. She said something strange. About the same time the Hoff woman was murdered, a man came into the chamber office and asked for a map of the area. She said he was definitely German. I mean real German, not from around here. He had an accent. He asked if there were any German descendents living in the area."

"What did he look like?"

"Tall, blond, well built, blue eyes. Looked like a perfect Nazi she said. A Hitler youth on steroids."

The call-waiting signal beeped on the phone. "Wait a second, Major, I've got another call incoming."

Before I could tell him not to take it, he punched off. I held the silent phone to my ear, waiting. I didn't like what I was thinking. Two deaths from broken necks—Hoff and Sader—both supposedly from falls? My training had taught me not to believe in coincidence.

No doubt, Strauss had been in Fredericksburg, and he had probably killed that Hoff woman. But why? What could he possibly want from an old woman? And who was the man that had lived with her? What did he have to do with it, and where was he?

"I'm back, Major. That was the sheriff. We've got more information." Cartwright paused.

"Yes," I said, thinking, come on, Sergeant. Spit it out.

Cartwright continued, "They found a small family graveyard on the property—only two graves in it. One was Rudolph Hoff's. The other was one of those double headstones. You know what I mean, like for husband and wife?"

"Yes, Sergeant, go on."

"Well, one side had Martha's name and birth date with a different last name. And, of course, there was no date of death for her." Cartwright paused again.

"Damn it, Sergeant, what did the other side say?"

"That's the good part," Cartwright replied. The last name on the other side was the same as Martha had used for hers. The sheriff checked and found out that the county coroner had signed off on the case as a natural death, cancer. Martha had arranged for the burial, and the funeral home director was certain it was the man who lived there, the one the Sheriff thought had disappeared. So he's no longer a suspect The date of death was just a few months ago.

"What was the name?"

"The inscription read, *In Loving Memory of My Husband, Eric von Speigel.*"

Chapter Fifty-Two
Tuesday, September 6

Monday night Bully begged off another search claiming exhaustion. Alec had gone anyway, driving the west end, hoping desperately to find some clue to the gold's location. He ended the night closing the Irish bar at two in the morning.

At three in the afternoon on Tuesday, someone knocked on his door. He shouted he was still in bed hoping they would go away. They could clean his room later. The knocking continued. He stumbled to the door half-asleep and opened it without thinking.

Mariana Villata pushed through the doorway and melted into his arms. They sank to the bed frantically removing what was left of her clothes.

They said little between them and afterwards, as they lay spent holding each other, Mariana lightly kneaded his shoulders and massaged his chest.

She kissed his cheek, then nuzzled his ear and whispered "Günter, I missed you so. I called you all week. I guess you didn't get the messages. My poor Auntie is gone. I could not stand living in that big house alone. I had to see you."

"I am so sorry about your loss, Mariana. You are right. I didn't get your messages. If only I had known."

Alec pushed her gently aside, then rose from the bed and moved to the window. Night shadows crept along the sidewalk below. It would be dark soon. Bully had promised him one more night of searching.

Why had Mariana come all the way from Argentina to Galveston? He had promised he would return. Had she not believed him?

He moved back and stood beside the bed looking down at her. "Mariana, I am so glad you have come. I missed you so. But...I told you I would return to Argentina as soon as my business here was finished. A few more days and..."

"Oh, Günter. I thought I could help, that's all. The faster you learn what you need to know about your grandfather the quicker we can both be happy in Argentina. Tell me what you know. How close are you to knowing what happened to him?"

Mariana straightened in the bed and rested her back against the headboard, motioning for Günter to sit beside her. He sat on the edge and put his hand on her naked thigh.

"He escaped after the war and went to Fredericksburg. He met his Abwehr contact there, Rudolph Hoff."

Mariana squiggled a little and reached for his hand, "Oh, Günter, this is exciting. You found him. Tell me more. But wait, I have a surprise for you."

Mariana rolled to the other side of the bed and reached into her tote bag.

"Look what I have for us. Ramefort '81. Your favorite cognac. It is our last bottle. We will celebrate." She moved closer to him. A coquettish smile enveloped her face. "Remember the night you first tasted it?"

Alec felt a stirring in his groin. He ran his finger along the inside of her leg and said, "How could I forget, my love?"

She moaned softly.

He moved his face over her and ran his tongue around her navel.

She scooted over the bed, giggling, teasing him. "You must have glasses, I'll look in the bathroom. I will just be a moment." She grabbed her purse and went past him.

Alec leaned against the headboard, thinking Bully would have to wait. They had all night to search. Germany seemed farther and farther away, his thoughts of the German Truth Organization but a distant dream.

A beautiful woman and a life of landed aristocracy beckoned to him. How could he refuse? Finding the gold would be the icing on the cake.

Mariana came out of the bathroom with two glasses of cognac. "A toast to us," she said. They sipped readily.

"So tell me more, Günter. What else did you learn?"

Günter finished his cognac, then said, "Eric von Speigel lived on the farm with the Hoff's. He even married the daughter, Martha. He died there a few months ago. I saw his grave and his marker."

"So he never returned to Germany? He never saw your grandmother, Anna Manfred, again?"

"No."

"How sad."

"I suppose so."

Mariana took a sip from her glass. "How about the funds for the operation, did they ever turn up?"

"The funds?"

"Yes," Marina said. "You know, the money for Eric's secret mission."

Somewhere deep inside an alarm bell sounded. He had never spoken of the money to Señora Rosas or Mariana. He had made it clear he was only interested in learning what had happened to his grandfather, Eric von Speigel. Why had she suddenly brought that up? He thought about the *estancia,* the weeds around the stable, the tarnished hinges and the smell of mildew. Now that the old woman

309

was dead, Mariana was afraid. So she needed money. So what? It was natural for her to ask.

They had been sitting side-by-side leaning against the headboard, looking toward the end of the bed. Not facing each other. He wished he could have seen her eyes when she asked about the money. But he had nothing to lose. He would play along.

"Rudolph Hoff buried the money, the gold, on the west end of Galveston Island. And I think it is still there."

Mariana sat up, "Really? He...he buried the money?"

"Yes, and they never went back for it. I have been searching the ranches out there with a local treasure hunter, Bully Stout. It is a long story, but he thinks I am looking for buried gold from the American Civil War era. Martha Hoff gave me some good clues, and we have narrowed down the search to one particular ranch. I am supposed to meet Stout later at The Garhole Bar. I think we will find it tonight."

"Where is this bar?"

"Out on the west side of the island toward the end."

Mariana bounced out of bed giggling, "Let us drink to it." She took the glasses back into the bathroom and refilled them. A moment later, she walked to the side of the bed and handed a glass to Günter. He sniffed the air quietly, then set the glass on the nightstand and reached for Mariana's hand.

He grabbed her arm violently and yanked her over him, then twisted her underneath and sat on top of her.

"Günter, you are hurting me. Get off my chest! I can't breathe."

Günter rose off her chest then slammed back down hard, squeezing the breath from her lungs.

"Günter, please!" she gasped.

"You lousy bitch! Who do you think you are? You think you can outwit me? I caught the aroma of burnt almonds when I sniffed the cognac. You forget cyanide was the poison of choice in Germany. Even Hitler used it. The Army trained me to detect the smell." He slapped her hard. Blood squirted from the edge of her mouth.

"So it was the money all along? The old woman scammed me, and you faked it too, you slut. Prostituted yourself. You whore!"

Mariana squirmed under his massive weight trying to break free, her lungs empty. She gasped, "Günter, no! She made me do it, please. I love you. We have the *estancia*. It is ours. Come home with me."

"Even now you lie, bitch. You are pitiful. She is still alive, isn't she? You came for the money. I was never to return there."

"Yes, it is true, but she is old. She will be dead soon. We can have it all!"

Günter lifted the glass containing the poison from the nightstand. He rose up slightly then pressed down on her chest with all his weight. When her mouth opened from the blow, he poured the cognac in and held her mouth closed with his hand.

He felt her weaken, a confused, dazed look on her face. She convulsed slightly. Her head fell to the side. Her eyelids rolled back, her pupils dilated.

Günter rolled his head back and laughed openly at the ceiling. Then he moved her legs apart and forced himself into her, slowly at first, then gradually increasing his rhythm, all the while caressing her breasts and whispering endearments.

Another late night search and a few hours sleep left Bully sitting at the table by the dock massaging the stump of his leg. When he felt the circulation return to normal, he reattached his wooden leg and went into the trailer. He slid a nitro pill under his tongue and absent-mindedly rubbed his chest. Lisa lay curled in a ball, sleeping soundly. He rearranged the cover over her, patted her shoulder and then stepped outside and hobbled to the bar for his morning beer.

He sat at the counter looking out through the back window, thinking about his friends. They had all called or stopped by to check on Lisa. Marvin Klaus had dropped in every day during his rounds of the west end. Neddie Lemmon was there, too, bringing fresh fish he had caught. Anything for an excuse to see Lisa or ask about her. Even Johnny Weeks, the jailer, came by for lunch on his day off. Everyone was anxious to reaffirm his "uncle" status. Harry Stein was out Sunday and had called every day. When the phone rang, it was Harry again.

"Bully, it's me. I'm still worried about Lisa. Is she sleeping okay? Anything I can do?"

"Jesus, Harry. You just asked me the same thing yesterday."

"Well?"

"Yeah, yeah. She's fine."

"I'm glad she's okay, Bully. Now listen, I'll be out this afternoon to help."

"Harry, damn it! I don't need no help. I can take care of Lisa myself."

"No, no, Bully, I know you can. I'm coming out to help you board up for Dorothy."

"What?"

"Hurricane Dorothy. It's less than three hundred miles out, due south of Louisiana. Son of a gun is huge. It could be a category four or five by the time it hits land. Winds are over a hundred now."

"Hell, Harry, I thought you was talkin' about Lisa. I ain't worried about no damn storm. Been through too many of them. You know that. Besides, last I heard it was going to Mexico."

"It's changed course," Harry responded. "Turned northwest, They've got all of Louisiana and Texas in the storm watch."

"Well, the tides are a little high here, that's all. Not even over the bulkhead," Bully said.

Harry panted into the phone. "Bully, you know how fickle these storms are. It could be in Galveston in twenty-four hours. Barometer's dropping as we speak. Mine read 29.974 when I left the office. That's a good indication and..."

Bully interrupted. "Come on, Harry, calm down. We're B.O.I., remember? Born-on-the-island. We've been through hurricanes before. Big ones too! Remember Carla in '61 and Alicia in '83. Screw it! Storms don't scare me."

"Right, Carla was huge, but we didn't get the brunt of it. It went in down the coast south of us. But Alicia spawned more than forty tornados. Doesn't that say something to you?"

Bully appreciated the concern in his friend's voice, but he wasn't about to back off.

"It'll probably go on into Louisiana," Bully replied. "And if it makes Sabine Pass, we'll be on the lee side of it."

"But it's headed northwest, Bully. If it comes in west of us, we would be on the dirty side of her winds. She would tear this island apart."

Bully stepped to the outside and looked over the water. "Winds are out of the northwest now about twenty." He tried to maintain an even tone. He could feel near-panic in Harry's words.

"Bully, I'm on the seawall. The swells are coming from the southeast. This is exactly how the 1900 storm came in. Winds out of the northwest, and then they changed to the northeast. The sea roared over Galveston. They had fifteen-foot tides and an eight-foot storm surge."

"Yeah, but we got a seawall now. Didn't have one then."

"And you still don't have one down on West Beach. What are you—two feet above sea level? You'll have water ten feet over the bulkhead. If it turns, you won't be able to get out. You know how fast high water closes 3005. Listen to me, Bully. I've been tracking this system since the beginning. It's uncanny. So far it's taken the exact same path as the 1900 storm."

"The same path," Bully exclaimed. "No hurricane's ever done that."

Harry had Bully's attention now. He had lost relatives in the 1900 storm—aunts, uncles, cousins. His own parents were visiting in Houston or he wouldn't be here today, fussing with Harry Stein.

"Exactly," Harry added, "but Dorothy has. She came up the Windward Chain and crossed over Cuba. Then she passed just northwest of Key West and looked as if she was going into Mississippi or Louisiana. Now she's turned west—same as the 1900 storm. It's the same track, and she's big. And that's not all, Bully.... She's coming on the same day!"

"What?" Bully screamed into the phone. "What do you mean, the same day?"

"I mean tomorrow, the eighth of September. The same date the 1900 storm came in. Damn it, Bully. Get Lisa and get out, now!"

Bully felt the exasperation in Harry's voice. Lisa! Yes, Harry was right. He did need to get Lisa out. Couldn't risk it with her. But he had another problem.

"I can't leave yet. I think Strauss is coming out again tonight."

"What! You and Strauss are still treasure hunting?" Harry's voice strained at the breaking point. "You're crazy!" Harry sounded as if he was going to stroke out.

Bully tried to calm him. "Harry, I promise I'll take care of Lisa, but I owe Strauss for saving Lisa's life. We went out last night and he said he'd be back tonight. But I gotta admit, Harry—I don't know about this Civil War gold thing. I know about every treasure story on this island and that one, well..."

"I know what you mean," Harry said. His voice was steady now, more relaxed. "Parker has his doubts, too."

"Parker?"

"Yeah. He came by to see me about Strauss. He asked what I knew about him."

"Damn that Parker. He has no right fooling in my business. I'm gonna tell him..."

Harry cut him off. "For Pete's sake, Bully, calm down. I just told him how Strauss approached me and how I referred him to you. You ought to be glad he's concerned." Harry hesitated, then, "Maybe I shouldn't have got you involved, Bully."

Bully felt for his friend. It hadn't been his fault. He was only trying to help.

"No, Harry. It's okay, really. At first I just did it for the extra money. But, now....Well, what Strauss did for Lisa."

"You feel obligated, huh?" Harry commented. "Where have you been looking?"

"The old Boehm ranch and the Schindler place. They're the only two ranches I could think of that were owned by Germans when the Yankees were here. There were a few farms but Strauss keeps talking about a cattle pen so we searched the ranches."

"I can't think of another place either," Harry added. "Both of those families were pretty well off in Galveston then. Boehm owned a large dry-goods store and Schindler operated a bank."

Bully said, "He claims he's done some research and has new information."

"Where did he get it?"

Bully noted the surprise in Harry's voice. It was a good question. Where would he have gotten it?

"Damned if I know, Harry. Maybe it was from Germany. Some family member of the Boehm's or the Schindler's might have written to a relative there."

"I doubt it," Harry replied. "He didn't even know about those two families until you told him."

"I guess that's right," Bully said.

Harry continued, "And I don't think he got it at the library. Yesterday I was thinking about the Civil War thing. I went over to the history room and researched it again—nothing. I'm convinced it was just a rumor."

Bully grunted into the phone but said nothing. His glass eye itched like crazy. Must be the wind blowing stuff in, he thought. He raised the patch to his forehead and rubbed the socket.

"Another thing," Harry said. "You have to sign in to do research there and list what you want to look at. I checked. There is no record of Strauss researching anything that occurred during the 1860s."

"So he didn't learn anything there?"

"I don't think so. The woman who runs the research department, Julie Hanna, hasn't been in for a few days. No one has seen her, so I haven't been able to check with her to make sure. She is the one who originally referred Strauss to me."

Neither of them spoke for a few moments, each one engrossed in his own thoughts.

Then Bully said, "You know Harry, maybe he's just making it all up. He heard what you said about the gold and he's makin' a story out it. A big tale."

"Fiction?"

"Fiction? What's that?" Bully questioned.

"Something the author makes up."

"Yeah, fiction. He keeps talking about trees and a windmill and corral. I guess he made that up too."

"Hey, you're right, Bully. The last time he was in my office he said he might write an adventure story about the gold if he didn't find any. Maybe that's what he is up to. Maybe he made up the part about the corral and windmill."

"But if he's writing a book, something he's making up, why does he keep talking about the windmill and stuff? Why is he paying me to search for something he knows ain't there? It don't make no sense."

"You're right, Bully. I don't get it either."

Bully said, "Well, anyway, I told him nothing like a windmill or corral on the west end of the island had survived over a hundred years—too many storms. Not to mention all the changes of ownership."

Harry interrupted. "Bully! Do you remember my cousin Laughman's ranch? It was out there between Ten and Thirteen Mile Road? We worked for him a little in high school."

"Of course I do."

"Remember that summer we built a new corral?"

"Yeah, what about it?"

"The old windmill. It was right across from where we built the corral. And there was a grove of salt cedars there, too."

"But Harry, none of that was there in the 1860s."

"Maybe so, but the scene fits his story. So maybe he is not making it up. Maybe he really knows something, and you've been searching the wrong property."

"You really think so?" Bully said, getting excited. "Is the windmill and all still there?"

"I think so. The front half of the old ranch is a subdivision now, but the land on the backside by the bay is too low for permanent development."

Bully jumped in, "Yeah, but that windmill and corral were built on a mound that old man Laughman bulldozed up to herd his cattle to in case of a storm. It's a good six feet higher than the marsh. You might have something, Harry. I'll bring it up and see if he's interested. Maybe I'll find out what this is all about."

"Bully, don't take him out there tonight. It's too dangerous. I know you feel like you owe him for Lisa. Just tell him you'll take him out again after the storm passes. It's only a few more days. You've got to get Lisa out now. If Dorothy changes her mind and comes into Galveston, it will be too late. If you need some help, I'll come out right away."

Bully said, "You're right, Harry. We'll pack up. No sense takin' a chance with Lisa. And thanks for the offer, but I can handle it."

"Well, okay. But get her out of there."

Worn down by the conversation, Bully reached over the counter into the cooler for another beer. He took a big gulp, then said, "I remember old man Laughman. He was a nice man. Always treated me right. He had a thick accent."

"Sure he did, Bully. He grew up in Germany. Barely escaped in the late 30s. He bought that ranch in 1940. Sure was proud of those cattle he had. Liked to show them off. Brahma's, I think. They were the only ones tough enough to live off the salt grass."

"Yeah, I remember that big white bull. Chased us one day out in the marsh. Laughman didn't have any family?"

"Just me."

"Yeah, but your family was Russian and his was German."

Harry laughed, "Yes, but we all started out in Poland. Way back, one brother went east and a sister went west. Laughman and I were second cousins. My side ended up in America."

"The lucky ones," Bully noted.

"We sure were. Anyway, Laughman left everything to me when he died. I was his executor too. A few years ago I sold off the front half of the ranch to a developer. He didn't want the back of it, too low. I donated the money to a Holocaust survivor's fund in Israel. I think the old man would have liked that. His entire family in Germany was picked up by the Gestapo. They were all loaded on boxcars. He never saw them again."

"Forkin' Nazis!"

"You said it."

Chapter Fifty-Four
Wednesday, September 7

I sat on a piece of driftwood in the afternoon sun timing the rolling swells. Unusually heavy and only a few minutes apart. It was like childbirth, the closer the contractions the more imminent the delivery. This storm was not going to Louisiana or Mexico. It was coming to Galveston, and it was time to get out.

I scrambled back across the neck of the island to find Bully stacking chairs on top of the tables. It was a futile gesture, but I didn't say anything.

He finished piling the chairs and moved to the back. He cut the wire holding the gar-head to the ceiling and slowly lowered it to the counter. Its huge open jaw and rows of jagged teeth covered the bar's width.

I pointed at it and said, "Bully, what are you going to do with the gar-head?"

"Don't know," he answered. "I took it down 'cause I thought you might want to try and save it."

"Well, maybe so," I answered. "Put it in your truck when we leave."

I stared at the white behemoth wondering if I would rebuild after the storm. For all my crazy ideas about leaving the island and not coming back, things seemed to have changed a little. I thought about Lisa and Claire. There was more to consider now besides myself.

I was under no illusion. Dorothy would wipe The Garhole out. The storm surge alone could reach as high as the ceiling. Everything not washed out to sea would be ruined. The rising salt water would flood the beer boxes, trashing the motors.

Bully went out on the dock and yelled through the back door. "Well, let's at least tie the boat off. Who knows, it might make it."

I knew better, but waited patiently as Bully raised the boat as high as it would go in the sling. Together, we tied ropes from each corner of the boat to the pilings.

As a last effort, we hauled several sheets of heavy plywood up the stairs and nailed them over the door and windows.

"This may help some," I commented. "But if the roof goes..."

We couldn't do anything about the camper. We both knew the storm would sweep Bully and Lisa's home out into the middle of West Bay. It would line the bottom of the bay along with a hundred other boats and trailers washed from the island.

We went back into the bar for one last look. I turned to Bully and said, "I thought Lisa would be back by now. I can't believe you sent her off for supplies. Now we have to wait for her. You were really thinking about staying here, riding this thing out?" The impatience in my voice showed, but so what. How could Bully be that stupid?

"Yeah, well I was," Bully replied. "I've ridden these things out before. But Harry convinced me not to this time. He was right. I guess I hadn't thought it through about Lisa and all."

"Thank God," I added. "The barometer's at 28.55 and falling. According to the reports, this thing is at least a category three, maybe a four. Winds could be over a hundred and thirty packing nine to twelve foot tides."

Bully took a six-pack out of the cooler, opened two cans, and handed one to me. Without thinking, I took the can off the counter.

We toasted the gar-head for the last time and drank the beer down. He opened two more and gave me another. The alcohol hit hard.

Foam dribbled down Bully's chin. He wiped his mouth with his hand and said, "I guess you're right, Parker. This could really be a bad one."

I nodded and said, "As soon as Lisa gets here, we're leaving. I want to go by Claire's condo. I haven't been able to reach her."

"It's getting late," Bully said. "You go on in. I'll bring Lisa out as soon as she gets here. I promise. We'll meet you at Claire's, and we'll all leave the island together, tonight. Plus, if Alec calls, I'll need to let him know we're leaving."

"Strauss? Why would he call?"

"I told him I would take him out again tonight, but to call first. Don't worry. I won't wait for his call. He's not stupid. He knows the storm's coming. I'll leave as soon as Lisa gets here."

I saw an opportunity to tell Bully what I had learned about Strauss. I put my hand on the old man's arm. "Bully, I want to talk to you about Alec. He..."

Bully jerked his arm back freeing himself from my grasp. His temper flared. "I don't want to hear it, Parker. I owe him and that's that. I'll just tell him he'll have to wait until after the storm."

I tried again, "Bully, just listen...please."

He shouted back again before I could finish. "And where do you get off going behind my back and talking to Harry Stein about all this."

I started to speak, but Bully continued his rant.

"Alec saved Lisa from that scumbag Denny Sader. You weren't here to help. You should've been here! I should've been here! We let her down, just like we have all along."

He stopped for air. His breaths came hard and fast. He walked in a circle rubbing his chest.

I let him vent. No sense stirring the pot anymore. He stopped suddenly and bent over.

"What's wrong, Bully? You don't look so good."

"I'm fine. Just get the hell out of here. You hear me, Parker? You don't believe Alec, but I do. So get out, now!"

I kept an even voice. "Bully, don't take it out on me. You're just upset that you weren't here for Lisa. Neither of us could have known what was going to happen."

Bully waved me off and turned to enter his trailer. His guilt had gushed out like the storm surge headed this way, but I wasn't about to buy into it. Not now. I had work to do. I had to find out about Strauss. And where was Lisa? Where was Claire?

I guzzled down the last of the six pack. My head swirled from the effect. I roared out of the parking lot toward town wondering if Strauss would show. If I met Lisa on the way into Galveston, I would take her with me. It would at least keep her away from the bastard. Then I would call Bully and tell him to meet us at Claire's.

Maybe if I told Lisa everything I had learned, she could convince Bully. Would she believe me? Probably not, I concluded. What's wrong with these people? Can't they see what's happening? Alec Strauss is *a* fraud, probably a killer.

Claire was my last hope. Maybe she would listen.

Who was I kidding? The way she had teased me about Lisa and Strauss. She had yet to take my feelings about Strauss seriously.

The pain in my joints returned. It sapped my stamina and gnawed on my willpower. As I drove, I pushed my shoulders forward and then pulled them back as far as I could. Nothing worked, the pain continued.

Pressure from all sides closed in—like an elevator, free falling, out of control. It scraped at my soul like sandpaper and would not leave. I swallowed and tasted the last remnant of beer sliding down my throat.

I thought of the beer dripping from Bully's mouth. A short drink would do it—just enough to kill the ache. I reached under the seat of my truck for the emergency stash—a pint of Famous Grouse, the good stuff. Just a sip, it was all I needed.

Along the road, I passed deserted sub-divisions. Except for an occasional empty pick-up or SUV left by one of the houses, the west end was empty. I wondered about the empty vehicles and hoped some hardheads hadn't decided to stay. There were always a few idiots who would try. If the wind and storm surge didn't get them, the tornadoes spawned by the hurricane would. They would be the ones found under a pile of debris with the rats chewing on them.

Thirty minutes later, I reached Seawall Boulevard. Out in the Gulf, huge, rolling swells lapped at the bottom of the great concrete wall that protected the city. Teenagers in wetsuits rode their surfboards with abandon, ignoring the double red flags with the black square in the middle. A brick-dust hue filled the sky, the last telltale sign of an approaching hurricane.

I hadn't passed Lisa on the way in. I realized she must have gone the back way. Bully would have to bring her out. I hoped they would get to Claire's condo before dark.

I pulled into the rear parking area of Claire's condominium units. Her car was not in its assigned parking space. I backed out, pulled to the front of the building, and yanked my truck to a stop. I pounded on her door, no answer.

Just then, the next door neighbor opened her door carrying an armful of clothes. I turned. "Have you seen Claire? I'm worried about her. I haven't been able to reach her."

"No, I haven't," the woman replied. "Haven't seen her since yesterday."

I asked to use the phone and the woman waved me inside while she took a load to her car. I called Claire's office. One of the realtors said she was closing the office, the last one out. She had not seen or heard from Claire all day. I went back to my truck and pounded the steering wheel in desperation, wondering where she could be.

Had she already left Galveston, evacuated without letting me know? This was her first storm. Maybe she panicked and ran?

I flipped on the radio. Evacuees clogged the freeways. The causeway was jammed. Too late to get out. It was best now to hunker down in one of the shelters and ride it out.

Thinking Bully and Lisa would be along soon, I sat in my truck and waited, drinking steadily. The whisky warmed my throat. I thought of Bully, and my anger returned. Why wouldn't the old man listen to me about Strauss? And why was Strauss so determined about this treasure-hunting thing?

I reviewed what I knew. Even thought there was no autopsy performed on Sader, I felt certain they had both been murdered. Günter Manfred aka Alec Strauss was at the scene when Sader died and probably at Hoff's as well.

And why the two names? What was he hiding? The image of Strauss's voice crossed my mind—the accent. He had lied about where he was from in Germany. Why? Of course! To throw off anyone tracking him. He was from eastern Germany, no doubt. With a map, I could probably pinpoint the city. Something Colonel Moore needed to know.

My watch said four PM. When Bully and Lisa arrived, I would send them on and wait for Claire. Just then Claire's neighbor came out again. She appeared to be locking the door, so I hustled back to call Harry Stein before she left.

"Parker! I'm glad you called," Harry said, his voice strained. "Listen..."

I cut him off. "Wait, Harry. I'm at Claire's and I told Bully to meet me here with Lisa. But Claire's not here and I don't know where she is. If you're going to be in your office awhile, I'll leave a note for them to come there."

Harry answered, "Well, I was planning to leave now, Parker. Going to a shelter. But I'll wait a while longer."

"Don't worry," I said. "They'll be along soon."

"Good," Harry said. "Now listen, Parker. About Strauss. He told Bully he had researched the Civil War gold story at the library. Well, I checked. The woman who runs that department hasn't been at work for a few days. Her name is Julie Hanna. Sweet girl."

I interrupted, "Listen, Harry. I'm in a big hurry and..."

"Wait, Parker. I finally tracked Julie down at her apartment. She didn't want to see me. Strauss beat the hell out of her. She was scared to death. He had threatened all kinds of harm to her. I'm going to call the police now. Maybe they can find him."

"I knew it, Harry. The bastard's a killer. I hope they can find him."

Harry continued, "And I'm worried about Bully and Lisa. Bully promised he'd bring Lisa out as soon as she got there. You don't think Strauss is out at The Garhole, do you?"

"Christ, I hope not, Harry. Bully said he'd tell him not to come. I'm sure he and Lisa are on their way in."

Chapter Fifty-Five

Alec decided the risk of removing Mariana's body from his room was too great. He had left the privacy sign on his door and spent the night searching for gold with Bully.

Now back in his room after a few hours sleep, he sat on the edge of his bed listening to the latest hurricane advisory. Below his feet lay the cold, still body of Mariana Villata. He had attempted to push her lifeless form under the bed but it only went in halfway. He looked down at a portion of her face, one eye and part of her nose and mouth. He reached down and ran his finger along her cheek. What a waste, he thought. Such a beautiful woman. Too bad.

The radio commentator predicted the full fury of the storm would reach Galveston the next afternoon. A note on his door announced the hotel was closing. All quests must be out by six o'clock today. He had told Bully he would be out to search again tonight. This was his last chance.

He hoisted Mariana's body to the bed and positioned it under the covers as though she had died in her sleep. With all the confusion of the storm, if her death looked natural, maybe it would buy him a little time. It was all he could do.

As he stepped out of the shower, he noticed the message light blinking on his room phone. He debated checking it. The blinking continued: off, on, off, on. He picked up the receiver and replayed the message. The voice came in quick short breaths.

"Hey, it's me, Bubba. I'm in Houston. I called just about every hotel in Galveston to find you. I left Denny's car behind a Pizza joint next to the motel I'm in. Oh, Christ, man, I...I...know I was supposed to dump the car in Galveston. I screwed up. Two cops are checking the license plate now. They're looking this way. I think they're coming to the motel. Oh, Christ! I'm sorry man, really. I'm cutting out before they get here."

Alec erased the message, slammed the phone down and yelled, "You stupid idiot." He rammed his fist through the wall, knocking a hole in the sheetrock. "You were supposed to take the bus so the police wouldn't find you with the car and tie you to Sader. Not drive it to Houston."

He slammed the wall again, smashing another hole. "Damn it!" He could not believe Shanks had called him. He must have put a terrific fear in the kid. He was too scared not to call.

Alec knew if the police caught Shanks he would squeal like a dying rabbit. Anything to save his own hyde. Even if Shanks got away, the police would search his room and trace any calls he made. The phone call would tie Shanks to Alec and probably to Sader.

He hurriedly started throwing his clothes into his luggage. The phone rang again. Was Shanks calling back? Without thinking, he picked it up.

An unfamiliar voice spoke in German, *"Truth."*

Alec inhaled deeply and held it. It wasn't Frankin. Who was it?

The caller repeated the password, *"Truth."*

Frustrated, Alec answered in his native tongue, *"Truth."*

Then the voice said, *"This is Wessler with the Committee. I know I am breaking the rules calling you, but we have just learned some vital information."*

Alec recognized the name. He knew Wessler vaguely from GTO headquarters. Alec said, *"What is it, and why are you calling and not Frankin?"*

Wessler said, *"We can't locate Frankin, and this is urgent."*

"How did you find me?" Alec asked, alarm in his voice.

Wessler said, *"We knew you were in Galveston, we knew your alternate identity. It wasn't difficult. Now be quiet and listen. There are problems here. Too many people with broken necks. Our man inside the police department says they have got you for a number of them."*

"You mean there, in Leipzig?"

"Yes."

"You are sure?" Alec replied. Pictures of his victims raced through his mind. The first one he remembered vividly, the Russian border guard he had killed in revenge for the raping of his mother. But the rest remained jumbled and confused. So many—the gypsies, the immigrants.

"Yes. And there is more," Wessler said. *"The police have received a request from U.S. Army Intelligence in Washington for your file and..."*

Alec broke in, *"Which file, which name?"*

"Manfred," Wessler shot back. *"They are asking if Günter Manfred is in the States and if so, why? We think you should get out now, quickly before you are caught. They might tie you to the Organization."*

The statement stunned Alec. Wessler called to protect the GTO, not him. But why the sudden police interest? How had they traced any of those deaths to him? And why did they suspect he was in the U.S. Unless...unless Frankin tipped them off. Yes! Alec decided that must be it. He had never trusted the bastard. The man had his own agenda. It would be much easier for him with Günter Manfred out of the way.

There was nothing else the GTO could do for him. Nor did he want them to. He was on his own now. *"Don't call here again,"* he ordered and hung up.

So, Alec thought. Frankin had betrayed him. But how did the U.S. Army figure into it? Had the police in Germany contacted them? If so, why the Army and not the FBI? No, someone here in the U.S. was attempting to check up on him. But who? Who had he made contact with that was connected to the Army. Certainly not Stein. Bully? That did not make sense. Bully was on his side now. Then who?

Of course. Parker McLeod! He had been in the Army, stationed in Germany. Is that why McLeod had spoken in German? To somehow test him? Maybe McLeod still had Army contacts and he had asked them to run a check. But why would he? What interest did he have?

Things were piling up. Alec knew he had to get out of Galveston quickly, but he needed money. One more attempt with Bully tonight. The storm would be good cover. The police would be too busy to worry about Alec Strauss or Günter Manfred. If Bully knew the right property, he would take him to it. He was sure of that. He had ways to make him.

And then what? Too risky going back to Germany. The police there suspected him in multiple killings, and they only had to prove one. He would take the gold and run. Screw the GTO. But where? Argentina? Mariana had confessed that Señora Rosas was still alive. He could make up a story about an accident with Mariana, prey on her emotions. The old woman was near death. He could hurry her along. There was no one left in the family. He would get a new identity, and with the gold and Señora Rosas's old connections, he would build a power base in Argentina.

Alec saw himself looking through the picture window in the parlor of Señora Rosas's home. Below him, the meadow was greener than ever and there were two stunning white horses drinking at the river. He and a beautiful, black-haired señorita were astride them. She with her head back, laughing. Her eyes alive with contentment. He visualized the form of her waist and the way her hair fell along the curve of her back. He smelled the sweetness in the nape of her neck.

The vision vanished as quickly as it had arrived. He forced himself to think. He still had a few hours before final checkout. He would leave the privacy sign on the door and leave early for The Garhole Bar. Hopefully, the hotel staff would honor the sign and not check the room until sometime after six.

Then it hit him—his passport at the bus station. He had almost forgotten it. Things were happening too quickly now. Too many things were cluttering his mind. He drove immediately to the bus station and retrieved his passport from the locker, relieved it was still there.

He called The Garhole. Bully told him not to come out. He and Lisa were leaving as soon as she got there. Bully said the gold would still be there after the storm. Alec knew he had to get out there now, before Lisa returned and they left.

He sat in his car at the bus station and considered his options. How long did he have? They would certainly find Mariana's body sometime tonight. And if they caught Shanks and he talked, they would be looking for both Alec Strauss and Günter Manfred.

What about the airport? How much longer would it remain open? With the storm coming in he couldn't take the chance. A break for the Mexican border might work. The police would be concentrating on the storm. He raced back to the Tremont, upset that he had left his clothes there. Another time-consuming mistake. He left the rental car at the curb front and hurried through the lobby to the stairs.

He slid the plastic card through the slot in the lock of his room and pushed the door open. Horst Frankin stood in the middle of the room pointing a small automatic at Alec's chest.

Frankin nodded toward the bed, then spoke in German, *"Hello Günter. Up to your old tricks with women, huh? Who is your girlfriend? I don't think she is feeling too well."*

Alec's mind reeled. What was this? Frankin here? The man was smaller than he had remembered and thin, very thin. His face was long and skinny, his nose thin and pointed.

Alec answered in German. *"Frankin! What...what are you doing here?"*

"The Committee sent me. Your reports have not been very forthcoming lately. If the money is here in Galveston, they want me to help you find it. What have you learned?"

The Committee! What a laugh, Alec thought. How could the Committee have selected this weasel for anything? Were they all this weak? But wait! Only an hour earlier he had received a call. What was the man's name? Yes, now he remembered.

"So, Wessler sent you, is that right?" Alec asked. He noticed a quick flare in Frankin's eyes. No doubt, Alec thought. Frankin knew he was on to him now. Wessler had called because they did not know where Frankin was.

"So you know," Frankin said. *"Well, no matter. You will cooperate."* Frankin waved the gun toward the bed. *"Sit down there, next to your friend, and tell me what you know."*

Alec sat on the edge of the bed. The lifeless body of Mariana Villata moved slightly as his weight shifted the mattress. They both ignored her.

Alec smiled. *"You are out for yourself now, huh, Frankin? You poor man. What has happened to your beliefs? The Fourth Reich? The master race? Although I have to admit, you do not look like a master race."*

Frankin pushed his gun hand out and stepped closer. *"Don't tempt me, Günter. I am just like you, you know. I knew once you smelled the money you would betray the Organization. You were never a true believer."*

"Like you?" Alec said. He smirked and shook his head.

"I was at first," Frankin said. *"It was a way out. I grew up like you, Alec. In East Germany, starving. Eating from garbage cans. We are not so different."*

Alec met Frankin's eyes and was silent for a moment. Then he said, *"Maybe you are right, Horst. Maybe we are not so different. I will make you a deal. We will work together and split the find. What do you think?"*

Frankin said, *"I can't trust you, Günter. You know that."*

"You don't have to. You have the gun. Besides, you really do not have a choice. You need me. You cannot find the money without me. But we have to get out of here. The hotel is closing soon."

Alec stood and moved toward the closet. He reached for his hanging clothes and turned his head toward Frankin, his hand still on the clothes bar. *"We don't have much time. The hurricane is coming. I do not have the money yet, but I think I can get it tonight. We must act quickly."*

Alec noticed a slight relaxation in the weasel's hand. The gun dropped just enough. He spun from the closet and hit Frankin across his arm and face with the hanging clothes. Then he dropped the clothes and grabbed Frankin's gun hand, pushing it down violently. Before Frankin could react, Alec flipped him over and kneeled astride his back.

"You gave me up to the Leipzig police didn't you, Frankin? You told them about the Russian guard and the others, didn't you?" Alec pinned Frankin's arms with his knees, then yanked his head back and smashed it onto the floor. *"Didn't you, Frankin? Didn't you?"*

Blood gushed from Frankin's nose and mouth. *"No, Alec. No."*

"Oh, yes, Franklin. Yes." Alec moved his hands to Franklin's head and twisted. The vertebrae cracked. He smiled and did it again, then dropped Frankin's limp head to the floor.

He got up quickly and moved Mariana to the side of the bed. He sat her up with her legs on the floor and shot her through the chest with the automatic. Her body fell backwards to the mattress. Then he hurriedly stripped Frankin of his clothes, moved his naked body to a chair across from the bed, put the gun between Frankin's lips, and fired a bullet into the roof of his mouth. He carefully wiped the gun clean, pressed Frankin's hand around it and dropped it to the floor next to Frankin's body.

Next, he removed all identification from Frankin's body. He searched Mariana's clothes and took her purse. If he could confuse the police for a few hours, it was all he needed.

Chapter Fifty-Six
Wednesday, September 7

I left a note on Claire's door telling Bully and Lisa to go to Harry's office. I had decided to give Claire a few more minutes. Maybe she would show. I sat in my truck and finished the bottle.

An hour passed. It was five o'clock, and Claire still hadn't arrived. Tired of waiting, I drove to the Tremont Hotel to check on Strauss. Like refugees in a war zone, a dozen guests lined the sidewalk waiting turns to load their cars. It was 1975, the American embassy in Saigon, helicopters landing on the roof evacuating the last desperate souls that had made it into the compound. I expected any minute a helicopter would swoop down onto the street.

Neddie Lemmon stood in front of the line, shoving luggage into the trunk of a car. I pulled him aside and said, "I'm looking for Strauss."

Neddie glanced around quickly, then whispered, "What's going on, Parker?"

"I don't have time to explain, Neddie," I replied. "Have you seen him?"

Behind Neddie, a gray-haired couple waited impatiently on the curb. Neddie slammed the trunk of the car and the next one in line pulled up.

Neddie said, "He came out about an hour ago in a big hurry."

The gray-haired man stepped off the curb, trying to get Neddie's attention. I stuck my palm up and gave him the evil eye. He backed off.

I put my hand on Neddie's shoulder to hold his attention. "You think he left town?"

"I don't think so, Parker. He hasn't checked out yet."

"Doesn't he know the hotel is closing?"

"We sent notices. But he's got until six tonight. Everyone has to be out by then. Strauss didn't have any anything with him. He must be coming back. He'll probably carry his own luggage, the cheap bastard."

The blinking neon on the Irish Bar across the street caught my attention. "Okay, Neddie. I'll be over there," I said, pointing to the Shamrock on the outside of the building. "If he comes back, you come get me, okay?"

"Right, Parker."

I ordered a double scotch on the rocks and sat at a table surveying the empty room.

The bartender, a forty-something man with saggy eyes said, "Well, I was going to close up, but since you're here, well...I got no place to go anyway. I just live up the street. Want another one?"

I nodded. I had no place to go either. After another drink, I borrowed the phone to check with Harry. Bully and Lisa were not there. I called The Garhole. The telephone rang endlessly, no answer.

I checked my watch. It was after six o'clock. I went to the window and caught Neddie's attention at the curb across the street. He shook his head. Strauss had not returned.

I went back to my seat. My thoughts flashed to Claire. Damn it, where was she? I fought back the effects of the alcohol, but finally exhaustion took over. I lowered my head on the table for a quick rest.

In a moment, Claire appeared at The Garhole, sitting at the table on the dock. She was smiling, moving a strand of windblown hair from her face. The freckles on her nose danced as she laughed. Bully was working with the skiff, his cigar glowing. Off to the side in the same picture, Lisa was sitting on a bench at the oak motte pointing excitedly at a bird across the pond giggling as she named it.

In the sky over all of these images, a huge white bird soared in the thermals, cruising in slow motion. Its wingspan blocked the sun. It seemed to be guarding them, protecting all that was below.

And there I was, standing apart from this, smiling as the scene unfolded. Suddenly the bird's wings collapsed. It spiraled toward the earth, out of control. And behind it, there was nothing but total and endless darkness.

Chapter Fifty-Seven
Wednesday, September 7

Bay water, pushed by the growing wind, lapped over the bulkhead and washed away the chalk outline of Denny Sader's body. Sheets of rain, slicing horizontally under the deck, pelted Bully's face as he stepped out of the back entrance to the bar.

He yelled to Lisa, "Hurry up, honey! It'll be dark soon. I told Parker we'd meet him at Claire's and we're already way late."

Lisa stumbled out of the trailer with an armful of clothes. "Sorry I was late getting here, Poppa. I had to go all the way to town. Everything on the west end was closed. The grocery store was packed with people buying stuff—flashlights, batteries, canned food, bottled water. I've never seen anything like it."

"You got everything? Need some help?"

"I'm okay," she answered. Some of her clothes dragged the ground. "I thought we were going to ride this one out here. Why did you have me buy all the food and stuff if we're leaving?"

"Well, I wanted to stay, but Harry and Parker talked me into leaving. They're right, honey. I can't take the chance with you being here. Now come on! Let's load the truck and get outta here."

"I'm coming, I'm coming."

They reached the corner of the building headed toward Bully's old pickup.

"Hello, Lisa," Alec said. "What's the rush?

Stunned by the sight of Alec, Bully yelled, "What are you doing here? I told you we weren't going tonight."

Bully attempted to push by, but Strauss kicked his wooden leg. Bully's two hundred and seventy pounds hit the cement like a demolition ball smashing the side of a concrete building. His wooden leg broke loose and rolled several feet. He scrambled toward it.

Alec reached past him and picked up the leg. Then he turned and tore the clothes from Lisa's hands. He slapped her hard in the face. She crumbled against the wall.

Bully reached for him. Alec hit Bully's arm with the leg, then turned and raised the leg toward Lisa.

Bully screamed, "No! Don't hit her."

"Listen to me, old man," Alec yelled. "We're going out now! And you'd better find the gold." He motioned toward Lisa.

Bully, desperate to protect Lisa, pleaded with Alec. "I can't find it. There ain't no Civil War gold."

"I know that, you old fool. Listen to me and listen good. During the war in '43, a German agent infiltrated Galveston."

"A spy!" Bully interrupted.

"Yes! He came here on a mission for the Abwehr."

"A goddamned Nazi," Bully interrupted again.

Alec ignored Bully's outburst. "The funds he needed for the mission were brought here in the form of paper money and gold and buried on the west end. It's still there."

The wind and rain howled over Alec's voice. Bully shook his head to clear his mind. What was he hearing?

Strauss continued, "It was buried on land owned by a German. Somewhere around a windmill and a corral. You came out here a lot back then. Think old man. You must know another place to search."

Bully hoped Strauss would come a little closer. If he could somehow trip him and get on top, his weight would handle the rest. But then he glanced at Lisa slumped against the wall, crying and shivering from the cold rain. No, he couldn't chance it.

The conversation with Harry came back to him. The Laughman place. That had to be it. Laughman was a German refugee and he owned a ranch in 1943. Was he a spy too? He had just come from Germany. Could he have been involved with the Nazis? No. Harry had said Laughman's entire family had been taken by the S.S. But what if they had held his family hostage? Made him participate? Was it possible?

Alec kneeled down and lifted Lisa's face with his hand. Tears streamed down her face.

"Your granddaughter is very pretty," Alec smirked. "I hope she stays that way." He grabbed the front of her hair and yanked it hard, pulling her head down to her chest.

Lisa moaned, her voice barely audible through the rain. "I'm sorry, Poppa. I lied. Alec told me to. He wasn't downstairs when Denny was here. He was up on the deck fighting with him."

Strauss laughed through the rain, a cruel grin on his face. "That's right, old man. I was on the deck with Sader." He grabbed Lisa by the arms, pulled her up and put both hands on her head. "Here, watch. I'll show you what I did to him."

Bully cried out, "Goddamn it, you bastard! Let her go! I'll find it. I'll find the gold for you."

Lisa collapsed back to the wall. Incensed, Bully determined to get up. He balanced himself on his one knee and placed his hands to his side, ready to push up from the concrete.

He screamed, "You're a damned killer, Strauss—a murderer. You didn't save Lisa. It was all a set-up to get me to help you. You're a Nazi too, aren't you?"

Bully steadied himself again. His chest pain returned—a load of concrete on his chest. He fought it off. Memories flooded in. The Battle of the Bulge—a minefield—his lieutenant. Friends dying all around—limbs torn from bodies. His body destroyed by a German mine. The massacre at Malmedy—machine guns—murder—blood on the snow. The hatred returned. Nazis bastards. And now this punk—one of them. He would not help him find the gold. More evil. No, he could not do it.

But what about Lisa? He needed to stall, to think, play along until he could come up with something. Parker wouldn't wait long at Claire's, he'd come back to check. Leave a signal, something to warn Parker.

"All right, I'll take you, damn you! Give me my leg." Bully reattached his leg and stumbled to the shed to gather his gold machine and an extra battery. Alec followed closely, holding Lisa by the neck.

Back inside the bar, Bully laid the machine on the counter next to the gar-head to check it. "Everything's working. Let's go," he said and picked up the machine. He glanced back at the gar-head. He had told Parker he would take it with him. He left the extra battery next to the head hoping Parker would get the signal.

Alec held Lisa's arm while Bully loaded the truck. Bully got in first and purposely flooded the engine. Anything to stall for time. He yelled out the window. "The damned old thing won't start."

"Get out," Alec said. "We'll take my car."

"No," Bully yelled back. "It's too low. We need the truck. Give it some time. I'll get it started."

They waited. Bully kept glancing at the road, hoping for Parker. Alec yelled at him again. Bully couldn't wait any longer. Maybe they would meet Parker on the road. They drove up FM3005 and turned on 13 Mile Road headed for the Boehm Ranch. He told Alec it was their best chance. But when they got there, water covered the area. The three of them got out of the truck and stood next to the fence.

Bully yelled, "This ain't gonna work. The winds are over forty now and the tide is coming up fast. We need to get out while we can."

"No!" Alec screamed back. He put his giant hand around the back of Lisa's neck. "We'll keep looking. But we've already searched here. Why are you stalling me, old man?" He pinched Lisa's neck.

Lisa moaned softly. Bully winced. He had to do something. Where was Parker?

"There's one more place we can look," Bully blurted out. "I just thought of it. We never tried it 'cause you kept talking about the Civil War and it wasn't a ranch then. It has a corral and some trees."

"Were they there in 1943?"

"Yes, yes, they were. I used to go there then."

A pounding rain blasted the windshield as they headed back down Stewart Road. The ditches on both sides overflowed onto the asphalt. Black clouds blocked the sun. Bully switched on his headlights. A few miles further, he turned onto a road that led back to the sub-division in front of the Laughman ranch. The homes were deserted. Bully turned down a shell lane that led to the back of the old ranch. He slowed at a sharp curve in the road and screeched to a halt.

Alec braced himself against the dashboard. "What the hell are you doing, old man? Trying to throw me into the windshield?"

Bully hit the truck's high beams. "Look at the road beyond the curve," he answered. "It's completely flooded as far as you can see. The water's at least a foot deep."

"Press ahead," Alec ordered. "We can make it!"

"No, it's impossible. I can't even see the road. If we slip off into the ditch, we're goners for sure."

"I said go, old man." Alec's left arm slid over Lisa's shoulder, his hand close to her breast.

Bully pushed on. Water flew up into the engine and steam hissed through the hood. Somehow the motor stayed alive. They crept forward, finally reaching the gate to what remained of the ranch.

The clues were perfectly aligned just as Martha Hoff had said. An old corral was a few yards inside the gate straight ahead. The windmill was to the left and a stand of salt-cedars to the right.

An aluminum gate, padlocked with an iron chain, blocked the entrance. In the darkened sky, the truck's headlights reflected water everywhere covering the entire ranch. Rolling bay water sloshed over the bottom railing of the corral.

Bully approached the gate and yanked on the lock. He signaled to Alec, then went back to the truck and yelled over the howling wind.

"The wind's shifted to the Northeast. That'll push the whole bay up on the island. We'll have five or six feet of water here in no time. It's almost to the floorboard of the truck now. We've only got a few minutes to get out."

"This is the place, I know it!" Alec exclaimed.

"We've got to go. We'll come back after the hurricane passes."

"No!" Yelled Alec. He opened the truck door. Water gushed in over the floorboard.

Bully shouted again, "We're gonna be trapped here. All the roads heading back to town are already closed. Our only chance is to get back to The Garhole and ride it out."

Bully wasn't manipulating this time. He was frightened himself. He looked at Lisa. She had shut down, her face void of color. What had he gotten her in to?

Alec slammed his hand on the dashboard. "Damn it, old man. If you're lying to me, so help me I'll..."

"Look behind us," Bully said. "The water over the road is already a foot higher than when we drove back here. It may be too late already."

Chapter Fifty-Eight
Thursday, September 8

Rain and wind hammering against my truck awakened me. I inched up in the seat and peered over the doorframe. Branches from downed trees and trash from overturned garbage cans swirled about. Where was I?

I straightened and glanced out the passenger side of the truck. Claire's condominium. How had I gotten here? My watch glowed— 5:00 AM—still dark. The last few hours were a total loss. The last thing I remembered was sitting in the pub across from the Tremont Hotel waiting for Strauss to return.

Where were Bully and Lisa? Where was Claire? I pushed the door open against the wind and struggled to the covered entrance in front of Claire's condo. I rang the bell and pounded the door. No answer. My note to Bully was still pinned to the door. I turned to the neighbor's apartment—no one there. The entire condominium appeared deserted. There were no cars in the street. The only movement was the incessant wind ripping objects down the block.

Wait! Headlights at the corner. A car approached and stopped at my truck. A sheriff's vehicle—Deputy Klaus. I jogged to the street. My brain jostled inside my skull. I felt every motion, every throbbing of my temple. I was still drunk. I raised my head to the sky to take in moisture. Rain soaked my lips. My body ached for liquid.

Marvin Klaus screamed out his car window. "Parker, where the hell have you been? I've been searching the whole city for you."

I stumbled to the open window and replied, "Damned if I know, Marvin. Damned if I know." I cupped my hand on top of the patrol car, pushed what water I could gather to the edge of the roof and sucked the gathering moisture into my mouth.

"Harry called," Marvin, shouted. "He said Bully and Lisa never showed at his place. We've been up all night worrying about them. The lines to The Garhole are down. I tried to drive out there but 3005 is flooded."

I joggled my head and slapped my face. A foul taste rolled across my tongue. "They were right behind me last night. Bully was going to leave as soon as Lisa got there. They should have been here hours ago. When did 3005 close?"

"Early last night," Klaus yelled back. "The storm's turned. It's headed straight for us—coming in now. Winds are already gusting to seventy. It's gonna be a real bastard. They're saying it may be a four."

"Something's wrong, Marvin! I don't like it. Where could they be?"

"Oh, and something else," Marvin continued. "The police in Houston found Sader's car next to a motel. You were right. They picked up that kid, Bubba Shanks. He sang like a mockingbird. Said he was with Sader the night he died. He didn't see it happen, and of course, he didn't have anything to do with it, but he thinks Strauss killed him. Strauss told him to dump Sader's car in Galveston, but he took it on to Houston instead."

"Jesus, that fits with everything I've learned. Strauss also murdered a woman in Fredericksburg."

"What?"

"I don't have time to explain now. Call the Tremont. See if Strauss is there." I went to the other side of the patrol car and got in.

Marvin said, "No use! The Tremont locked up tight at eleven last night. And, oh!" Marvin slapped his forehead. "How could I forget. They found a man and woman dead in Strauss's room. Looked like a murder-suicide. He shot her and then himself. No identification on either of them."

"Could the man have been Strauss?"

"No such luck. He was small, wimpy looking."

I hit the dashboard with my fist. "Damn it! It doesn't make sense. Two people dead in Strauss's room. No identification. Who were they? This thing turns weirder every hour. And where the hell is Strauss?"

Klaus said, "Good question. Galveston police have an APB out on him. He hasn't been to the airport, and he hasn't checked his rental car in."

I turned to Marvin. "Strauss has gone to The Garhole, I know it! He must have gotten out there before the road flooded over."

"Oh, God," Marvin exclaimed, "I hate the thought, Parker, but it might explain why Bully and Lisa haven't come in."

"Yeah," I said, my jaw tightening. "And Bully did say Strauss wanted to search again last night."

Marvin's cell phone rang. "Klaus here."

"Yes, Deputy Klaus, this is Colonel Pat Moore, a friend of Parker McLeod. Do you have any idea how I can reach him. It's urgent!"

Klaus handed me the phone. "Pat, it's me, Parker. What's up?"

"Been trying to reach you all night. Then I remembered you mentioned Deputy Klaus's name. Glad I found you."

"Our connection is weak. The storm's coming in right now. I may lose you."

"I'll talk fast. We heard from the German police. Seems your man Günter Manfred alias Alec Strauss is a real humdinger. He's a member of a neo-Nazi outfit called the German Truth Organization. The police have it pretty well infiltrated. Bunch of goddamned skinheads. They're fanatical. Think they can take over the government. They talk about a Fourth Reich. Only problem is, they're short of funds. Your man Strauss is on a mission to get money for the organization."

"Money? How, Pat?"

"It's crazy, Parker. According to Nazi records, in 1943, a German spy named von Speigel..."

I interrupted. "Eric von Speigel? The name on the gravestone in Fredericksburg? Martha Hoff's husband?"

"One and the same," Moore answered. "Anyway, this von Speigel was supposed to have landed from a U-Boat at Galveston for a secret mission, but the Coast Guard sank the sub off Louisiana and he was never heard from again."

"I don't get it, Pat."

"Well, a German officer was rescued off the U-Boat and transferred to the POW camp at Fort Crockett. He escaped and was never found."

"So, you think this officer was actually von Speigel."

"Yes. Von Speigel wouldn't have used his real name. This happened in 1943. Von Speigel would have known about the case in 1942 in New York. Remember that?"

"Vaguely," I noted.

Moore continued, "Eight German agents came ashore in a rubber dingy off a U-Boat. They all had forged documents—birth certificates, driver's licenses, even social security cards. The leader had seventy thousand dollars cash on him. They had duffel bags full of explosives. A Coastguardsman on patrol spotted them. They had orders to kill anyone who discovered them, but they made the mistake of trying to bribe him. He reported them, but they had gone. Later, one of them squealed to the FBI. He was actually an American citizen who got cold feet. Anyway, they were all rounded up and six were executed.

"They fried them?"

"Sure did."

"Well, you're right, Pat," I said. "Von Speigel probably figured they would've executed him too, so he used an alias."

Moore continued, "If Hoff was von Speigel's contact, von Speigel probably went to Fredericksburg when he escaped."

I broke in, "That fits with what Sergeant Sanders said. Von Speigel must have stayed there and lived with the Hoffs. Even married the daughter, Martha. That explains why he never left the farm. But how does Strauss's search for gold figure into all of this?"

"Well," Colonel Moore said. "Like in the New York case, German agents were well financed. If Hoff was his contact, he might have also been responsible for supplying the funds."

I considered Moore's theory. "Do you think the funds were U.S. currency? Strauss talked about finding gold. Is that possible, Pat?"

Moore seemed to hesitate. I could hear him breathing into the phone. "It's possible," he replied. "Hoff was probably a sleeper agent, activated for this mission. Gold and currency, both for that matter, could have been smuggled to him in advance."

"You may be right, Pat" I broke in. "But if Hoff had the money, what did he do with it? Cartwright said it appeared he never left the farm."

"We think that Hoff must have taken the money to Galveston to meet von Speigel when he was supposed to have been smuggled ashore. But von Speigel never showed because he was in the POW camp."

"That explains Strauss's interest in the POW's at Fort Crockett."

"Exactly. So somehow, Strauss must know that Hoff brought the money to Galveston. He must think it's buried on the west end. Hoff probably had a connection with someone out there."

"Of course, Pat. That's why Strauss hired Bully. He's been badgering him about searching on farms owned by Germans. He's using the Civil War thing as a cover. Strauss must be out there now! I've got to go, Pat. And thanks."

"Wait, Parker. There's more. There may be another one of them there. A man named Horst Frankin flew in to Houston yesterday."

"Was there a woman with him?"

"Not that we know of, why?"

"The police found a man and woman dead in Strauss's room."

"You think Strauss murdered them?"

"They said it looked like a murder-suicide, but who knows? Anything is possible with Strauss, I mean Manfred."

"They're probably all paranoid," Moore added. "Like Hitler and his bunch. Crazy bastards. Strauss is a highly trained killer—especially with his hands. There has been a series of murders over the past few years around Leipzig, Strauss's hometown. They think it was Strauss, or should we say Manfred. All of them killed the same way, broken necks. Even a Russian, an ex-border guard."

I jumped at the reference, "Leipzig...East Germany. I knew it, his accent."

I terminated the call, handed the phone back to Klaus, and opened the car door. I got out and leaned in toward Klaus. "Bully and Lisa are in big trouble. I've got to get out there."

"Impossible!" Klaus replied. "The road has disappeared."

Chapter Fifty-Nine
Thursday, September 8

Marvin hit his flashing lights, waved me back into the patrol car and sped down the boulevard to where the seawall ended and the road descended to sea level. As far as we could see down 3005, water covered the island.

Marvin shook his head and exhaled a long slow breath. "Well, Parker. We're done for. The Gulf has met the bay."

Less than a hundred yards out, a small car stalled in the rising water. A young couple from the vehicle saw the flashing overheads and waded up the ramp toward the patrol car.

A large board, propelled by the swift current, rushed toward them from behind. I ran down the ramp into the rising water and shouted over the roaring wind. The board sailed past them but smashed through the glass door of a service station, inundating the entire store with seawater.

When the couple finally struggled to the top of the seawall, Marvin herded them into his patrol car for safety.

I knew it would only get worse, the water rising as the storm approached. It was now or never. I turned to Klaus, "I've got to get out there, Marvin. I've got to."

Just then, a lone pickup pulling a small aluminum boat on a trailer drove up a side street to the seawall. I pointed at it and shouted, "Block that truck!"

Marvin gunned his patrol car and jammed it in front of the escaping vehicle. I ran to the driver's side and yanked open the door. The man stared at me, speechless, obviously shaken by the flashing emergency lights.

I screamed at him, "I need your boat! Out on the west end, family in trouble. I must get out there."

The man seemed to understand. He quickly got out of the truck and motioned for me to get in. I backed the truck down to the water's edge. We unloaded the boat and started the motor.

A wind-whipped tide heaved over the sides of the small boat almost, capsizing me into the storm. I found a small bucket and bailed water with one hand while keeping a steady grip on the motor handle with the other.

I dodged the floating remains of everything not tied down— pieces of lumber, lawn chairs, tables. Anything that would float twisted around in the rising tide. The motor sputtered, trying to quit. I raced the throttle, hoping the engine would hold out. The Garhole Bar was eighteen miles away down the storm tossed island.

The turbulent water kept pushing the bow of the boat making it difficult to maintain a straight course, slowing me to a crawl. If only the motor would keep chugging.

Somehow, I had to stay on course. The road had disappeared beneath the water. I could be swept off the island completely, out into West Bay or the Gulf of Mexico. And that would be adios to good old Parker McLeod. I decided to hug the power line that paralleled the road.

Dark skies and a pounding wind and rain surrounded me. Half an hour later, I recognized the Pirates Beach development ahead. The strip center on 3005 was built several feet above ground level. Water lapped at the doors and windows, and the hurricane wasn't even here yet. A bitch of a storm was coming.

I passed the stores, keeping a row of houses along the beach on my left. Huge waves pounded the pilings of the homes facing the Gulf. The houses appeared empty. Sheets of plywood covered many of the doors and windows. Towers of salt spray cascaded onto the upper decks, washing deck furniture over the side.

I steered closer to the power line. Suddenly, a cable broke and the wire hit the water. Thousands of volts danced and snaked around in front of me. The motor sputtered again and quit. The boat's momentum pushed me toward the wire. Frantically, I pulled the cord, twice, then three times. The motor started, and I shoved the handle hard to the right, just missing the jerking power line.

I shook the five-gallon gas tank connected to the motor. Empty. A moment later, the gas in the carburetor ran out. The motor coughed once more and quit. I was at the mercy of the storm.

Roaring tidewater heaved my boat toward an empty field that separated Pirates Beach from Jamaica Beach, the next subdivision. There were no houses in sight, nothing to keep me from washing across the island into the bay.

I grabbed the small paddle in the boat and pushed hard diagonally across the field, desperately trying to intercept a house before I hit the bay.

My shoulders felt as though they were being sliced with a razor, and my arms drooped like rubber, every muscle exhausted. I not only had to reach a house, I had to find gas for the motor. I couldn't make The Garhole without power.

Most of all, I couldn't quit. Lisa and Bully needed me. I paddled hard across the field, desperately tired. As I neared the first house, a swirl of water pushed me away. I jumped out of the boat, the water waist high. I pulled the boat to the stairs and tied it to the railing. I ran up the stairs, only to find the window and doors boarded over. I yanked on the plywood with both hands—nothing. I needed a tool of some kind to peel it off. But then what? People kept their gas cans in the garage not upstairs. Getting inside was useless...unless an internal stairway lead into the garage.

I retrieved the aluminum paddle from the boat and pried on the plywood. Slowly, slowly, the board came away. I gained some leverage, and pulled with both hands. The board popped off. I shoved the paddle through the glass window and hustled inside.

I found the stairway, kicked open the door to the garage below, and went down. A foot of water had seeped in around the garage doors covering the floor. There were two five-gallon gas cans. The first was empty. My heart sank. The second one seemed half-full.

I raced up the stairs, back out the broken window and down the outside staircase. No! The boat was gone! I hit the bottom stair and thrust into the water, searching. Nothing! I pushed further into the driveway. A board hit my back, knocking me into the water. I came up coughing, spewing saltwater. My kidneys ached.

A banging noise. I spied the boat at the house next door crashing against the outside wall. I shoved off toward it, knowing it would break loose soon and be blown out to sea or sunk.

Something scraped my leg. Blood gushed to the top of the water. I couldn't stop now. The boat flipped over, drenching the motor. I grabbed underneath the gunnels and heaved, flipping it right-side up, hoping the drowned motor would start. I towed it back to the house where I had left the paddle and gas can. Then I hoisted the boat up the stairs until the bow rested on a rung out of the water.

Blood streamed out of a three-inch slice in my leg. The cut was deep, almost to the bone. I ripped off my shirt and managed to stop the blood flow with a tight bandage. I felt my back and twisted to see a large abrasion seeping blood. I grew weaker, slowly losing consciousness. Nothing to eat for over 24 hours. Blood lost.

I held the bow rope and laid back on the stairs, exhausted. The water continued to rise fueled by the wind-whipped waves. I needed rest. My eyelids dropped closed as the wind and rain swirled around driving me down.

And I saw Lisa. She had been sitting beside me on the bench by the oak motte, but had gotten up and moved closer to the bird pond. She looked very small and innocent. She beckoned me to her to see a bird. But something held me back. I could not get off the bench. She waved frantically now, urging me to come. I still could not move. But, I saw her more clearly now. She was crying, calling to me.

Chapter Sixty
Thursday, September 8

Not wanting to risk flooding the engine, Bully crept all night against the rising water. In many places, the roads had vanished and several times Alec had to get out and lead the truck on foot. Bully wanted to run him down, but if the motor died, he knew he wouldn't be able to get back to The Garhole alone. Lisa wasn't strong enough to handle the rushing water.

Just as they reached the turn-off to The Garhole, the motor died. They would have to wade the last hundred yards. A torrent of water swirled around their feet, making it difficult to keep their balance. Any loss of footing and they would be swept off the lane at the mercy of the growing storm.

The wind drove the rain at a hard, piercing slant, strong enough to penetrate the skin. Bully and Lisa held tight to each other, struggling to make the front door. The leg muscle that controlled Bully's prosthesis weakened under the pressure of the moving water. More and more of his weight shifted to Lisa.

Alec was close behind, his head down against the rain and wind. Bully thought he could turn quickly and push him off the path into the storm surge. But what if it didn't work? He might lose his balance. The swirling tide could pull both Bully and Lisa off the path into the current. Too risky. Better to catch him off-guard inside.

He yelled back to Alec. "It's safer to go in the front. Around back we could be washed off the patio into the bay."

Alec nodded. Bully pushed through the front door. A foot of water covered the floor. At least they had gained a temporary respite from the punishing wind and rain.

Bully hollered to Lisa, "Open the back door and latch it. We'll leave the front door open too. Let the water flow through."

He leaned on the counter to brace himself, then turned to Alec. "Listen to me. We'll have wind over a hundred miles an hour here soon. Could be seven or eight feet of water down here. Our only chance is to get into the bedroom upstairs. We've got plywood nailed over the door. I can't make it up there. You'll have to go up and tear it off so we can get in. There's a crowbar and hammer in the shed behind the camper."

Lisa sat at a table with her head down and eyes closed, her feet in swirling water. Alec yelled across the room. "Lisa, come with me!" She didn't respond. Alec moved toward her.

"No!" Bully screamed. "Leave her alone. She's too weak to go out into the storm again." His last chance was to get Alec outside the bar.

"Can't you see we're exhausted? You're the strong one. You can do it. We've got to save our strength to get up the stairs."

Alec stared at Lisa for a few seconds, then looked at Bully. "Okay, old man. Neither of you move." He retrieved the tools from the shed and went upstairs and began ripping the plywood off the bedroom door.

Bully's chest pounded, the pain growing more intense. His breaths came quick and short. He had little time left. He thought of Lisa. He had to try. He gathered his last remaining strength. For her, one last effort—everything he had. The war memories erupted again. Nazis...evil. He positioned himself behind the counter just inside the door like a cat ready to strike. His only chance.

Alec appeared in the doorway, his head lowered from the driving rain. With his last ounce of stamina, Bully pushed off the wall. His arms enveloped Alec. The momentum generated by Bully's massive body pinned Alec against the wall. They crashed to the floor. Bully struggled to hold Alec's head under water. He needed a few more seconds. He felt him weaken. The effort was almost over. He and Lisa would be free.

But then, the pain came again. There was no air, no intake. Bully instinctively released his grip on Alec and grabbed at his chest—the effort futile. He collapsed onto Alec.

Alec exploded from beneath Bully. He heaved upward out of the water and pushed Bully aside. The Nazi lay back against the wall gulping huge breaths.

Lisa ran to Bully's side and lifted his head out of the water, cradling it in her arms. She kissed his face. "Poppa! Poppa! Say something—please! Don't leave me!"

Alec sat buckled against the wall, his hands to his side, his breaths fast and deep. Water rushed over his body's lower half. In a subdued voice, weak but triumphant, he said. "You bitch. Can't you see he's dead?"

Lisa ignored him. She continued her plea. "No, Poppa, please! No!"

"You're next," Alec screamed. He grabbed Lisa's hair and yanked her away from Bully.

Bully's head dropped below the gushing water.

Chapter Sixty-One
Thursday, September 8

I exploded through the door behind Strauss and slammed my fist into the back of his head. As Strauss crumbled, I leaped over him and propped Bully's head against the wall.

Lisa screamed, "Parker, watch out!"

Too late. Strauss yanked me backwards, his massive hands on my neck, positioned for a quick jerk. In an instant, a vision of twisted, broken vertebrae flashed through my mind. I thought of Denny Sader lying dead on the cement. I grabbed Strauss' fingers and tried desperately to bend them backward. They tightened.

Lisa slammed a chair against Strauss's back. He buckled. I broke free from his death grip and gasped for air. I grabbed an empty beer bottle that had floated from behind the counter and swung hard, striking Strauss in the forehead. He fell back, his head going under water. With the help of the swirling tide, I managed to push Strauss's body out the door, knowing the rising water would float him out into the bay.

I glanced at Lisa cradling Bully's head. For a brief moment, our eyes met. I saw the surge of relief in her face. Alec Strauss was gone. We were safe.

I turned to rest against the counter, totally spent. Hours with no food, nothing but alcohol to drink. My mind drifted, weak from lack of energy. I stared at the gar-head on the counter. Its razor teeth seemed to snarl and taunt.

My knees gave, too weak to stand. The bandage on my leg was gone. The cut oozed blood. I slid to the floor.

Lisa screamed, "Parker! Parker, for God's sake, help me!"

Bully's head had slipped back into the water. My eyes focused on her, but nothing else seemed to work. My arms and legs wouldn't function. I heard Lisa's voice shouting at me and felt her pulling my arm, but I couldn't respond.

She somehow managed to prop Bully up against the wall and yell back at me, "Parker, we've got to get Poppa upstairs."

An arm responded, then a leg. I managed to stand. I bent over the counter and pulled a beer from the cooler. I needed nourishment—anything. The warm beer soothed my throat. I gulped it quickly, then turned to Lisa.

"How is Bully?"

"Not good. I think he's..."

I moved to Bully and felt the pulse in his neck. "No, he's alive. Help me with him."

We pushed and shoved until I had Bully over my shoulder. Too much dead weight, I couldn't lift him. I sat him down and together we dragged him out the door to the bottom stair. He regained consciousness.

I yelled above the howl of the blowing rain and screaming wind. "Bully, listen to me. You have to help. We can't get you up these stairs by ourselves. You hear me! Help us! Grab the railing and pull yourself up."

Lisa took his other side and together we pushed and shoved until we had him standing. Slowly, one step at a time, we reached the top and moved him to the bed. I checked his pulse again—weak and thready—his skin pale and damp.

I turned to Lisa. "He's very weak. Maybe even a heart attack. It'll be touch and go. All we can do is try to battle out this storm and survive. You stay here with Bully. I'll be back in a minute."

At the bedroom door, I stopped to look at the bay. A torrent of rain obstructed my view. Visibility ended at the dock's edge. Water swirled three feet over the bulkhead. At that moment, a gust of wind pushed a wall of water under the boat. It propelled upward hitting the underside of the dock. The moorings broke and the skiff smashed against a piling and floated out into the bay.

I had only moments now. In the bar, I gathered what provisions I could find—canned foods, bottled beer—any type of nourishment available. I waded past the back door and started up the stairs.

Out of nowhere, hands encircled my waist, pulling me down. The provisions washed away. Strauss was back. Blood gushed from his forehead, pouring into his eyes. I realized he couldn't see, but his strength hadn't diminished.

I refused to go down. I pulled his wrists to break free, but Strauss held on. I dragged him through the door into the bar, then pried his fingers back and broke his grip. I twisted around and slammed my hands on both sides of his head. He fell back against the side of the counter and slid to the floor, his head barely out of the water.

I had only seconds before Strauss would regain his strength and come at me again. I ran to the stairs and yelled, "Lisa! Help me! Help me!"

I grabbed Strauss's shoulders with both hands and began to pull him up, shouting again, hoping she would hear.

Lisa ran into the bar, sloshing through the water. I motioned with my head, hoping she understood. She put both of her hands on Strauss's back and pushed upward. I lifted and pulled, and together we twisted him over the counter. I slammed his head on the bar as hard as I could, stunning him again. Blood gushed from his nose and mouth. His eyes rolled back into his skull as through he were unconscious.

But this evil bastard had already come back from the dead once; and I wasn't about to give him another opportunity to reincarnate himself again. Thoughts came in a rush. What Strauss had done to Lisa. To Bully. The poor woman in Fredericksburg. The librarian he had beaten. Anger took over. My mind reeled in disgust. I had the power now, and I would be damned if Strauss would have another chance to hurt another soul.

From somewhere deep inside me, knowing this had to be my final effort, I summoned one last adrenalin rush. I pushed his neck into the jaws of the gar-head, and lunged over the top of the skull crushing the top jaw down into Strauss's carotid artery.

His hands reached for the jaws. Too late. His life-blood poured from the gashes in his neck and spilled across the counter. He tried to speak, a gargled word mixed with blood.

"Mari...Mariana..." Then, nothing. It was over.

With the gar-head still stuck into Strauss's neck, his lifeless body slid from the counter and splashed onto the water-covered floor below.

I eased to the floor beside him and leaned back against the side of the counter. Something warm dropped steadily onto my shoulder. Strauss's blood spilled down from the bar. Thick, red goblets rolled off my shirt and mixed with the swirling water around me. I remember reaching over to Strauss and pulling the gar-head from his neck and then—nothing.

I was sitting in the middle of my bird pond wondering why it was filled with pink flamingoes. Flamingoes, not roseate spoonbills. Why were they here, in Galveston? I reached out and touched one and smoothed its feathers. And I was grateful for its presence.

Chapter Sixty-Two
Wednesday, September 13

Four days had passed since Hurricane Dorothy destroyed The Garhole Bar. The evening, of the storm, the barometer plummeted to its all-time low for Galveston, 28.4 inches of mercury. The sustained winds reached one hundred thirty miles per hour with gusts to one hundred sixty. The storm surge crested at seven feet above sea level.

During the height of the storm, a tornado took most of the roof, the stairs, and half the back deck. Lisa and I had managed to get Bully into the bathtub. We huddled beside it with the mattress over the three of us.

Late the next day, Claire arrived with Harry Stein and Deputy Klaus. The authorities had closed FM3005 to all traffic, but Klaus in his official vehicle was allowed to pass. A normal thirty-minute drive had taken them three hours, stopping every few feet to clear debris from the road.

Bully was alive but weak and delirious. Together, we rigged a hammock and lowered him to the deck. We loaded him into the patrol car and Marvin sped off to the hospital in Galveston.

Since then, Claire had been out each day to bring supplies. I had just finished a four-mile run on the beach and was jogging down the lane to The Garhole when she pulled along side me in her Lexus.

She lowered her window, "How was your run?"

"The beach is still packed with debris," I answered. "Had to jog around the piles."

"Glad to see you following doctor's orders," she said, smiling.

"Well, I am feeling a hell of a lot better, thanks. Maybe my new best friend, Colonel Kennon, had a plan after all." I gestured toward her car. "I hope you brought some more water. We're almost out."

"I brought another five gallons. I guess they still haven't certified the water out here yet, huh? "

"Nope. We can shower in it, but that's all."

She parked and strolled to a redwood table that had washed up next to the house during the storm. I came up behind her.

"How about some fried chicken?" She set the box on the table and strolled to the bulkhead, inspecting the empty spot where Bully's trailer had rested.

She turned and said, "Any news on Bully's trailer?"

With a mouth full of chicken, I said, "We'll never find it. Not worth bringing it back if we did."

She shouted from the back door, "Hey, you've still got the gar-head! I've got to get a drink and toast it."

In front of Claire, hanging from a wire in the ceiling, the gar-head offered it's grotesque smile.

I said, "Yeah, the last thing I remember was giving it to Lisa in the bar. She took it upstairs and saved it."

A vision of Strauss's neck caught in the gar's teeth came back to me. So where was Strauss? His body hadn't been found. It would probably turn up sooner or later somewhere across the bay, washed up in some reeds. Good riddance.

My mind played tricks on me. I could not remember parts of the day of the storm. I had no idea how I had traveled the last few miles. I remembered finding the extra gas can and getting the boat back after it had washed away. And I remembered crashing down on Strauss at The Garhole, but nothing in between. Maybe it would come to me, maybe. I shook those thoughts from my mind and walked over to Claire.

"Must be an omen," Claire said.

I gave her a confused look, "An omen? What do you mean by that?"

"Saving the gar-head," she answered. "The omen is you are supposed to reopen The Garhole Bar'."

I waved her off and went back to the fried chicken on the table. Claire finished surveying the damage, then returned to the table.

It all seemed so natural, so comfortable—Claire beside me in an old pair of faded jeans and denim shirt. A crimson scarf matched her hair. The morning sun accentuated the freckles on her nose.

Something still bugged me, though. Where was she the day the storm arrived? I couldn't bring myself to ask. Maybe she'd had a momentary panic attack. Who knows? Anyway, who the hell was I to judge her after my fall from grace with the Famous Grouse? After that screw up, I was damned lucky things turned out as well as they had.

After a moment, she spoke again. "You know, Parker, you and Lisa have really accomplished a lot around here in a week. The place is looking pretty spiffy."

She waved toward the house. We had stretched an army surplus tarp over the top of my bedroom, and Lisa and I had hosed and scrapped the sand and mud off the floor of the bar and the dock behind it. We had burned most of the trash that had washed into the yard and the parking lot. I saved a few pieces of lumber, a couple of plastic ice boxes and the redwood table.

I turned toward Claire and said, "Yeah, look at The Garhole. Ready for business." I grinned at the lame joke, then picked up the chicken leg for the last bite.

"Just trying to cheer you up," Claire said. "Look at the bright side. The three of you made it through the storm and Bully's out of the hospital."

Claire placed her hand on mine. "You're still upset with me, aren't you, Parker? We haven't discussed it, but I know your feelings are hurt that I left Galveston before the storm without saying anything to you."

I threw the chicken bone into the water and reached for a biscuit. Claire closed the chicken box and moved it to the bench beside her. "Okay, Parker McLeod. No more food until you talk to me. I asked you a question."

I shoved the entire biscuit into my mouth and pointed to my filled cheeks signaling I couldn't speak. Her eyes bored into mine. No where to run.

"Answer my question, Parker. Talk to me. If I didn't care about you, I wouldn't be here. I think you know that, but that's as far as I'm going without some response from you."

I chewed quickly and swallowed the remaining piece of biscuit, then said, "Claire, what if I was just worried about you? A storm was coming in after all."

"Worried? I'm a grown woman, Parker. I can take care of myself. You'll have to do better than that."

I hesitated. A group of blue-winged teal hurried low over the water, whistling as they passed. They made a wide arc, then turned back over us roaring by like a group of jet fighters on a run. It comforted me that nature had not given up on the island. More importantly, Claire had not given up on me.

I turned to face her. "Okay, Claire. The truth is...I was disappointed. I expected to see you. Maybe I took you for granted. If I did, I'm sorry. My feelings were hurt, I admit it."

A car turned off the blacktop and braked into the parking lot. Harry Stein and Marvin Klaus stepped out.

"Where are Bully and Lisa?" Harry asked. "We thought they'd be here with you."

"They went out early this morning to your cousin's place looking for that damned gold," I answered. "Bully's convinced it's buried there."

"Think he'll find it?" Harry asked.

"Who knows," I responded. "But here is the funny thing. After the storm, I searched Strauss's car and found three gold coins—real doubloons. I gave them to Bully. At least he's got something."

"Why would Strauss have gold coins?" Marvin asked.

I shook my head. "Can't figure it out," I said. "But Bully was really happy about it. You know he had two coins just like those, but he lost them in the storm. Forgot to get them out of the trailer."

Harry said with a smile, "Well, he's got three of them now. Not a bad trade, I guess."

Marvin spoke, "I hope he's not out there doing all the digging himself. He's only been out of the hospital two days."

"Yeah, but he's a tough old coot," I added.

Marvin said, "But if he finds something on someone else's land, it wouldn't be his. It would belong to the land owner."

"You're right," Harry said. "But if he finds it on the Laughman property, he can probably work out a deal. I know the owners. They're good folks." Harry winked as he said it.

Marvin slapped his forehead. "Oh, hell, Harry. I forgot Laughman was your cousin. You own the ranch, don't you?"

Harry nodded.

Marvin Klaus turned to me and said, "So what do you think? Are you going to rebuild?"

Claire chimed in, "Of course he is. There has to be a Garhole Bar. And he still has the gar-head. What would the west end be without it? Right, Parker?"

"I don't know," I responded. "Maybe I ought to get a real job. Besides, I didn't have it insured. Couldn't afford it."

Claire said, "Just a minute Parker, I've got something for you." She got a folder out of her car and handed it to me. "Here, look this over."

"What is this, Claire, an offer? I told you I would never sell."

"Read it first, Parker, before you assume the worst. I went to a lot of trouble for this. It's where I was on Friday before the storm

369

when you couldn't find me. I was in Houston negotiating this deal. I wanted to surprise you."

I opened the folder. "The Houston Audubon Society wants to buy my land?"

"Just part of it," Claire responded. "A hundred acres that border West Bay, including the oak motte where the birds stop during migration. It's a good offer, Parker. It will be a reserve, protected."

"Great idea," Harry added. "A hundred acres withdrawn forever from development."

"And with the money, you could rebuild The Garhole," Marvin concluded.

Just then, Bully's truck slid to a stop in the parking lot. Lisa jumped out and ran over to join them squealing, "We found it! We found it!"

Claire said, "That's great, Lisa! How did you find it?"

Bully excited, cut her off, "Well, I figured all Strauss's talk about the corral and windmill and trees must've meant something. So I got to thinkin', where would a German spy bury loot? You know what happened then?"

Harry and Marvin said in unison, "No, what happened then?" "Well, a German swastika jumped into my mind. You know how it looks, crossing lines. So I just triangulated to the center between the well and the corral and the trees and bingo."

"Pretty darn smart," Marvin said. "I guess your gold machine went off right over the spot, huh?"

Bully stammered and rubbed his hand over his mouth. "Well, uh, that's a secret. Can't be giving out that valuable information."

Lisa winked at Marvin. He shot back a wide grin.

Bully opened a rusted tin box. "It ain't much, but here it is." He pulled out a wad of disintegrated paper and held it for the rest to see. "The paper money's destroyed. Too much water seeped into the box over the years. Looks like there must have been a lot of it at one time."

"No gold?" Claire and I said in unison.

"Just a few coins, maybe three or four dozen of them. Not worth much I reckon. There're so small."

"Let me see," Harry said. He reached into the box and withdrew one of the coins. "Why there're...there're genuine United States twenty dollar gold pieces."

"But they don't weigh nothing," Bully interjected. "Ain't more than a few ounces of gold altogether."

"You don't get it, Bully," Harry said. "These are collector's items."

"So?" Bully said as he examined one of the coins.

"Last quote I saw, twenty dollar gold pieces were selling for over eight hundred dollars each. You've got thirty or forty thousand dollars worth here."

"What?" Bully clutched his chest and eased to the bench by the table.

Lisa said. "Are you all right, Poppa?"

He looked up with a wide grin. "Oh yes, honey. I am....I sure am. Looks like you'll be doing all the schooling you want."

Just then a loud squawk came from the boat dock. A night heron had roared in from nowhere and perched at the top of the remaining deck. I squeezed my eyes and studied the bird. Was it Charlie, the bird whose wing I had fixed and turned loose?

The heron faced us and squawked again. It seemed to be offering a message. If it was Charlie, it was healed, totally normal. I liked to think I had healed myself a little as well.

The night heron arched its back and stretched its wings out as far as they would go—wide and proud. I raised my hand and returned the salute. "Hello, Charlie," I said with a wide grin, "Glad you're back."

About The Author

As a fourth generation Texan and Galveston resident, A.Hardy Roper writes from a wealth of knowledge about the island's storied past and vibrant present. Mr. Roper's great grandparents arrived from Germany in the 1840's and entered through the Port of Galveston, at the time, second only to New York for immigrant destination.

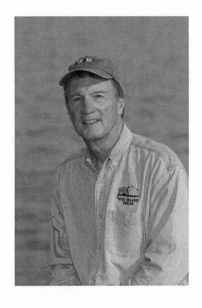

A. Hardy Roper

Today's Galveston is an eclectic mixture of 'old money' and Victorian mansions checkered among indigent neighborhoods of African Americans and Hispanics, all weaved tightly together, as if huddled against the onslaught of the next storm like the epic 1900 hurricane that claimed 6,000 lives.

From its 19th Century past of pirates and buried treasures, to its 20th Century lifestyle of bootlegging, bawdy houses and gambling, Galveston Island offers an endless setting for mystery and intrigue.

A. Hardy Roper has studied its culture and its history. His Parker McLeod mysteries weave an intricate path of deceit and mayhem as the city struggles to balance its colorful past with the inevitable collision of sleepy 'island life' and the hurried weekend rush as the playground of Houston's wealthy baby-boomers.

Contact Hardy at: Hardy@westbay-publishing.com